MW01132290

Reign *A Royal Military Romance*
Loaded *A Bad Boy Romance*
Ride *A Bad Boy Romance*

Shifter Country Wolves Series
Running with Wolves
Betting on Wolves
Fighting for Wolves
Uncaging Wolves
Longing for Wolves

Shifter Country Bears Series
A Bear's Protection
A Bear's Nemesis
A Bear's Mercy
A Bear's Journey
A Bear's Secret

North Star Shifters Series
Grizzlies & Glaciers
Shifters & Soulmates
Forests & Fate

Copper Mesa Eagles Series
Predator
Prey
Protector

Find them all on RoxieNoir.com!

TORCH

A Second Chance Romance

Playing with fire gets you hot, but playing with a fireman gets you wet.

Fighting wildfires is dangerous as hell. If I fuck it up I get a hundred-foot wall of flame coming at me with nowhere to run, no escape, and no rescue - but it's still the best damn job in the world.

And women? They practically line up to slide down my pole. I never did like repeating myself. Not since she broke my heart into a thousand pieces, anyway.

Clementine's that ex. The one I thought I was going to marry until she dumped my ass while I was on active duty.

The one who's suddenly next door. She's still hotter than any fire I've ever fought.

We already went down in flames once, but I've never wanted anyone like I want Clementine. Not even close.

Fuck it. I need to have her again, even if it's just one more time, and to hell with the consequences.

I've already gotten burned once.

Hunter and I were over a long, *long* time ago, and there was a good reason why. Actually, there were a hundred good reasons, and I remember them *all*.

Until he shows up in my town. He's left the Marines to become a wildlands firefighter. He's rugged, hardened, dangerous, and...

...he looks at me *just* like he used to. He makes me laugh just like he used to, like the last eight years may as well have been eight minutes.

And when he gets close, I can't help but think of everything *else* we used to do - the sweaty, naked, toe-curling things. The way he could take me from laughing to moaning in half a second.

Playing with *this* kind of fire may get me hot — my *God* does it get me hot — but it also gets me burned, and once was enough.

...or was it?

Available now on RoxieNoir.com!

CONVICT

A Bad Boy Romance

I never wanted to be good. Not until I met her.

Five years in prison was supposed to reform me, but it didn't teach me shit.

I tried to start fresh: new name, new town, new *life*. No more raising hell, no more women whose names I don't bother learning, no more running from the law.

Yeah, I fucked *that* up in no time at all, but it doesn't matter. I've never liked anything but trouble - and Luna is trouble with a capital T.

She's whip smart, headstrong, fucking *gorgeous*... and a cop.

I know I can't have her. She'll see through my lies in seconds. She deserves a happy ending I know I can't give her.

Hell, with the demons from my past chasing me down, I can't even keep her *safe*.

All I can give Luna is trouble. But I can't stay away.

I don't mind being a little bad.

I date nice men. If I keep saying it, it'll be true, right?

That means I *don't* date the sexy, rakish, tattoo-covered mechanic who's got one dimple and a lifetime of working with his hands. I don't need a man who lies to the police, *obviously* has problems with authority... and who growls *filthy* things into my ear when we're alone.

It doesn't matter if one glance from Stone makes me want to tear my clothes off, I *don't* fantasize about someone who's a suspect in a double arson.

Even if the way he calls me *detective* turns me into a puddle.

I can spot trouble from a mile away, and trouble's the last thing I need.

...right?

Available now on RoxieNoir.com!

A Royal Military Romance

Some fairy tales start after _midnight._

The crown prince and I have nothing in common.

He's a rugged, battle-hardened soldier who spent four years in the Royal Guard, an elite military unit. I met the King and Queen for the first time wearing leggings and a sweatshirt.

He's the serious, quiet, straight-laced heir to the throne, and I accidentally got drunk at a formal dinner.

But there's the way he looks at me, eyes blazing with hunger. Like he knows _every_ dirty thought I've had about him - and he _likes_ them. There's the way my pulse _skyrockets_ every time his hand brushes mine.

I'm the ambassador's daughter. I _know_ better than to mess around with a foreign head of state.

But I don't know how long I can resist.

Not all princes are charming.

I spent years in the Royal Guard, our most elite military unit, fighting like _hell_ so I could rule one day - not so I could give my father an heir with some well-bred rich girl.

I have a f*cking country to run. My love life can take a back seat. It's not like I've ever met a girl I _had_ to have.

Until _her_. The ambassador's daughter. She's so... _American._ Lowborn, brash, wildly unsuitable... and _gorgeous._

I'm disciplined, tough as hell, and I don't f*ck around. But I can't stop thinking about the way she laughs, about how she might _taste_. My father's threatening to strip me of my title if I touch her, but she makes me want to break _every one_ of my own rules.

F*ck titles. F*ck rules. F*ck my father's threats. I want her. I _need_ her.

She's _mine_.

Available now on RoxieNoir.com!

RIDE

A Bad Boy Romance

Save a horse. Ride a cowboy.

Bull riding is dangerous as hell, but that's half the fun. Guts, glory, and cute country girls lined up for days. It may only take eight seconds to win, but I can go all night.

Yeah, I've broken almost every bone in my body at some point, but I've been the World Rodeo Champion two years running. Nothing's gonna keep me from making it three.

Not even Mae Guthrie, a spitfire who's as hot as a Texas wildfire and one hell of a distraction - and who acts like she doesn't remember me at all.

...I'll just have to remind her that we've been acquainted.

I bet she'll remember once she's screaming my name.

Jackson Cody nearly ruined my life.

I was dumb, drunk, and eighteen. He was a rodeo star with a smile that could melt steel, and I was this close to giving him everything.

Thank god for that close call with the cops.

I learned my lesson, grew up, and moved on. Now I've got my first huge assignment as a photographer, and if I play it right, this rodeo shoot could make my whole career.

There's just one problem, and it's got spurs, boots, and hazel eyes.

He's grown up too - Lord has he grown up - and he's only gotten hotter, cockier, and more dangerously alluring since the last time I saw him.

But now I'm older, wiser, and not interested in a fling with a cowboy...

...right?

It's only a couple of days. How hard can he be to resist?

Available now on RoxieNoir.com

Never Enough

ROXIE NOIR

ISBN: 1544135270
ISBN-978-1544135274

PROLOGUE
Gavin

Marisol walks through the lobby door, and I hold my breath. I almost always do when she walks into a room, because I swear she lights it up.

Even when she looks unhappy, like she does right now. I can't blame her. I don't want to be here either, but according to my publicist we've got *damage control* to do, so here I am.

"You're early," she says as she walks up to me, people rushing by on either side.

"I've actually been here for ages," I say. "Valerie's already thrown the book at me. I came down so I could see you before the piranhas moved in."

Her gaze flicks away from me, to the elevator bank, and she nervously adjusts her briefcase on her shoulder. My chest tightens.

I know that last night was a complete catastrophe, and my manager and publicist are losing their minds over it, but it wasn't her fault. It's nothing we can't fix.

"Good," she says, her voice nervous. She's still not looking at me. "I wanted to talk to you."

"Don't worry about last night," I say. "It's my fault, I should have never—"

She shakes her head, cutting me off, and takes a deep breath.

"I think we should start discussing our breakup because I'm clearly not the right person to be playing your girlfriend," she says, the words spilling out of her in a rush.

I'm stunned.

It feels like an arrow through the heart. I know this is all pretend, that she's only my fake girlfriend, but I can't let this happen.

I *can't* let Marisol go. Not like this. I don't care what the people upstairs think or do or say.

"No," I finally say, shaking my head.

Marisol blinks.

"What do you mean, *no*?"

"I mean *no*," I say, and swallow hard. "No to you, no to this, no to all the bloody play-acting—"

This is going horribly, worse than when I asked her to be my fake girlfriend in the first place. I can't explain myself in here, convince her to stay while there are people in suits rushing around on their phones, so I take Marisol's hand and pull her toward the exit beyond the elevators.

There's a sign that says FIRE DOOR, DO NOT OPEN, but I don't give a fuck. I push through it and an alarm goes off in the building, then quiets as the door shuts behind us.

Marisol's already talking a mile a minute, clearly nervous, upset, and unhappy.

"You could find someone much better," she says, not looking me in the eye. "I'm terrible at this. I got high by

2

accident and freaked out, I don't know *anything* about music, I'm awkward in front of cameras—"

I lean down and take her face in both hands, feeling as if my nerves might burst through my skin.

"I don't care, and there's not anyone better," I say, my heart thundering.

I don't know what to do, what to say to make her stay. I only know that I absolutely have to.

She keeps talking, her voice almost a whisper.

"—I was almost too nervous to kiss you on the cheek, and then the lip-on-lip kiss was really awkward and bad—"

I kiss her.

It might be the last time. It might be the *only* time I get to kiss her without cameras, without others around, without being *watched*, but I have to do this.

I'm not letting Marisol go without a fight, without telling her that I'm no longer holding her hand in public or kissing her goodnight so that the cameras will see. I'm doing those things because I *want* to.

Because I've taken to pretending that this fake relationship is real.

I end the kiss and pull away from her, suddenly so nervous that it feels as if there's live wire under my skin. She looks up at me, her brown eyes wide with surprise.

I take a deep breath.

"Marisol, I'm not pretending," I say.

CHAPTER ONE
Gavin

One Month Earlier

Valerie holds her finger on a button, her body perfectly motionless as the blinds lower slowly. It cuts the sunlight down by about half, but it's still too bloody bright in here. Hell, everything in Los Angeles is too bloody bright.

Wake up in the morning: sun. Go for three-mile run, one of my new, healthy, *replacement* habits, and there's sun. Lunch, dinner, when I go into the studio: fucking sun, sun, *sun*. The only respite is at night, though then the whole city is lit with screaming neon, so it's not too terribly different.

It'll make a man miss his rainy gray motherland, that's for sure.

"There we are," Valerie says, and walks to sit at the head of the conference table, facing away from the window. Larry and I sit as well, him in his five-

4

thousand-dollar suit and me in my nicest black t-shirt and least-ripped jeans.

Can't say I haven't made an effort. I rejected two other pairs of trousers as I was getting dressed. Across the table, our manager Nigel is wearing a short-sleeved button-down shirt and a windbreaker, so at least I'm dressed better than someone.

"Is Miss Fields running late?" Larry asks, checking his Rolex. He couldn't be less subtle about it.

Valerie's face doesn't move. I'm not sure it *can* move.

"A few minutes, yes," she says, her voice perfectly placid and calm. Her dark hair is parted neatly in the middle, both sides waving gently away from her perfectly smooth, even face.

She makes me think of a porcelain doll come to life, if porcelain dolls were particularly crafty, manipulative, and bossy — and since she's the band's new Public Relations manager, I consider those things compliments.

"Tonight is Gavin's first show since the tour ended," Larry says, lacing his sausage-like fingers together on the table. "We can't wait forever, you know, and he should be arriving early at the venue, making sure everything is—"

"I'm fine, Larry," I interject before he can really get going. "It's been three minutes, surely we can give her three more."

"I'm just saying, your time is valuable, and if—"

"I'm known to be late on occasion as well," I say, starting to get impatient with my lawyer. He's good at his job, but he's set on having the advantage in every situation, even one like this.

"She'll be here very soon, I'm sure," Valerie says, her tone still neutral and pleasant.

I hate this.

I hate this sterile, shiny, *bright* conference room and I hate that now I've got to listen to people who lecture me about *my image* and *my brand*. Once upon a time I played guitar too loud in tiny clubs and howled at the top of my lungs and didn't give a shit what anyone thought, but now I'm *here*. With these wankers.

My old self would make fun of me now, that's for sure. At least until he saw the house I live in. That might shut him up.

Larry sighs dramatically, checking his watch again, but just as he does the door swings open and four people enter: a man, two women, and a girl.

My heart plummets when I see the girl, like a ball of lead straight into my gut. If I had doubts about this already, now they're doubled. Tripled.

She's blonde and blue-eyed, practically cherubic. I don't think she's old enough to drink legally, but she's got that calm, blank affectation that people who grew up in front of the camera tend to have. As if she only comes alive when someone's recording.

One of the women leans over the table, and I stand to shake her hand.

"Margaret Sorenson," she says, all business. "I'm Daisy's PR person. This is her lawyer, Michael Warren, and this is Karen Fields."

"Lovely to meet you," I say automatically, though she's already moved on to Larry.

I look at Daisy Fields, then at Karen Fields, who *must* be her mother, and I realize two things.

One, she brought her mother to a business meeting; and two, Daisy Fields is her *given* name. I'd assumed she changed it when she went on television, but I guess her parents actually named her *Daisy Fields*.

They must have really wanted their little girl to go into showbiz, as they say out here.

Then Daisy herself is across the table from me, leaning forward, holding out her hand. It's small and soft, and she barely grips me at all. It's like shaking hands with a mitten.

"It's so nice to meet you!" she bubbles.

"You as well," I say.

"I love *Half-Asleep*!" she goes on. "It's such a beautiful love song."

It's *Half-Awake,* not *Half-Asleep*, and it's not a love song, but I let it slide.

"Thank you," is all I say.

We all sit, and Valerie starts talking, but I'm hardly listening, my mind swirling as I stare at the girl across from me.

I can't do this. There's no way I can do this, not with *her*. I'm sure Daisy Fields is nice, but she's a child. She brought her mother to this meeting, and even now, she's watching Valerie intently, as if she needs to hang onto every word that comes out of the other woman's mouth or she might lose the thread of conversation.

"And that's all amenable to you?" Valerie asks Daisy's side of the table.

Wide-eyed, Daisy looks at her mother. Karen nods, then Daisy nods too.

That's it. I've had it.

I no longer give a single fuck about *rehabbing my brand* or *making over my image* or any of that.

I'm not doing this. I'm not pretending to date a former child star who might not even know where Britain *is* so that the music-buying public will think I've turned over a new leaf and discarded my old, sordid ways.

I have. They're gone. It's been months since I so much as had a drink, but I'm not hauling this girl around town on my arm to prove it.

I stand, shoving my expensive leather executive chair back, all eyes on me now.

"Larry, Nigel," I say, my tone clipped. "A word?"

I don't wait for them to answer, just walk out of the conference room and into the hall. Both men follow, and they shut the door behind them.

"Gavin—"

"I'm not doing this," I say, gesturing at the door. The wall dividing the hall from the room is frosted glass, so I know they can see me, but I don't care.

"Come on, Gavin," Nigel says, holding his hands out like he's trying to console me. "We talked about this, and you *know* the record label isn't—"

"Was I unclear?" I ask, my voice rising a little. "I'm not pretending to shag that sweet moronic poppet so that housewives on Long Island will buy our records, and *fuck* the label."

Nigel's face drops, his mouth sagging at the corners. Next to him, Larry's face is perfectly, carefully neutral.

"Gavin, this is what we—"

"How can I get you to *yes*?" Larry interrupts, a phrase I'm certain he learned from some negotiation seminar.

I didn't think I could hate this moment more, but *now* I do.

I just shake my head and push one hand through my hair, the narrow leather straps around my left wrist sliding down. There's seventeen of them, one for each week I've been clean.

"You can't," I say, turn, and leave the building.

CHAPTER TWO
Marisol

My feet are already screaming as I walk through the doors of the campus library, toward the reserve desk. I *really* wish I hadn't forgotten my flats, but I keep telling myself it's good practice for next year, when I'll have a job where I'll be wearing shoes like this six days a week.

Well, if I'm lucky I'll have a job like that. If I'm not lucky I won't have a job at all, but I can't think about that right now.

"Need a book?" asks the undergrad behind the reserve desk.

"Yes, please," I say, sliding an index card across the counter. On it I've written, very neatly:

```
Meyers, Law 341
Contemporary    Issues    in    American
Asylum Law, Second Edition
KZ6350 .S27 2014
```

"Cool," she says, reading the card. "Be right back."

She walks away and I hang on to the counter, carefully lift one foot, and circle my ankle above the floor, wiggling my toes. There's a small knot of anxiety in my stomach, because I *still* haven't been able to get a hold of the book, and I need to do my reading by Monday.

Since it's a small seminar class, participation counts as fifty percent — *half* — of our final grade, meaning that each once-weekly class session is 3.125% of that grade. And sure, if I don't participate once, a 96.875% is still an A, but why risk it?

The undergrad doesn't reappear. I think calming thoughts. My phone buzzes in my briefcase, and I crouch down to grab it.

Brianna: *You're still coming to the secret show tonight, right?*

Crap. I squeeze my eyes shut, put the phone down on the counter, and rub my temples. I totally forgot to put Brianna's birthday thing in my calendar and now it's tonight.

Just say you forgot and don't go, I tell myself. *You know it's going to be her and a bunch of her new, rich friends, and they're just going to talk about celebrities and designer purses or whatever it is she likes now.*

I wish. It's a nice fantasy, but I text her back.

Marisol: *Of course! The Whiskey Room at 10, right?*

Brianna's my oldest friend. We've known each other since kindergarten — almost twenty years now. I *have* to go.

True, about a year ago she married Larry, who's forty-three, mega-rich, and bills himself as "the attorney to the stars." Since then she's found a new crop of friends, but I should still go to her birthday party. It's the least I can do.

The undergrad finally reappears, frowning. My stomach sinks, because she doesn't have a book.

You have to be kidding me.

"It's checked out," she says, handing my index card back.

"Would you mind looking again?" I ask, as politely as possible. "It was also checked out yesterday morning, yesterday evening, and earlier today, and there's a two-hour limit on checking out reserve books."

She taps at a computer for a few moments, then nods.

"Yeah, it's still checked out," she says. Then she frowns. "Actually, it's been checked out for two days. That's weird."

I close my eyes and take a deep breath. I *need* that book to do the reading, and someone's taken it.

No. Worse.

They've taken it *against the rules*. Those rules are there to make sure that *everyone* can do the reading, whether or not they can afford insanely expensive textbooks, and someone's just *ignoring* them.

And *now* I'm furious.

"Could you tell me who has it?" I ask, still perfectly polite through sheer force of will. "It's a small seminar class, so I'm sure I know whoever it is."

"I can't," she says, sounding apologetic. "It's against the law."

It's not, actually, but I'm not going to argue about it with her. It's probably against library policy.

"You could just buy it?" she asks, obviously trying to be helpful.

I almost laugh in her face. It's a two-hundred-dollar book. Short of a fairy godmother, I can't *just buy it*.

But I don't. It's not her fault that some jerk hasn't returned it.

"Thanks," I say, even though my heart is pounding.

"No problem!" she says brightly, and pulls her phone back out.

I take a deep breath, heave the strap of my briefcase over my shoulder, and walk deeper into the library. I take the elevator to the basement and fall into the ugly wooden chair at my carrel, glad to finally be off my feet.

Two undergrad girls walk by, whispering about some party tonight, both wearing Tiffany bracelets and casually carrying laptops worth as much as my rent. A pang of jealousy stabs through me.

I should have married a rich guy too, I think. *Or just been born to rich parents in the first place.*

I feel guilty instantly. My parents didn't pay my college or law school tuition because they *couldn't*, not because they didn't want to.

But while my classmates' parents were smoking pot in college, mine were escaping a decades-long civil war in Guatemala. When their parents had their first full-time jobs, mine were picking strawberries on migrant worker visas, entering the lottery for permanent resident status over and over again. When their parents were in their twenties, working office jobs and going to happy hour, my parents were learning English, navigating a labyrinthine immigration system, and studying to become U.S. citizens.

And now, when they're in their fifties and they *should* be slowing down, working less, enjoying what they've earned? Their scumbag landlord's evicting them. The part of town where they live, Highland Park, has suddenly become the preferred neighborhood of white hipsters, and that means rent has skyrocketed.

Their apartment is rent-controlled, so instead of raising their rent, they're just getting kicked out. The landlord *says* his son is going to live in the apartment — one of the few reasons you can evict someone — which I know is bullshit. But I can't prove it, so now my sister and I are helping them look for another place to live, and it's not going well.

I sigh, pull my five-year-old laptop out of my bag, and fire it up. If I can't actually get the book, maybe I can find something written *about* it and still contribute to the discussion on Monday.

But then, watching my laptop's load screen, I have a flash of genius.

The bookstore has a fourteen-day return policy. I've got a credit card that I hardly ever use.

As long as I don't damage it, I *can* buy this stupid book. I can get my reading done, get my participation grade, and then return it. Of *course*.

I grin, shut my laptop, and shove it back in my bag. Today's got *nothing* on me.

CHAPTER THREE
Gavin

I'm backstage, forty-five minutes before we go on, and of course the band is having a row.

"You're kidding, right?" Darcy says, her arms crossed over her chest, her stance wide, like she's ready to fight. Which she most certainly is.

"I'm not going to make gaga eyes at this *child* for months to prove that I'm fucking clean," I say, crossing my own arms.

"God*damn* it," Trent says, then turns and walks away, toward the door.

"God fucking *damn* it," I hear as he jerks the door open and stomps through. For a split second, I can hear the screaming, thrashing guitar of the opening band before he slams the door and it's muffled again.

I let him leave. I knew they'd be angry.

"I can't do it," I say to Darcy. "I can't fake interest in someone just so we're photographed properly and the fucking gossip blogs can write about how former junkie Gavin—"

"This was our way back!" Darcy suddenly yells, throwing her arms wide. "We finally got Crumble City to agree to something, and it was *so fucking easy*, Gavin, you just hang out with a cute girl for a while and *voila*, we keep our contract."

Crumble City is our record label. They're the ones insisting that I *improve my image* or they'll be dropping the band.

"As if there are no other record labels," I say. "As if *Lucid Dream* didn't go triple-fucking-platinum and buy the head of Crumble City another *fucking* Aston Martin."

Darcy's nostrils flare, just slightly, her pale face flushed with anger.

"That was before you made headlines by *nodding out on stage* and we had to refund all those tickets," she says, her voice tight and furious. "That was before people stopped *buying* tickets because they all learned you were a junkie who might nod out on stage. It was *way* before Allen died and Liam nearly did."

"We used to be a rock and roll band, not a collection of arseholes spit-shined and polished to present the nicest public image to grannies in Florida," I shoot back. "You think anyone's going to buy an album from Gavin Lockwood, Nice Family Bloke?"

"There's not going to *be* an album from any other Gavin," Darcy snaps.

She's started pacing back and forth in the small room, growling guitar licks leaking through the thin walls separating us from the stage where we're due in forty-five minutes.

"No one's interested in the liability of Junkie Mess Gavin, no matter how good his songs are."

And there it fucking is, the worst truth, the ice pick to the heart. I wrote great fucking songs when I was high as a kite and since I got clean I haven't written a note.

Suddenly I can't be here, in this room, with Darcy any more. I stride for the door Trent left through.

"I'm not pretending to fuck some angel-faced child to make a fat asshole in a suit happy," I say, and yank the door open.

"Jesus fucking—"

I shut the door before Darcy can get to *Christ*, walking down the passageway along the back wall of the Whiskey Room, a ratty black curtain the only thing separating me from the musical overtures of Skullfuck, our opener.

I open another door to another room, and then stop short. It's half-filled with young blonde women in sky-high heels and tight dresses, all holding glasses of champagne, and for a few moments I wonder if they're lost.

Then one of them comes over and *hugs* me, kissing each cheek like we've met before.

"Gavin!" she says, flashing a very white smile. "Thank you *so much* for letting me hang out with the band."

Bingo. It's Larry's trophy wife whose name I can't recall. I just smile and nod at her, doing my best to be congenial.

"Not a problem," I say, crossing the small room away from her. I grab a guitar off a stand and hoist it over my shoulder, because I need an excuse to leave. I've had more than enough blonde girls for the day.

"It's *so* cool," another one gushes. I nod at her.

"I've got to go tune, but have a lovely time, yeah?" I say, my hand already on the doorknob.

They look like they're about to pout, but I head through the door before I have to see it, a faint "Bye!" trailing after me. I'd completely forgotten that Larry talked me into letting his new wife and ten of her closest friends come backstage before the show. I think it's her birthday or something.

Down another hallway, Skullfuck loud as ever, through a door, right, and then I'm outside at last in a near-quiet alleyway. It's set up as a smoker's outpost with Christmas lights and two plastic chairs, but no one smokes any more so I'm alone.

I ease the door closed carefully, leaving it just barely ajar so I can get back in, and lean against the wall, taking a deep breath of the cool, dry Los Angeles air.

And I begin to feel guilty.

Maybe Darcy's right. I've fucked up spectacularly, and Dirtshine isn't just my band, it's theirs too. Maybe I owe it to her and Trent to pretend to date Daisy for a few months, no matter how little she interests me. Surely there are worse things than having dinner with a pretty girl who's a bad conversationalist.

I thumb the A string. A hair flat. The sound is quiet and twangy when the guitar's not plugged into an amp, and it feels muffled in this alleyway as I twist the knob, tightening the string.

I do the same to the E string. Realistically, I'm sure I could get away with a single date a week, maybe two hours. Just two hours, how bad could it be?

Someone pushes the door open, steps outside, and stops.

Holy mother of God.

I can't see much more than a silhouette, but I freeze, thumb poised above my guitar strings.

And I just *stare* at this woman.

It's been ages since I actually found someone attractive. It's been even longer since I found myself simply staring at someone, but there's something about the curves of her body, the way she's standing, the arc of her neck as she looks around.

Then I notice the door swinging shut behind her, and I'm unfrozen.

"Oi!" I shout. "Don't let that door—"

It shuts. She whirls around, one hand on her briefcase, and then lunges for the door but of course it's already locked. That doesn't stop her tugging on it for a moment while I watch her, suspicion unfurling in my chest.

She's carrying a briefcase and dressed like she's on her way to the board meeting of Pointless Wankers, Inc.

I wouldn't put it above Crumble City to keep tabs on me, the fuckers. In fact, given all our recent communications, I'd almost be surprised if they *didn't* send spies to this show, to make sure that I'm not high or strung out.

And they think that if they send a fucking *gorgeous* woman to spy on me, I won't mind.

As I said: fuckers.

The sexy spy woman pulls on the door again, pointlessly, then finally looks up at the wall.

"Useless," I call, standing, arms crossed over my chest. "It's locked tighter than a spinster's arsehole."

She turns and looks at me, surprise written all over her very pretty face.

Busted.

CHAPTER FOUR
Marisol

I yank on the door one more time, but it's obviously not going to work. Instead of finding Brianna's birthday party I've locked myself in an alley with a man who just used the phrase *spinster's arsehole*.

The door doesn't open. I admit defeat and turn toward the voice.

"Sorry, love," he says, arms crossed over his chest. "Tighter than a spinster's *butthole*."

I think he's a roadie, because he's out here, leaning against the wall, a guitar slung over one shoulder. But instead of apologizing, like I should, I don't say *anything*.

Because he's really hot. Probably the hottest roadie ever.

Not that I've met a lot of roadies. I don't go to a lot of concerts, and especially not a lot of *secret, cool* concerts, but my impression of roadies was that they were mostly dour, stringy-haired guys with weird facial hair.

This guy, on the other hand, is wearing a black t-shirt that's bulging at the biceps and chest, all broad shoulders and powerful arms. He's got two full-sleeve tattoos, deep brown eyes, and a square jaw.

And he's looking me up and down, taking in the heels, the briefcase, the whole dressed-for-success outfit that is *wildly* out of place right now.

I'm trapped in an alleyway. There's an *extremely* attractive man here, with a British accent no less, and he just used the phrase "spinster's butthole."

Law school has not prepared me for this, but I open my mouth anyway.

"I'm shocked at *spinster*, not *asshole*," I say. "I don't think I've heard anyone say *that* since my great-grandma died."

I take a good look at him, one hand steadying my briefcase on my shoulder, sizing him up. Hot but smug, and there's something else I can't put my finger on about his expression — there's something just a little dangerous about it, like he's challenging me to something.

He raises one eyebrow. Surprise: it's very attractive.

"I'm sure your great-grandma and I have quite a lot else in common," he says. "I also fancy a good knitting session and a nice cup of tea on my nights off. Staying in, watching telly, bedtime at ten, that's me these days. Not a lick of fun."

"Well, Nana stays in all the time, being dead," I point out, my eyes narrowing.

I have no idea why this man is telling me how quiet and uneventful his life is. Is he hitting on me?

Do I look like someone whose knees go weak at the phrase *knitting session*?

"Then our lives are about equally interesting," he says.

"You've had five children and hide the good tequila in the Guadalupe statue by the stove?"

"I haven't got any good tequila to hide," he counters. "Nor any children."

"Sounds like your life is actually *less* interesting than hers was," I say.

We're definitely arguing, and I *definitely* have no idea why.

"Leaps and bounds less," he says, and then we just look at each other for a long moment. I pull my phone out.

"Let me text my friend," I say. "She can come open the door."

"Right," he says, and sits down in an ugly plastic chair. I text Brianna that I'm trapped in an alleyway and hope she's not too annoyed to come rescue me.

I wait. She doesn't text back. My feet are screaming because of my shoes and my shoulder's screaming because of the heavy bag, so I brace myself against the door and give it one more good, hard *yank* because I don't really feel like being in this alley with a standoffish jerk, no matter how hot he is.

The door doesn't open. The standoffish jerk laughs.

"It's quite locked," he calls, tooling around a little on the guitar.

I take a deep breath, eyes closed, and then I walk over to the other plastic chair and sit in it, because if I'm going to be stuck out here I may as well not be on my feet.

"Just double-checking," I say, trying to keep my voice neutral. "I'd feel like an idiot if it weren't locked and we were out here for no reason."

"No worries, there's a reason," he says. "You ruined my carefully executed plan."

I snort. *Screw* this guy.

"Your half-assed plan was not *carefully executed*," I say.

"Like hell it wasn't," he retorts, fingers still plucking at the guitar strings, a faint melody issuing forth. "It does take finesse to leave that door *almost* closed."

"I'm *certain* you could have found a chunk of cinderblock out here to prop it open if you'd tried," I say, leaning my head back against the concrete wall. "*That's* a plan."

"There's a trick," he says. "If you leave the door too far open the alarms go off, and then you've got management up your arse when you're just trying to tune an instrument in peace."

"And you'd prefer your ass stay tight as a spinster's," I say without thinking.

He stops tooling around with the guitar and looks at me. I meet his gaze.

He's not smiling, but he's kinda close.

"I'd prefer management at least buy me a few drinks first," he says, his eyes just barely crinkling at the corners.

I raise my eyebrows.

"And you tried to tell me that your life is all knitting, tea, and television," I say. "Not that I believed you."

That was the wrong thing to say, because his face changes. The almost-smile disappears, and he looks down, both hands back on the guitar, half-playing some fast, angry melody that sounds vaguely familiar.

"Nah, of course not," he mutters, half to himself. "It's not as if people can change without a bleeding nanny around to supervise, right?"

I have no idea what he's talking about, but it sounds weird and paranoid, and I'm starting to get nervous. I stand, pain throbbing through my feet, and hoist my briefcase over my shoulder.

"I'm gonna walk around front," I say.

"There's a fence," he says without looking up.

"Then I'll walk around the block."

"Fence both ways," he says.

I frown. *That's* a pretty serious code violation.

"This is a fire exit," I say, pointing at the door.

He glances at it.

"Indeed," he says.

"You can't have a fire door open onto a blind alley," I say. "What if the building catches fire? People will just be trapped here instead of inside."

"Perhaps you could tattle to the fire marshal as well," he suggests. "Two birds with one stone."

I take a deep breath, letting it out slowly. I probably *shouldn't* get in a yelling match with a stranger who's got a good eight inches and eighty pounds on me in a mostly-dark alley, but today has been *stupid*.

"What the hell are you *talking* about?" I finally ask, my voice raising. "I don't know *what* crawled up your butt and died, but if you've got some prob—"

The door opens, cutting me off, and Brianna teeters out in a tiny dress and sky-high shoes.

"Mare?" she calls.

Thank *Christ*.

"Bree!" I say. "I'm so sorry, I got weird directions from the bouncer and then this door locked by accident and I—"

She's not even looking at me anymore, she's looking at the British jerk.

"Gavin!" she says, cutting me off. "Jeez, good thing I found *you*!"

He smiles tightly and stands.

The thought crosses my mind: *maybe he's not a roadie*.

Brianna would never in a million years know a roadie's first name.

"I do turn up in the strangest places," Gavin says.

23

"Come on!" Brianna says brightly, stepping back. We both follow her into the Whiskey Room, silently, as I wish I hadn't just lost my cool.

Once inside, Gavin pushes open one of the other doors — apparently it sticks, that's why I thought it was locked — and disappears while Brianna grabs my arm, practically dragging me along.

"You didn't tell me you were out there with *Gavin*," she says.

I didn't know I was out there with Gavin, I think.

"I was hoping I was important enough to get rescued on my own," I say.

She squeezes my arm and laughs.

"Stop it, you know what I meant," she says, and opens another door, leading me through.

On one side of the room is a gaggle of women dressed to party, all clearly her friends, all holding champagne glasses. On the other is a slightly grungier collection of people who look considerably more at home in the Whiskey Room, all ripped denim and t-shirts.

The two halves aren't interacting.

"Here," Brianna says, pushing a champagne flute into my hands. "They told me the show is starting in ten minutes, so make sure you have a drink!"

We clink our glasses together. I wish her happy birthday. Then I put down the plastic bookstore bag and briefcase and try to join the girl-gaggle conversation.

It could go better. They mostly talk, and I mostly stand there politely, mind elsewhere. I've got a growing, gnawing suspicion that Gavin is someone of note, maybe even someone in the band.

Someone Brianna would prefer that I *not* have been an asshole to.

Thankfully, after five minutes Brianna waves her arms for attention.

"Hey, the show's gonna start soon so we should all head upstairs!" she says brightly. "We're in the *vee-eye-pee* section."

She pronounces each letter loudly and thoroughly, as if to make sure that we all fully understand that we're VIPs tonight. I grab my briefcase from where it's leaning against the wall and join the troupe of sequined blonde girls as we parade out of that room, through the maze backstage, and then up a staircase to the balcony.

Half of it's roped off, filled with couches and chairs and tables. There's more champagne in ice buckets up here, and when she sees it, Brianna squeals and claps her hands together.

I try not to think mean thoughts. It's her birthday, she's drunk, and we're friends.

I lean against the balcony railing, hoping I look casual, like I'm a totally cool, hip person who goes to secret rock shows all the time. Even though I can't actually remember the band's name right now.

Floor polish? I think. *Sparkle... something. Sparklehorse? Mudhoney?*

Nope.

A girl leans on the railing next to me. She's less blonde than the rest, but not by a lot.

"I am *so excited*," she says, carefully pushing her hair behind one ear, champagne in her other hand. "Earlier *Gavin* said my dress was *brilliant* and I just can't believe it!"

So he's definitely not a roadie. My stomach flutters a little.

"That's great!" I say with all the enthusiasm I can muster.

"Right?!" she says. "I was totally — ooooooh!"

The lights over the audience dim, and a huge cheer goes up from the crowd. I take the opportunity to slip my feet out of my shoes, because right now I don't care if this floor is covered in a mixture of saliva, old beer, and drugs, I *cannot* wear them anymore.

Lights go on at the back of the stage. Now I can make out the big drum that says DIRTSHINE in ornate-but-grungy letters.

The name sounds vaguely familiar.

The other girls gather around me, clustering at the railing. For once, I'm glad I'm short so the blondes in heels can see over my head.

The crowd cheers. The girls squeal. Even though I don't know a thing about the band, my heart starts to beat faster, because there's something exciting about being with people this amped up — I can't help but feel it, too.

A guy comes out, backlit so I can't see his face. The crowd cheers louder, and he sits behind the drums and waves. Another guy walks out and picks up a guitar, then a woman who also grabs a bass.

I think one of them might be Gavin, but I can't tell.

Now everyone is screaming, stomping, and clapping. *I'm* clapping. The floor below my feet is vibrating with the noise.

Another guy comes out, and now everyone in the entire place *loses their minds*. It's so loud I nearly cover my ears, only I don't want to seem like an even bigger dork than I already am.

He's backlit, and I can't see his face. He's got the right haircut and the right build, but mostly, it's the churning in my stomach that tells me it's Gavin.

Okay, so he's the singer of some band, I think. *Who cares?*

Probably-Gavin grabs a guitar. He steps up to the microphone. The drummer raises his sticks in the air, and they all pause.

Then the drummer counts off one-two-three-four and all at once, a wall of sound crashes over the audience and the stage lights go on.

It's Gavin, his head thrown back, the muscles in his forearms knotting as he plays hard and loud, the same thing he was half-playing out in the alleyway only now they're all together, playing as one on stage even as he seems like he doesn't notice that the crowd is there, going *crazy*.

And it's loud, but it's *good*, nothing like the dissonant noise of the opening band. I can almost feel the heavy guitar surround me in the air, like it's lifting me up, taking me somewhere that's not this grungy club or this balcony full of screaming girls.

I think I recognize the song. I think I've heard it before, somewhere.

The guitar stops, leaving nothing but a scant drumbeat and a bass line. The audience holds its breath as one, like a monster with hundreds of throats. *I* hold my breath.

Gavin steps forward. He takes the microphone in one hand and leans into it, like he's whispering to a lover. It's so intense that I can almost feel his breath on my ear, sending a shiver down my spine.

Then he starts singing.

Wrap me in sunrise...

His voice is deep and melodic and rough in exactly the right ways, and I realize: I've heard this song at least a million times.

I *do* know who Gavin is.

At least he's so famous you'll never have to see him again, I think.

CHAPTER FIVE
Gavin

God, I'd almost forgotten how this felt.

Playing together with Darcy and Trent again, all of us so close and so *together* that it feels like our hearts are beating in rhythm as the music flows from my fingers, through the guitar, out of the speakers and over the crowd.

We've practiced together since the tour ended abruptly, of course. Eddie joined the band when Liam left and we had to break him in, so to speak, and that was good, but there's absolutely nothing like hundreds of people standing and watching you in awe, mouthing the words to the songs you wrote, screaming for you.

Makes you feel like a king. A *god*. This is why rock stars become complete tossers.

The first song ends. The crowd *roars* but Darcy slides her hand down the neck of her bass, strings squealing, the throb coming through the soles of my feet and just like that we're together again, into the next song, all parts of the same animal.

Right now, I don't miss being high. Not at all.

As we play, I look out over the crowd, the people who were either lucky enough or in-the-know enough to come to our "secret" show at this tiny, ugly, dirty club on the Sunset Strip. In this moment I fucking *love* every last one of them.

I glance at the balcony. It's a riot of sparkles, so that's where the party girls must be, but they seem into it so it's fine.

No: it's great. Everything is great.

At the front of the balcony is one person *not* in sequins, and even though it's hard to see with the lights in my eyes, I can just barely make her out: white blouse, black skirt, standing still like she's rapt at attention.

The girl from the alley.

My heart beats just a little faster.

• • •

We play until one in the morning, and then we play two encores, and we'd play a third if the Whiskey Room didn't turn its house lights on.

When I walk offstage, I'm buzzing, high as a kite, my blood humming through my veins even though I'm covered in sweat and the fingertips of my left hand are a bit sore. I haven't played that hard or that long in *months*.

Not to mention that it's been even longer — years, probably — since I took the stage sober.

I do wish Liam had been there. I can't help it. Eddie's a wonderful bloke, great drummer, nice as can be, but it's not the same. It still feels a bit like driving on three tires and a spare, but I just have to trust that after a while it'll all be as good as it ever was, only without Liam, because some messes are beyond saving.

Backstage, everything feels like it's happening in

hyper-speed, and I'm just standing in the middle as people rush around, carrying instruments and microphones and sound equipment. The party girls seem to be gone, probably off to another party, and though I didn't need to see *them* again there's a tiny pang of regret in my gut that I won't see Alley Girl.

She wasn't exactly nice, but I don't think I want *nice*. There are thousands of people who'll be *nice* to me.

"Great show, man!" a voice behind me shouts, just as a hand lands on my shoulder so hard it makes my skin tingle. "That was awesome, just awesome!"

It's Eddie, grinning so bright he could light up a football pitch at night. I slap him on the shoulder.

"Not bad for your first show with the band, huh?" I say, grinning almost as wide as him.

He shakes his head, hair flopping around.

"You know, I was really nervous beforehand, like, butterflies and all that, but once I got out there it was just—"

He whistles, gliding a hand through the air, possibly to indicate *smooth sailing*.

"You've got it down cold, mate," I say. "That was fucking perfect."

Darcy and Trent appear to my left, both looking somewhere between cautious and relieved. Eddie looks at them, looks at me, and jerks a thumb over his shoulder.

"I'm gonna go make sure they're not... you know, with the drums... catch you guys later," he says, backing away.

We watch him go.

"He's sweet," Darcy says.

"He's a good drummer," I say.

Then we stand there in silence for another beat. Darcy sighs.

"Fuck," she says, and wraps me in a hug. "Just, *fuck*,

Gavin, what the fuck."

She squeezes me harder.

"This is why I write the lyrics," I say, and she laughs, then lets me go.

Trent shrugs.

"Fuck?" he says.

We hug as well.

"Listen, guys," I start.

Trent shakes his head.

"We'll work it out," he says, then points over his shoulder, back toward the stage. "I'm still pissed at you, but *that*? Worth working it out."

Another twinge, deep down, the missing piece that's Liam. He knows the show was tonight and he's probably piss-drunk somewhere, if not disastrously high.

"I'm also still pissed," Darcy offers, not sounding cross at all, and I laugh.

"That's fair," I say.

They glance at each other.

"Listen, we're going to this bar a couple blocks away where some people are getting together, and do you want to... come or anything?" Trent asks, his voice very careful.

I can feel the weight of seventeen thin leather bands on my wrist, and I shake my head.

"No thanks," I say.

They both look *relieved*. There's a big part of me that wants to go, but I know I'll end up following the old pattern. Rounds of shots, then lines of blow in the men's room, partying until dawn. Near-inevitably finding myself in a room with a needle and someone who wants a story about shooting up with Gavin Lockwood.

My therapist and I have talked a *lot* about changing habits.

"Okay," Darcy says, and squeezes my shoulder. "Chin up, all right mate?"

It sounds goofy as hell with her American accent, and I smile.

"Right-o, spot on," I answer, and they walk away.

• • •

I hang around back stage for a while, long enough that anyone waiting for me outside will have given up, or at least I hope so. Fans I can deal with, but paparazzi? Not so much.

I'm just not sure I'm up for that yet, the shouted questions about *do you think you can stay clean* or *what's the band like without Liam* or *what do you want to tell your detractors*?

I don't want to tell them a damn thing besides *sod off*, so I stay backstage and annoy the roadies by being underfoot for another while, but there's nothing doing here either.

It's strange as hell and a little lonely, being bored after a show, even as I'm still amped up from being on stage, from the screaming crowd. It seems like there ought to be *something* happening now, something properly enjoyable that doesn't involve substances, and as I put my jacket on I think, *maybe one drink.*

You can hold your liquor. You were a junkie, not an alcoholic. Just one.

I should know better. I *do* know better, but the thought of everyone else celebrating without me while I go home, sip tea and watch telly grates on me like sandpaper. It was my show more than anyone else's, and fuck this, I *deserve* to celebrate, just a little.

One drink. Maybe two. Two drinks is fine.

I leave the room and I'm heading down the hall, the space between the wall and the stage, when I hear a voice, pleading, maybe on the verge of tears, and I look over my shoulder.

It's Alley Girl, arguing with a security officer nearly twice her size.

"I don't *care* about Gavin or the band," she's insisting, her voice getting louder. "I was with Brianna Diamant's birthday party and I left something really important back there. I just want to look for it, I swear."

I can't hear the answer, but I can tell from her face it's not good.

Don't get involved, I think. *You were a right cock to her last time you spoke and you're unlikely to make it better now by trying to swoop in and save the day.*

Doesn't matter. I've already turned and I'm walking toward the guard's back, the girl's eyes tracking me suspiciously.

"Hey," I say, putting a hand on the man's shoulder. "She's all right."

The security guard shrugs and steps aside, but the girl just stands there, looking surprised.

"What's the problem?" I ask, nodding her backstage.

CHAPTER SIX
Marisol

I'd like a redo on today.

First the library didn't have the book, then I forgot my flats and have been wearing these stupid heels for hours, then I locked myself out of the Whiskey Room and got into a fight with a famous rock star, and now I've left behind the book that I bought and planned to return.

The book I *need* to return. I don't have $200 to throw away on a stupid, champagne-fueled mistake, not if I'd like to eat *and* pay my rent next month.

Of *course* the person who's taken up my cause is the one I was hoping not to see again.

"Thanks," I say to Gavin, because I know my manners.

Maybe he's slightly less of a dick than I thought. Or maybe he just wants to bring me backstage again so he can keep being a dick, but right now, I don't care.

I've only had two glasses of champagne, but I drink so rarely that I'm pretty tipsy, and that means I'm on the verge of tears. About this stupid, expensive book.

I take a deep breath.

"I think I left a book back here by accident," I say, eyes ahead and not looking at him, voice steady. "I already checked outside and it's not there."

"A book," he says thoughtfully.

For some reason, *that's* what makes me snap.

"Yes, a *book*," I say, grabbing the strap of my briefcase tightly in one hand. "Made of paper, has words and sometimes pictures, weighs about two pounds, generally used by the moderately educated to impart important information to others."

He looks at me, eyebrows raised.

I'm a jerk. He's not even being a dick right now.

"Crap, I'm sorry, I've just had a really stupid day and now *this*," I say, putting one hand over my eyes. "I just really need this book and I'll be out of your hair."

I hear a low, throaty sound and look up. He's laughing.

"I've always been told that stupid questions get stupid answers," he says.

"It wasn't that stupid of a question," I say apologetically.

"What does this method of imparting information look like?" he asks, still laughing.

I describe *Contemporary Issues in American Asylum Law, Second Edition* as he leads me through the backstage area and then opens a door. It's the room where we were earlier, before the show.

"I should warn you, I've not seen it," he says, stepping inside and looking around. "And frankly, back here a book would stick out like a nun at a stag party."

My stomach is in knots and my face is hot, because as much as I need to find the book, I don't want to admit to him just how much I can't afford to lose it.

"It was in a plastic bag," I say. "And I put it down against that wall, next to my briefcase, and then didn't pick it back up..."

There's no book by the wall, but Gavin shrugs. Then he strides over to the couch and starts pulling cushions off, though one's already missing.

"I can look," I say quickly. "You looked like you were leaving, I don't want to keep you here if you've got somewhere else to be."

"Just my tea and my telly," he says, pulling off another cushion. No book.

I sigh, bending and looking under a table, moving aside a few boxes.

"Okay, I give up," I say. "What's that code for?"

"What, tea and telly?"

His voice is muffled as he peers down the side of the couch, his hand in the crevice.

"Right," I say, crawling under a table so I can turn everything upside down. "You said it earlier, too."

I go through a couple boxes: nothing, nothing, nothing. Panic is starting to give way to the dull, numb feeling of inevitability that I'm never going to see that book again.

Now I can't do the reading *or* get my money back, which is the worst of both worlds. Now my participation grade will be shit, I'll have to do *spectacularly well* on that final essay, and I'm going to be eating ramen, rice, and beans for a month.

I wish I'd never had the brilliant idea to buy it and return it.

"It just means tea and television," he says, straightening up. "There's no code."

I'm on the floor, and I lean on one hand, tucking my legs under me. Hopefully I'm not flashing the very hot rock star, but I don't even care any more. I'm sure he's seen panties before, and how much worse can tonight go?

"So, right now, you're going to go home, drink tea, and watch television," I say, my voice doubtful.

"You don't sound like you believe me," he says, collapsing onto the sofa, arms stretched wide, one cushion is still missing.

"Would you believe yourself?" I ask, still on the floor.

"Not likely," he says, half-smiling. "And with good reason."

"Okay," I say. I feel like I'm adrift in this conversation, because we've had it before and it went differently then. "Last time I said that, you got weird and started acting like I was Big Brother."

"I thought you were someone else," he says.

I wait in silence for him to finish explaining. There's still no book and I'm *not* in the mood for games. He sighs.

"I thought the record label had sent you in secret to keep tabs on me because you're dressed as if you're going to a job interview," he says. "They've not been too happy with me lately."

I stretch my legs out and lean against a table leg. I don't think I'm ever getting *Contemporary Issues in American Asylum Law* back, and I need to figure out a way to do the reading *and* come up with $200.

But right now, I'm going to sit here and talk to this famous, hot rock star for five minutes. Everything's already screwed up, so why not?

"What did you do?" I ask.

He leans forward, his elbows on his knees, and rubs his hands together slowly.

"You can sit on the couch, you know," he says.

"I'd rather sit here than stand in these shoes again," I say. "Answer the question."

He grins at me instead.

"Law school, right?"

"I'm not going to forget I asked."

"You know you haven't told me your name?"

"Marisol. Tell me."

"Marisol. Three syllables, tripping off the tongue..."

He stops, eyes narrowing, then looks at me and laughs.

"That's all I can remember."

It sounds familiar, but I can't place it.

"Is that..."

"*Lolita*," he says, leaning back onto the couch. "Not only do I know what a book is, I've read one before."

"That's an odd choice to read if you've only read one," I say.

"All right, more than one," he says. "And I read *Lolita* during my one year of college when it was assigned, I don't seek out books on pedophiles."

"So your record label must be pissed for some other reason," I say. I'm trying not to smile, but I can't help it. "What did you do?"

Gavin laughs again, and the sound makes *me* laugh, because it's warm and friendly and even if he's kind of a jerk who apparently behaves badly enough to piss off record labels, I kind of like him.

Also, he's hot and I'm tipsy.

"Where does one start?" he asks, putting his hands behind his head and looking at the ceiling. "I guess Crumble City *first* got angry a few years ago, when—"

There's a crash, somewhere far away, a crunchy, *squealing* crash. A shriek. Something slamming against a wall, yelling, footsteps running around.

Gavin's already to the door by the time I'm on my

feet, briefcase in hand because I am *not* losing anything else, and I follow him as he rushes through the hall, between the wall and the curtain, to a huge double door that leads to the outside.

It's open, people rushing back and forth. As I get closer I can hear someone shouting at the top of his lungs with a British accent so thick I can barely understand it.

"Fassroit!" I think he says. "Got meunshoo *nae*."

Maybe it's not English.

"Jesus Christ," mutters Gavin. "Fuck me fucking bloody, that fucking twatheaded *fuck*."

He charges through the door. I'm not sure if I should follow him, so I slow down. Before I can see through the doors I can hear him.

"What the *Christ*?" Gavin shouts. "The shit have you done *now*, you fucking lunatic?"

I stop, back against the opposite wall, and peer through the big double doors onto the Whiskey Room's parking lot.

There's a large van, its nose crunched against a concrete post, steaming from under the hood. The driver's side door is wide open, the interior light on, one front tire flat.

Between the building and the van is a loose circle of people, all standing and staring, the drunken British shouting coming from the center. They give Gavin a wide berth as they let him through, still shouting.

"—Can't just come here and nearly run people over, you madman, you almost killed the valet you fucking idiot, and then what — JAYSUS what the fuck is that thing?"

Gavin practically leaps away as everyone in the circle takes a step back all at once, a quick flash of orange lighting up the parking lot. I keep lingering inside the building, curious, but not terribly interested in getting involved.

"Yoocin geh' *ennufing* 'ere," the drunk guy says. He laughs. There's another flash of orange.

I realize that there's a faint trail of smoke coming from the center of the circle, and I step to my left, then my right, trying to see around the people blocking me.

"Give me that," Gavin commands. "God*damn* it, Liam."

The drunk guy — Liam, I guess — just laughs again and holds something up in one hand. Six inches of flame shoot out of it, and I involuntarily step back, pressed against the wall.

I think the smoking thing on the ground is a pillow, not burning but *smoldering*. Liam says something back to Gavin and now they're arguing, both shouting, and I can't understand anything either of them is saying.

I should go before this gets too crazy, I think, though there's already a drunk man burning pillows in a parking lot.

Liam kicks the pillow. He picks up something from beneath it, still shouting back and forth with Gavin, backing away, shooting his mini-flamethrower or whatever the fuck that thing is, and laughing maniacally.

Then, just as I'm about to turn away, he holds something up.

A light blue, hardcover book.

"HEY!" I bellow, already through the door before I can think. "Put that DOWN!"

I shove past the people standing around, but I feel like I'm moving in slow motion, much too slow.

Liam holds the book up by the spine. The pages fan out. He turns on the tiny flamethrower.

"NO!" I shout.

He's holding the flames to the pages, and they go up like *that*.

"What the *fuck*?" I shout, and I lunge for it.

A strong hand grabs my arm and pulls me back before I can actually grab the flaming book.

"You mother*fucker*!" I shout, trying to wrest my arm away. "What's fucking *wrong* with you? That's mine!"

Liam just laughs, still holding the burning book.

"Finders keep— fuck," he says, dropping it onto the ground, shaking his hand.

"Move!" A female voice bellows, and seconds later someone's there with a fire extinguisher, dousing *Contemporary Issues in American Asylum Law,* the pillow, and Liam, spraying Gavin and I some in the process.

I'm just staring at my book, half-burnt and doused in white foam. Tears are pricking at my eyeballs, and I think I've got about three seconds before I start sobbing from pure rage.

Liam's still laughing.

"Iss joost some—"

"FUCK YOU!" I scream.

"Marisol, I'm—" Gavin starts.

"FUCK YOU TOO!" I shout. I turn in a circle, taking in all the wide eyes and alarmed faces. "Fuck all of you! FUCK!"

I storm away, across the parking lot. Someone shouts after me and I ignore them, sobbing by the time I reach the street.

No one comes after me.

CHAPTER SEVEN
Gavin

"FUCK!" Marisol shouts, tears glittering in her eyes, and before I can do or say anything, she's hightailing it through the parking lot.

Liam shouts after her.

"It's a sodding book, you posh cu—"

I grab his shirt and heave him backwards, up against the side of the equipment van he stole, silencing him mid-sentence. The modified lighter drops to the ground, his head bounces off the sheet metal, and he just laughs.

I guess I should have done this in the first place.

"What the *fuck* is wrong with you?" I shout in his face. "You can't *do* this, crash cars and burn people's things—"

"You can't have a band without me!" he shouts, our faces inches apart. "This was supposed to be us, not you and three American wankers!"

His speech is slurred, his accent thick as mud though I can still understand it. He reeks of cheap tequila, the stuff practically oozing from his pores, and his pupils are pinpricks. Alcohol, coke, and God only knows what else.

"You think this'll get you back? Showing up at a gig with a stolen van and a bleeding homemade flamethrower?"

"Least I'm still living a little," he says, his eyes focusing and unfocusing on my face. "Better than being some stupid boring twat who goes home and puts his feet up by the fireplace every night."

"And who's the stupid twat when I'm alive and you're dead in the gutter, Liam?" I shout.

I slam him against the van again, his head bobbing slightly like it's come loose. I want to rip it off his neck, partly because of what he did and partly because he's bloody right, this *was* supposed to be us.

But only one of us got clean enough to carry on, and it wasn't him.

"Is that what you want, both of us rotting in our graves by thirty?" I yell. "Because that's the end you're coming to, you—"

Sirens wail, and I stop shouting. Blue lights flash across the parking lots as we both turn our heads and see two black and white cop cars screech to a halt, officers running out, leaving the doors open.

I unhand Liam. He stumbles, nearly falls, then rolls his eyes and puts his hands over his head as the cops shout for him to get on the ground.

I back away and nearly trip over the burned wreckage of *Contemporary Issues in American Asylum Law.*

Shit. Marisol.

I turn and push past a security guard, standing there with his mouth open, then jog through the parking lot in the direction she went, the night air cool against my skin.

What if she's gone, I think. *She can't have gone far, and I need to—*

Well, that part I don't know since it's fucking unclear how I could possibly improve this situation. I take a guess and jog left when I get to the sidewalk, scanning the busy Sunset Strip for someone in black and white, carrying a briefcase.

Nothing. No one. I stop at a corner, wondering if I should have gone the other direction, trying to pick out one form from the hundreds along the street.

Then I spot her. She's across the street, sitting on a bus bench, *glaring* at me.

There's a bus a block away. Of course.

I wave at her. Marisol looks away, and even in the light of the street lamps I can see her face is pink and puffy. The traffic on Sunset right now is heavy and fast, all the drivers probably half-drunk and texting while also shouting at their mates and fiddling with the radio.

There's a very small break in traffic. I step out, tentatively, as the bus pulls up wheezing. I'm on the double yellow line in the middle of Sunset, cars hurtling past me on both sides, honking and flashing their lights but not a single one slows.

I hate Los Angeles drivers, I think.

Marisol gets on the bus, and through the windows I watch her pay her fare and then walk down the aisle, not looking at me again. Another tiny break in traffic and I sprint across three lanes, the bus already lumbering away even as I'm waving my hands for it to stop.

The driver just honks. I pound on the door as it passes me only for him to ignore me as the bus slides past with all the grace of a skier in the mud.

I look at the windows, searching for Marisol, and for a fleeting second, there she is: head against the window, staring into space. She doesn't even see me.

"Fuck!" I shout, and kick the ugly green bench, an advertisement for a real estate agent smiling back.

I rub my eyes. I pace back and forth, trying to get a handle on things, trying to figure out why I'm so upset about this one book, this one girl who's had a bad night.

Beautiful as hell with an arse *made* for grabbing, yeah, but that's not it.

She's the first person in weeks, months maybe, who's interested me. Who I want to *talk* to again, even if I never get to see her naked. Marisol's woken up some part of me that I thought was dead, snuffed out by booze and smack and an endless supply of women.

I take a deep breath. I shake my head, and I turn to walk back to the corner and cross Sunset *properly* when I realize there's a line of people standing there, staring at me, half of them with their phones out.

I pause a moment, staring back at them. It's not as if I was doing something shameful or wrong, but I feel like I've been caught in a private moment, one I'd prefer not to share with the gossip-hungry world.

"Cheers," I say, and half wave.

Then I walk to the traffic light and wait patiently for it to change.

• • •

The police take Liam off to jail on charges of driving under the influence, reckless driving, attempted arson, public drunkenness, and probably ten other things. They hang around for a bit, but it's not as if there's some great mystery to unravel: a good twenty people saw everything that happened.

As I'm standing around, waiting to be questioned, I get out my phone and find *Contemporary Issues in American Asylum Law* on Amazon.

It's two hundred dollars. Christ, no wonder Marisol was upset.

I put the book in my cart and email Larry to get her address, the least I can do. Then I sit there, on the steps into the Whiskey Room's back door.

Liam's headed to jail again, probably pissing himself in the back of a cop car right now, no doubt to have a miserable night in a holding cell. Darcy and Trent are going to be angry at me again when they find out what's happened here, and when video of me trying to chase down some girl surfaces tomorrow, because no doubt it'll have some asinine caption like BACK TO SMACK? GAVIN LOCKWOOD SIGHTED IN HOLLYWOOD CHASING THE DRAGON!

Maybe I ought to fake-date Daisy Fields, I think. *There are far worse punishments than trying to talk to a vapid young starlet for an hour once a week.*

God, the thought makes me shudder. It's not me. I don't date young starlets and smile for cameras, I'm some bloke from so far north in England it's almost Scotland who played the guitar a lot and got lucky.

But I don't think I can lose Darcy and Trent, or even Eddie. Liam's already out of the band, and since I'm clean and he's not, it's nearly impossible for me to be around him.

It feels as if I've gotten divorced, my family split in half, and I ought to bite the bullet and take Daisy out, but I *desperately* don't want to.

Then I have an idea.

It's probably not a good one. It's not likely to work, but it *does* make me smile and that's got to be worth something, yeah?

I pull out my phone and dial up Valerie, because I know she's still awake near one a.m. on Friday night, probably telling someone else how they ought to behave.

"What's wrong?" she answers her phone.

Lots, but I don't go into that with her.

"Nothing, I've had a thought," I say, watching a tow truck pull the crashed van away.

There's a moment of silence while she waits.

"And?" she finally responds.

"What if I pretended to date someone besides Daisy Fields?"

Valerie sighs into the phone. I can hear noise and thumping bass behind her. She's probably out somewhere, bossing around another famous person.

"Do you have someone in mind?" she asks.

"I do," I say.

CHAPTER EIGHT
Marisol

"Next!" calls the lady behind the register. The girl in front of me heads up, handing over a physics textbook practically the size of a cinderblock.

I tighten my grip on *Contemporary Issues in American Asylum Law, Second Edition*. It showed up at my door mid-day Saturday, and after I gawked at it for a full minute, like it was a rainbow unicorn offering me a box full of rubies, I cried with relief.

And then I felt guilty.

I left it backstage in the first place, and yeah, Liam shouldn't have *lit it on fire*, but I'm almost positive he isn't the one who sent me another copy the very next morning. My only problem now is that my receipt was sandwiched *inside* that copy, so it's also a small pile of ashes in a club parking lot.

"Next," the lady says again.

I walk to the counter and hand over the book. She holds it up, examining it, and I hold my breath, even though I *know* it's in mint condition.

Finally she nods and sets it on the counter.

"Receipt?" she asks.

I clear my throat.

"I don't actually have it with me," I say, as apologetically as I can. "There was an accident and it got… destroyed."

She raises one eyebrow.

"We don't usually take returns without a receipt," she says.

I use the sincerest, most hopeful tone I've got.

"I know, and I'm so, so sorry," I say. "I've got my credit card with me, is there any way you could look up the transaction history instead? It's just that it's a two hundred dollar book and it turns out I don't even need it for class, and… that's a lot of money."

She sighs. I look down. At least I got the reading done and participated *hard* in class this afternoon.

I can always sell it some other way, I remind myself. *I probably won't get the full price for it, but one-fifty is better than nothing.*

"And I could *really* use the two hundred dollars," I say, my voice quieter now.

She taps her finger on the counter and looks at me for a long moment.

"All right," she says at last. "Don't tell my manager."

I thank her again and again, then practically dance my way out of the bookstore, mentally promising to never, ever try to cheat the system like this again.

As I walk across campus toward my bus stop, I'm almost *giddy*. Like the weight of the past week is finally off my shoulders and I can relax again, just a little.

Well, not that much. I've got to do my reading for my next class, write a paper for my Special Topics course, prep for next week's mock trial, review a few hundred pages of documents for my research assistant job, and edit a very bad twenty-page undergrad essay for my side gig, but at least I don't have two hundred dollars hanging over my head.

Plus, this weekend I told my parents I'd come out to Highland Park and spend Saturday helping them look for a new apartment.

So, yeah, I'm busy, but at least I'm not stressed. I've just gotta get it done.

I'm heading past the library, sun shining, birds singing, when my phone rings with a Los Angeles number I don't recognize. I answer.

"I'm calling from Diamant and Skeller on behalf of Lawrence Diamant," a polite female voice says.

I stop in my tracks instantly, back straight, holding my breath as if she can see me somehow.

"It's nice to hear from you," I say, the first polite phrase I can think of.

"I'm sorry for the short notice, but are you available to come in for an interview tomorrow afternoon?" she asks.

"Yes!" I say, nearly shouting. "Yes, of course, what time?"

Even though I'm standing on the side of a walkway, I drop my briefcase, kneel next to it, and dig out paper and pen, writing down meeting details like a crazy person while students swarm past me. Once I'm scheduled, the receptionist and I say our polite goodbyes and hang up.

Then I jump up and down, pumping one fist in the air. A couple people look at me weird, but I don't care.

Even though I'm friends with Larry's wife, I didn't seriously think they'd call me about this position. For starters, the posting says they *prefer* someone with 1-2 years of experience, and I'll be fresh out of law school when I start.

Plus, they're a huge, wealthy firm with one of the biggest and most respected immigration law practices in town. They're hired by Saudi oil barons and Japanese bankers, people with lots of money to drop on getting green cards and citizenship.

I almost can't believe my luck today. I feel like I should head to Vegas or something and try the roulette table or something.

You need to prepare, I think. *For job interview questions, about law, about where you see yourself in five years, and you need to do laundry, make sure your shoes look good, put together your resume and CV and work samples, brush up on the names of everyone who works there...*

My to-do list swirling through my brain, I practically run to the bus stop.

• • •

The following afternoon, I get there half an hour early, which means half an hour to anxiously walk around Century City, the part of Los Angeles where virtually every business big enough has its offices. While most of Los Angeles is low and flat, with buildings two or three stories at most, Century City is all shining high-rises, steel and glass, people in suits bustling back and forth.

There's hardly a flip-flop in sight, which is pretty strange for L.A.

Finally, five minutes before I'm due, I head up to the twenty-first floor of the Chaplin building, where Diamant & Skellar have their offices. Then I check in with the receptionist, sit down, and wait.

I try to sit still, but I'm as nervous as a box of bees after several cups of coffee, so I look around the small, expensive-but-tasteful waiting area, and try to find something to occupy my hands.

A magazine on a glass coffee table catches my eye, and I frown, tilting my head.

It's *Rolling Stone*, in the middle of a spread of *Sunset*, *The New Yorker* and *The Atlantic*, so it's already out of place. But that's not what catches my eye.

Gavin's on the cover. At least I'm ninety percent sure it's him, so I reach out and pick up the magazine.

Definitely him. And he is definitely not wearing a shirt, just ripped jeans, boots, lots of tattoos, and a glare that I feel inside my ribcage, even though it's only a picture.

Well, I think, trying not to let my eyes linger on the lines of his body even as I ogle this picture, *he's both the hottest and the most famous person I've ever screamed profanities at.*

Not to mention he sent a replacement copy the next day. I should send a thank you card.

I scan over the page. The rest of the band is there, too, all in various states of disarray, glaring at the camera under a headline that shouts:

DIRTSHINE: THE REBIRTH

The band on death, departure, and drummer drama.

Vaguely, I wonder who died, but it's probably someone's dog and they wrote a sad song about it.

Those abs, though, I think, giving Gavin's picture one last good look. *Jeez, he's got that V where the muscles on his hipbones point straight down to—*

"Marisol," Larry's voice booms. "Glad you could make it."

I practically throw the magazine at the coffee table, my face already heating up at getting caught staring at a half-naked man.

"Of course," I say, standing. "It's my pleasure."

We shake hands, and he leads me out of the reception area, down a hallway. The offices are modern and high-end — half-frosted glass walls, floor-to-ceiling windows, everything white and steel and pristine and uncluttered.

Larry's office is at the end, a corner office, the walls completely frosted so I can't see inside. He opens the door and gestures me through, my heart beating double-time, maybe triple-time.

I'm not even past the threshold when I stop short, because someone's already in here, sitting in an expensive white chair, facing Larry's desk.

"Cheers," Gavin says.

My mind goes perfectly blank with surprise. There's a long delay before I finally speak.

"Hi again," I say.

I glance at Larry, because I thought I had a handle on today, but suddenly Gavin's here at my job interview and I don't have a single solitary clue what's going on.

Am I going to be working his immigration case? I wonder.

Does he have an immigration case?

"Have a seat," Larry says, gesturing at the other chair in front of his desk. He sits heavily, unbuttoning his jacket while I perch on the edge of the white leather, my heart thumping in my ears.

"You've met Gavin already, and this is Valerie and Nigel," he goes on, waving at the back of the office.

There's two other people there, one in another chair and one sitting on a couch. I didn't even see them, but they both stand and we shake hands.

"I didn't know this was a group interview," I manage to say. At least my voice isn't shaking.

Larry laces his fingers together atop his desk, his mouth a straight line.

"This is a different kind of interview," he says.

No shit, I think.

"Is it still for the junior immigration attorney position?" I ask, trying to regain a handle on this situation.

"It's not *only* for that position," Larry says, starting to speak in his most convincing, cajoling Lawyer Voice. "Rest assured that Diamant and Skellar is, in fact, *very* interested in making you a part of our team, but today we have a slightly different proposal in addition to that one."

Oh, God, this is going to be some sort of weird sex thing.

My face instantly feels like the surface of the sun.

"Nothing salacious," Larry says quickly, though it doesn't help much. "But I'm afraid it's somewhat sensitive. My client Mr. Lockwood here is... in need of a suitable relationship partner for the media."

I stare at Larry, because I don't think I can even look at Gavin right now.

"A media partner?" I echo. I have no idea what that means.

"My client needs someone respectable with whom he can be seen around town, going on dates, holding hands, that sort of thing," Larry explains.

But why am I here?

There's silence again. Probably the most uncomfortable silence I've sat in since I cluelessly asked my mother what a blowjob was at age eleven.

Finally, Gavin speaks up.

"I need a fake girlfriend," he says.

"Okay?" I say.

I can tell that there's something huge here I'm missing, some important aspect of this conversation that's going straight over my head, but I don't have a clue what it is.

They think I can help Gavin find a fake girlfriend? Is that it? Why on earth do they think that?

"I don't really know anyone, but I could ask around," I say tentatively, because I want to help — and I still want this job — but it's not like I know anyone who does this for a living.

Do people do this for a living? Is *fake celebrity girlfriend* a job?

Gavin grins, leans back, and pushes his fingers through his hair.

"Jesus, we're bollixing this up," he says. "I'm not asking for a reference, love."

Wait.

"I'm asking if you'll do it," he finishes.

CHAPTER NINE
Gavin

There's a rather long pause. This whole meeting has been half pauses, I think, but it's an odd topic so I'm not surprised.

"The fake girlfriend job?" Marisol finally asks.

She's sitting bolt upright in a swivel chair, looking from me to Larry and back, and even though now she's in full attorney gear — high-necked light green blouse, gray suit, trousers, sensible heels, hair tied back — she's still fucking *astounding.*

I have to force myself not to think about peeling her layers off, her warm skin on my lips, the way her blazer would look *perfect* in a pile on my bedroom floor.

"The very one," I say. "It's not much of a job, really. We'd go out once or twice a week, dinner dates, smile for cameras, you'd be back home—"

"I'm not an actress," she says.

Her face is flushing again, and I think this time her voice is trembling.

Fuck, this is going wrong.

"We don't need—" Larry starts.

Marisol cuts him off, standing, one fist balled tightly at her side, her jaw flexing.

"If you'd like to talk about the junior attorney position, I'm still very interested in being considered for that job," she says.

Her voice is tight, rising in pitch, and I can tell it's hard for her to keep it under control.

"But I'm a law student, not someone desperate for fifteen minutes of fame, so I'm afraid I'll be declining the *fake girlfriend* position. Thanks for the interview."

She nods once, briskly, and strides out of Larry's office. I jump to my feet.

"Marisol!" I shout after her.

I'm an idiot. This is how you approach someone like Daisy, not a girl like Marisol, and now she's angry and she'll never say yes.

That's not how it was supposed to go. Not at all. I thought she'd be surprised but I didn't think she'd be angry, not at something simple like getting paid to go on a few dates a week with a famous bloke.

But it's not like I know a lot of girls like her. That's the whole idea.

"Marisol!" I call again, but she's out the office door as her shoes click down the hallway, quickly. Like she can't wait to get out of here.

I can't let her leave. I need her for the band, for the record label.

And I simply don't want to watch her walk away.

"Marisol!" I shout, striding after her, my voice echoing down the glass, steel, and marble hall. Heads turn, but not the one I *want* to turn. That one just keeps going, walking faster if anything.

I break into a jog and a young man carrying a file box dodges out of my way. Two professionally-dressed people scatter to either side of the walkway and then she's there, almost to the end of the hall and I dodge in front, turning to face her, holding my hands up.

"Marisol," I say again, though I'm not shouting this time.

She doesn't even make eye contact, but her eyes are filled with tears, threatening to spill over as she moves to her left, trying to get past me.

"Marisol, please."

She dodges to her left without responding, but I move in front of her that way too.

Then she just stands there, staring straight ahead, not making eye contact.

"I grew up playing football on a muddy field filled with gopher holes," I say. "You're not going to get around me unless you've got fancier footwork than that."

Marisol takes a deep breath. She lets it out, and finally, she looks me dead in the eye.

"I've still got a *nasty* scar from the time I slide tackled Ramón Bautista in fifth grade soccer and scraped my leg on a piece of broken glass on the field," she says. "He didn't want to let me past him either."

"Slide tackle me and I *promise* to let you leave without another peep," I say.

"I ought to," she says. "Apparently I was invited here because I've got a vagina, not because of my GPA, so I've got nothing to lose."

A head down the hall turns toward us, then quickly away. It *can't* be the first time someone's said *vagina* in this hall.

"That's not why," I say. "It wasn't even a requirement. Frankly I'd get loads more press if I suddenly came out as gay."

"*Are* you gay?" she asks, raising one eyebrow.

She looks me up and down, realizes what she's doing, and looks away. I have to fight back a grin.

Marisol could check me out all day if she wanted, no arguments.

"Not at all," I say. "And I don't think I could fake it very convincingly for the cameras."

"So a vagina *is* a requirement."

Not even a lawyer yet and she's talked me into a circle. I'd be annoyed if I didn't rather like it.

"Yes, all right, it's a requirement but I didn't ask for you to be my fake girlfriend just because you've got one," I say.

"You asked because you know so much about me," she says, more than a little sarcastic.

"I asked you because — bugger, hold on," I say. There's a gaggle of well-dressed young attorney-types coming down the hall, toward us, and I don't feel like begging publicly right now.

I take Marisol's hand and pull her to the nearest open door, closing it behind us. The lights are off, but it's clearly someone's office.

Oh well.

"You're the first person in weeks I've been able to stand talking to," I start.

Marisol pulls her hand out of mine, and I feel a tiny, sharp pang of disappointment.

"Sounds like a pretty low bar," she says, tilting her head and crossing her arms in front of herself. She doesn't look thrilled, but she doesn't look like she's leaving.

"It's not like that," I say. "It's that, Marisol, I feel like everyone around me is ready to strike or waiting for me to fuck up for the last time, like they're wolves crossed with vultures or something, and — I've cocked this up already, haven't I?"

Marisol looks like she might be trying not to smile.

"You could go back to the part where I'm capable of a conversation," she offers. "Amazingly, that's been the best thing so far."

It *almost* sounds like she's teasing me.

"I'm not very good at this," I say.

"No," she agrees.

I take a deep breath, trying to straighten things out.

If I were good at talking I wouldn't have wound up a musician, I think.

"I'm a fucking mess," I start. "During the last record and tour — and, all right, for a long time before that but I won't go into it — I had a slight heroin problem."

"Can you have a *slight* heroin problem?" she asks.

"Okay, I had *quite* a heroin problem and it fucked up the tour rather dramatically," I say. "I'll tell you every detail you care to ask, but I went to rehab, got clean, and the strongest thing I've used in over four months is coffee."

She waits, quietly.

"Everyone I know is pissed at me. The band. Our record label, our manager, our fans. The media is slavering outside my door waiting for me to open it and tumble out, needle in arm, so the record label wants me to start dating a nice girl who seems like a good influence, convince everyone I've turned over a new leaf, yeah?"

Marisol just nods. My stomach tightens, just a little, because even as I talk I'm realizing how much I want this. It's more than I thought.

It might be way more.

"Only I don't know any nice girls. Ever since getting clean, everything seems just a little too sharp and pointy, and everyone's angry with me, and all the new people I meet are interested in me because of what I can do for them, not my charming wit and sparkling personality," I go on.

"Can't imagine why," she deadpans.

"I owe it to the band to stop fucking them over, but I can't spend a few hours a week with some empty-headed blonde who'll just remind me why I picked up the needle in the first place," I say.

"And there's no possible route back to respectability besides pretending to date someone," she says, even though she clearly believes otherwise. "You couldn't volunteer at a soup kitchen or adopt a puppy."

"I could, but those are obvious photo-ops. Valerie — she's my public relations minder — says that dating someone is evidence of a *lifestyle change*, and that's what the people who buy tabloids from the market checkout really want to see."

Marisol sighs. She walks to one of the swivel chairs, drops her briefcase, and sits down, one elbow on the arm of the chair, her face leaning on her hand.

"It's been ages since I wanted to see someone again just to finish a conversation," I say. "And — Christ, this sounds tawdry — I chased after you on Friday because you were the first person who I *didn't* want to see leave."

She makes a face.

"Sorry about that," she says, her voice quiet and less angry now. "And thanks for the book. It really helped."

I sit opposite her in a pristine swivel chair and lean my elbows on my knees.

"That's all it is," I say, my voice quieter now. "I like talking to you and I need someone I can spend time with. It's not a sex thing, it's not some complicated way of getting you into bed. I need a friend is all."

We look at each other for a moment.

Of course I'd *like* it to be a sex thing. I've spent the past three nights thinking about Marisol's thighs around my ears while I had a wank.

61

But I'm not stupid. If I were to say *oh and also let's shag* she'd be out of here like a rocket.

"And I'll pay you a million dollars," I say. "Sorry, buried the lede again."

Marisol freezes.

"You're joking," she says.

"I'm not," I say. "Though I did get a bit carried away there and neglect to mention that quite important aspect of this transaction. It's not just for shits and giggles."

Marisol's slowly going pink, the color creeping up her neck, clashing with her light green blouse even in the dark.

"Is that legal?" she asks.

"*You're* honestly asking *me*?" I say, grinning. "I've not been too concerned with legality so far. That's more your department, love."

She stands suddenly, clearing her throat, glancing through the frosted glass wall.

"I have to think about this," she says, sounding almost apologetic.

Fucking unbelievable. I'm on the cover of the *Rolling Stone* in the lobby, I just offered her a million dollars, and she's got to think it over.

Any other girl would have said yes ages ago. Before I got a second sentence out. I wouldn't have even needed to take over some stranger's office.

But I don't want any other girl. I want Marisol to be the one pretending to like me, so *thinking it over* is what I get.

I *did* ask for this. Quite literally.

"Are you going to negotiate?" I tease. "You want a million dollars, posh dinners, diamonds, *and* a vacation to a private island, is that it?"

"Is that what I should hold out for?" she asks, her brown eyes sparkling. "You must be a terrible poker player."

"I am, but because I can never remember the rules and bugger it up," I say, standing as well.

I grab the door handle. She's standing in front of me, but I hesitate for a moment, long enough for her to look back.

"Marisol," I murmur, suddenly so close that I can smell her shampoo and all my nerves sing at once, suddenly alive. "Say yes."

I know she won't, not right now, so I pull the door open without giving her time to answer and we walk down the hall, to the receptionist's desk, in front of the elevators. She shifts her briefcase on her shoulder as the elevator doors open.

"I'll call you," she says, and walks into one. The doors close.

I turn back toward Larry's office, catching sight of myself on *Rolling Stone*.

Smug cocky bastard, I think at my photo.

CHAPTER TEN
Marisol

I take the elevator down in a daze, because I feel like someone's inserted a hand mixer into my ear and scrambled my brains, because all at once I'm angry, confused, and slightly offended, but *a million dollars.*

A million dollars.

I could buy my parents a house. Real estate prices in Los Angeles are completely insane, but a million dollars would get them something small but nice in a good neighborhood. Their rent would never go up again. They'd never get *evicted* again. They could actually save that money for retirement.

I don't think they've ever actually *considered* retiring.

I could pay off my student loans, even the ones from law school. I could pay off my sister's student loans.

I could study for the bar exam and look for a job without worrying about stringing together enough work to pay for rent and food in the meantime. When I get a job, I can save my money instead of putting most of a paycheck toward my student loans.

That's what a million dollars would mean.

It would mean *not worrying about money*.

I have no idea what that feels like. Thinking about money, putting a cost on nearly everything I do, is second nature to me. I just assumed that I'd always worry about money, every day, for the rest of my life.

When I get to the plaza downstairs I sit on a bench for a moment and just stare into space, trying to think. It seems like it can't be real, but we were in Larry's office. I may not be crazy about the guy, but he's a real lawyer, and I don't think signing a contract to be a fake girlfriend is illegal.

And then despite myself, I think about the Rolling Stone cover again. I think about watching Gavin on stage Friday, the way Dirtshine made hundreds of people all lose their minds at once. The way he moves on stage, his deep raspy voice, his hands moving on the guitar.

At least I know I'm not alone in thinking that he's ridiculously hot, pure British sex. The mystery is why the hell *he* wants *me*.

I know he was just saying what he thought I wanted to hear, piling on the sort of flattery he thought someone in law school would like, but it *worked*. He's sweet. He's funny. He's a little broken — okay, he had a heroin problem, so a lot broken — but I wouldn't mind spending more time with him.

We seem to get along, after all, but this is still insane. No respectable person would do it, I know *that* much.

Except: a million dollars.

And the way he murmured *say yes,* just before I left.

I shake my head and stand. I've got a day or two to think this over, so no need to decide right now.

I heave my second-hand briefcase over my shoulder, adjust my sale-rack suit, and walk to the bus.

. . .

Million-dollar fake boyfriend aside, I make myself stick to my priorities. That means going over the notes I took on my reading for class tomorrow, studying for a possible quiz Friday, starting *next* week's reading, and editing the first ten pages of this terrible undergraduate essay.

Then, when all the things on my to-do list under "Tuesday Priorities" are finished, I put everything away, get another mug of tea, and tackle this Gavin problem in the best way I know how: with research.

It takes *hours*, because *wow* is there a lot on the internet about Gavin Lockwood.

Here's the short, sweet version: he grew up in a village in Northern England along with his close friend and future bandmate Liam Fenwick. Yes, *that* Liam. They formed a band in high school, went to college — sorry, *university* — for a short period, then dropped out and moved to London.

That band broke up. They formed another, and it broke up as well, but one fortuitous night they met Darcy Greene and Trent Ryder, both Americans, and Dirtshine was born.

Then came the usual struggle in obscurity, though after a while they managed to get signed to a label and release an album that did okay, so they released a second album, *Lucid Dream*.

Lucid Dream was huge. Triple platinum, world tour, TV shows and magazine covers and constant radio play, the whole nine yards.

It was around then that, according to his Wikipedia article, "Gavin's heroin addiction became more serious and problematic, and the Dirtshine frontman grew erratic."

Gavin's *erratic* behavior culminated in the night that he and Liam didn't show up at a gig, and they were found strung out in Liam's hotel room, along with a roadie named Allen Liddell. All three were transported to a hospital, where Allen died of an overdose, Liam was in a coma for two days, and Gavin came out of it the next morning.

Then: thirty days in rehab, possession charges reduced to misdemeanors, community service. Dirtshine is reportedly "hard at work on their next album," albeit with a new drummer, not Liam. Apparently Liam also went to rehab, but if I had to hazard a guess based on his behavior Friday night, I'd say it didn't stick.

I get up, make another cup of tea and a sandwich, and get back to it. This time it's endless articles about recovering from heroin addiction: the Mayo Clinic, Narcotics Anonymous, addiction.org.

I put books on hold at the school library. I use my law school login to read articles on the cutting edge of addiction science, and even though I don't entirely understand all the neurochemistry involved — okay, I don't understand it at all — I keep going until it's nearly one in the morning and I've still got no answer.

Everything I've read says that addicts recovering for the first time are pretty likely to relapse, and the scholarship suggests that it often takes more than one try for recovery to "stick." But at the same time, the people least likely to relapse have a support network of non-addicts. They "form social bonds outside the sphere of addiction," meaning they make non-junkie friends.

I fall asleep still not knowing what the right answer is. Yeah, I'd love to have a million dollars, but I don't know if I can take it from someone falling back under the drug's sway, and I don't exactly think I'll be the difference between him staying clean and relapsing.

But on the other hand, I *am* a social bond outside the sphere of addiction. And I *like* Gavin.

Maybe I could at least help.

• • •

The dream decides it for me.

It's not about Gavin. It's not even about the money and what I could do with it.

In the dream, I'm sitting at my laptop, scrolling through an endless list of apartments for rent. None of them have prices on the listing, and they're all shitty — one-bedroom basement apartments, places with no kitchen where you can *see* roaches, hovels within spitting distance of the freeway — and yet, when I click to see the price, they're all hundreds more than my parents can possibly afford.

When I wake up, my heart is racing and my palms are sweaty, but I've got an answer.

If Gavin relapses, he relapses. It won't be my fault.

But my parents have worked their hands to the bone, for their whole lives. If I've got the chance to buy them a house, I'm taking it.

It's six-thirty in the morning, but I leave Larry a voicemail saying *I'll do it*.

CHAPTER ELEVEN
Gavin

The light turns green, but no one moves. The intersection is completely gridlocked, cars head east-west blocking the path of cars attempting to travel north and south, but that doesn't stop several people from laying on their horns.

"Keep honking, it's sure to do the trick," I mutter to myself.

Finally, I inch forward, getting about fifty feet before the light turns red again, and look at the time. Already late, *and* we've got to get all the way up to Malibu in Friday night traffic.

My God, we may not be there by tomorrow morning.

"In one hundred feet, turn right," the pleasant female voice of my phone's GPS says.

At the current rate of travel, that's only five minutes.

I text Marisol and tell her that I'm on my way and should be picking her up sometime before sunrise. She texts me back a thumbs up. The butterflies in my stomach churn.

I'm still surprised she agreed to it. I know it's the million dollars and not me, but I really didn't think she'd say yes, particularly after she spent an extra twenty-four hours deciding.

And then, of course, the meeting where we signed the paperwork went two hours over schedule, entirely her fault as she went through the contract with a fine-toothed comb and requested probably a hundred minor changes, resulting in the first time I've ever found paperwork sexy.

The agreement is pretty simple, or at least, I think so: no fewer than two dates a week, totaling at least three hours, at a location that Valerie's PR firm has pre-approved, meaning one with plenty of paparazzi.

Until such time as we can no longer avoid acknowledging a romantic entanglement, Marisol and I are to tell all interested parties that she's a member of my legal team, and we are *getting to know* one another. This, according to Valerie, will entice members of the press in a way that saying, "Right, she's my girlfriend," will not.

Hand-holding, arm-touching, and kisses on the cheek and eventually the lips are all explicitly discussed in our contract, though it's silent on further "physical affections." We are to smile and laugh in one another's presence. We are not to argue, at least until it's time for us to end our fake relationship.

Two months. The contract is for two months.

I haven't got a plan. I haven't got anything, except for the ceaseless sensation that no matter what I've said, I want more than *this* from her, though I barely know what myself.

The last time I dated someone was years ago. It ended badly, as relationships between two junkies often do, though I wrote a hit song about it. Then came a parade of one-night-stands, groupies, whoever was soft and warm and the moment.

And then there was nothing much except the needle, which has a way of dulling everything. Not least your very own wants and desires.

That is to say, it's been a very long time since I really wanted something from *any* woman. Hard to remember what it feels like or what it is I'm supposed to do next, but I think it's something like this, a warm sizzling sensation not unlike electricity crackling along a wire.

"Turn right," the GPS chirps. "Then turn left."

I grit my teeth, steel myself, turn right, and then merge across three lanes of traffic into a left-turn lane with no light and wall-to-wall traffic facing me.

"Turn left *now*," the GPS says.

"Fuck you," I tell it.

We go back and forth until I've finally gotten onto a residential street, large apartment buildings on either side. I check her house number again, but before I can find an address I see her, waving from the front steps.

I double-park, grab the bouquet from the passenger seat, and get out.

"It's a date," I say, as she squeezes between the bumpers of two parked cars. "I'm supposed to come knock on your door and hand you these."

I hand over the flowers. I don't know what they are, but they're colorful and I picked them out myself.

"Sorry," she says, laughing as she smells them. "Should I go back upstairs while you look for parking?"

I glance up and down her block. No empty spots.

"You'd be a while," she says. "Or we could just go on our date."

I at least open the car door for her, then get in myself.

"Swanky car," Marisol says, running one finger along the leather seat.

She's wearing fairly tight jeans, heels, a blue top, and a tailored jacket, her hair down. It's the first time I've seen her wear anything so casual, and I'm a bit afraid I'll crash my car staring at her.

"I admit I bought it with dreams of speeding down the California motorway, stereo blasting, sun shining in my windows," I say. "So far I've not found California to be a very speedy place."

"Not around here," she says. "Drive out to the desert sometime, that should do you."

"Make a U-turn," the GPS says.

"Why?" Marisol asks it, frowning.

"I think I've put her on difficult mode or something," I say. "She's trying to kill me."

"Don't make a U-turn," Marisol says, and takes my phone from its holster on the dash. "Drive forward and turn left in two blocks."

"Oi, I need that," I protest.

"You don't trust me?" Marisol teases.

"That's not what I said," I say, easing the car forward to the next stop sign.

"Good," she says. "Make a left here and a right at the light onto Vermont."

I drive and let Marisol guide me. Not having the map does make me uneasy, but Marisol at least doesn't seem interested in having me take our lives into our hands every few minutes, so I relax after a bit.

She narrates as I drive, pointing out hole-in-the-wall restaurants with great food, the Korean place with ox-blood soup, dive bars, bowling alleys, the apartment where she used to live, the subway stop she uses. I've only been through this part of town a few times and it never seemed like much to me, but it comes alive as we drive south.

Plus, she gives good directions, far better than the woman in the GPS. Before long I realize: I don't *care* if we actually get to the restaurant in Malibu or not.

Once we hit the freeway traffic moves better, and before long we're through the final tunnel and then suddenly driving on the coastal highway, Santa Monica beach next to our left, ten minutes after sunset with the sky still fading pink and orange.

"Good sunset," Marisol says approvingly.

"Aren't they all good sunsets?" I ask.

"They're *mostly* good sunsets," she says. "When it's too cloudy or too clear they're a little lackluster."

I come to a stop light and look over at the sun setting over the Pacific Ocean.

"*Lackluster*," I say, and she laughs. "You've clearly never been to England."

"I may be somewhat spoiled when it comes to weather and sunsets," she says.

CHAPTER TWELVE
Marisol

The sun fades as we drive up the coast in the nicest car I've ever touched. Or, at least, I'm pretty sure it is — it's black, low slung, two-door, has butter-soft leather seats and more knobs and dials than a spaceship.

Plus, it purrs like a tiger, even at stoplights. Frankly, it's a shame to drive this in the city of Los Angeles, where its top speed can't be more than forty-five miles per hour.

"You've not forgotten about giving me directions, have you?" he asks after a while, during a lull in our conversation.

I had, completely, and I switch his phone back on to look at the map. We're not there yet, but we're getting pretty close.

"Of course not," I say. "But it's gonna be coming up on the left. I think it's that second stoplight up there."

"You did forget," he says. "You'd have let me drive clear to Santa Barbara."

I laugh. He might be right.

"I would've noticed before too long," I say. "You might be drive-to-Point-Dume-by-accident interesting, but you're not all-the-way-to-Santa-Barbara interesting. Plus we're already half an hour late for our reservation."

"I'm not sure what you've just said but I think it might be an insult," he says, his voice teasing as he slows the car, waiting at a stoplight with his blinker on.

I laugh.

"You'll learn your geography sooner or later," I say. "We're far enough from Point Dume that you shouldn't be insulted."

"If you say so," he says.

There's a break in the traffic and he turns left, down a smaller road, past some very expensive houses, to a classy-looking backlit sign that just says NORU in big gold letters, a valet parking stand next to it .

Clustered around, on the sidewalk, are about a dozen people with cameras around their necks, and they all turn as we pull up, peering into the car's windows, already snapping pictures.

Panic suddenly wells inside me, bubbling up as I watch these people close in before the car even stops.

I knew this was coming, but I have this sudden sense of being surrounded, of eyes pinning me down as they scrutinize me, my second-hand purse, my drug store lipstick, my shoes from Target. Not to even mention the fact that we're faking this whole relationship and I'm not even an actress, just some student who needs money.

I *freeze,* breath caught in my throat.

In the driver's seat, Gavin looks out the window and sighs.

"Here we are at the circus, then," he says, sounding resigned.

I don't answer, because I'm staring past him at the paparazzi, so close they're practically fogging up his car window.

What the hell have I done? I think, still frozen. *Oh my God, I'm going to be in tabloids and on the internet and they're going to post horrible, unflattering photos of me, they'll probably say mean things and they're going to know this is fake in three seconds flat—*

"Marisol?" Gavin's voice breaks through my crazed inner monologue. "You all right?"

I look at him and clear my throat.

"Yeah?" I say, though I couldn't sound less convincing.

He reaches over and takes my hand in his, warm and calloused, and squeezes it.

"They're bumblebees," he says. "Buzzy and irritating but so long as you don't try to fight them off, they're harmless. Just smile and wave and it'll be over in a flash."

"Right," I say, and take a deep breath. "Harmless."

He gives my hand another squeeze.

"Ready?" he asks.

"Ready," I say, and Gavin lets me go.

He unlocks the doors and the valets, two men in deep red vests, open them. One offers me his hand and I take it, thanking him to the *click click click* of cameras, and I look up directly into a round, black lens.

The lens lowers, and there's a frowning man behind it, his black hair pulled back.

"Who are *you*?" he asks.

I just smile and hope I look normal, not crazy.

Gavin walks around the front of his car, a knot of people with cameras following him, all shouting at once.

"Gavin! Are there any more Dirtshine shows planned?"

"Gavin! Does the new album have a title?"

"Are you still clean?"

"Is it true you assaulted your former best friend Liam?"

"Is he pressing charges?"

Click click click click.

He just smiles, holds up one hand, and keeps walking.

"Just trying to get to dinner," he says, and then he's at my side, one hand on my lower back, and I remember to move forward.

"Gavin, who's the girl?" someone shouts.

He opens the big glass door to the restaurant and I step through, the frantic clicking cut off when it closes behind us, and for a moment, warm, fuzzy relief washes over me.

And then I look around.

This is the fanciest place I've ever been, and it's fancy in a sleek, modern, California kind of way — lots of highly-polished surfaces and sharp vertical lines, the architecture wood and slate at right angles. One wall is sheer glass, and it's facing the ocean, nothing but beach between the window and the water.

"Welcome to Noru," says the very pretty, polished hostess as she looks Gavin up and down, clearly recognizing him. "If you'll give me *one* minute I'll be right back with you."

"Not a problem," Gavin says, putting his hand on my lower back again as she walks away quickly.

Then his voice is quieter, closer.

"You did great," he says.

"I didn't do anything," I point out.

"Exactly," he says. "It's impossible to win, you can only draw."

"Sorry for panicking," I say. "I knew what to expect, I just... wasn't expecting it."

He chuckles quietly, his hand still around my hip. Like we're an actual couple out for a very fancy dinner.

"You're doing loads better than me already," he says. "The first time someone tried to take my photo like that was after a show in London, and I was shitfaced and stoned. So naturally, I showed him my John Thomas and he snapped a picture of it."

My face heats up just at the thought, and I laugh to cover it up.

I *definitely* imaged-searched Gavin. And I definitely *didn't* see that one. I probably shouldn't. Seems unprofessional.

"It is *literally* my job to be the respectable one here," I point out.

"And you're doing a bang-up job of it," he says as the hostess walks back toward us, smile still plastered on her face. "Hardly even a flash of ankle."

She steps in front of us, wearing massive fake eyelashes, which she bats at Gavin.

"I'm *so* sorry about the wait," she says. "Right this way."

We're the ones who were half an hour late, I think, but I don't say it out loud. I get the sense that apologizing is somehow déclassé.

Gavin's hand on my back nudges me forward and I follow the woman past a room full of people to a table by the huge window, looking out over the ocean. He pulls my chair out for me, and I bite back a teasing comment about studying up on manners before we came.

There's already sparkling water in an ice bucket on the table, and the hostess pours us both glasses before she leaves. I guess they don't just know who he is, they know his entire back story as well.

"Cheers," Gavin says, lifting his up, and I do the same. "To making it this far."

"You know it's bad luck to toast with something non-alcoholic, right?" I ask without thinking.

Gavin grins at me.

"Except for people in recovery, cheers!" I say hurriedly and too loud, lifting my glass off the table.

"So I tell you that I once drunkenly flashed my todger to a paparazzo, and next thing I know you're trying to get me on the sauce," Gavin says, his eyes dancing.

I turn *scarlet*, my face like the surface of the sun. Any possible response dries up in a sudden storm of nerves, and I'm left, staring at Gavin, practically gawping.

It feels like everyone in this restaurant is watching us, like I'm an exotic bug under a microscope, and they're listening to Gavin tease me about wanting to see his penis.

Which I don't. He's sexy and charming and oddly sweet, but I've never even *thought* about his penis. Except when he mentioned it a few minutes ago.

Really. Never crossed my mind. Not for even a second.

Okay, maybe one.

"I'm just teasing, love," he says, leaning slightly forward, and it breaks the spell of my awkwardness.

We clink our glasses together and take sips, but I can still feel everyone's eyes on me. When I look around at the other tables, I'm almost certain everyone glances away just in time, murmuring to their dinner partners.

Probably wondering who the hell Gavin Lockwood is with and why she's got a three-year-old purse and fake leather shoes, I think.

To make matters worse, almost *everyone* in here right now is white — there's a black guy at a corner table and an Asian woman laughing along with a Caucasian man, but that's *it*. I stick out like a short, brown, *poor* sore thumb in this sea of tall, well-dressed blondes.

"What sort of bad luck?" he asks.

I blink at him for a moment, because I've got no idea what he's talking about.

"The toast," he says. "What sort of bad luck am I to expect now?"

"Oh, right," I say, and look down at my place setting. "Just regular, I think?"

"It's not something specialized, like seven years of shoddy cocktails or always getting to the subway platform as the train pulls away?" he asks.

My shoulders relax a little.

"You'll break slightly more dishes than you would normally," I say.

Gavin smiles. He puts his hand over mine. I realize I was twisting my napkin through my fingers, and I stop, his hand warm and solid and comforting.

"No one in this restaurant gives a shit that you're here," he says, his voice soft and a little raspy. "I promise they're all far too busy hoping to get noticed themselves to think about who you are or what you're doing."

I can't help but smile, shaking my head a little.

"Sorry," I say. "I've never been on a very expensive date with a very famous person before. It's kinda weird."

"It's weird as a frog in trousers riding a bicycle," he says. "But you're managing a bang-up job of it."

"Thanks," I say.

Someone steps forward silently and waits to be noticed. We notice him.

"Welcome to Noru," he says. "My name is Aidan, and I'll be your server. Would you like to hear the specials?"

Gavin doesn't let go of my hand.

• • •

The waiter suggests the Chef's Tasting Menu, so that's what we both end up getting. I'm not exactly a sushi expert — it's *expensive* — so anything that keeps me from having to figure out the difference between all the different fish is perfect as far as I'm concerned.

It also doesn't take me long to remember that I'm not crazy about sushi. I don't exactly dislike it, but something about the taste and the texture just doesn't do much for me, and this is... *creative* sushi.

Creative meaning raw octopus tentacles that wiggle when the waiter pours soy sauce on them. Creative meaning fermented fish paste as a topping, which *must* be an acquired taste, and plates arranged with shrimp heads staring up at us beside the main dish.

"Do we eat these?" I ask Gavin, as quietly as I can.

He prods one with a chopstick.

"I'm baffled," he admits.

There's large caviar that explodes between my teeth with a strong, fishy taste I don't enjoy. There's fish liver doused in squid ink.

And finally, there's the sea urchin. It looks kind of like a pale orange brain atop rice, and from the way it wiggles *just slightly* as the waiter puts it in front of us, I can tell I'm not going to be crazy about it.

"The final course," the waiter intones. "Noru's famous fresh-caught *uni*. Please enjoy."

I don't really want it, but *not* eating it seems incredibly rude. Gavin and I each take a piece and, after a pause, I put it into my mouth.

I was right.

It's *squishy*, slightly slimy and somehow the tiniest bit gritty all at the same time. It tastes vaguely like the ocean, but the way it coats my tongue makes it overwhelming.

Plus, it's *squishy*, very squishy, and did I mention squishy? It's my least favorite texture.

I swallow, then quickly lift my glass to my lips, washing it down. Across the table, Gavin's doing the same.

We lock eyes, still drinking, and he starts laughing. Then *I* start laughing, because we both just acted like children forced to eat brussels sprouts.

When we put our glasses down, he leans forward again, beckoning me in.

"Can I tell you something?" he asks, his voice low.

His face is only a few inches from mine, the closest he's been all night, and my heart is thumping like a bass drum.

This is for show, I think, over and over again. *It's an act. You're getting paid.*

"Depends on what you're going to tell me," I answer.

"I don't think I like *uni*," he says. "And when Valerie booked this date, I didn't realize it was for sushi, or I think I'd have requested something else."

I'm trying hard not to laugh.

"I think you just spent a *lot* of money on a dinner you didn't enjoy," I tease. "Maybe look up the restaurant next time?"

"No, I spent money on *food* I didn't enjoy," he says, his eyes still sparkling at me. "It's the best fake date I've ever been on."

My stomach flip-flops, and I try to cover it up by taking another sip of water and sitting back in my seat.

"Have you been on many fake dates?" I ask.

"Just the one," he admits.

"Then it had *better* be the best," I tease. "Though by that logic it's also the worst."

"If you're done talking yourself in circles, I'm trying to tell you I had a good time paying you to act as if you like me," he says.

We lock eyes for a moment and a small, slight shiver runs through me.

I'm not sure it's acting, I think.

"Thanks," I say.

CHAPTER THIRTEEN
Gavin

I pay the bill without letting Marisol see it, because frankly, I feel a bit guilty signing away that much money on a single meal. Even though I'm flush *now*, it's hard not to look at a restaurant bill in the mid-three-figures and think of how many weeks' food budget it would have been a few years ago.

She wants to know, of course.

"What if I guess," she says. "And you say higher or lower."

"No," I say, enclosing my credit card in the leather folder.

"How many numbers? Five? Six? Including decimal places," she goes on, her eyes laughing.

I glance at the bill again.

"All right, it's five, but that's all you're getting from me."

"So it's in the hundreds," she says. "Over or under five hundred?"

The waiter comes by and I hand him the check along with my credit card. He thanks me and disappears.

"I could have sworn I *just* said I wasn't telling you," I say.

"Is the first numeral odd or even?"

I take a drink of water and say nothing.

"Okay, is it prime?"

"You think I'm going to know off the top of my head whether a number in the hundreds is prime?" I tease her. "I'm a musician, love, not a calculator."

She laughs.

"I just meant the first numeral," she says. "*Those* shouldn't be beyond you, right?"

"It's not prime," I say.

She grins at me.

"Shite," I say. "That's it, no more questions. Why do you even want to know?"

"Because you don't want to tell me," she answers. "So the first numeral is two, four, six, eight, or nine, since one, three, five, and seven are all prime."

The waiter returns and hands me the credit card receipt in the leather envelope. I stare into space a moment, calculating the tip.

"If you need help I can figure it," she offers.

"I know what you're doing and I'm not falling for it," I say, and quickly write the tip, add the two together, write the total and sign it.

Then I put my hand flat on the leather folder containing the check, just in case, but she glances at the front door and looks somber again, nerves creeping back onto her face.

"You do exactly as before," I tell her. "Smile, walk through, sit in the car."

"I know," she says. "It's going to take some getting used to is all."

I stand and offer her my hand, and she takes it, hers small and soft in mine, though she grips me back with surprising strength.

She's just nervous, I remind myself. *It's not more than that.*

The hostess, whose face might have been transformed into a permanent smile via plastic surgery, has the valet retrieve my car while we wait inside the restaurant, away from the paparazzi on the sidewalk. When I see my Ferrari glide up, I thank her, squeeze Marisol's hand, and open the door for her.

The vultures are right there, black camera lenses staring like massive, dead eyes. They all shout questions, and they're all old hands at using my first name liberally, knowing how hard it is not to pay attention to *that*.

"Gavin, how's recovery?"

"Gavin, did you have a good dinner?"

"Gavin, who's this?"

We ignore them. A valet holds Marisol's door open and I see her in, not leaving until the passenger door is closed behind her. The vultures keep shouting as I walk around the car, cameras a foot away from me, maybe less.

I've got the urge to shove them out of my face and hear that satisfying *crunch* of delicate equipment on asphalt, but I resist.

I tip the valet. I get in my car, already purring, and I close the door, turning to Marisol.

"Still doing aces," I tell her.

She exhales, leaning her head back against the leather headrest, ignoring the cameras right outside the windows.

"Is it like this everywhere you go?" she asks incredulously.

I slip the car into gear and rev the engine. Paparazzi move out of the way, just barely.

"God, no, thank Christ," I say. "Valerie had us come here because she knows it's essentially an observation tank for celebrities. Most places I go there's a few curious people with their phones out, if anything."

I ease the car forward, quite careful of the men *still* taking photos, and drive the car down the street.

"That's why they've got the valet stand out on the street," I say. "Because the paparazzi are allowed on public property. They could easily move the valet stand into their parking lot and eliminate the entire song and dance, but then the restaurant wouldn't get all the free publicity and celebrities would go elsewhere to be seen."

"Oh," she says, and she sounds relieved.

I come to a stop at the traffic light on the Pacific Coast Highway and wait, blinker on to head back into Los Angeles. I can't say I particularly want to go home, but this is what we've agreed upon — one date, to Noru — and it's already a little past ten.

As I wait, my stomach growls. Loudly.

"I guess we should have eaten the shrimp heads," Marisol teases.

"I've got no idea *what* we were meant to eat," I admit, still waiting for the light to change. "And exotic cuisine is all well enough, but it just left me wanting a proper basket of nice, greasy fish and chips."

"I know where you can get that," Marisol says.

"Is this going to be organic-battered artisanal fish with hand-globbed ketchup and chips arranged in pleasing architectural formations?"

"It's a shack full of bikers up near the county line," she says. "Sound acceptable?"

"Lord, yes," I say. "Take me there."

The light turns green.

"Left," Marisol says.

• • •

Poseidon's Net is, indeed, more or less a shack, and its gravel parking lot is full of the sort of big, chrome-and-leather motorcycles I believe Americans call *hogs*. Parking looks haphazard, so I pull into something that seems like a spot and we get out.

It's a gorgeous spot. The restaurant is just inland of the Coastal Highway, and on the other side, the land slopes downward to a row of houses lining the shore and a strip of sandy beach. Though the shack itself is small, it's got a massive wrap-around veranda filled with wooden picnic tables and large, loud men wearing leather vests.

"This work for you?" Marisol asks.

"Beautifully," I say.

We walk across the gravel parking lot, and I take her hand. She glances over at me.

"We ought to get into the habit," I say. "Besides, you never know when some bloke on the street is going to photograph us and sell it to TMZ."

It's true but it's not why I took her hand. I just wanted to.

"Good point," she says.

"Plus, you're not terribly stable in those shoes."

"I didn't think I'd be trekking cross-country."

"You're the one who suggested this," I point out.

"*Hours* after I picked my outfit," she protests.

"This might go faster if I carried you," I tease.

Marisol just sticks her tongue out at me.

Eventually we make it to the shack itself, where the veranda is packed with gray-haired bikers, surfer types, hippies, and regular people out on a Friday. The inside is small, sweaty, and hot, the menu consists of faded handwriting on a chalkboard.

I can already tell it's going to be good.

We read the menu, still holding hands. I grab a bottle of water from a refrigerator and see that Marisol's glancing at their beer selection.

"D'you want one?" I ask, my hand on the door's handle.

"I'm all right, thanks," she says.

"You've certainly earned it," I say. "And just because I don't drink doesn't mean you shouldn't."

She eyes the selection again, and I laugh.

"Go on, have one," I say, opening the door for her. She grabs a Negro Modelo.

I get the fish and chips, *obviously*, she gets fried shrimp, and we sit on the veranda at one end of a picnic table, overlooking the highway, the row of expensive houses, and the ocean. A few people give me a second look, the *don't I know you from somewhere* that I'm used to, but no one shouts my name. No one so much as snaps my picture.

"I think this is better," Marisol says, dunking a chip in ketchup.

"This is certainly better," I agree. "I can't say I feel particularly at home in high society, even the version that California offers."

Marisol narrows her eyes.

"What's *that* mean?" she says.

I laugh and dip a chip in her ketchup.

"It means that I saw a bloke in flip-flops at the restaurant," I say. "I'm sure they were gold-plated designer flip-flops that cost a thousand dollars or something, but they were still flip-flops."

She laughs.

"I didn't even notice," she admits.

"And I'd wager that not a single person in there carried a hereditary title," I say. "Nor had a family crest, or had a suffix larger than *junior* after their name."

"There's a Robert Hampton the Third in one of my classes," she says.

"I used to be mates with Cornelius Archibald Fairfax the Seventh when I lived in London," I say. "Raging coke fiend. *Piles* of family money."

"All right, you win," she says.

I look at her beer. It's sweating on the table but she hasn't touched it.

"You're welcome to *drink* that," I say.

She picks it up, takes a sip, and then looks at it in her hand.

"It feels weird," she finally says.

"The beer?"

"Drinking around someone sober," she says. "Everything I've read about recovery says that people are most likely to relapse if they're in the conditions where they used in the first place, like being *around* alcohol and drugs, and I know beer isn't, you know, hard drugs, but it still feels weird."

"It's true, that's half the point of going to rehab. You break out of old habits," I say, eating another chip. "But I'm on the beach in California, out under the stars with an aging biker gang and a pretty girl who *happens* to be drinking a beer. It's is a pretty far cry from the moldering basement flats and backrooms of dirty clubs where I used to get high."

"Point taken," Marisol says, and drinks more beer.

I'm a bit jealous. I miss drinking. I miss beer and whiskey and even gin, sometimes, the fantastic way your head feels when you've had just a few and everything is funny and you're on top of the world.

Stop, I tell myself. *This is how you talk yourself into drinking again.*

There's a long pause, and we both look out over the water.

"It was Liam, huh?" Marisol finally asks. "Who got you... started?"

"My addiction was no one's doing and no one's responsibility but my own," I say.

"They taught you *that* in rehab."

"They did," I admit. "But Liam also never got me to do a single thing I didn't want to do all by myself."

She watches me, taking another drink.

"Not that Liam was ever a good influence," I say. "He certainly never talked me *out* of bad decisions. But if it hadn't been him I'd have found someone else. The problem was always *me*."

We haven't spoken in a week, though I know he posted bail for himself last Saturday morning so at least he's out of jail. I imagine someone will be pressing charges against him as well, possibly several someones.

And I don't think there's a single damn thing I can do to help him. Not before he wants to help himself, at least.

Marisol's bottle is nearly empty and she's spinning it back and forth between her palms, looking at it with great concentration, like she's trying to put something together.

"If you've got more questions you can ask them," I offer. "I've been to so much therapy in the past five months that I'm an open book."

"They're not really first date questions."

"This isn't really a first date," I say. "Speaking of which, you've already put in overtime tonight if you want to leave."

"Do you?" she asks, the bottle still rolling between her palms.

"I don't," I say. "It's nice here, and I'm renting a big empty house in the hills that's gray and white and sterile as fuck."

"Where you knit and drink tea."

"Right," I say, grinning.

"We could go down to the beach," she suggests.

"It's private here, there's houses."

Marisol finishes the last sip of her beer, then smiles at me, raising one eyebrow.

"We're in California," she points out. "The beach isn't private anywhere."

CHAPTER FOURTEEN
Marisol

"Hurry *up*," Gavin says, pulling on my hand.

I'm tottering as fast as I can in these stupid shoes. I'm pretty sure I've already got blisters from them, and now I'm crossing four lanes of fast traffic, trying to be as quick as I can.

"I'm trying!" I say, but I'm already on the sandy, grassy shoulder of the coastal highway, my heels sinking in precipitously.

"For a moment I thought I was gonna have a flat fake girlfriend," he says, taking my hand again.

It's because he can tell you're having trouble balancing, I tell myself.

"Can you imagine the headlines?" he asks.

"Probably something like, 'Megastar's girlfriend dies tragically. Sex tape to blame?'" I guess.

Gavin looks at me, one eyebrow raised as we make our way along the shoulder of the road.

"Sex tape?" he asks.

That was the beer talking.

"It seems like every other headline on those tabloids is about a sex tape," I say. "I figured they'd work it in somehow."

"Have you got one?"

I just laugh.

"Please," I say. "I wouldn't even let my last boyfriend—"

I stop myself before I say *put an enormous mirror in his bedroom*, but my face is already hot.

"You *can't* just stop there," Gavin says. "How am I to know what false salacious details to give to the press?"

"I wouldn't let him record us having sex is all," I say lamely. "So, the beach is public and it's mandatory that there be access points every half mile, so look for a passageway between the houses to the beach. They're usually marked by a County of Los Angeles trash can."

Gavin points in the dark.

"Like that one?" he asks.

"Right."

"Does the sex tape have a title?" he asks.

"I don't *have* a sex tape."

It's true. Obviously.

"What about 'Legal Action,'" he says. "Since you're in law school, and there's sexy action in it."

"There's really no sex tape," I say.

"'The Jury's In My Box,'" he guesses.

We get to a set of concrete stairs down to the beach. He goes first, holding up his hand behind himself, helping me balance.

"That doesn't even make sense, and it's gross," I point out.

We go down the rest of the stairs silently as I try to keep my balance, and then I stand on the bottom stair and take my shoes off before hopping onto the sand, the cool grains between my toes.

There's a half-moon just about directly overhead, so the ocean is dark with occasional ripples, the white of the surf the only thing we can really see.

Gavin takes his shoes off as well and we walk toward the ocean, hand-in-hand, equally slowed by the sand, and we stare into the water for a long moment, neither of us speaking.

"I know you don't have a sex tape, by the way," he says. "I was just having a go."

"I got that," I say.

"But I do want to know what you wouldn't let your boyfriend do," he says, grinning.

My stomach flips over, and I look away, into the surf, feeling like a huge loser. Gavin's not one of those rockstars who's bragged about banging hundreds of women or anything, but I'm not an idiot. I've seen the way women look at him while I'm standing *right* next to him.

He's famous. He's rich. He's ridiculously handsome.

I'm *sure* his sexual past is more interesting than mine, and even though it doesn't matter, I don't want him to think I'm a prude or something.

"Don't make fun of me," I say. "Please?"

"Cross my heart."

"He wanted to put a mirror in his bedroom so we could watch ourselves have sex and I wasn't into it," I say quickly, looking away.

Gavin laughs, and I shoot him a glare.

"You promised!"

"I thought you were going to say you wouldn't let him see you topless or touch you without rubber gloves on or something," he says.

"Rubber gloves?" I ask.

I start laughing as well.

"I don't know," he protests. We start walking, still hand in hand, on the part of the beach where the sand is still wet but the waves are gone.

"Is *that* how I seem?" I ask, half teasing and half really wanting to know. "Like I require rubber gloves before someone touches me?"

"No, not that, specifically," he says. "You're just quite cautious is all I was getting at."

That's hard to argue with, honestly.

For a moment I consider firing back at him, asking Gavin if *he's* got a sex tape or something, but I don't want to know.

Because if he does, and he tells me, I'm going to look it up. I won't be able to stop myself, and *then* I'll have to watch him have sex with some other girl, and even though this relationship is completely fake, I don't want to.

I'm just being respectful, that's all. Really.

"When did you break up?" he asks.

I glance over at the houses. We've walked past five or six already, and I'm hoping we can remember where the exit back up to the road is.

"A little over a year ago," I say.

"Was it because of the gloves?" he says, very seriously.

I roll my eyes, but I'm smiling.

"It was a really boring breakup," I admit. "We just sort of... stopped making time to see each other until one day I called him and said, hey, I think we're broken up now."

"That's incredibly boring," Gavin agrees. "At least tell me he cried and begged you to take him back or something."

"I think his exact response was, 'Huh, you're right.'"

"Disappointing."

"I was relieved," I say. "There's not much worse than listening to someone cry because you don't want to see them anymore."

"There's being the crying bloke who's had his heart stomped on," Gavin points out.

"Oh, right," I say. "That's true."

He looks down at me.

"You've never been dumped."

"Yes I have," I say defensively. "I've been dumped *twice.* Once in college and once right after."

"But you've never had someone tear your heart from your chest and set fire to it," he says.

"I was upset," I say, but he's right. Both times I got dumped I was sad for a little while, but I got over it pretty quickly. I didn't feel like I'd lost the love of my life or something.

"You should *see* some of the things I wrote after my first girlfriend dumped me when I was sixteen. Maudlin rubbish," he says.

"You kept a diary?" I ask.

"Worse," he says. "I wrote *poetry.*"

I laugh.

"I'm an artist, we're very dramatic."

"Then I expect at least a song about me when we break up," I say.

Gavin doesn't answer for a moment. He shifts his hand in mine, just slightly.

"The problem there is 'Marisol' doesn't rhyme with much," he says, his voice just a little different somehow, like there's a hint of edge that wasn't there before.

"What about *very tall,*" I say.

"*Rather small* is a bit more accurate," he points out. "*In the fall.*"

"*Climb a wall,*" I offer.

"How am I to use *that* in a song?" he teases.

We keep walking, slowly, barefoot and holding hands. After a while, the houses end and to our right is a sheer cliff leading back up to the coastal highway, headlights streaking up and down as cars go past. We stop there and turn back, our footsteps still visible in the sand.

In his car, Gavin turns the heater on full blast and directs all the vents at me.

"Sorry I don't have a jacket," he says. "I'd give it to you."

"Thanks," I say. "I wasn't even cold until I got in the car, honestly."

"Your hand was *freezing*," he says.

I flex my fingers in front of the heater vent. They're pretty stiff.

"That was fun," Gavin says. "I liked our long walk on the beach."

"Too bad there were no cameras, it would have been good press for you," I say. "'Famous rock star enjoys long, romantic walk on beach with new girlfriend.'"

There's a pause.

"Yeah, it would have been," he says, and puts the car into gear.

• • •

The next afternoon, I'm studying for my Political Crimes and Legal Systems class when I get an email from Valerie.

From: Valerie Derian
(vcderian@firstplacepr.com)

To: mgomez@law.ula.edu;
gl3553@email.com

Subject: PERFORMANCE NOTES ON YESTERDAY'S DATE

Good afternoon Gavin and Marisol,

You got a brief mention on TMZ and RockGossip today though not much buzz yet.

Next date needs physical affection. Recommend hand-holding, arm around Marisol, affectionate glances.

Marisol, good job looking nervous about the camera. Very natural, normal, girl-next-door but you can back off a little. The camera is your friend!!!

Next steps: touching, cheek kissing. Goal is lip-on-lip (no tongue) within the next week or two.

You're gonna go VIRAL!!!!!!

Warmly and Respectfully,
Valerie

She also includes links to the two posts about us, so I take a deep breath and click on the first one. Thank God, it's pretty tame: the headline is just "New arm candy for Dirtshine frontman Gavin Lockwood?!" with a picture of us, taken from the side, walking into Noru together. The other is basically the same thing with an extra line added about how they don't know who I am.

It could be way, way worse but it still makes my stomach flutter. *Now* there's no turning back — my face is out there, publicly linked with Gavin's. There's no chance of getting out of it quietly.

I scan Valerie's exclamation point-laden email one more time. There's something very weird about seeing a pattern of physical affection laid out like this, and something weirder about her telling me that being nervous about cameras is "very natural," as though I did a good job acting, but I can take that all in stride.

Besides, the weirdest is definitely "goal is lip-on-lip (no tongue)." I don't think I've ever heard kissing on the lips described in a less-sexy way, almost like it's mouth-to-mouth. And the last time kissing was a stated *goal* of mine was the "What I Plan To Accomplish This School Year" entry in my eleventh-grade diary.

I accomplished it, by the way. Robert Azucena, in the movie theater. Underwhelming.

After a few more minutes with Legal Systems, my phone buzzes again.

> Gavin: Good job looking normal.

> Me: Thanks. Never been described as arm candy before.

> Gavin: Just wait until they find out you're Latina. Then you'll be 'spicy' arm candy.

> Me: Great. Can't wait to go VIRAL.

> Gavin: I'm not sure Valerie knows what that means.

> Gavin: Still on for lunch Tuesday?

> Me: Still on!

I don't mention *lip-on-lip*, and neither does he. But I spend most of the next few hours trying not to think about it.

• • •

It's more or less like that for two weeks. We go on dates, mostly to fancy places with lots of paparazzi. They figure out my name and that I'm a law student, but they're not that interested in me.

We hold hands in front of the cameras and the most interesting thing either of us is recorded saying is, "Just eating dinner."

Valerie sends us a performance evaluation every time. Sometimes Gavin looks too tentative for her liking, sometimes she thinks we're holding hands wrong, once she excoriates him for not holding the door for me properly.

After a few emails informing us that she "really needs a CHEEK KISS," we plan one. Gavin doesn't think we need to orchestrate something that simple, but I'm nervous, so we do.

It's a Saturday night, and we have dinner at La Rosette, a super-trendy French "fusion" place with $16 cocktails and a whole squadron of photographers lurking just outside. I have a glass of wine, the first time I've drunk anything since the night at Poseidon's Net.

"Am I so bad you've got to take the edge off?" Gavin teases me as we're done eating and I'm draining my glass, the check paid.

I swallow the last sip and put it down, half-rolling my eyes.

"You *know* it's the cameras, not you," I say. "You're basically, I don't know, a mannequin or something to me by now."

He raises his eyebrows, grinning.

"I'm a mannequin," he says, and I feel myself blushing.

"Something I don't mind kissing on the cheek," I say. "You know, it's no big deal, like my brother or my gay friend or European people when you meet them for the first time."

This is half-true. I don't mind kissing Gavin, and I'm definitely nervous about the cameras, but I've worked myself into a *state* about putting my lips on his face. For days now, I've been thinking about it again and again: the feel of his skin under my lips, our faces touching, probably our *bodies* touching.

And I'm worried that the second I kiss him, he'll *know* that I've thought about this way too much, that I've stared at the phrase *lip-on-lip* over and over again and imagined what it would be like, that sometimes when we're innocuously holding hands on one of our dates it makes me feel warm and squirmy in a way that fake relationships aren't supposed to.

Basically, I think I've got a crush on the incredibly handsome, famous, rich, *notorious* rockstar, and I feel like the world's biggest cliché, because even though the rockstar is sweet and funny and I'm pretty sure we're *friends*, there's no way he reciprocates the warm-and-squirmy feelings.

He taps a few fingers on the table and glances back at the paparazzi.

"All right, then," he says. "Let's get on with it."

We rise. He takes my hand and squeezes it. The wait staff all smile at us as we leave.

Gavin pushes the door open. The valet nods and jogs off to get his car.

"Gavin! How's your night going?" someone shouts, swooping in front of us.

My stomach writhes.

"It's going well," he answers.

The moment he does, two others swoop in, because Gavin Lockwood rarely says anything.

"You enjoy your dinner?" the first one asks, a totally inane question.

"I did," he says, and looks down at me. "You have a nice time?"

I'm way, *way* too nervous to answer. I just laugh, squeeze his hand, and stand on tiptoe.

Then I press my lips to the side of his face, his skin warm, stubble just prickling through his skin, and then it's over. Done. I did it. He squeezes my hand and his car drives up.

Once we're inside, he turns to me and grins.

"Was that so bad?" he asks.

It wasn't bad. Not at *all*.

"Tolerable," I tease, and we zoom off.

CHAPTER FIFTEEN
Gavin

When we get to Marisol's neighborhood, I circle her block and the blocks around it for nearly twenty minutes, looking for a parking spot because I'm determined to walk her inside, properly.

There's no cameras. Valerie's not going to mention whether I did or didn't walk her inside in her review email tomorrow. I just want to do this fake date *right*.

"It's really okay if you just drop me off," Marisol finally says. "Or we could keep driving around Koreatown very slowly for another half hour."

"There's just literally nowhere to park," I say, astonished.

I wouldn't be surprised if I were in, say, London or New York, but here there are so many cars and so many places to park. They're just all filled.

"Yup," says Marisol. "Literally nowhere."

I sigh, give up, and drive back to the front of her apartment building, double-park, and put my flashers on. At least I can walk her to the front door of her building, which I do, the sidewalk flooded in the orange glow of street lamps.

"I think Valerie ought to approve," I say as she fishes her keys from her bag.

"That won't stop her from sending us pointers," Marisol says.

She looks away quickly, then back at me.

"Sorry I was so nervous," she says. "It wasn't that I minded or something, it's just... cameras make me nervous, and I'm always afraid I'm going to screw up and suddenly everyone will know I'm just your girlfriend for hire and everything will be ruined."

I hate it when she says that, *girlfriend for hire,* because even though I know better, I've taken to pretending it's real. That when she takes my hand, it's because she wants to. That when she kissed my cheek, there was real affection behind it.

It feels that way sometimes, but then I remind myself that it's *supposed* to. That's the point.

"I don't think you'll ruin everything," I say. "See you Wednesday?"

"For sure," she says.

Then she opens the door to her building, steps inside, and it's just me, my car flashing its lights, and scattered pedestrians walking here and there. I get back in and drive away, back to the house I'm renting in the hills, wishing that Wednesday were sooner.

• • •

The moment I turn onto my street, a winding road up above Hollywood, something feels *wrong*. Sure enough, the gate to my driveway is open and the skin on my back starts to crawl.

Did I leave it that way? I think. *Did someone break in? Am I being robbed right now?*

I stop my car in the street and peer in, squinting through the dark. There's movement on the steps leading to my front door.

Someone looks up, then stands.

It's Liam.

Fuck.

I knew this was coming. I knew we'd have to talk, hash out what happened at the Whiskey Room, why Dirtshine is going ahead without him, how I can even think about continuing alone what we started together.

He waves. I pull into my driveway and hit the remote button that closes the gate behind me, take a deep breath, and get out of my car.

"Hey," Liam calls, and just from the way he pronounces that one syllable I've already got a feeling he's been drinking.

"Hey," I call back, walking toward him. "Did I leave the gate open?"

"Nah," he says, shoving his hands into his pockets. "The control panel lets you guess the access code five times. Got it in three."

"So you remember the address of the house where I grew up but not that I've asked you a thousand times to fucking *call* first?" I ask.

Now we're both standing in front of the house. It's got desert landscaping, most of the yard covered in smooth gray pebbles, with various succulents and bushes dotted around for decoration.

"You ever heard the phrase 'better to beg forgiveness than ask permission'?" he asks, one side of his mouth ticking up in a hopeful little smile.

I don't answer.

"I knew you'd say not to come here if I called so I just came," he says.

"What do you want?" I ask, folding my arms in front of me.

Liam shoves his hands into his pockets and looks away, back toward the road, before he answers me.

"I need a place to stay," he says, very, very quietly.

I wish I were surprised, but I'm not, especially after what happened the last time we saw each other.

"You can't go to your flat?" I ask, though I already know the answer.

"Got booted," he mutters.

"When?"

"Few weeks back. Broke a window and singed the carpet a bit, management overreacted and changed the locks. I'm still fighting them but—"

"You haven't got a new place?" I interrupt, because I know that Liam's got some story about how his landlord's got a grudge against him specifically.

Seems that *lots* of people hold grudges against Liam specifically, and never once has it been his fault. According to Liam, at least.

"It's been a bit tricky finding a new lease," he says. "I guess I'm being sued, plus I haven't got my deposit back on the old apartment yet and it was quite a lot of money. It was a nice flat..."

Lights flicker through the slots in the fence, and he turns his head to look at them, like he's desperate not to make eye contact with me.

I stare at him.

"You haven't got enough money for a deposit on another flat?" I ask, incredulous. "You can live somewhere that's not a glass-walled penthouse in a posh neighborhood by the ocean, you know. Like we used to live in."

"I haven't got the cash on hand right now is all," he says. He's still not looking me in the eye. "I've been staying with friends and such, but I don't want to wear out my welcome, you know how it is."

"You haven't got money for a motel?" I ask, incredulous.

I'm fucking gobsmacked. As the songwriter of Dirtshine, I made more money than the rest of the band — that's how intellectual property works — but Liam still made a fucking *mint*. Even after hospital bills, rehab, and renting an utterly ludicrous flat, he ought to have been able to live like a king for a long time yet.

"I'm trying to save for another flat," he says. "Come on, mate, just for a few nights. I'll be quiet as a church mouse."

I start pacing from the steps to the driveway and back, so worked up that I feel like I've got to keep moving or I might actually explode.

I keep thinking *I can't believe this, I can't believe this*, but I'm just lying to myself. Liam, here, out of money and asking for help might be the most believable thing that's happened in months.

"Where'd it go?" I ask.

"Where'd what go?" he asks.

"The money, you fucking muppet!" I say, my voice rising. "What the *fuck* did you spend all that money on?"

He's silent for a moment. I realize he's just the slightest bit unsteady on his feet, his eyes not quite tracking me properly. Not only has he been drinking, he's been *drinking*.

"What, you're my mum now?" he asks.

"No, I'm the man whose house you're asking to live in," I say. "And since you're here, hat in hand, without a pot to piss in, maybe you could be less of a *fucking* arsehole right now."

Liam laughs. He throws his head back and laughs, stumbling backward a step as he does.

"Sorry, I forgot I was in the presence of *royalty*," he says. "I spent my money on the same fucking things you did, Gavin. A pile on that fucking worthless rehab, a pile on a flat, on a car, a bit of travel. Only we can't all be angel-voiced musical geniuses, can we, and for some of us money runs out."

"And on bail, yeah? And on buying drinks for everyone you meet so your party doesn't stop, and on piles of coke for all your new *friends*, and on wrapping your car around a light pole and trashing your overpriced flat?" I snap.

"Least I'm a man and not my own granny," he says. "Sorry, for a moment there I could have sworn we were in a rock and roll band or something. Maybe your next album can be all about the *sinful pleasures* of waking up by nine in the morning and jogging three miles before breakfast."

If ever there was one person who knows exactly how to stab me deep and then twist the knife, it's Liam *fucking* Fenwick. Not that it's surprising. When you know someone for most of your life, when you're more or less brothers, of *course* they know how to twist the knife.

That knife cuts both ways, though.

"Actually, *I'm* in a rock and roll band," I say. "Last I heard *you* were a free agent."

"We can't all be the golden boy, can we?" Liam snarls. "Must be nice to be Gavin *fucking* Lockwood instead of just some junkie drummer."

Now he wants me to say *you're not just some junkie drummer*, but I grind my teeth together and force myself not to, because then I'll be having the argument that *he* wants to have.

I don't say anything for a long moment. I can't think of anything to say that isn't going to lead further into this same stupid argument that we've already had.

Liam rubs his hand across his mouth, then along the back of his neck, like he's getting antsy for something. Likely a smoke, maybe a bump.

"Look, it's only for a few days," he says, his voice quieter. "You're the last person I've got right now, and I just thought..."

He trails off, but I know exactly what he's getting at. He thought that since he's my oldest friend, my *best* friend, I'd have mercy and give him another chance.

He thought that maybe I'd be reluctant to write off twenty years of friendship in a couple of months. He thought maybe I'd feel guilty that I couldn't help him, that I didn't talk Trent and Darcy into sticking with him a little longer, or that my life is actually looking up while his spirals the drain, yet again.

And goddammit, the fucking bastard's right.

"Only a few days," I say.

Liam starts to smile, but I hold up one hand, stopping him.

"I'm clean and I'm fucking serious, Liam," I say. "*Nothing* stronger than caffeine in the house. No alcohol, no drugs, not even pot. You smoke *outside*."

"Got it," he said. "Just pretend I'm living at a nunnery."

"Bloody fucking—"

"Oi, mate, I'm just having a go," he says, holding up both hands at once. "I got it. There's rules, and I'll follow them."

I unlock the door with a sinking feeling in my stomach, because I already know it won't be a just few days and he won't follow my rules for more than forty-eight hours.

But I don't feel right doing anything else.

It's *Liam*. Even though he's a fucking train wreck, he's the one who was there for me when my parents split, when my first girlfriend dumped me, when I dropped out of university. *We* were Dirtshine, fucking around in his mum's basement, playing open-mic gigs at the local coffee shop, before we ever met Darcy or

Trent.

I can't live in this palace and turn him out on the street. I just can't.

"There's a guest bedroom upstairs and on the right," I say. "That can be yours."

He claps me on the shoulder.

"Thanks, mate," he says, and disappears up the stairs.

I stand there and wish, for at least the thousandth time, that things had gone differently.

CHAPTER SIXTEEN
Marisol

Gavin and I have started texting each other. It makes sense, obviously. We're supposed to be dating, and people who are dating call and text and generally communicate when they're not actively together. But people who are *really* dating haven't signed contracts stipulating the amount of time they're required to spend together.

They don't get email from publicists suggesting that they "raise the physical affection stakes" or, with increasing insistence, requesting "lip-on-lip" action.

We don't mention to Valerie that we're texting and sometimes even calling. Neither of us tells her that he texts me pictures of good sunsets to ask if they meet my high standards, or that I call him from the bus stop sometimes, just because I'm bored, and we end up talking until long after I've gotten all the way home.

It's not that she would mind, but it feels like a secret, like it's something just between us that can't be wrapped up prettily and presented to the public. Those dumb pictures and phone calls are for *us*, not them.

• • •

I'm in the middle of class Tuesday when my phone buzzes in my pocket. I hit the button to turn the buzzer off, but a few minutes later, it buzzes *again*, and then again.

One missed phone call is no big deal, but a bunch? Something is *wrong*.

My hearts beats a little faster as I stealthily pull my phone from my pocket, and I mentally run through a list of people who might be in trouble.

My parents, my sister, Brianna. One of my cousins. Gavin.

I swallow, my mouth dry, and finally get the phone out of my pocket.

Four missed calls from Valerie. I roll my eyes, set my phone to Do Not Disturb mode, and pay attention to class. She *has* my schedule. She demanded it, and she demands to know any and all changes to it, and yet calls me without ever consulting it.

After class I'm done for the day — well, except for the pile of homework that I need to get through — and after checking my student mailbox, dropping a book off at the library, and doing a few other things on campus, I finally call Valerie back.

"*There* you are," she answers her phone. "My god, Marisol, I was about to form a search party."

"I was in class," I point out, rolling my eyes as I walk down the street. "Which is on my schedule, actually."

"This is *important*," she says. "Emergency meeting, can you get down here?"

I walk a little faster.

"What's the emergency?" I ask. I don't really know what qualifies as an *emergency* to Valerie, because I suspect it could range anywhere from real, actual life-or-death situation — Gavin in the hospital? — to a blog that said something slightly uncharitable about us.

"I don't think it's an emergency, Val," Gavin's voice says.

Apparently we're on a conference call. You know, like couples routinely do with their publicists.

Valerie huffs into the phone.

"Please just get to my office," she says. "It's rather *confidential* in nature and I'd prefer not to discuss it over the phone."

"It's not *that* confidential," Gavin's voice says, but the phone line goes quiet.

I guess I'm not studying much this afternoon.

• • •

The offices of First Place PR are less expensive-looking but more trendy than Diamant & Skellar's offices, but they're not any less sterile. My footsteps echo when I walk in, and a receptionist snaps her head up.

"Marisol, meeting with Valerie, right? Big conference room on the end," she says, all smiles and perfect teeth.

"Thanks," I say.

When I get to the door, Valerie practically runs me over, rushing out of the room.

"Oh, thank *God*," she says. "Give me one minute, all this kale juice is really moving through me."

She doesn't wait for a response, just power-walks to the women's bathroom as I walk into the conference room. Gavin's already sitting there, in an executive leather chair, and I sit next to him.

"Tell me this is actually important," I say.

He grins at me and leans back in his chair.

"It's important," he says. "But it's not an *emergency*. We got invited to play at the National Music Awards on Saturday so now you're on for a whole red carpet do."

My heart squeezes slowly, and I try to think about what the red carpet at an awards show even *looks* like. All I can remember is hundreds of photographers and celebrities looking polished and perfect, smiling in every direction while people ask *who they're wearing*.

Oh, my God, that means there are TV cameras. From real TV stations, not just GossipNewsDaily and TMZ or whatever we've been dealing with. Actual reporters will be asking me actual questions and expecting me to actually respond while people at home talk to each other about whether I'm cute enough to date Gavin Lockwood.

And it's in *four days*. And I'm supposed to wear something red carpet-worthy, not that I have any idea where one even *gets* that sort of outfit.

Crap. *Crap*.

"Hey," Gavin says, leaning forward in his chair. He loops one arm around my shoulders, and suddenly our faces are six inches apart. "You all right? You went quiet."

"Sorry," I say, swallowing. "I spazzed for a minute there. Red carpet sounds like a big step up."

His fingers trace a slow circle on my shoulder blade, and it's soothing and heart-pounding all at once, but I relax a little with Gavin's arm around me.

Even if it's fake, even if it's *practice*, it's safe and warm and *nice* like this.

"It's fine," he says. "It's just a bunch of gibbering idiots who shove cameras in your face and ask idiotic, easy questions, like 'Don't you think music is nice?' and you say, 'Yeah, it's brilliant,' and everyone's happy."

I laugh, and as I do I fight the urge to reach out to him, put a hand on his knee or something, lean my forehead against his. More and more, every time I'm near him — even alone, like this — the deep, instinctual part of my brain is whispering at me to touch him, make all those little gestures that couples do.

I don't, but for just a moment, I glance up, into his eyes.

The air sucks out of the room and suddenly the conference room doesn't exist, the fluorescent lighting doesn't exist, this high rise doesn't exist. It's just us, his deep brown eyes staring into mine, every inch of my skin charged and crackling with sheer electricity.

Gavin doesn't say anything. I don't say anything. His fingers curl around my shoulder and I lean toward him, just a little more, my heart beating so fast I think it might explode.

"Marisol," he murmurs, so close I can feel his voice vibrate. "What if this—"

The door opens so fast it practically explodes.

"—why it's called a juice *cleanse*, wow!" Valerie's saying as she marches in. "I'm still waiting for that clean, calm energy it says I'm supposed to have, though."

We both practically leap backwards, like teenagers afraid of getting caught. Even though we're adults who weren't *doing* anything.

Valerie doesn't seem to notice.

"All right, Marisol," she says, sitting at the head of the table and opening a folder. "There's a lot to do to prep you for Saturday, so here's your schedule and itinerary and by God, once you're on that red carpet you'll be buffed and shined and ready for the spotlight."

She slides a stapled bundle of papers over to me, across the perfectly polished table, and I catch them, looking at the first entry.

Saturday, 7:00 a.m., arrive at Dean LaMont salon to begin skin and hair prep.

Valerie's still talking, going over my incredibly-detailed itinerary, so I just interrupt her.

"I can't," I say.

She stops, mouth slightly open, and stares at me.

"Are you allergic to one of the treatments?" she asks. "We can change them, there are other things that'll fix your—"

"I'm busy most of Saturday," I say. "I'm volunteering at an immigration law clinic from nine until four. I mean, I can still make the awards at six, but I'm gonna have to skip the Miracle Clay Mud Wrap."

She looks down at the paper, then back up at me.

"I don't think you understand," she says. "This event is going to take all day, so you need to reschedule your volunteer thing."

"I volunteered *months* ago," I say, the butterflies in my chest starting to flutter. "I can't just back out now. People are depending on me to be there. I'm halfway through their green card applications."

"You're doing it for free, they can find someone else," she says.

My mouth is going dry, because I *know* that I'm getting paid a ton of money to be Gavin's girlfriend, and that means last-minute awards shows, but the volunteer gig is actually a big deal, and it's important to my career — the one I'm going to have once I'm not Gavin's fake girlfriend any longer, and the money has been spent on my parents' house and my student loans.

"I really don't want to ask them to do that," I say, trying to sound as reasonable as I can. "This is a big—"

"Val, Marisol's not coming to the awards show," Gavin interrupts. He's leaning back in his chair, one hand drumming on the table, restless.

Valerie rolls her eyes.

"This is why you're *paying* her, Gavin," she says. "She is getting a million dollars to come places with you, and I think that outweighs—"

"She said she's busy, so she's busy," he interrupts her. "She's got real work to do, not faffing about in a pretty dress watching the rich and famous pat each other on the back."

Valerie looks down at my carefully-scheduled itinerary for a long moment, quickly tapping a pen against the table, her face perfectly expressionless, smooth and blank in a studied way.

Then, finally, she looks up at me.

"Can you at least make the after party?" she asks, sounding annoyed.

"Yes," I say. We were supposed to have a date that night anyway.

"Good," she says. "*Whirl* magazine rented a mansion for their annual party, and you're both coming to that, at least you'll still be seen by plenty of people. Gavin, I'm going to put it around that the reporters should ask you about the rumor that you're dating someone, and you say yeah, she's out saving the world or whatever..."

Valerie is furiously scribbling on the packet of paper in front of her, slashing through line items, half muttering to herself and half to me and Gavin. I start taking notes, hoping that I look like I'm paying attention and being studious, because I am.

I *want* to do this right, be the best possible fake girlfriend that I can be. I just can't do two things at once.

Gavin, on the other hand, couldn't be paying less attention to Valerie. He glances over at me, sees me writing, and grins.

I stick my tongue out at him.

He puts one hand on my knee, holding it there for a long moment, and I feel the butterflies and tension drain out of me, only to replaced with that same electric feeling, a shiver passing over my whole body. Valerie doesn't notice a thing.

After a little while, Gavin takes his hand off.

I wonder what he was about to tell me earlier.

CHAPTER SEVENTEEN
Gavin

"At least you don't have to worry about whether we win something or not this time," Eddie says brightly. He's looking out over his shoulder, through the window of the stretch limo, as we come up on the theater where the National Music Awards are being held.

"Right, we can just sit there and wonder if we should have had another dress rehearsal," Darcy says dryly.

"I'm sure all the pyrotechnics will go off without a hitch," Trent says. "Just don't miss your cue."

Darcy, Eddie, and I all snap our heads around to stare at him.

"Fireworks?" Eddie blurts, but Trent laughs.

"Kidding," he says. "Chill, you guys, you'll be fine."

"*You'll* be fine," Darcy says, tugging at her dress again. "You haven't got half a mile of duct tape holding up your tits right now."

"You don't know that," Trent says.

"Well, whatever's going on in there, they look great," Darcy teases.

"Thank you," Trent says. "And, for the record, you look nice as well."

"Thanks," Darcy says. "I somehow got talked into a *glam makeover* and I think I might live to regret it."

"Do you need one of us to walk on either side you just in case you topple suddenly?" I ask. "Perhaps there'll be a strong breeze or something, and those shoes look quite risky."

Darcy just laughs. I've only rarely seen her wear something besides combat boots or maybe flat sandals, so I have a feeling she's not accustomed to heels.

"You're joking, but it's not a bad idea," she says. "Though I might make headlines if I fall ass-over-tits and show the nightly news my snatch."

"I wouldn't mind having someone else take the heat for a bit," I say. "Maybe I'll push you."

The limo comes to a stop, and we all look through the windows at the red carpet, dotted with other celebrities swanning along slowly, row after row of cameras pointed at them.

"If you push me, I *will* kill you," Darcy says. "God, I hate this part."

"Just fucking get it over with," Trent says grimly.

Only Eddie looks kind of excited, but it's his first time at one of these events.

"Three, two, one," I say, taking the door handle, since I'm the closest. "Geronimo!"

I open it and step out to the sound of shutters clicking away, adjusting my jacket as I do.

"He's been in the U.S. too long," I hear Trent mutter behind me. I turn and offer Darcy my hand as she gets out. She bravely steps up on the curb, not wobbling more than a little.

"Fuck," she whispers to me, dropping my hand.

A handler, holding a clipboard and wearing a microphone, comes over and starts telling us how to stand, where to go, what to do, which cameras to look at. About a hundred of them ask Darcy who she's wearing, and I hear her make up four different designers, because of course she has no idea.

Earlier today, one of Valerie's minions tried to talk me into wearing a suit, and I had the thing on, nearly ready to go, but then I remembered something Liam said.

We used to be a rock and roll band.

Now I'm wearing jeans and a leather jacket.

We walk down the red carpet slowly. We smile big. And finally, we reach the end, where the video cameras are rolling, with pretty, polished reporters ready to ask questions.

A brunette practically leaps onto Darcy, whose smile is frozen in place, and asks her who she's wearing.

"Mister Camino," I hear Darcy answer.

The reporter's never heard of that designer, and I try not to laugh as someone pulls me in, practically yanking me in front of a camera, which she then faces.

"I'm here with Dirtshine lead singer Gavin Lockwood," she says, then turns to me. "How does it feel to be playing your first big show with your new drummer after you kicked out longtime member Liam Fenwick?"

I hate these questions. What am I supposed to say, it feels great that we booted my best friend? But I smile anyway.

"I'm quite excited," I say. "Eddie's a fantastic drummer and we're very lucky he's agreed to join."

She moves right on to the next question, like a shark onto the next kill.

"You've been seen around town with a mystery woman on your arm," she says. "But I don't see her anywhere here, have you already broken up?"

I smile at the thought of Marisol as a *mystery woman*,

and also at the thought of how much she'd hate being here right now.

"Marisol's in her final year of law school," I say, giving the camera my most charming smile. "I'm afraid she's out fighting for truth and justice at the moment instead of being here, playing dress up with me."

The reporter laughs, a semi-forced laugh, showing me all of her teeth.

"Well, I think you dress up *quite* well," she says. "Thanks for talking to us, Gavin."

"My pleasure," I say.

That exact scene, more or less, gets repeated a good six or seven times before we finally make it inside, where we wait around more before we sit down in the theater to wait around for our performance.

By the time we head backstage to get ready, I feel like I might explode.

• • •

It's been ages since I played a show this size, even though it's not nearly as big as some of the shows we did last tour. But it's much larger than the Whiskey Room, and the crowd is completely different — rows and rows of seated people wearing suits and ball gowns, politely watching as you sing your heart out on stage.

Harder to get excited when that's what's staring back at you. Harder to feel in sync with your bandmates when the stage is the size of the house where I grew up and we all may as well be in different rooms.

I'm not nervous, not exactly. I've done this a thousand times, just not recently, and hardly ever stone cold sober. I didn't start shooting up before shows until near the end, but before the Whiskey Room it had been *years* since I went on stage without at least a drink and usually more.

The presenters are on stage, reading out the nominees for the night's final award. We're the last performance, closing out the show, and then everyone leaves and goes to whichever afterparty they're attending.

That means I get to see Marisol soon, and *that* thought makes me stupidly happy.

I keep catching myself wishing she were here. I keep imagining what she'd think of this whole thing, of sitting around watching people pat themselves on the back for being able to sing songs well, whether she'd find it wonderful or stupid or somewhere in between.

And more than anything, I wish she were here to see the show itself. I don't think I care if all these people in their shiny outfits with their carefully arranged faces like the songs we'll be playing, but I want to impress *her*, want to share something I love with her.

The audience bursts into applause, and backstage, I start paying attention again. Five young men wearing matching suits come up to the stage, take the shining statue, and start speaking into the microphone.

"We're next," Trent's voice says behind me.

I turn. The four of us are all here, and we're all back to the way we normally look: torn jeans and flannel shirts and combat boots and ripped fishnet, too much eyeliner on Darcy, messy hair.

It's us. Us minus Liam, but recognizably *us*.

"Okay, you fuckers," I say.

Darcy and Trent grin. Eddie looks nervous, and Darcy rubs his shoulder.

"Let's go play some fucking rock and roll, yeah?" I ask as the lights all dim.

"Fuck yeah," Darcy says.

"Right on," Trent says.

"Yes," Eddie says.

We walk out to our places on the pitch-black stage. The stagehands are busily rearranging all the set pieces, and I pick up my guitar in the dark, looking out at the audience. It's the only time all night I'll be able to see them: excited but sedate, sitting politely.

The rush of stagehands stops as they leave. Everything goes still for a moment. I take a deep breath, feeling the most sober I've ever felt, everything crystal clear and sharp, and in that second I'd give *anything* for some chemical assistance.

But there's nothing, of course, so here we go with the new version of Dirtshine, the new version of *me*.

Eddie counts off. Darcy's bass line dives and hums, going so low I can feel it in my bones before it climbs again. The crowd cheers just as Trent joins in, the two melodies intertwining, trading back and forth for a few bars.

The lights come up slowly, and I close my eyes. I pretend I'm at the Whiskey Room, where it's hot and stuffy, the lights are blinding, it smells like stale beer and I can barely hear myself think over the screaming.

The guitars squeal and fade. My heartbeat buzzes through my veins, and I imagine the Whiskey Room's balcony, a girl wearing a skirt and blouse in the very front, looking utterly out of place. She's watching me, not excited but *intrigued*.

We lock eyes. She smiles, just barely.

I take a deep breath, shut out everything else, and sing to *her*.

CHAPTER EIGHTEEN
Marisol

The auditorium hushes, and suddenly the only sound is the click of my heels as I half-walk, half jog along the ugly backstage hallway.

Shit, they're starting, I think. *Crap. CRAP.*

After the immigration clinic, I got rushed to a salon, where there was an *entire team* of people waiting to do my hair, buff my skin, paint my face, polish my nails, tell me I should drink more water and probably do a juice cleanse as well, and finally stuff me into the little black cocktail dress that Valerie and I agreed on earlier this week.

When they were done, I barely even recognized myself in the mirror. In my regular life I wear lip gloss, mascara and maybe a little eyeliner at *most*, but now?

Hello Marisol, Rock and Roll Girlfriend.

I turn a corner in the backstage hall, and a guy in a black suit and an earpiece holds up one hand.

"Badge?" he asks.

Out on stage, the bass line starts, and a spike of

urgency flashes through me because *I'm missing it*. I fight the urge to sprint past this guy, and instead I open my clutch and grab the *very* last-minute VIP pass Valerie got me.

As I hand it over, I see that she's texted me a few minutes ago: *I NEED LIP-ON-LIP TONIGHT!!!*

I switch my phone off. The guard looks at my pass skeptically. He looks at me.

"Please?" I say.

He squints at it again in the near-dark. The guitar part starts. I grit my teeth together, and tell myself I've still got time. Finally the guy looks over his shoulder, then shrugs.

"Don't cause any trouble," he says, and hands me my pass back.

"Thank you!" I whisper.

From there it's chaos, but I can see the curtains that make up the back of the stage. There are people running and talking into headsets everywhere, but I dodge around them as I make for the side of the stage, and they don't even seem to notice me.

I dart in front of someone pushing a light and then I'm *there*, standing in the wings of the stage between two dark velvet curtains, watching Dirtshine play.

It's different than the Whiskey Room. Different crowd, different song, I'm at a different angle, but the thrall feels the same. The music wraps itself around me like a snake, sensuous and dangerous but I'm totally transfixed.

I don't think I could leave unless someone dragged me away.

I stand there for their entire set without moving. I can't tear my eyes away from Gavin, the way he sings, the way he plays, the way his body *moves* with the music like he's a part of it. He's always hot, but when he plays? He's practically a god, all of us enthralled by him.

Now I get why girls throw their panties on stage. I'm half thinking about it myself, since I *did* wear a nice pair.

They finish with a final, sonic roar. The stage lights all shut off at once, throwing them into near-total darkness and the crowd goes *insane*, shouting and clapping and stomping their feet, even the well-dressed celebrities standing. I'm grinning and clapping too, swept away in the energy, giddy that my fake boyfriend's done so well.

Even so, there's a kernel of anxiety jammed deep inside my chest as the band walks off the stage toward me, because Gavin doesn't know I'm here.

Quit it, I tell myself. *He'll be happy to see you and you know it.*

Then the four of them are coming through, their faces hard to see in the dark, but Eddie and Trent just nod at me. Darcy glances at me, looks away, looks back, and narrows her eyes quizzically, like she recognizes me but can't quite place my face.

"Is that Marisol?" Gavin's voice says as he materializes.

He's grinning.

"Hey," I say, my heartbeat speeding up again. "I got done with stuff early so I wanted to come—"

He picks me up in a hug and before I know it I'm spinning around in a circle, Gavin laughing as I yelp, then dissolve into laughter myself.

Someone with a headset shushes us, and he puts me back down, grinning.

"I thought you weren't going to make it," he says. "Thanks."

Now I'm blushing, heat creeping up my cheeks. Everyone backstage is acting like they don't notice what's going on, but I can see sideways glances, eyes gazing up from clipboards.

"Of course," I say, smoothing down my hair, trying to compose myself after flying through the air. "I didn't want to miss it."

"Wait, is *this* the... you know, *that* girl?" someone whispers, and I realize that Darcy, Trent, and Eddie are all standing nearby, in a line, watching us.

"Eddie, be cool," Trent mutters.

"Right, sorry," Gavin says, and turns to the rest of Dirtshine, one hand on my back. "Guys, this is Marisol. Marisol, this is Darcy, Trent, and Eddie."

"Great show," I say, nerves fluttering again. I have no idea if they know *our deal* or not. "It was really—"

"And here's Dirtshine, fresh off their big comeback show! Let's go see what *they* think," a woman says, *very* loudly, stomping her way into the middle of our little circle.

She's wearing a formal dress, holding a microphone, talking into a camera, and nearly runs poor Eddie over before he moves.

"Hi there!" she says, smiling hugely. "I'm Peyton Donovich with MTV's Undercover Backstage All-Access Camera! How'd the show go tonight?"

The band looks at each other, and after a moment, Gavin answers.

"It's really great to be back out there," he says.

She keeps going, asking them questions that are all variations on *isn't this wonderful* and *how cool is everything* while I just stand there at Gavin's side, his hand still on my back, and try to stay off her radar. Really, that's what I'm here for: to look like a nice, normal girl who doesn't like drugs and who's a *good influence* on Gavin.

Just as Peyton's wrapping up, putting everyone on edge with her manic energy, she locks her crazy eyes on me.

Please no, I think, but I'm stuck and helpless.

"Now, *you* must be Gavin's *mystery girlfriend!*" she says.

I force myself to smile, even though I feel like the black hole of the camera lens is trying to swallow me.

"I didn't know I was a mystery," I say.

Peyton laughs way, way too hard.

"This is my girlfriend, Marisol," Gavin interjects. He's still got his hand on my back and he's stroking my spine gently with his thumb, almost absent-mindedly.

"Well, I'm glad you made it," Peyton says, half-turning to the camera. "Because welcome to the BACKSTAGE KISS CAM!"

She's going to kiss me?! I think in terror.

Then Gavin pretends to laugh, and I realize: she means me and Gavin.

Valerie's text flashes in my head: *LIP-ON-LIP*.

Gavin looks down at me, smiling, and I try to smile back.

LIP-ON-LIP, LIP-ON-LIP, my brain screams at me.

And then our faces mash together.

There's not another way to put it. I thought he was going to my left so I move my head that way but I half-miss his mouth, so really, our lips are only partly touching. I turn my head and try to save it, scrunching my face towards his, but now somehow my teeth are on his lip, his nose is squashed against his face funny, and the camera's getting all of this.

For a long moment, Gavin doesn't move. I don't move. Then we both back away, and he turns to smile at the camera.

"Beautiful!" shouts Peyton, and she keeps shouting but I can't pay any attention.

That was terrible. Absolutely the worst kiss I've ever experienced, hands down. Worst than my first kiss, worse than the guy who had braces, worse than the guy who shoved his tongue into my mouth and just let it *flop* there.

I'm reeling. Thunderstruck. I've thought about kissing Gavin at least a thousand times, *fantasized* about it, but... the reality was awful. Bad.

Maybe I've been wrong this whole time, I think. *Maybe there's really nothing between us, and we're just going to kiss like awkward adolescents and that's all.*

Plus, now it's going to be on TV, so that's *extra* great.

"Earth to Marisol?" Gavin's voice says, breaking through my mental whirlpool.

"Hi," I answer, blinking.

"Hi," he says. "Come on, we've got to get changed and then go to this party."

"Right," I say, and follow the band.

• • •

The dressing room for the band is a lounge area, with couches and snacks, and a couple of smaller changing rooms branching off. The band heads off to change, and I wander over to the snack table, my mind totally elsewhere.

It was an awkward kiss in front of a camera, I tell myself. *You weren't prepared. It happens. It doesn't mean anything.*

But it was *bad*, and if two people are compatible shouldn't kissing be *good*? How hard is it to kiss well? It's not as though either of us had never done it before.

Maybe you should stick to planning things like this, I think. *Talk about it beforehand, script it out.*

Planning a kiss on the lips so it's good enough isn't the most enticing thought I'd had. Shouldn't that kind of thing be, you know, spontaneous? Spur of the moment?

You're overthinking this, Gomez, I tell myself. *Quit it. Have some candy and then go party.*

The snack table is mostly junk food — chips and packaged cookies and candy. There's a whole bowl of M&Ms, along with fun-sized candy, Twizzlers, and *two* bowls of gummi bears, a small one and a big one. I don't know why. Rock and roll stuff, I guess.

I grab a small handful from each bowl, just to compare. Gummi candies are my weakness, especially when I'm stressed.

"You know the story about Van Halen and brown M&Ms, right?" Darcy's voice says behind me.

I turn, mouth full of gummi candy, and swallow quickly.

"I don't think so," I say.

"They got a reputation as prima donnas because, in their concert rider, they specified that they needed a big bowl of M&Ms backstage, but with all the brown M&Ms removed," she says, grabbing a handful of candy.

"Did they just hate brown?" I ask.

She shakes her head, chewing.

"Years later, David Lee Roth explained it," she says. "When they went into their dressing room, if there were no brown M&Ms, they knew the venue had actually read their whole concert rider, and the important stuff — like lights and sound and everything — were probably set up right. But if there *were* brown M&Ms, everything needed to be double-checked."

I pop another few gummi bears into my mouth. They taste a little strange, but I figure they must be *gourmet* gummi bears or something.

"That's actually pretty smart," I say.

"And now *every* venue has M&Ms, just because," she says, popping more into her mouth. "So, what kind of law are you studying?"

• • •

The party house is *gorgeous*. It's up in the hills above Los Angeles, and the terraced back yard has a view of nearly the whole city, from the skyscrapers downtown all the way to the spinning lit circle of the Ferris wheel on the Santa Monica Pier.

There's a camera set up with a backdrop near the front door, since the party's thrown by a music magazine, but it's mercifully fast, and there's no insane, toothy reporter demanding that we kiss for show. Inside is crowded but not jam-packed, and in few minutes, I'm drinking a glass of champagne while Gavin has club soda with lime as we talk to another musician he knows.

"I think it's an awful remaster," the other guy — Billy? — is saying. "The originals are just so gritty sounding and real, you know? You can't remaster demos. It's like showing videotape in high definition, you just see the scratches better."

"That's the thing, though," Gavin says. "I rather like hearing all of that stuff, the pops and the scratches. Makes me feel as if I'm in the basement with Dylan, not listening to him in the car."

Billy laughs.

"I like feeling as though I'm listening to them in the car," he says. "Reminds me of being nineteen and having snagged a bootleg tape that I could drive around all night and listen to."

A waiter with a tray passes by, taking my champagne glass and offering me another. I glance sideways at Gavin and his club soda, his other hand protectively on my back.

Despite myself, I think about the awful kiss again, my teeth mashed against Gavin's lip.

And I take another glass of champagne.

"I admit to getting precious few bootlegs myself," Gavin says. "There were quite a lot of very loud shows in very dirty bars, though, where you really could hear each and every flaw in the wiring."

I'm still listening, but I haven't got all that much to contribute. Besides, the two of them somehow seem really far *away*, and it's making it hard to pay attention to them, almost like I'm looking at them through a telescope and a microscope at the same time. Like they're really close but also far away, and it's *weird*.

Billy laughs. Gavin laughs. I look from one to the other.

Laugh, I think. *You should probably laugh right now because you're being a little weird and you don't want them to know you're weird, act normal, are you acting normal now? Come on.*

I laugh. Reflexively, I take another sip of champagne, then look down into my glass at the bubbles rising slowly to the top. It's *really* cool.

"Well, everyone's only listening through headphones now is the problem," Billy's saying, but now he feels *extra* far away and something about him seems off, like I'm looking through a kaleidoscope I can't actually see.

Crap, I'm drunk. Am I drunk? Is this what drunk feels like?

I touch Gavin's arm, and he looks down at me.

"I'll be right back," I hear myself say, as though I'm visiting the ladies' room.

"Sure," he says.

I smile. I nod. These are actions I am supposed to do, and then I walk away thinking *right foot, left foot, right foot.*

I don't head for the bathroom. Instead I head outside, because I think I might need fresh air. I've only had one drink — the second glass is still full — but maybe I'm locking my knees or something as I stand, which I know you're not supposed to do because the blood flow from your feet to your brain is very important, even though it's really *weird* that the same blood is in your feet and your brain because they're really different, you know? Feet and brains?

I reach the edge of the terraced back yard. There's a stone wall, and I rest my champagne glass on it, looking out over Los Angeles.

These lights are the most beautiful thing I've ever seen, I think, looking at the buildings, watching the slow crawl of headlights on the freeway.

They just keep going, like stars on the ground or like snakes with stars on them. There's so many people here, and they've all got their own individual lives, every one of those lights down there, and—

I have a quick, bright moment of clarity.

I'm not drunk. This isn't what *drunk* feels like, not at all.

I didn't lock my knees, I'm not hyperventilating.

Nope. I'm stoned.

Really, really stoned.

CHAPTER NINETEEN
Gavin

"I know it's cliché but I really did like their first album better," Billy says.

I drain the rest of the club soda from my glass, the lime hitting my upper lip.

"It's cliché for a reason," I say. "The first album is five, ten years in the making sometimes, the stuff you've been working on for ages. The second album you've got two, *maybe* three years and everyone expects it to be genius."

"True," he says, looking thoughtful.

I glance around the room again, looking for Marisol. She's been gone for a few minutes now, and I'm starting to hope she hasn't gotten lost or something.

I'm not exactly worried — she's an adult, I trust her ability to navigate a party perfectly well — but if she's gotten sucked into a tedious conversation with some executive's wife or someone's trying to quiz her about me, I should probably go rescue her.

After all, good boyfriends don't just leave their girlfriends to fend for themselves around wolves. Or vultures, for that matter.

"I'm going to go make sure Marisol's not trapped in conversation with that bloke Titus or something," I say.

Billy laughs. Titus is a drummer for a band called Black Acid Rain, and he's known for cornering people and simply listing different types of drumming equipment. Impossible to escape.

"I'll catch you around," Billy says, and we walk in separate directions.

I'm taller than most people here, but there's still no sign of Marisol as I glance through different rooms, looking for curly hair and a black dress. Nothing, anywhere.

It's odd. It's very odd.

She ran off because of your dreadful kiss, I think.

It's a rubbish thought, but it still stings. I know she wouldn't just leave without telling me, but for the past hour or so she's seemed a bit quiet, a bit distant.

I can't help but think it's because we kissed like a couple of toddlers imitating adults.

It caught me off-guard, and it caught her off-guard, and I doubt that kissing for a camera is ever a particularly enjoyable or natural thing to do, but *still*. I hate it. I knew that we'd have to get to *lip-on-lip*, as Valerie's increasingly urgent communiqués call it, but I hadn't meant it to be like that.

I didn't want our first kiss to be for the cameras. That's half the reason I haven't done it yet, because I've kissed dozens of women but I wanted it to be *right* when I kiss Marisol.

And, well, I buggered that up.

I head through room after room, but she's nowhere at all. Not outside, not near the bathrooms, not in any of the massive house's half-dozen rooms filled with well-dressed people and lounge furniture, so I start asking people if they've seen her.

Trent and Darcy haven't. Billy hasn't, and neither have any of the other several people I ask.

Until it's Eddie to the rescue. He's waving his arms about, a beer in one hand looking precarious, talking to a few other blokes dressed almost exactly as he is.

"That's your *girlfriend*, right?" he asks, practically winking at the world *girlfriend*.

"Yes," I say, holding up one hand, palm down. "About this high, black hair, black dress?"

"Oh, I think she went upstairs," one of Eddie's mates says.

I frown.

"Upstairs?" I ask.

He shrugs.

"Yeah, some girl went up there. I figured the bathrooms down here were full or something?"

"Has she come back?"

He scrunches his eyebrows together as if remembering is quite a task.

"I don't *think* so," he says.

"Thanks," I say, and make for the stairs myself.

The grand staircase leads around a landing and then into a dark hallway, and I walk into it slowly, heart pumping.

"Marisol?" I call softly.

Maybe she got too drunk, I think. *Maybe she's upset about something — about me — and wants to be alone. Maybe she just wants to be alone.*

No answer. I walk into the dark, and as my eyes adjust, I realize there's a sliver of light near the end of the hall, a door partly open.

I head for it and call her name again.

There's a slight rustle inside, then Marisol's voice.

"Shit," she says.

I push the door open. It's a palatial bathroom with a huge glassed-in shower, two sinks, marble floors, a walk-in closet, and a jacuzzi tub in the corner.

Marisol's curled up at one end of the empty tub, perfectly dry, head against the lip, eyes closed. I've no idea what's going on.

"Is everything all right?" I say.

It's a stupid question — she's in a tub in a dark bathroom at a party, obviously something's awry — but I don't know what else to ask.

Marisol clears her throat without opening her eyes.

"Yeah," she says, her voice a little too high-pitched, the tiniest bit shaky. "Everything's fine. I'm fine. Totally fine."

I don't believe her. Alarm bells are going off in my head, big screeching sirens, so I walk over to her and kneel.

"You're curled in a bathtub at a party," I say, trying to sound as calm as possible.

"I'm really stoned and I think I might be dissolving," she says. "And on one hand, I know that sounds a little insane but I also can't prove that I'm *not* dissolving and I would really prefer to stay in this tub so that if I *am* dissolving, I can just plug the drain and collect myself later."

"You're not dissolving," I assure her.

"I have to stay here, though," she says. "I don't want to dissolve everywhere, it would be a huge mess, and if I move I'm just going to dissolve faster."

I've got no idea what's happened. A few minutes ago she was fine and now she's completely toasted.

"Did you smoke?" I ask. "Did someone give you something?"

Not that I think Marisol would just smoke something that was handed to her.

Even so, anger starts a slow simmer somewhere beneath my sternum that someone, somehow did this to *my* Marisol.

She just shakes her head.

"I hate this," she says, her eyes still closed. "I'm dissolving and I broke my brain. I'm never going to be able to think again, but I'm also not even going to have a body unless I stay here and all my atoms get collected in the tub..."

I take her hand in mine and kiss the back of it. She doesn't respond.

"Is this my brain forever?" she whispers.

I swallow hard, flexing my other hand into a fist, because even though I've got no idea *how* she got this high, I'm fairly sure it wasn't her idea and I'd like to hit whoever's made her this miserable.

I swing my legs over the side of the enormous tub and sit with her. She doesn't move.

"I'll tell you if you open your eyes," I say.

"You're getting my molecules *all over* you," she says.

I don't *think* she's on anything besides enough pot to get a horse stoned, but you never know.

"Come on," I say, putting one arm around her.

She looks at me without moving anything but her eyelids. Even in the near-dark I can see that her eyes are bloodshot red but her pupils are fine.

"Your brain's not broken," I tell her. "It's going to be a little while but you'll get back to normal."

Marisol just shakes her head and closes her eyes again.

I'm going to kill whoever did this, I think, even as I put one arm around her. *Did they think it was fucking funny?*

"*Did* you smoke?" I ask, even though she doesn't smell as if she did.

Marisol just shakes her head.

"I had champagne," she says, her voice slow and dreamy.

Everyone had champagne, so I doubt it was that.

"Anything else?"

"I can't..." she says, her voice trailing off. She swallows again, her mouth probably dry. "My brain is dissolving kind of fast right now but maybe that piece will go by."

"You don't look as if you're dissolving," I say. "You seem in one piece."

She shakes her head, but I don't argue with her. I've been here before, so high I was utterly convinced that my teeth were melting out of my mouth, and someone trying to argue with me didn't help in the least. The best I can do is stay calm and tell her, every few minutes, that she's still intact.

But it doesn't mean I'm not angry. Fuck yes I'm angry. I want to hit whatever utter imbecile did this to her, stuff pot down their throats until *they're* too high to move and in a bathtub, see how they fucking like it.

"There were those mini tacos," she murmurs.

Then she sighs.

"What if the tub dissolves too?" she asks. "I think maybe everything is dissolving."

"Porcelain can't dissolve, everyone knows that," I say, thinking furiously about what she might have had. Couldn't have been the mini tacos, I had them as well. Couldn't hardly be any of the hors d'oeuvres here.

"Did you eat anything backstage at the concert?" I ask, keeping my voice light and casual.

"Hold on," she says.

She's quiet a long moment.

"The concert," I remind her quietly.

"Sorry, I forgot, because I can stop myself from leaking out of my skin if I concentrate on it really really hard, and what did you say? Concert?"

"That's right."

"There was candy. No brown M&Ms, but I ate a bunch of the—"

Her head snaps up and she looks at me with bloodshot eyes, her face alarmed.

"There were gummi bears," she says, her voice dropping to a whisper. "They were weird."

I've never heard anyone sound sadder about candy.

"Are gummi bears poison now?" she asks, sounding completely baffled, as if the fabric of the universe has changed and no one warned her.

Which is sort of true.

"Just those," I reassure her. "But you're fine. Still don't look dissolved yet."

Marisol closes her eyes and drops her head onto my shoulder, and my anger flares white-hot again because someone *did this* to her. Intentionally or not, and I'm going to fucking find out who.

She sighs into my shoulder and my insides twist because I can barely stand to see her like this. I kiss her hair, but I don't think she notices, and then I take a deep breath.

I need to get her out of this bathtub and home. That takes priority over finding someone to blame.

"Marisol," I say gently. "I need to leave for five minutes, but I'll be right back. You should stay here."

"Go to your party and don't forget me when you leave?"

"Five minutes," I say again.

"I'm going to be mostly puddle so please don't step in me," she says.

"You still seem quite whole," I say, but she doesn't respond, so I leave the tub, close the bathroom door behind me, and head downstairs.

Yeah, I'm a fucking hypocrite. For years I did anything and everything I could find, but I never got someone *else* high without their permission. Now I want to kill whoever's made Marisol think she's dissolving and can't leave a bathtub.

Past the bathroom there's a second staircase, a smaller one, and I take that one down into the bustling kitchen where all the servers and cooks ignore me. I call the limo driver and ask him to come around to the side driveway, *quietly*.

He says he'll be there in a few minutes. I hang up, and before I go get Marisol, I head back into the party to see if I can't find my bandmates because we need to have a *fucking* word.

Darcy's the first one I spot, in a corner, looking at her phone and drinking a tumbler of whiskey like she'd rather be anywhere else. She looks up as she sees me coming, taking in the look on my face.

"What happened?" she asks.

"Pot-laced candy in the dressing room," I say, crossing my arms in front of me and glaring, willing myself not to make a scene. At least not *yet*. "Marisol's in the bathtub upstairs, stoned out of her mind."

Darcy blinks, taken aback.

"Her?" she asks. "She didn't seem like the—"

"On accident, you dumb bint," I snarl. "Someone left their edibles around."

"Chill the *fuck* out," Darcy says, standing up straighter, her voice rising. "I'm not enough of an asshole to bring pot goodies to a show I'm playing with a *goddamn junkie*."

The people around us get a little quieter, and I realize we're being watched. I take a deep breath and flex both hands. I'm angry, but I know Darcy's not lying. Fuck, she's as interested as anyone in Marisol being a good influence.

"Sorry," I say, forcing my voice calm. "Have you seen Eddie or—"

Darcy points, and Trent steps up beside me, a beer in his hand.

"Gavin's fa... Gavin's girlfriend is super high, and he thinks it was pot candy backstage at the show," Darcy says, her words still clipped. "You leave anything lying around?"

Trent frowns.

"No," he says, like it's the world's most obvious thing. "You're in recovery. Is she okay?"

"She'll be fine, I'm taking her home," I growl, glancing around. People have gone back to their conversations and stopped watching us, but there's no sign of Eddie anywhere.

As much as I *want* to give him a piece of my goddamn mind, getting Marisol home is more important. I turn away without saying goodbye, head up the back stairs again, into the dark hallway, and open the door to the bathroom.

She hasn't moved. My heart lurches just looking at her, curled in the tub.

"Splish splash," she says.

CHAPTER TWENTY
Marisol

I only have two thoughts right now: *my body is slowly breaking into a billion pieces and leaking through my skin, atom by atom*, and *I hate this*.

"You're still not dissolved," Gavin's voice says as he walks toward me.

"It's a process," I point out.

"All right, love," he says, his voice much closer, like he's kneeling by the tub. "There's a car downstairs to take you home if you can just get up."

Obviously, that's not going to work. I can't leave this bathtub, but saying all that seems much too hard, so I just shake my head. My atoms fly everywhere.

"There's a back way out. Super secret. You've just got to get up," he goes on.

"I have to stay here."

"It's fifty meters away."

I don't respond. Something takes my hand.

Oh, it's his hand.

"Marisol, I promise you aren't dissolving but you *are* disastrously stoned and in a bathtub and if you want to feel any better, I very much need you to stand up and come with me, all right?"

Gavin stands. I open my eyes. I don't know why I believe him, but I do.

I take a deep breath, exhale, and then slowly push myself up until I'm standing in this huge jacuzzi tub, straightening my dress and remembering to breathe, even though I can feel every molecule of oxygen enter my lungs and then my bloodstream and then zoom around my body.

I can feel *everything*, even if it feels like I'm in stop-motion.

Gavin holds out a hand, palm up. I take it and step from the bathtub carefully, still in my heels. My balance is fine — I'm not drunk — it's just everything else. I walk because my body remembers how, not because I do, and he leads me down the stairs.

At the bottom is the kitchen, but Gavin keeps me moving and before I know it we're exiting through a door to the outside, the cool night air settling over my face like a thousand feathers falling softly onto my skin.

"It's different air," I say out loud.

There's a car. Gavin opens a door and guides me inside and then I'm sitting on the plush back seat of a limo, and it's warm and kind of nice.

I remind myself that he's sober and *swore* I'm not dissolving. I remind myself again. And again.

Gavin's about to get in, but someone calls his name, and he steps back away from the car.

Close the door, I think, though I don't move too close. *Close it. No one can see me. Close it. Close it.*

"Hey, man, I'm really sorry," says voice I recognize, and I flip through faces in my mind like a rolodex. Flip flip flip.

"You fucking *idiot*," says Gavin. "Did you really just leave those things out and not tell a single fucking soul what they were?"

There's a dangerous, wild, feral note in his voice that I've never heard before, and it's a little scary but also strangely thrilling, like a low flame held just off my skin. Like I'm seeing Gavin's *animal* nature.

A thrill runs through my entire body and I think of his fingers on me, my shoulders, my neck, his lips on mine, him pulling me onto his lap in the back of this car—

"I meant to leave a note, but I had to go find paper and then they called me for a sound check, and I... sort of forgot?" the voice says, distracting me.

My rolodex lands on Eddie, the drummer.

"You fucking *forgot*," Gavin says. "I found Marisol upstairs curled into a bathtub, miserable and stoned out of her fucking gourd because you *forgot*."

"It was a mistake, man," Eddie says. "It was just pot, she'll live."

"That's not the question," Gavin says, his voice rising quickly. "She's got real fucking responsibilities. She could have a drug test and you'd have fucked her over."

That sounds terrible, I think.

"But she doesn't, right?" Eddie says, his voice pitching higher. "Look, I'm sorry, but just chill, okay? It's not the end of the world if your pretend girlfriend—"

"You stupid *cunt*," growls Gavin.

There's a thump.

"Motherfucker!" shouts Eddie.

Alarm works its way into my brain for a moment and I lurch across the seat, flat on my stomach, looking out the open car door. Gavin's flexing his right hand and Eddie's holding his face, mouth gaping open.

"Goddamn it, what the fuck, dude?" shouts Eddie.

"Don't *fucking* leave your shit around!" says Gavin.

"You *punched* me!"

"I'll do it again if you've not fucking learned!"

Eddie stares at Gavin, one hand on his face. Gavin stares back, shoulders squared, all the veins in his tattooed forearms standing out.

"Goddamn maniac," Eddie mutters.

Then he walks away.

"Bloody right I am," Gavin says, then turns and gets into the limo. I sit up and scoot over, and he closes the door. The limo starts driving but I'm just staring at Gavin, eyes wide, mind going a thousand miles a minute.

Did that just happen? I think that just happened, right? Do I really remember that? Am I still dissolving? A thump plus Eddie saying 'you punched me' equals punch, right? But just because I remember it did it happen?

Is memory even real? I guess reality is just this very instant and everything else is a construct, right?

"Did you..." I start, staring at Gavin's knuckles. They're bright red, already starting to bruise, and I force myself to collect the rest of that thought. "...just punch Eddie?"

"I did," Gavin says, sounding resigned. "And I definitely shouldn't have done."

"No," I say.

Then I remember he's in the limo with me.

"Where are we going?" I ask.

"Your flat."

"You don't have to," I say, leaning my head back against the head rest and closing my eyes. "I stopped dissolving. I think I'm a little less high. Go party. I'm sorry I was in the bathtub. It was just really nice in there."

Something soft touches the top of my head lightly. I *think* Gavin just kissed me. I *think* he also did it before, but again, I'm not quite sure if the concept of memory is real or an elaborate ruse at the moment, so I don't spend much time on it.

"Parties are less fun sober," he says. "And I just clocked Eddie in the face, so I may not exactly be welcome back."

I think about this for a long moment, which turns into thinking about fingers, faces, parties, champagne glasses, the way bubbles rise, and the way my brain feels like saltwater taffy, being stretched and pulled and squished and stretched again.

Then Gavin's hand is on my shoulder, and he's saying my name.

"I'm awake," I say, opening my eyes.

"Come on," he says, opening the door. "We're here."

He opens the door, gets out, and offers me his hand. We seem to be on my street, in front of my apartment building, and he shuts the back door of the car.

"I'm okay from here," I say. "Really."

"You've got your keys, then?"

I exhale, closing my eyes, because I have no memory whatsoever of what happened to the clutch I was carrying. Was I carrying it? Do I have hands? Have I always had hands?

"I can't hold them because I don't—"

Gavin holds up my clutch.

"Oh," I say.

"I think it's best if I see you in," he teases gently. I stop arguing.

As we head up the three flights of stairs, I quietly pray that my underwear drawer is shut and my vibrator isn't out somewhere, since I may as well have named the damn thing after him by now. My apartment is usually pretty neat, and I'm not in the habit of just leaving things like that around, but I also know that if it were going to happen it would happen now.

Maybe if he sees your underpants or vibrator he'll get some ideas, I think. *You could put the moves on him, and if he turns you down, next time you see him act like you don't remember.*

I unlock my apartment door, his hand protectively on my lower back, sparks shooting up my spine. It makes my heart beat faster whenever Gavin touches me, but right now everything is amplified ten times and it's driving me *crazy*.

I want his hands on my skin. I want his mouth on mine. I want to run my fingers over the chiseled abs I've still only seen in pictures. I want—

"Were you going to open the door, or just stand there with it unlocked?" he asks.

I pull the key out, turn the knob, push my door.

"Sorry, I forgot," I say.

My apartment's *tiny*, a studio with a two-burner stove, no oven, and a miniature sink. The bathroom's too small for a tub, so it's just got a shower. The main piece of furniture is my bed — which I'm pleased to discover I made this morning — along with a loveseat I got for free when a friend got rid of it.

The only table is my desk, next to an ugly-but-sturdy and completely full bookshelf that I got from the Salvation Army for ten dollars. There's one chair. My dresser is also my bedside table, which, *thank God*, doesn't have my vibrator sitting on it.

It's not fancy, but I can just barely afford it without roommates, and that's all I want.

"This is a nice place," Gavin says.

I toss my keys onto my desk, then flop onto my bed, shoes and dress still on, and close my eyes.

"No, it's not," I say.

"I like it," he says. "It's cozy. Feels like home, you know? All the cheap flats I've ever lived in were infested rat holes. Possibly because dirty junkies don't always keep the cleanest quarters."

"I've seen roaches," I admit. "It's the neighbors. They come through the walls. I hate it. There's nothing I can do."

A quick, vivid memory: opening a drawer to bugs scuttling away from the light.

I think I'm less high. Am I? Yes? Yes.

"I did once have a long conversation with a rat while he was sitting in my sink," he says.

"Did the rat tell you to stop doing drugs?" I ask. "I wish I had a rat to tell me that right now."

Gavin just laughs.

"You'll be surprised to learn I don't recall what the rat said," he says. I can hear him opening and closing my cabinets, then the sound of glasses clinking softly. The water goes on, then off, and he walks over to the bed.

"Here," he says. "Sit up and drink some water at least."

I let him pull me up and take the water without opening my eyes. I don't like opening my eyes. I'm fairly certain I've stopped dissolving, but sight just reminds me how terrible everything feels.

"Thanks," I say when the water is gone.

"Where do you keep pajamas?" he asks.

I don't.

I sleep naked, but I definitely cannot tell him that right now.

Take your dress off and tell him that this is your pajamas, I think. *You're already in your bed, and he probably kissed you in the limousine. It could work. The terrible kiss was just a fluke.*

ROXIE NOIR

Just thinking of it ties my stomach in a knot, but I take a deep breath and look up at him. Seductively. I hope.

I feel like I'm looking at him through a kaleidoscope I can't see, tiny particles of everything, of me and him and the bed and the room and the universe all flying through the air and crashing together haphazardly.

I close my eyes again. I don't think my seduction is working.

"Pajamas," he repeats softly.

CHAPTER TWENTY-ONE
Gavin

I *cannot* give in right now. Marisol's still high as a kite, and even though I'm in her flat, right by her bed, and she's looking up at me with wide eyes and lips parted, I'm not giving in.

I'm not even going to kiss her. Much less push her backward, pull her dress down, and run my lips down her neck as she gasps. Absolutely not, no matter how badly I'm aching to touch her.

No matter that I'm fighting a losing battle with my own dick right now, and I'm at half-mast despite my most desperate attempts to visualize the Queen.

"I'm not leaving until you're in bed," I tell her, wishing I meant it anything but literally. "Otherwise I'm afraid you'll sit here and stare at your own hand all night."

She rubs her face, then reaches for a dresser drawer and pulls out shorts and a t-shirt, tossing them on the bed next to her, and stands, reaching behind herself.

It takes every bit of self-control I've got to turn around.

"Wait," she says. "Unzip me?"

I wish I was high, or drunk, or *anything* besides perfectly sober, because then every curve of her body and every inch of her skin wouldn't be taunting me in crystal-clear detail.

I wish Marisol were sober instead of completely off her head, because sober I could kiss her again and not feel like I was taking advantage.

Her back's to me. I move her hair from her neck, my fingertips brushing her warm skin. A thrill runs through me, and I grit my teeth together, grasp the zipper, and slide it down as a slim oval of Marisol's back is revealed.

I almost fucking lose it. I'm struck by the urge to kneel, press my lips to the base of her spine, and then climb her vertebra by vertebra until I'm at her neck. It's so strong that I almost can't help myself, and I rock back on my heels, strung tighter than piano wire.

"Thanks," she says.

"Right," I say, and turn my back while I still can.

There are rustling noises. Her dress falls to the ground, softly, while I breathe and wait, trying to think of *anything* besides Marisol naked, right behind me.

I distract myself by looking at the books on the top of her dresser, all of which have a library sticker on them. The bottom one is *Clean: Overcoming Addiction*, then *Addiction Recovery for Dummies,* then *Twelve Roadblocks to Recovery*, then *The Neurochemistry of Opioid Addiction*.

I blink. Something squeezes in my chest.

She didn't have to, I think.

Then I hear her voice again.

"Okay," she says.

I turn. She's wearing a University of Los Angeles Debate Team t-shirt and plaid shorts, taking off her shoes.

"I'll leave when your head's on the pillow," I say. I know I sound like a particularly strict nanny, but I can't help it. She's so small and vulnerable right now that I'm driven by the weird urge to take care of her, give her water and make sure she gets enough sleep.

And the urge to punch Eddie. *Jesus* I wish I was drunk, because at least being tits-over-arse is an excellent excuse for violence.

Marisol gets between the covers, then kicks them half off.

"I think the bathtub was better, just in case," she says. "I wish my apartment had one."

I laugh softly.

"All this and you wish I'd left you there," I say.

"I'm sorry I made you skip your fun rock and roll party."

"It wasn't that fun," I say. "Nor was it that rock and roll."

"Still," she says, and then we both go quiet for a long moment.

Marisol doesn't move, her chest rising and falling. I refill her water glass as quietly as I can, set it by her bed.

And give in to the wild urge to kiss her on the forehead.

"Stay," she murmurs, her face just underneath mine.

"Go back to sleep," I tell her, nerves suddenly jangling.

"Please?" she says, her voice soft and sleepy and distant.

"Your couch isn't big enough," I point out.

"Don't sleep on the couch."

I nearly kiss her on the lips, because she's soft and warm and tempting and I'm stretched near my breaking point, but I don't. In the last few months, since rehab, I've done a lot of teaching myself to think about consequences, so now I think about waking up tomorrow, Marisol remembering I've kissed her while she was incapacitated, the betrayed look on her face.

And I know I should do the same about staying here. I should call an Uber and go to my own house, my own bed, but I don't.

"All right," I say. I take off my jacket and shoes and I lay down next to Marisol, still wearing my shirt and jeans. She turns to face me and puts her hands in mine.

I can't believe I'm doing this. I can't believe I'm dead sober next to a girl who's out of her mind, I can't believe I'm fully clothed in her bed, and I can't believe I'm not going to do a thing about it. If Gavin from six months ago saw this, he'd laugh his arse off.

"Thanks," Marisol murmurs.

Past Gavin can go fuck himself.

• • •

I wake up because it's too hot and too bright and I've clearly slept in my clothes.

Hungover and jonesing again next to some groupie slag, I think automatically, more asleep than awake.

My eyes open onto an empty pillow, and I brace myself for the crashing headache. It doesn't come.

You stopped doing that, you pillock, I think, but it's somehow still a pleasant surprise that I don't feel like a clammy wreck itching in my own skin, and that I can remember everything from last night perfectly well.

I'm at Marisol's, in her bed, because she asked me to stay. Being sober feels like life on easy mode sometimes, and I roll over, looking around her cozy flat in the daylight.

She's not there. It's easy enough to see her whole place from the bed, and she's not anywhere in it. Half-awake disappointment crawls through me, and I sit up slowly, feeling a bit stupid.

I'd thought, as I fell asleep holding her hand last night, that maybe I'd wake up with her in my arms this morning. That maybe she'd look at me, whisper my name and we'd kiss properly as she rolled over, straddling me, my hands sliding up underneath her shirt—

But she's not here. All that's here is a note on the table.

Gavin—

I went to study group & didn't want to wake you. Help yourself to coffee & breakfast if you want it. Lock the knob when you leave.

Valerie's called a meeting at 5pm in her office. See you there.

Marisol

I'm gut-punched, and last night is fading away, replaced by the constant, unforgiving hard sunlight of Los Angeles.

She was toasted off her gourd, I think. *She barely even knew she was asking you to stay.*

I feel like an idiot. A sober idiot, but an idiot to think it meant anything. Now all I've got is a drummer with a black eye, a furious band, and a pretend girlfriend who's really just pretending no matter what I tell myself, not to *mention* the fucking train wreck of a human staying at my house indefinitely.

It doesn't fucking matter, I think. *You've cocked this up beyond repair and you didn't even need to be high. You just needed to be you.*

I stand and put my shoes on again, shove both hands through my hair, and stuff the note in my pocket.

I at least deserve a fucking drink, I think. *If everything's going to hell in a handcart, might as well drink while it does.*

As I turn to go my eyes sweep across the dresser, stacked with Marisol's books. The ones about getting clean and sober. My stomach turns. I take a deep breath.

If you still want one after the meeting.

Then I lock the knob on Marisol's door, shut it behind me, and leave.

CHAPTER TWENTY-TWO
Marisol

All day there's been a feeling of grinding dread deep in the pit of my stomach, and walking toward the skyscraper that contains Valerie's Public Relations firm, it's only getting worse.

Everyone's angry. Gavin's angry with Eddie. Eddie, Darcy, and Trent are angry with Gavin. The record company is angry with Gavin. Nigel's probably on his fourth scotch already, and it's barely four in the afternoon.

Every gossip website is running stories about how he's out of control on a drug and alcohol-fueled bender. It's rumored that Dirtshine is breaking up because Gavin's a total maniac and they've completely had it with him.

And it's my fault, because I ate some gummi bears like an *idiot*. I knew they tasted weird, and I ate them anyway without stopping to think *hey, Marisol, you're backstage at a rock concert, maybe don't eat things that taste weird.*

And because there are probably *children* who can keep it together better when they're super high than I can. Who the hell curls up in a bathtub and babbles on and on about dissolving just because they're stoned? Who makes their very famous fake boyfriend spend the night in their shitty apartment just because they had a little pot?

I don't think I'm cut out for this. I don't think I'm helping anything at this point. My contract specifies that I still get some of the money, and I think it's enough that I can get my parents another apartment, just until I've got a real job and can help them better.

I pull open the heavy glass door on the building's ground floor lobby and try to steel myself for what's coming. If I don't get fired, I'm going to suggest that maybe I'm not the right choice, and maybe Gavin and I start having our public breakup.

Walking through the lobby, I go over my reasoning one last time. This isn't fair to him; he needs someone who can handle the attention without getting awkward. After all, I had to work up the nerve to kiss him on the cheek, and when it came to lip-on-lip I botched it *completely*.

Plus, I can't act for shit; he deserves someone prettier than me; he needs someone who won't turn down important things like awards shows. Overall, I'm just the wrong choice, and we'll go our separate ways professionally and amicably.

And yet, I want to cry, because I went and got attached.

It's just more proof that I'm not the woman for the job.

I round a corner toward the elevator bank, then stop in my tracks. There's a very familiar form leaning against the wall, and he looks up from his phone.

"There you are," Gavin says, walking toward me.

"You're early?" I ask, because that's not exactly his normal style.

"Just this once," he says. "I wanted to see you before the piranhas moved in."

Tell him now and get it over with, I think. *He's going to be the hardest one to tell, so just do it first.*

"Good, I'm glad you came down," I say.

I straighten my back and take a deep breath.

"I think we should start discussing our breakup because I'm clearly not the right person to be playing your girlfriend," I say, all in one breath, spitting it out before I lose my nerve.

Gavin docsn't react. He just stares at me, in the hallway by the elevators. Two women in suits walk by. One of them turns to give him a second look.

"No," he finally says.

There's a huge lump in my throat, and I'm holding my breath, trying to act normal and not get emotional in near-public like this.

"What do you mean, *no*?" I ask.

"*No*," he says again, shaking his head. "No to you, no to this, no to all the bloody play-acting—"

He breaks off, looking around. Then he takes my hand and pulls me toward a door marked EXIT.

It's also marked FIRE DOOR, DO NOT OPEN, but he ignores that and pulls me through into a narrow-but-sunny alleyway. An alarm goes off in the building, silenced as the door shuts behind us.

I start talking.

"I got high by accident and freaked out, I don't know *anything* about music, I'm awkward in front of cameras—"

Gavin turns and takes my face in both hands.

"I don't care," he says.

I keep talking, an anxious train that can't stop.

"—I was almost too nervous to kiss you on the cheek, and then the lip-on-lip was really awkward and bad—"

He kisses me.

His lips are warm and firm on mine, his fingers in my hair, and for a split second I'm so surprised that I don't move.

Then I kiss him back. There's no one else around. No cameras, no reporters, no other people at all. Just us. I drop my briefcase and slide one hand around Gavin's neck, his skin hot underneath my fingers as our mouths move together, slow and deliberate.

He pulls back a fraction of an inch, one thumb stroking across my cheekbone. In a heartbeat, I close the distance between us again, pressing my body against his, one of his hands trailing down my back as my spine turns to molten liquid.

It's *nothing* like the kiss yesterday.

When we finally separate, he leans his forehead against mine, and I try to breathe, my heart slamming against my ribs.

"I'm not pretending," he says, his voice low and quiet and rough.

"I'm not either," I whisper.

He kisses me again. It's almost deliriously slow, our mouths moving together, our bodies drawing closer as we explore each other for the very first time.

A river of heat floods my body, and I'm swept away in it. I didn't really think *this* was in the cards. I thought we'd kiss politely in public and shake hands in private.

I thought I'd just be fantasizing about Gavin's body pressed against mine like he *needs* me, his tongue slow and deliberate against my bottom lip, his fingers curled into my hip. But this isn't fantasy, this is real — his arm around me, his mouth on mine.

His massive erection making me ache fiercely.

We pull back again after a long time, both breathing hard. Even though it's our first kiss — sort of — I still want to wrap my legs around him, right here in this alley, feel his hips move against mine.

"I don't care if you dump me in front of the cameras," he murmurs. "As long as this is real."

I just nod, breathless.

"It is," I whisper.

He kisses me.

"Fuck all this," he says, and kisses me. "Fuck tabloids, fuck record companies, fuck publicists."

"Fuck reporters," I add, and he laughs.

"Fuck Valeric's suggestions of next steps and physical affection benchmarks," he says, and we kiss again, deep and slow. I put one hand on his chest, the hard muscle rippling under his shirt, and I slide it down slowly, my entire body tingling until I stop right above his belt.

Gavin pulls away, kisses my jaw, bites my earlobe, and I gasp.

"You don't have to stop," he murmurs.

I know we're in an alleyway. It's public. There's a dumpster twenty feet away and graffiti on the wall facing us, and I know better than to get any further than first base *here*. But my brain's not really in control any more.

Gavin's phone dings, and I can feel it buzz in his pocket. We both freeze.

"I think we're late," I whisper.

He pulls his phone from his pocket and glances at it.

"Nigel?" I ask.

"Just asking where I am," he says. "I did tell him I was headed to the loo, which he's figured out by now is rubbish."

I pull out my phone as well. I turned the ringer off earlier today, but I've got a feeling I might have a few messages waiting.

There's a wall of them. The latest one is from Valerie and says **THE MEETING STARTED AT 5PM**.

"Same idea," I tell Gavin.

We're both quiet for a moment, and we look around for a moment, from the dumpster to the graffiti to the swish of traffic out on the main street as we remember *where* we are. I lean against the wall, trying to collect myself, remember what I'm doing and why I'm here.

Gavin gives me a long look, from my toes up to my head. By the time his eyes meet mine I've forgotten why I'm here again.

"Fuck meetings," he says, stepping forward and taking my hip in his hand.

I grab the front of his t-shirt and pull him toward me and then his mouth is on mine again, hot and hungry, need like I've never felt surging through my body.

Alleyway, I think again, but Gavin slides his fingers underneath my shirt, his callouses rough against my skin, and I forget about it. I do the same to him, his body warm and hard beneath me.

I feel like I'm careening down a hill with the brakes cut.

Slow down, my inner voice keeps telling me. *You've only just kissed—*

Gavin kisses my neck, just barely nipping at the skin, and I *grunt*. Then he grabs my ass and lifts me, pinning me against the concrete wall of the alley, and now my legs are wrapped around his hips, his erection pressing against me with pure, delicious need.

Slowing down isn't gonna happen. My inner voice can take a hike.

Suddenly there's a loud *bang* at one end of the alley, and I jerk my head back.

Still tangled together we turn our heads as one, mouths open in surprise.

There's a truck coming toward us, and as it hits a pothole it lurches with another *bang*.

I freeze. Gavin slides his hands out from under my shirt, and the truck slows to a crawl. The driver's side window lowers, and I pull myself off Gavin, standing on my own two feet again.

"You all right, Miss?" the driver calls out.

I can feel myself turn bright red, the color of a ripe tomato.

"Fine!" I call, smiling as big as I can and giving the thumbs up.

Gavin doesn't turn around. It's not like he needs *more* headlines.

"Just checking," the driver calls. He revs the engine and turns into a loading dock, disappearing around a corner.

I think Gavin's laughing.

"We should go somewhere else," I whisper.

He turns and glances at the alley, thumb edging back under my shirt and stroking my skin, sparks skipping through my veins. There's an open door into an empty hallway, leading to the basement of another tall building, and he looks at me and grins.

I *meant* my place or his, but the words dissolve before I can say them, along with my objections that it's too fast, too soon.

I want this. Technically, we've been dating for weeks. It's not as if I don't know Gavin, and besides, I don't care *what* kind of girl it makes me.

We make for the dark hallway, hand-in-hand, a thrill running through me.

CHAPTER TWENTY-THREE
Gavin

I have no idea where we are and I don't *care*. It's the industrial cinderblock corridor to some high-rise building, gray and fluorescent. I've got her hand tight in mine and we're both laughing as we try every door on the hall.

A knob turns in Marisol's hand.

"Here," she whispers, and opens the door, looking back at me. I glance up and down the corridor but there's no one there so I push her inside and close the door after myself.

It's dark, lights blinking, the warm hum of electronics echoing off nearby walls. Marisol's right in front of me and I pull her in, warm and soft and yielding as I press my mouth to hers again.

Our tongues entangle. She makes a soft noise, somewhere between a gasp and a moan, and it sends lightning down my spine.

"Shh," I say, pulling away. "Don't get us caught."

I kiss her jaw, the spot under her ear, her neck. Her heartbeat races beneath my lips, her hands on my back, fingers digging into me as I move to her collarbone, then the space underneath it.

I can't remember the last time everything was this clear and *sharp*, the last time every single one of my senses was so overwhelmed with desire, like fire burning underneath my skin.

For *years,* every time I've been with a girl I've been dulled, the edge taken off, desire foggy as if I was looking at it through wavy glass.

Not now. It's as if I've grown extra nerves just so they can shiver as well, desire like a thousand pencil points against my skin, hard and real.

Whatever's behind Marisol is only hip high, and I lift her onto it. She wraps her legs around me again and I pull her to me, the delicious friction so overwhelming that I can't even kiss her for a moment, just press my face against her, hand in her hair, trying to gather myself.

"You okay?" she whispers. "We can stop if you're not okay."

I just laugh and bite her earlobe softly, listening to her tiny gasp.

"I'm far better than okay," I say.

Her fingers curl into my shoulder as I speak, and I laugh.

"This do it for you?" I ask, letting my lips barely brush the shell of her ear. Her fingers curl into me again.

"Yes," Marisol whispers.

"I *do* like how you say that word," I murmur.

I slide one hand under her shirt, my heart racing.

"The way I say yes?" she asks, her voice low and musical.

I run one thumb along the very bottom of her bra, feeling the soft skin underneath, and she tightens her legs around me. I'm hard as iron and I *know* she can feel it as she rocks her hips against mine.

She runs her hand through my hair and puts her lips to my ear.

"Yes," she whispers again.

That's all it takes.

Whatever self-control I had snaps, and I kiss her hard and deep. Marisol arches her back into me as she reaches behind herself, and suddenly her bra is loose under her shirt and my hands are on her small, full breasts, her nipples hard between my fingers.

I pinch. She makes a noise into my mouth, her hands under my shirt, short nails on my back, tiny slivers of white-hot pleasure spiking into me, and I groan.

"Shh," Marisol teases me.

She slides one finger underneath the waistband of my jeans and my cock twitches even harder, my balls tightening for an instant.

Jesus, what's wrong with you? You're acting like you've never been with a woman before.

I run my thumbs over her nipples again, circling slowly, feeling the delicious way they pucker as Marisol presses herself into me, our mouths together. She pulls harder on the waistband of my jeans and then, so slowly it feels like torture, slides one hand down the length of my cock from tip to root.

I nearly lose my mind. I have to fight the sheer primal urge to tear our clothes off, push her back and bury myself hilt-deep inside her, right here in this storage closet.

I don't. I just want to, desperately, as her hand closes around me in my jeans, and I hear myself *growl*. Marisol pulls back a fraction of an inch.

"Was that noise—"

"Good, *yes*," I whisper and cover her mouth with mine again.

Her hand tightens. White heat slithers through my veins, and for the first time in at least ten years, I'm afraid I'm going to come in my pants.

And I'm not big on rules, but I've got at least one: ladies first.

I roll her nipples one last time, grab her hips, and pull her forward to the edge of the table. I unbutton her jeans. She bites my bottom lip between her teeth and I slide my hand beneath her knickers, over her mound, my fingers slipping between her folds.

Marisol's wet as hell, her knickers soaked through, and she leans her face against mine and moans softly as I draw my fingers back and forth, between her lips and up to the nub of her clit. She wriggles off the table, her legs unwrapping from me as I lean her back, over the table.

I stroke her again, and she gasps raggedly so I keep going, circling my fingers around her clit, rubbing her harder and faster, too far gone to tease.

We kiss again, her hand wrapped around the back of my head, pulling me down as she takes my cock in her other hand. She unzips my jeans and before I know it she's grasping my erection, fist around the base as she strokes me long and hard.

"Jesus," I whisper, and her other hand closes around my hair, her body tense and tight, a wire ready to snap, her fist stroking my cock.

"Don't stop," she whispers. Her hand tightens in my hair, loosens, slides down to my neck.

As if I'd *stop*.

"Oh," she says softly, and gasps, our foreheads together, eyes closed. Her nails dig into the back of my neck and she makes another noise, like she's trying to swallow a moan.

She comes. Her whole body tightens at once, her hand on my neck, her grip on my cock. She sighs and gasps for breath, moaning in a whisper, her face against mine. I keep circling her clit with my fingers as her chest rises and falls against me, until her mouth finds mine again and she kisses me deeply, her mouth opening under mine.

It's the sexiest thing I've ever seen. I want to make her come a hundred more times, but now she's stroking me harder, faster, her fist around my cock as needy and urgent as her mouth on mine.

Fuck, I can't take this.

"Marisol," I murmur, pulse racing, breath coming in hard gasps. "I'm gonna—"

She bites my lip and strokes me harder.

I explode.

I have hardly any warning, just barely covering my cock with my hand in time so I don't come all over this supply closet. Marisol's lips are on my neck. I have to force myself not to shout as I come so hard I feel like I've been hit by a train, my toes curling, every muscle in my body bunching and tensing again and again.

When it's over, Marisol takes her hand from my cock. She kisses me again, slow and long, until finally we separate.

We look at each other in the dark, and I realize that neither of us planned this far.

"So..." she whispers.

"You haven't got a tissue, have you?" I ask. "I could use one."

"Shit," she says, looking around.

Then she starts laughing.

"I didn't quite... hold on," she says, and slips away from me. I can hear her zip her pants and can just barely make out her outline in the dark.

I stand there, softening cock out, one hand full of jizz, hoping that she's got a plan. I certainly haven't. I haven't got much of anything besides a lazy, satiated feeling and the desire to do this again as soon as possible.

"Here," she says, her voice low. I reach out with my non-jizz hand and she presses a warm piece of fabric into it.

"It's a sock, isn't it?"

"It's all I've got," she says. She sounds apologetic, but I can tell she's trying not to laugh.

I wipe my other hand. The sock's not very absorbent, but it's better than nothing.

"I feel like I'm thirteen," I whisper.

"You did this when you were thirteen?"

I can hear the smile in her voice.

"I certainly thought about it," I say, turning the sock inside out. My hand's still sticky, but at least I'm no longer dripping. "The end result was the same."

I tuck my cock into my pants and zip up. Marisol puts her shoe back on. Electronics hum around us as she stands and I skim her back, pulling her in for one more kiss with my non-sticky hand.

"We should go," Marisol murmurs. "Now we're *really* late to the meeting."

The thought of going upstairs and talking to Nigel and Valerie, having them pick Marisol and I apart like we're characters in their story, *actually* makes my stomach turn.

"There is *nothing* I want to do less," I say. "Let's not."

"We said we'd be there."

"I don't think I can stand it," I say slowly. "I can't sit there while they discuss what angle we ought to be kissing at or whether we should hold hands or what physical affections markers will be most palatable and convincing to the American public."

She hesitates.

"Run away with me," I say.

170

"I can't just *leave*," she says. "I'm supposed to be—"

"We've just broken into a closet in an unknown building and rounded third base," I tease. "Don't start being the good girl *now*."

Marisol sighs.

"A proper date," I say. "No fucking cameras, no tabloids, no reporters, no trying to convince onlookers that this is real, no one watching or listening. Just us, together, on a date."

There's a short silence, filled with the hum of machinery.

"Okay," she finally says, and in the dark I can barely see her smile. "We'll go on a date."

CHAPTER TWENTY-FOUR
Marisol

Miraculously, the hallway is still empty. I can hear a door open and then shut behind us as we walk out, Gavin gingerly holding my sock in one hand, and my blood pressure spikes at the thought of being caught.

But nothing happens. We leave the building, cross the alley, throw away the sock, find an entrance to the parking garage, and get into Gavin's car.

I check my phone. There's a solid wall of texts, emails, missed calls, and voicemails, and my stomach plummets. I *hate* not following through on things I said I'd do, even for good reasons.

Good reasons like Gavin's mouth on mine, hot and hungry. Good reasons like hand jobs in a closet and coming so hard my face went numb.

I can't believe I did that, I think, staring blindly at my phone. *We could have gotten caught, we could have been arrested and then we'd both be felons as well as on the sex offender registry...*

"How bad is it?" Gavin asks, pulling out of the parking space.

I swallow, focusing on my phone.

"Bad," I say. "I've got sixteen missed calls from Valerie and ten from Nigel, plus a ton of text messages about how I need to come in for damage control, put out fires, reassure the American public, asking if I know where you are..."

I scroll.

"...asking if we're together, saying that we can't be seen together before we've got a strategy for re-gaining the media's trust and goodwill..."

Gavin just laughs.

"Is that irony? *Now* we're supposed to pretend to no longer be seeing each other?"

"It's sort of ironic," I say, distracted.

One minute ago, Valerie forwarded something that isn't in all caps, and that's weird for her. There's no panicked commentary on this email at all, which makes *me* nervous, so I click the link.

GAVIN'S LADY LOVE A LIE?

DRUMMER DISHES DIRT!

Shit.

I freeze. Gavin pulls out of the parking garage and then stops in the driveway, looking over at me.

Then he takes the phone from my hands.

"No, wait," I protest.

He pops it into the cupholder on his side of the car.

"I promise it'll all be there in the morning," he says.

"Eddie told someone we were faking," I blurt. "I think, I only read the headline that Valerie sent."

"That fucking *cock*," Gavin says, pulling his own phone out. I reach over him and grab mine, and for a few

173

moments, we're both just reading and scrolling.

After Gavin punched him, apparently Eddie got drunker, there were cameras, and long story short, he spilled the beans on us, trashing us to the paparazzi who were waiting outside the party.

I hold my breath. A car honks behind us and Gavin rolls down his window, waving them around.

"I don't know that they *believe* him," Gavin murmurs.

"I can't tell either," I say, scrolling back up. There's a blurry picture of Eddie above the headline, his eye dark, though it's hard to say whether it's a bruise or a shadow. "The article at least sounds... skeptical."

"He was quite drunk as well as angry with me," Gavin says. "I wouldn't believe what he said."

"Even if it was true?"

There's a quick pause as we look at each other, and then Gavin smiles slowly.

"Well, it's not true any longer," he says, and my heart does a little flip.

I take a deep breath, filling my lungs to bursting, then tilt my head against the headrest and exhale. The last twenty-four hours have been almost too much — the concert, the bad kiss, getting stoned, Gavin taking care of me, and now to have it suddenly become real, *very* real, *bodily fluid* real only for Eddie to tell everyone it's fake?

"Am I living in a telenovela?" I ask, eyes still closed. "This is absurd."

"Hard to say, given as how I'm also in it," Gavin says. "But you've not fainted dramatically nor met your long-lost twin who's turned out evil, so I don't *think* you are."

"I *did* think I was dissolving."

"That's less telenovela and more after school special about the dangers of drugs," he teases. "I should have filmed you, could have scared a whole generation off the devil's weed."

"They had those in England, too?"

"Of course," he says. "And they didn't work there either, *trust* me."

Another car honks and then goes around us, squealing its tires as it turns onto the main road. My phone buzzes, another regularly-capitalized email from Valerie, something more about Eddie and Gavin's supposed feud from the looks of it.

Gavin reaches over and takes my phone. This time, I don't argue.

"Fuck this," he says, dropping it into his cupholder and adding his. "We're going on a bloody date with no phones, no one else, and no bullshit."

He takes my hand and kisses it.

"And we're going to have a *delightful* goddamn time, though I do have a problem."

"Get in line," I tease. "Everyone's got a problem."

"I've got no idea where to take you that we'll not be recognized."

Now I laugh.

"It won't be hard," I say.

"I'm quite famous, you know."

"Turn left and trust me."

He grins, kisses my hand one more time, and then we drive off.

• • •

We slide into a half-circle vinyl booth, and a waitress hands us menus, then disappears. Gavin looks around curiously. No one looks back. He puts one arm around me.

"What's this place called again?" he asks.

"It's 'the Korean restaurant with the booths near 6th

and Vermont,'" I tell him. "If that needs clarifying, it's the one with the random portraits of European royalty everywhere and the lamps shaped like weird Cupids."

He's quiet for a moment, looking at a huge painting of a woman with a huge dress and a neck ruff on the wall opposite us, over another couple in another booth. I have no idea why this Korean restaurant has these huge paintings everywhere, but they do.

"Is that our Queen Bess?" he finally asks.

I tilt my head.

"Bess?"

"You know, Bessie Tudor, the virgin queen?" he says. "Do American schools teach you nothing of proper history?"

"I know all about how we dumped your tea into a harbor and then kicked your asses," I say.

Gavin grins at me, rubbing my shoulder with his thumb.

"You colonials have always had *quite* the attitude."

"We earned it via that ass-kicking," I say, laughing.

"Can't even spell correctly," he goes on. "Call it *soccer*, make abominable tea."

"Do you even drink tea?"

"Not here I don't," he says.

"At least we don't have a dish called *mushy peas*," I point out, laughing. "I still remember the day that I found out it really *was* just peas mushed together."

"And what's wrong with that?"

"Everything," I say.

"I bet you've not even *had* blood pudding or haggis," he says. "Then you'd know questionable food."

"Is haggis the sheep stomach?"

"It is. Technically it's Scottish, not that they're known for fine cuisine either, just bloody good alcohol."

"The drunker you are, the better haggis is?" I ask.

"Right," Gavin says.

The waitress comes back. I order the same thing I always get, spicy tofu soup, and Gavin says he'll have what I'm having. She looks skeptical of him but doesn't say anything.

"I told you my father was Scottish, right?" Gavin asks. "He made it a point of pride for us to have haggis at least once a year when I was growing up. It's actually not quite as bad as you'd imagine."

I settle back against his arm and lean into his shoulder. He's told me his father was Scottish at least twice already, but there's something oddly comforting about the re-telling. It feels *intimate* that I already know this about him, that we've talked so much he's forgotten what he's told me.

"I refuse to believe that," I say.

"Hand to God, I swear he's Scottish. Talks like the fat bloke from *Austin Powers*."

I roll my eyes, because we both know what I meant.

"And he plays the bagpipes while climbing mountains in a kilt?" I tease.

"Now you're just parroting stereotypes," Gavin says, taking a long drink of water. "Though I did used to own a kilt. Might still be somewhere in my mum's house."

I narrow my eyes, looking at Gavin and trying to imagine him in a kilt, because I can't quite.

"And now you're thinking exactly the same thing all American birds think about men in kilts," he says, leaning back and grinning.

No underwear?

"No pockets?" I ask, doing my best to sound innocent.

"That we've got naught on underneath," he says, laughing. "I swear it's the only thing women know about Scotland."

My face gets warm. I try to act nonchalant, but suddenly all I can think about is Gavin's dick, huge and hard as steel in my hand. How I want him somewhere *besides* my hand.

"Is that even true?" I ask.

"Depends on the Scotsman, doesn't it?" he says, leaning in closer. "Unless you're asking *me* what I wear underneath. In which case I could give you a definitive answer."

"And if I'm not asking?"

I'm trying not to smile.

"Then you'll never know, will you?"

"I think I've got a pretty good idea," I say. "Unless you were going to bring all that up to confirm that, yes, you've got your Kermit the Frog underpants on whenever you're wearing the kilt."

Gavin just laughs.

"Would that at least be a letdown?" he asks. "If you're going to talk me in circles, the least you can do is admit you were thinking about what I've got underneath."

And *now* my face is on fire, because yes, I was thinking about his junk, *of course* I was thinking about it.

You just gave him a hand job in a closet, I remind myself. *Shouldn't you be a bit beyond blushing at the thought of seeing Gavin's dick?*

"It's quite all right," he goes on. "Think about it all you like, you're very pretty when you blush."

"I don't know *why* I'm blushing," I say. "I've only got one sock on right now because..."

I trail off, fumbling for words.

"The other's spunk-crusted and in a dumpster?" Gavin says, though he at least keeps his voice low.

I cover my face with my hands, trying not to laugh and praying that no one can hear us. When I finally look up he's still grinning.

"Sorry about that," I say. "It was very spur of the moment and I didn't quite, uh, consider the consequences."

"Don't be," he says, pulling me in and kissing the top of my head. "It was perfect."

"*Was* it?"

"No, but I wouldn't trade it."

The waitress appears, two bowls of soup on a tray, and sets them in front of us. They're both in stone bowls, both still boiling rapidly. I thank her and grab my chopsticks, while Gavin does the same.

"Not quite what I was expecting," he says, poking the chopsticks at the bubbling red broth.

CHAPTER TWENTY-FIVE
Gavin

"You like Korean, right?" Marisol asks. "I didn't actually think to ask."

"And you don't think it's a bit late now I've got a bubbling cauldron in front of me?" I tease.

"I did think you'd speak up if you wanted something else."

"As far as I know I quite like it," I say. "We played in Seoul last year."

I swish the chopsticks through the broth and come up with a complete-but-small shrimp, head and all.

"Just eat it whole, it's so small the eyes aren't even squishy," Marisol says.

I shrug and pop it into my mouth. She's right. The eyes aren't squishy.

"What's Seoul like?" she asks.

I just stir my soup for a moment, trying to think of what to tell her because to be honest, I hardly recall Seoul. I hardly remember anywhere that we went on tour. I've been to incredible places around the world —

Tokyo, Melbourne, Moscow, Rio de Janeiro — and they're not much better than a hazy smudge in my memory.

Strangely, one of the worst parts of being clean has been realizing everything I missed.

"I don't really remember," I say, finally. "I just know that every time I showed up in a new city there was inevitably someone waiting for us with some high-grade junk. It was one of the benefits of being quite famously strung out."

"Oh," she says. "That... sucks."

"It was quite convenient at the time," I say. "It meant I didn't do a lot of sight-seeing, but I also didn't wander the alleyways of a foreign city at three in the morning looking for a fix."

"Would you have?"

I almost laugh, because of course I would have.

"Yes," I say simply. "And I've done far stupider."

"Do I want to know?"

My heart clenches in my chest, because I know she doesn't *really* understand. If she has to ask whether I'd have gone to the worst parts of dangerous cities alone, late at night, to get a fix, she doesn't understand.

Because books can't explain *that* part of it, only ugly experience. I can't help but want to hide that part of myself from Marisol. I want her to think of me as *this* Gavin, clean and sober and charming, not the track-marked junkie mess who couldn't finish a sentence. Not the guy who once traded his girlfriend's shoes for a dime bag.

Even if that bloke is right below the surface, waiting for me to slip up. Even if I think he'll probably *always* be there and I'll always have to live with knowing it.

"If you do, I'll tell you," I say.

She swallows. I steel myself, because the mood between us has suddenly gotten somber and serious. As it does when you discuss heroin problems.

"I'm sorry, this got dark all of a sudden," she says, stirring her soup and not looking at me. "I didn't mean to be such a downer."

"Right, *you're* the downer here," I say, half-laughing. "Not the years-long addiction to fucking *heroin*."

She smiles and makes a face, concentrating on grabbing a piece of slippery tofu with her chopsticks.

"You can ask me anything," I say. "I'll answer. Promise."

She grabs another shrimp out of her soup and holds it in her chopsticks, waiting for it to cool, looking at it like the question she wants to ask is written on its shell.

Finally, she looks at me.

"Do you still miss it?"

I'm tempted to say *no, of course not, it was terrible and I'll never go back,* but I tell her the truth.

"Every day," I say. "Shooting up feels like floating on a magical cloud and drinking good whiskey while getting a blowjob from an angel, not a single care in the world. Like nothing at all can touch you."

"That good?"

"I barely remember my first kiss or the first time I got laid," I tell her. "But the first time I got high is still seared perfectly into my memory, fucking clear as daylight."

"So it's better than sex?" she asks, looking me in the eye.

"It's better than *some* sex. My first experience in that department didn't exactly produce fireworks."

"Is it better than fireworks-producing sex?"

I swear she's faintly turning pink. I resist the temptation to ask if she'd like to help me find out and instead answer the question, like I said I would.

"Hard to say," I tell her. "Being on heroin does make one's sexual abilities a bit lackluster, so it's been quite a while since there were fireworks."

I *have* nodded out during the act before. More than once. I don't mention that part.

"Everything else was rubbish, though. When I wasn't high, I was waiting to get high, figuring out how to get high, or finding my next fix. I've blown out half my veins, so drawing blood or getting an IV into me is a complete fucking disaster. The strongest painkiller I can ever take is ibuprofen."

That's not to mention the nasty things I've done, the relationships I've destroyed, the people I've alienated. For fuck's sake, someone died, and even though it wasn't my fault, I'll always carry it with me.

But that's all deeper and darker than I want to go into right now.

"How did you start?" she asks.

I feel a bit like I'm on the witness stand and she's questioning me. But then again, that's what I get for going on a date with a lawyer. Future lawyer. Whichever.

"The first time I snorted heroin I was seventeen," I say. "A friend of a friend was playing a show over in Yorkshire and some bloke backstage offered."

Liam was there. He'd never done it before either, and I think the two of us together were braver and more foolish than one of us alone. I don't mention that to Marisol.

"I thought cocaine was what people snorted," she says, frowning.

Now I *have* to laugh.

"If you really put your mind to it and believe in yourself, you can snort near *anything*," I say, grinning at her.

She's got a huge chunk of tofu half in her mouth, and

she just rolls her eyes at me, the message *you know what I meant* perfectly clear.

"But snorting heroin is fairly common," I say. "Shooting it is a bit more advanced, but that's what will really fuck you up."

"Because snorting it doesn't?" she says, raising both eyebrows skeptically.

"Comparatively speaking," I say. "But as I got further in, snorting got me less and less high until I finally stuck a needle in my arm. And then I did that more and more frequently until someone died."

I'm making it sound both more and less complex than it was. The facts are easy, but they don't say anything about the terrible romanticism of addiction, the way it feels like a love that eats you whole from the inside out, how easy it is to think you're nothing without it.

How all your time is split into *when I'm high* and *when I'm not high and wishing I were*.

Musicians do love the *tortured artist* stereotype. Some do. I did. Or I thought I did.

"Why'd you do it?" she asks. "The first time, when someone said *hey, do you want to try heroin*, why'd you say yes?"

"Because I was seventeen and not about to back down from *anything*," I say. "Because I was curious, and I didn't really think I could get addicted, and because I didn't have a lot else going on at the time."

She's quiet for a moment, looking at her soup, thinking.

"You're not impressed with my reasons," I say.

"They're pretty bad," she agrees. "Though I'm not sure what a *good* reason to try heroin is."

"Perhaps if you've just had a leg amputated and the hospital's out of morphine, it could do in a pinch," I say. "But that's a bit extreme."

"Did you ever share needles?" she asks.

I very much want to lie to her, but instead I steel myself and take a deep breath.

"Yes," I say.

Dead silence.

"But I haven't in a few years, since the band took off. And I've been tested monthly since I went to rehab and it's all come back clean," I say quickly, desperate to erase the horrified look on her face.

Her eyes drop to my left wrist, the one with twenty-one thin leather bands on it.

"Four months ago?"

"Four and a half," I say.

Get it over with.

I take a deep breath.

"I've also slept with loads of women and had the clap twice, syphilis once, and wound up with crabs after a particularly ugly night," I say. "I've not always been terribly concerned with safety, which is probably not a surprise coming from someone who used heroin intravenously every day for several years."

She swallows.

"But I haven't got any kids," I say quickly. "And I've been thoroughly treated and didn't pick up anything permanent, thank Christ. And I haven't got anything now. I've been a monk ever since rehab."

"Define *monk*," she says.

"I've not so much as kissed anyone."

"Until this afternoon. Well, yesterday," she points out.

I smile.

"Right." I say.

She stirs the dregs of her soup for a moment. I wonder if I've given her too much heavy information too quickly, but then she pushes her bowl away and looks at me.

"Is there anything else?" she asks.

I frown.

"Anything else like what?"

"Like you've ever shot a man just to watch him die," she says. "Or you can't get off unless your sex partner starts barking or quacking or something."

"I'm afraid it's *just* the rampant drug abuse and general willingness to shag anyone who presented herself," I say, leaning forward on my elbows. I'm trying not to smile. "But if *you're* into barking or quacking I think I could manage."

Marisol leans back in the booth and puts one ankle on her opposite knee, her leg lightly touching mine.

"Well, if we're trading histories," she says, "I've had sex with two men total, performed reciprocal oral sex on another, have always used condoms, am on the pill, and haven't been tested for STDs in the past six months but everything was fine at my last checkup."

It's the first time I've found the phrase *reciprocal oral sex* enticing.

"And I got bitten by a dog when I was seven but I'm pretty sure I don't have rabies," she finishes.

There's a long pause, and I realize: I've not frightened her away.

"How sure is *pretty* sure?" I finally ask, and she laughs.

"Nearly positive," she says. "But you might want to be careful."

I reach over and take her hand, lacing our fingers together, and she looks down.

"You've got bruised knuckles," she says. "I'm surprised you didn't cut them on his teeth."

"I learned to fight properly well before I hit puberty," I say. "My village growing up wasn't a particularly kind place for sissy boys who enjoyed books."

She gives me a quick once-over.

"Sissy?" she asks.

"Defined as enjoying anything that wasn't football, punching, or committing misdemeanors," I say. "Including musical instruments and not wanting to harm cats."

"That does sound terrible," she says. "And not unlike my neighborhood."

"We've got loads in common after all," I say, grinning. "Virtually the very same upbringing."

Her fingertips find the valleys between my darkened knuckles, cool and gentle.

"I punched him because he said you were fake," I admit. "And also because he's a half-cocked idiot who got you miserably high. But I wasn't going to actually hit him until he said *that*."

"It was true," she points out.

"That made it worse."

"Sorry you had to take care of me," she says. "And thanks for not letting me dissolve."

"I didn't mind," I say. "And I wasn't lying when I told you that party wasn't terribly fun."

"I know it wasn't very rock and roll of me."

I just laugh.

"Marisol, I'm going to tell you something and it may quite upset you," I tease.

She raises one eyebrow.

"You're not very rock and roll either."

"You're kidding," she deadpans.

"Truth be told, you're a bit square."

"*Square?*"

"I began to suspect when you told me you didn't allow people to touch you sexually without rubber gloves," I say.

"—okay, you *know* that's not true—"

"And then you got *quite* tipsy off of one drink, passed up an invitation to an awards show to volunteer for people who needed your help—"

"—I had a prior commitment, also, that's not a bad thing—"

"—gave me the world's most awkward kiss and couldn't even identify the taste of pot—"

Marisol grabs the front of my t-shirt and pulls me in for a hard, long kiss. When she pulls back she bites my lip, and the sensation sizzles through my whole body.

"I'm not *that* square," she says.

"I didn't say it was a *bad* thing," I murmur. "I rather like you as you are."

"Which is square."

"Yes," I say, and kiss her again, because now that I've started it's difficult to stop even though we're in the middle of this restaurant.

Marisol's other hand finds my thigh as she turns toward me. I was already half-hard but I stiffen instantly despite my best efforts against it.

"Would a total square tell you her apartment is only two blocks away?" she murmurs, her eyes teasing as she looks up at me.

"It depends whether you're asking me over or not," I say. "Because doing such a thing after everything I've just told you is probably unwise and borderline reckless."

"I've got plenty of rubber gloves and a hazmat suit," she says, laughing.

"Alluring."

We kiss again, and then I pull her out of the booth, praying that the entire restaurant isn't staring at my erection.

CHAPTER TWENTY-SIX
Marisol

The moment my key's in the lock, Gavin's lips are on my neck, his hands on my hips pulling me against his massive erection, as if there were any doubt what we're here for.

I close my eyes and arch my back, pressing myself into him as his lips move slowly around from the back of my neck to my throat, then travel up toward my ear, his hands under my jacket and shirt.

"Marisol," he whispers, his voice low and rough.

His lips brush the shell of my ear. A tingle rushes through my entire body, and I squeeze my eyes shut, trying to fight it.

"You're absolutely terrible at opening your own door."

My eyes fly open, and now Gavin's laughing quietly, his forehead against my temple.

"Shut up," I murmur, snapping the deadbolt back.

"You were rubbish last night, too," he says, and even though he's teasing me it still sends shivers down my spine.

I open my door. We step through, and before I can think, it's closed and Gavin's pushed me up against it, his mouth hot and hungry on mine. My briefcase drops to the floor and he pulls my jacket off, then his.

He swipes my lower lip with his tongue and I open my mouth, his hand on my face, in my hair. His erection feels like an iron rod in his pants, massive and insistent against my belly, every movement of our hips together making me wetter.

My shirt flies off, the door cool against my bare skin as he looks at me for a long moment and I try to catch my breath, one hand on his chest, slowly tracing down over the hard muscles of his abs, all the way down until I hook one finger into the waistband of his pants.

We kiss, hard, tongues together. I think I moan and he digs his fingers into my back, tugging me further into him, and I slide both my hands under his shirt, letting my fingers explore every ripple of muscle before I finally pull it over his head.

Then I take a second to just *look* at him. He's got two full tattoo sleeves that extend to both pecs, some bright and colorful, some older and faded. I run one hand over his shoulder and onto his chest.

"You approve?" he says.

"I've never seen you shirtless in real life before," I say. "Only pictures."

Gavin grins and rests his hands on the door, one on either side of my head, then leans in.

"And how many of those did you look at?" he asks.

"Some," I tease, my hands still making their way downward.

"You should have told me," he says, and now his face is up against mine again. "I'd have been happy to pose for more if I knew you wanted them."

He's against me again, skin to skin, his tongue curling into my mouth as he feels behind me for the hook on my bra, then fumbles with it for a moment. I try not to laugh, and almost succeed, until he pulls away.

"Fucking hell," he mutters, so I reach back and undo it myself.

Gavin slides his palms over my nipples and I shiver, feeling them pucker under his hands while I bite my lip and try not to moan again.

"Oh, come on," he says, kissing the spot below my ear. "It's only fair that I get to hear the noises you make."

"I've got neighbors," I whisper.

Gavin chuckles, his mouth at the hollow of my throat.

"Then I see I've got a new objective," he says. "Make sure they know my name."

Suddenly he pulls me forward and before I know it he's sitting on my couch and I'm straddling him, topless but still wearing jeans, and he's got my hips in his hands, staring at me with a ferocious, almost feral look in his eyes I've never seen on *anyone* before.

For a moment, all I can hear is my heart beating while his eyes crawl over me, lust written on every inch of his face.

Then I lean in and kiss him as hard as I can, and I swear he *growls* again, rolling one nipple between his fingers. He kisses my jaw, my neck, pulling me in so I'm on my knees and our bodies are touching as his lips trail down my neck, past my collarbone until he closes his mouth around one nipple and runs his tongue across it.

I gasp. My hand tightens on the couch cushion behind his head and he grabs me harder, pulls me in, takes my nipple lightly between his teeth until I moan, then switches to the other one.

I'm aching like I've never ached before, my core filled with molten heat that doesn't let up, that demands *more*. My whole body tingles with every heartbeat, even as I push my fingers through Gavin's hair while he flicks his tongue over my nipple one last time and then lifts me even higher, his lips in the valley between my breasts, then the space above my bellybutton.

He pulls me back down to face him. I kiss him desperately, rolling my hips against his hardness, my body responding in a pure, animal way as he unbuttons and unzips my jeans, then slides one hand inside.

This time I moan, my mouth still on his, as he finds my clit and moves his hand past it, his long fingers dancing around my entrance, just barely teasing their way inside before circling my clit again, pleasure pulsing through my body as I writhe against him.

Then he pulls his hand away, and before I know what's happening, he's flipped me so we're reversed and I'm sitting on the couch, my legs still around him as he tugs my pants off and I lift my hips, finally wriggling out of them.

Gavin's on his knees on the floor and he kisses my belly again, presses his lips to my hips and then nips me softly and I gasp, making him chuckle against my skin.

He pulls me to the edge of the couch, pushing my thighs apart. My whole body is ramrod-tense with anticipation, and for a split second, he looks up at me, dark eyes filled with lust as he kisses the inside of one thigh, running his thumb along the very edges of my soaking-wet lips.

I gasp, hold my breath, and grab the cushions behind my head as his thumb is replaced by his tongue, just barely pushing between my lips, moving up, flattening as he flicks it across my clit.

I make a noise somewhere between a grunt and a moan, but his hands tighten around my thighs and he flicks his tongue across my clit rhythmically, circling it gently, lapping at me as I get closer and closer and then slowing.

I'm pretty sure he's torturing me, and by the second time I'm about to come, only for him to slow down and slide his tongue to my entrance, teasing me there, I think I might just explode from sheer frustration. My fingernails are probably about to tear holes in my ratty couch cushions, and as he circles me again with his tongue I whimper, already panting for breath.

His tongue moves faster. My toes curl and I moan again, turning my head to one side as Gavin takes one hand off my thigh, runs his fingers along my opening and then enters me, stroking my inner wall as he flicks his tongue across my clit furiously.

"Oh my *God*," I half-moan, half-whisper, and I come. Every muscle tenses at once and I arch my back, fists digging into my couch, toes curling behind Gavin's back, but he doesn't stop, even as wave after wave runs through my body.

His tongue slows and I put one hand on his head, trying to collect myself for a moment since I feel like I've just had an out-of-body experience. He stops licking me, pulls his fingers out and kisses the inside of my thigh again so I lean forward and kiss him on the mouth.

He tastes like me, but I couldn't care less, I let him pull me in until I'm also on the floor, my back against the couch, the flat of my hand pressing hard against his erection as he groans softly.

"That was fucking beautiful," he whispers. "You should have warned me."

I undo his jeans and pull at them until he's in my hand, long and thick and hard as a rock as he groans into my shoulder while I stroke him, his whole body wound like a spring. We're wrapped together on the floor, and it would be the easiest thing in the world to wrap a leg around him and let him enter me bare, feel him skin-to-skin.

Every single fiber of my being wants it, almost like some other force has completely taken control of me. Even though not an hour ago, he told me himself *exactly* how bad that idea is.

The head of his cock bumps against my thigh, slick with precum, and I stroke him one more time, nearly trembling as my self-control shreds.

Then he pushes himself away and kisses me.

"You've got condoms, yeah?" he murmurs.

I swallow and nod.

"Yeah," I whisper, and get off the floor, taking a deep breath.

I've had sex before, and I've been horny as hell before, but never like *this*. *This* feels like some other force has taken me over completely, so much that I'm nearly powerless against it.

I grab a condom out of my underwear drawer, glad that at least one of us can still think straight, and glad that I stay prepared.

When I turn, Gavin's sitting in my desk chair, cock sticking straight up, massive and proud, his fist closed around the base. It's sexy as hell, and for a moment I can't believe that this is real, that this incredibly hot man is in my apartment, with *that* body and *that* dick, hard like that for *me*.

Then he strokes himself and I walk over and straddle him, condom in my hand, his thick cock sticking up between our bellies as I wrap my fist around it. He kisses me yet again, hard and deep and I rock into him, tempted to put him inside me right this second, even though I'm actually holding the condom.

I don't. Gavin kisses my neck and takes the foil package from me, rips it open, and bites my collarbone a little too hard as he unrolls it onto his length, my fingernails digging into his shoulder.

He lifts me, my toes barely on the floor, my face against his as I guide him to my entrance, so wet I'm nearly dripping. I've got my forearms on his shoulders, holding myself up, my whole body coiled and tense with desire, with the promise of what's about to happen.

"Say yes again," he whispers.

"Yes," I breathe.

In that instant he lowers me and I let myself down, finally taking his length inside me in one slow, long stroke. We both groan as he hits every sensitive spot inside me and suddenly I'm sitting on him again, our hips together but now he's buried inside me and *Jesus Christ* it feels good.

"God, you feel fucking *perfect*," he growls, his face in my neck.

I'm panting, eyes closed, and I move my hips so that Gavin rocks inside me as he wraps one hand around my shoulder from the back, the other on my hip, shifting me back and forth.

We move together like that, harder and faster, and it feels so good I can't think. I can only hang on, holding Gavin to me as tight as I can, my lips against his ear as I moan louder and louder.

"Fuck, Marisol," he whispers, kissing my neck as he holds me, thrusting hard.

I swear he's found a deep, *primal* spot inside me that I didn't know was there. He's hitting it over and over and it feels so fucking good I think I might lose my mind, spiraling up and up, threatening to explode as our bodies move together in a furious, delirious rhythm.

Then suddenly I'm at the top and everything is pure white light for a single instant.

"Yes," I whisper into Gavin's ear, and I explode.

I feel like I'm on fire, bursting into a million pieces, and all I can do is hang on, still moving against Gavin as I moan uncontrollably and he holds me so tight I think I might burst. He groans again and pulls me down as hard as he can, his face in my neck, then against my ear and he growls something I can't even understand.

Gradually, it fades, and even though I'm still gasping for breath, my heart beating out of my chest, my hands nearly shaking, I kiss Gavin on the temple, hands in his hair. He turns, my face in his hands, and kisses me full on for a long, long time as we sit there, him still inside me.

After a long time I pull back, resting our foreheads together, and I touch his face, his chin, letting my fingers trail down his neck. I can feel his pulse, beating fast and hard, and I take a deep breath.

"Did you, uh..." I say, and let the sentence trail off, because suddenly I have no idea what to say. I'm not exactly a dirty talker.

He laughs softly, stroking my back.

"Achieve orgasm?" he teases. "I did."

"Me too," I say.

He kisses me.

"I was hoping that's what happened when you clawed the skin off my back and nearly screamed in my ear," he says. "Otherwise I'd be a bit afraid to see what it *actually* looks like."

"Shut up," I say.

We kiss again.

CHAPTER TWENTY-SEVEN
Gavin

We sit in Marisol's office chair for a good while. I'm a little afraid she'll cut off the circulation to my legs, but I like this so much, being inside her even soft, being this *close* to her that I don't say anything until she finally gets up.

I throw away the used condom in her bathroom, and when I come out into her still-dark apartment she's lying on her belly on her bed, sprawled like a starfish atop her covers, blinking at me sleepily. I crawl onto her bed as well, kiss her on the temple, and lay on my back.

Marisol scoots over. I put my arm around her and she rests her head in the hollow of my shoulder, one arm draping across me.

"This was more or less my plan to seduce you last night," she says.

I look down.

"You were going to flop on me naked?" I ask.

"Something like that," she says. "I think my plan was to get naked while you were turned around, and then

197

when you looked at me, say, 'This *is* my pajamas.' And then I didn't have a plan from there."

"You probably would have asked me to wrap you in a sheet so your body parts would all stay attached."

"Well, I couldn't remember my master plan long enough to make it happen," she says.

"I'm quite glad you didn't," I say, lightly stroking her back with my hand. "I nearly caved undoing your zipper."

"And that's bad?"

"You thought you were *dissolving*," I say. "I'd have been taking advantage."

She's quiet for a moment, and then she looks up at me, her dark eyes deep in the dim light of her flat.

"Was it hard?" she asks.

I grin.

"If you mean my cock, yes," I say.

Marisol scrunches her face up, and I laugh.

"Cock," I say, just to watch her squirm. "*Cooock.*"

"Okay, okay, I get it," she says. "I meant was it hard being sober while I was high? I know that's supposed to be a trigger."

I glance over at the books on her dresser about addiction, which are still there in the same order. Even though we've just been *quite* close, for some reason that's the thing that makes my insides turn to goo right now. Her *research.*

"Only a little, but due mainly to the particulars," I say carefully. My fingers trace a slow oval around a midsection of her back, her wild, curly hair tickling my face. "If you'd been having an excellent time I'd have been quite tempted, but given that you were miserable and didn't even have the pot *on* you any longer, the idea wasn't terribly alluring."

She sighs.

"I can't believe I just *ate* those gummi bears after

specifically noticing that they tasted weird," she admits. "I had common sense once, I think."

"It's been pushed out of your head by all that book learning," I say.

"I think I've just gotten soft in college and law school," she says. "I *used* to be a street-wise badass."

I just laugh.

"Okay, I used to be *more* street-wise," she says. "I did grow up in East L.A."

"I can't imagine you walking around with brass knuckles and punching the snot out of your rivals," I say.

"I *did* punch a punching bag with brass knuckles once," she says. "It didn't go that well, I wasn't holding them right and I managed to bruise my hand really bad. I was actually afraid I'd broken it."

"Such a badass," I murmur.

"I kicked a boy in the nuts for bothering Brianna," she goes on. "And the only reason his friends didn't come after me was because they thought it was hilarious that a *girl* had taken him down like that."

"Brianna," I say. I *know* I know that name, but I can't place it.

"Larry's wife," Marisol says. "The blond who invited me to your secret show."

"She's from your neighborhood?"

"She grew up down the block from me," she says. "We used to play Barbies together. Well, knockoff Barbies."

"And now she's married to *Larry*?"

Marisol just laughs and rolls over until her chin is propped up on my chest and she's looking at me.

"Her dad's... Salvadorean, I think," Marisol says. "She dyes her hair blond and wears blue contacts so she can pass for white."

"I really thought she was a spoiled rich girl from Beverly Hills or something," I go on. "Though it does explain why you're friends in the first place, I always found that a bit strange."

"When I went to college, she started getting low-level modeling jobs," she says. "She'd waitress at clubs, be that girl who walks around half-naked with a tray of shots, and eventually she started getting hired for private parties and... poof, now she's married to a rich lawyer with fancy celebrity friends."

"I think *clients* is the word you're looking for," I say. "Larry and I aren't exactly getting pints down at the local together."

"She would be *very* upset to hear you say that," Marisol murmurs, rolling her cheek down so now she's on my chest, looking at me sideways, the upper half of her body draped across me.

I've got one hand in the notch of her waist, though alluring as she is right now, it might take an act of God for me to get hard again.

"To hear Brianna tell it, you and Larry are close, *personal* friends, and you're over at their house for dinner practically every night."

"I've been to his house *once*."

"Then she talks about that one time a whole lot," Marisol says, her eyes dancing with amusement.

"This is the problem with being *incredibly* famous, wealthy, and good looking," I say.

"Please, tell me your problems," she teases.

"Everyone's only interested in you until your star dims," I say. "And then they're onto the next hot young thing."

"I've already got the phone number of the lead singer from... that band that wore the matching suits to the awards," she says. "Monkey Avenue Riot or something?"

"I can tell you're a huge fan."

"The second your next album doesn't go palladium, I'm calling him."

I just grin at her.

"What?"

"Then you'd better call right now, given it's *platinum*," I tell her.

She rolls off of me and lays on her back, her head still on my arm.

"I started the new album," I hear myself say.

Then I shut my mouth in surprise. I'd decided not to tell *anyone* I was writing songs again, not until I'd gotten a few done I was happy with. I still believe in jinxes, after all.

"When?" Marisol asks.

I roll over toward her, the bed frame creaking, and put one hand on her belly, stroking the soft skin there. She puts a hand on top of mine.

"A week or two ago," I say. "I found a few demo tapes from the tour I'd recorded that I thought I'd lost, and they're a bit rubbish, but they got me going again at least."

That's not precisely the truth. I did find the tapes, and I have been writing again, but I don't think the tapes were what did it. It's not the only thing that happened a few weeks ago.

"Did you tell Darcy and Trent?"

"Well, not exactly," I say. "They both think I've been hard at work on the album this whole time."

Marisol gives me a very skeptical look.

"Or, rather, I've been telling them that and what they believe is up to them," I correct myself. "But I can't exactly go back now and say, hey, guess what I've got three tracks done already, I know I said I had more last week, would you like to hear them?"

She goes quiet for a long moment, tracing the outline of my hand on her belly with one fingertip. It's hypnotic and soothing, and even though it's not yet ten at night, I catch myself starting to drift off.

"I know I'm a pretty recent addition," she says, suddenly. "But I think they're so angry with you because they love you. You guys are practically family."

Practically, I think. *Excepting Liam, the one who really is almost my brother. Him we just threw away like rubbish, and now he's living in my guest bedroom because he's got nowhere else.*

"I'll tell them," I say. "I just need a little while to work on the songs on my own."

I don't say anything to Liam about her. I've not even told her that he's living with me, and though I almost bring it up now, instead I go quiet and let her trace my fingers until I'm nearly asleep.

I've failed. I've failed Liam by letting him spiral down again, and I've failed my own recovery plan by letting an addict stay with me. I don't know that he's shooting up again, but I'm neither blind nor stupid, and I can see the path he's on.

But I like this, lying peacefully in Marisol's bed, in her tiny flat, her research books on addiction next to us. I need her to know that I'm trying, because I *am* trying, and admitting that Liam's in my house right now feels like letting her down.

I'll boot him. I'll figure out something to help him, send him back to rehab or something, and then I'll boot him before she ever even asks.

"You're staying, right?" she says softly, and her voice filters through my nearly-asleep brain until I wake up.

"If I'm allowed," I say, murmuring into her hair.

She doesn't say anything but she turns her back to me and snuggles into my arms. I fall asleep feeling her breathe.

CHAPTER TWENTY-EIGHT
Marisol

I'm awake at six, the sun just starting to nose through my curtains. Gavin's still in my bed, still sound asleep, face down on his pillow with one arm thrown over me.

I stretch. He rolls over in his sleep and pulls me toward him, one arm under my head and one across my torso until I'm half-wrapped in his hard, warm body. Carefully, I kiss him on his shoulder, a black-and-gray rose tattoo beneath my lips. He doesn't move.

We stay like that for a while, and even though I know I need to get up, make coffee, have breakfast, read over my notes one last time and then get on the bus for my 8 a.m. class, I let myself drift in and out of sleep for a while.

At last, he makes a deep grumbling noise and rolls over onto his back.

His morning wood looks like a circus tent, and I get out of bed blushing furiously. I pee and make coffee, but my eyes keep coming back to it, because this is the first time I've really *seen* it in all its...

...Well, *majesty*. Let's use the correct word here. Not that I'm all that experienced — two sex partners plus oral, remember? — but I'm fairly certain that Gavin's dick is *way* at the upper end of the bell curve.

And right now, standing in the designated kitchen area of my little apartment, I'm getting kind of wet looking at it. That and remembering last night and how ridiculously *good* that thing felt.

He grunts again and rolls over, his erection under him now. It's 6:45, and I need to leave by seven at the *latest*, so I turn back to making coffee, then drink it while flipping through my reading notes from yesterday.

Though it's pretty hard to concentrate with Gavin in my bed, even asleep. I'd *much* rather spend the day there, with him, than a seminar about tort law and then proofreading articles for the Los Angeles Law Review, where I'm the managing editor.

Or reading the ten *thousand* emails and texts I have from Valerie and Nigel. I slide my phone into my bag, because I can read those on the bus.

At seven, I'm packed up and ready to leave, so I sit next to him on the bed, lean over, and kiss him on the forehead. His eyes open slowly, and he just blinks at me for a few seconds before lifting his head off the pillow and looking around.

"Hey," he finally says.

"I've gotta go to class," I say. "Can you lock the knob when you leave?"

He pushes one hand through his hair, then rubs my back lightly, frowning a little.

"Yeah," he says. "Where are you going?"

"Class."

"Right."

He looks at the clock, then closes his eyes, opens them again like he's trying to read hieroglyphs, and his hand settles on my lower back.

"Have you got to leave *right* now?" he asks, his lips curving into a smile, his voice still rough and dusky with sleep. "I've got a legal briefing you could study."

I've never been more tempted by something, possibly ever, but I take a deep breath. I *cannot* start missing classes or showing up late just because of a guy, not even this guy, so close to finals and graduation.

"I'll study it later," I promise, grinning.

"Why not study now *and* later?" he asks, his accent thick and rough as he takes my hand and kisses the back of it.

There's the circus tent again, and my whole body pulses with desire this time even though I'm trying to ignore it. I can't *believe* I'm turning into goo at the mere silhouette of a penis.

Even though it's a hell of a silhouette.

"I'll text you later," I say, and kiss him on the lips.

He winds his fingers into my hair and holds me down, against him, lazily curling his tongue into my mouth. My body thrills all the way to my toes, and I'm a hair's breadth from tossing my bag to the floor and climbing on top of him, because I can be late *once* right?

But Gavin ends the kiss.

"Better get going," he says. "*I* don't want to be responsible for you failing out of law school."

He kisses my hand one more time, and then I leave. I hold my breath as I walk through the hall of my apartment building and down the stairs, trying to slow my heartbeat and calm my nerves, because I've got a whole day of *law stuff* before I can even think about seeing him again and finally—

I open the exit of the staircase and stop in my tracks.

My building has a glass front door, and outside on the steps, there's five men with cameras, standing around and shooting the shit.

No. Six. *Shit.*

I duck back into the stairwell.

Maybe it's a coincidence and they're here to photograph someone else, I think. *There's a ton of people living here, I can't be the only one...*

Yeah, right.

I shake my head, then peek around the door again to see what they're doing. Still just standing around, talking to each other, not paying a ton of attention, so I cross my fingers and say a quick prayer to whichever saint is in charge of not getting stalked by paparazzi.

Then I exit the staircase and turn left, away from the front door. I don't look back, and I just pray they're not interested or haven't figured out who I am as I head through the laundry room and leave my building through an alley door.

Thankfully, they're not out back, and they're not by the alley, so I walk a few extra blocks to a different bus stop, and I text Gavin on the way.

> Me: Photogs by the front door. If you head away from them you can leave through the laundry room out back.

> Gavin: Bugger.

> Gavin: Thanks.

> Gavin: I've an unpleasant sensation that we missed quite a lot of news yesterday.

Waiting for the bus, I start going through my emails and texts. The articles that Valerie sent us yesterday — **Drummer Dishes Dirt** — was just the beginning. *That* post didn't have the video.

There's a video now. My stomach curls around itself. I really, *really* don't want to watch, but I put in my headphones and make myself do it.

It's blurry. It's shaky. It's shot on the front driveway of the house where the party was on Saturday, and then it focuses in on Eddie, holding a can of beer up to one eye.

"Eddie! What happened?" a voice says.

"That goddamn asshole punched me," he says.

"Gavin?"

"Yeah."

"Why'd he punch you?"

"Because he's a fucking psychopath, man!"

"He just punched you out of nowhere?"

Eddie turns away from the camera and paces back toward the house, beer can still held to his face.

"Eddie, why'd he punch you?" the disembodied voice says again.

Eddie turns toward the camera.

"Because he's a fucking dick!" he shouts, waving one hand in the air. He's pretty obviously drunk, even on this blurry, shaky video.

"Is that all?"

"No, he's a fucking stuck up British *asshole* who thinks that just because he got clean he can just be a dick, like, to whoever he wants!" Eddie says, his voice rising. "Like, great fucking job, man, I've been off heroin for twenty-four years! I don't even have a pay a girl to hang around me! The fuck are you punching *me* for, man? He's the fucked up one."

I clench my jaw and take a deep breath, staring into the middle distance. He makes it sound like Gavin's hiring prostitutes or something.

Plus, he's obviously leaving out the part where he *left drugs disguised as candy* just sitting around. I'm slowly getting furious, watching him act like Gavin just punched him for no reason.

"What do you mean, he pays girls to hang around? Like prostitutes?"

Eddie waves the arm that's not holding the beer to his face again.

"No, man, not prostitutes, but that chick he's with?"

"Marisol?"

"Yeah, whatever her name is. He's fuckin' *paying* her so he looks like he's got a regular girlfriend, but she's just. Like. Getting *paid*. To be there."

"She's an escort?"

The voice behind the camera is clearly starting to get excited at this huge, juicy scoop.

"No, I think she's in law school, dude, but like. He paid her. To come tonight. They're totally faking it."

There's a commotion off the screen, and the camera turns, tracking a red blur marching toward Eddie. Darcy glares at the camera, holds one hand out toward the lens, and then pretty much drags him away.

That's the end.

Shit.

CHAPTER TWENTY-NINE
Gavin

Eddie's a *fucking* unbelievable prick.

I punched him because I'm the asshole? I finally got off heroin while he *drugged someone without her knowledge or permission* and I'm the psychopath?

If he thinks that's what I am he's not *seen* psychopath, though I'll show it to him happily. This first punch was a little girl's tea party argument compared to what I'll—

The phone rings. Darcy. I take a deep breath and answer, still lying naked in Marisol's bed.

"Glad you finally turned your phone on," she says.

I swing my legs over the edge and stand up.

"That cock-headed prick virtually fucking *poisoned*—"

"Yeah, I saw the video," she interrupts me. "Eddie's a dipshit who ran his mouth off without thinking. We're in agreement."

"Is the goddamn imbecile trying to ruin everything?" I ask. My voice is rising and I'm pacing back and forth in Marisol's apartment, in front of her tiny kitchen counter.

"The goddamn imbecile was drunk, angry, and had *just been punched*," Darcy says. Even though we're on the phone, I can picture her perfectly: standing still, one hand on her hip, staring stonily into space. Her *master of reconciliation* pose. "You can't tell me you would have reacted much better."

"But this is *his* fault to begin with," I say, gesturing with one hand. "He's the one—"

"I'm not siding with him!" Darcy says. "And I'm not siding with you! I'm trying to keep this *stupid* gossip tabloid fake girlfriend shitshow from being a total goddamn clusterfuck. Because we were a band again for a few weeks there and it was pretty fucking nice!"

She has a point and I know it, though I'm still mad. I don't say anything, just pace back and forth, stewing silently.

"Gavin," she says.

"He's an absolute wanker," I mutter.

"*Gav.*"

"And a *fucking*—"

She just clears her throat loudly.

"Fucking *Christ* woman, Jesus, I'm finished," I say, but there's no real force behind it. Talking to Darcy always makes me swear at least twice as much as I do normally.

"Thanks," Darcy says. "Have you or Marisol talked to *anyone* in the media?"

I walk to the window, part the curtains slightly, and peer down. There are still a few men with cameras standing around, looking at their phones.

"No," I say. "Though there's paparazzi outside her apartment, so getting out may be a bit exciting."

There's dead silence on the other end of the phone as I peer through Marisol's window, watching them below.

It takes me several seconds to realize what I've said.

"Are you *at* Marisol's right now?"

Fuck.

"No?" I say. "I'm in my own house, obviously, only she just texted me and let me know that there are—"

"You're at Marisol's at eight in the morning."

"I just *said* I'm not."

"Is she there?"

I give up.

"No, she left for class already."

Another long silence.

"I'm so fucking confused," Darcy admits.

"It's all a bit complicated," I agree.

She sighs.

"Look, can you come to my place for lunch?" she asks. "Nigel's developing two more ulcers and he's called a meeting for this afternoon, but you and Eddie need to fucking figure it out before that. And then you can explain to me how you're banging your fake girlfriend, and maybe also how I ended up living in an episode of *Days of Our Lives*."

I lean against Marisol's counter, still pissed at Eddie, but I know Darcy's got a point. She usually does, even if she expresses it like a particularly blunt and foul-mouthed sailor.

"I'll be there," I say.

. . .

Darcy lives in a top floor loft of an old building down in Hollywood, so it's got lots of features that I say are rubbish and she says add charm. Like the elevator with a wrought-iron cage that cranks shut, clicking and clacking all the way to the top.

Inside, her place is all flowing curtains, cushions, houseplants, and graffiti-style canvases on exposed brick walls. Trent is already there, sitting on a cushion in front of a low wooden table with a platter of tacos in the center, and Darcy comes out of the kitchen wearing torn jeans and a Joy Division shirt with two bottles of sparkling water.

"No Eddie yet?" I ask, sitting on a massive cushion at the table. It's a bit uncomfortable — not my preferred position at *all* — but I keep my mouth shut and don't say anything.

"He just texted that he's running ten minutes late," Trent says, his voice deep and stoic.

"So, fifteen minutes, minimum," Darcy says.

"At least he'll show up."

I don't say anything. Trent's making a point about Liam, and he's right, and I know it.

"We should just eat before the tacos get cold," Darcy says, and heaves a couple onto her plate. "Speaking of which, a photographer paid the taco delivery guy to let him bring the tacos to my door, so expect a picture of me flipping off a camera to surface in the next few days."

"I'll put it in my scrapbook next to all the others," Trent deadpans.

"You ought to change up your pose sometimes," I join in. "Try something else. Both hands maybe."

"Stick out your tongue," Trent suggests.

Darcy rolls her eyes.

"Okay, I get it," she says, and takes a huge bite of taco.

It takes Eddie twenty minutes to show up, and when he does, he's wearing shorts, thong sandals, and a t-shirt with a cartoon on it. His eye is splotchy purple, the edges of the bruise already turning that ugly yellow color. It wasn't my best punch, but right now I'm glad for that.

He looks around Darcy's apartment like he's already forgotten how he got there, and then finally kicks off his shoes and walks over to us.

"Sorry I'm late," he says, sitting on a cushion. "But it's kind of a madhouse downstairs, I had to run the gauntlet pretty much."

The three of us are quiet for a moment. I'm tempted to remind him that he had to run the gauntlet precisely because he managed to make the news yesterday with his video, but I think Darcy might stab me with a plastic knife if I say that.

Besides, I've spent the morning reading completely moronic internet speculation about the "feud" that's "heating up" between the two of us. According to the gossip mill, Darcy's on Eddie's side while Trent's on mine, Eddie's threatening to reveal lots of horrible secrets about the two of us, and Marisol is either a high-class hooker or an innocent victim in all this.

It's a fucking mess, and even though it's been a mere twenty-four hours, I'm tired of it.

"Next time go in through the car park," I say. "They weren't watching that entrance very well."

Eddie looks at me. He clears his throat. He looks at his plate, then back at me.

"Sorry, man," he says stiffly. "I shouldn't have left the pot candy around."

I know a canned, Darcy-coached response when I hear one. Eddie's not looking at me, he's looking at the table with a dark glare that says he's not really very sorry at all, that he still thinks what I did is worse than what he did.

Darcy and Trent both look at me.

It's up to you to not fuck this worse than it's already been fucked.

"I'm sorry as well," I say, my voice too formal. "I shouldn't have punched you."

There's another long, awkward silence. It's a shitty reconciliation, that's for sure, but it's better than nothing. It's a first step.

Eddie clears his throat.

"Is Marisol okay?" he asks around a bite of taco.

"She's fine. Slept it off."

"Tell her I'm sorry," he says. "She's nice. Probably too nice to be your fake girlfriend."

From the corner of my eye, I can see Darcy shoot Eddie a glare.

Rise above it, I tell myself. *Rise above it, rise above it*.

"I'll pass the message on," I say.

"I like her too," Darcy says. "And she's cute."

"Seems actually sane for once," Trent agrees.

"Probably a secret freak, though," says Darcy. "I bet she's into something weird, like being—"

"Could we not?" I ask.

Eddie frowns, confused. Darcy laughs. Trent rolls his eyes at her.

"I'm just saying," Darcy goes on. "She's in *law school*."

"Try calling her 'counsel' in bed," Trent suggests.

Darcy's told him already, of course. They tell each other everything, being best friends.

Eddie looks even more baffled. I stay perfectly and politely silent, because while I'll admit that Trent and Darcy may know more than they ought to about my sex life in the past, there's no reason that needs to continue.

"He's less fun sober," Darcy says. "We'll never hear about her weird tattoos."

"She hasn't got any," I say.

Then I sigh. Darcy grins.

"We'll get there," Trent says to Darcy.

Eddie seems to have given up entirely on the conversation, and for the rest of the meal, it's just the two of them versus me. In short: almost like it used to be.

CHAPTER THIRTY
Marisol

When I finally finish my hours at the Law Review, it's nearly six in the evening. The sun is lowering as I walk out of the law school building and onto the quad. Since the law school is on the same campus as the University of Los Angeles, and it's a gorgeous day, it's full of undergrads tossing frisbees back and forth, studying on blankets, and a few simply taking naps outside.

I lean against the brick building and stand there, watching. All day I've either been in class, trying to avoid my classmates' eyes, or dealing with the slew of texts, emails, and messages from Valerie, Nigel, and Gavin.

Gavin's texts I like getting, at least, and even though we've been texting for weeks now, my stomach still flutters a little when I see one from him. He's had lunch with the band, where he and Eddie apologized to each other. It sounds like it could have gone better, but at least it's no longer a total disaster.

He also texted me that the band knows we're actually dating and not fake-dating now. I've got no idea what this will affect, but I know I like it. Not that I've had time to really wonder *how much* I'm his girlfriend or *how real* this is or whether it was a secret.

At least, none of my classmates have said anything to me. Even though for the past few weeks it's felt like the entire *world* was watching my every move, it turns out not very many law students follow the gossip press religiously. Small mercies, though I've got a feeling that's going to change before too long.

But none of that's really where my mind is. Even my classes aren't where my mind is, because my mind is still stuck on last night and this morning, on Gavin in my bed with his arms around me. On getting to see him again tonight, which makes my toes curl in excitement like a teenager on her first date.

Even though we're going to be in a meeting with his manager, his publicist, and the rest of his band. Not really romance material, but I don't care.

I take a deep breath, my back against the warm brick, and exhale, trying to calm my nerves a little. I'm already late to the meeting in a hotel conference room near Valerie's office, and even though I *told* them I'd be late, I have a feeling that information might not have stuck.

My phone buzzes in my hand. I take another deep breath, then look at it.

The information didn't stick. Valerie's wondering, in all caps, WHERE I AM.

• • •

The emails all said "The Orange Grove conference room at the Varnish Hotel," but they didn't communicate that it's more like a bedroom-less suite than a conference room, complete with a kitchen, a lounge area, a huge TV, *and* a room with a giant wooden table.

The kitchen and lounge have snacks, so I grab a quick handful of cheese and crackers before I head in. I figure they're almost *definitely* not full of pot.

"You need to regain the trust of the American people," Valerie is saying.

I close the door behind me, trying to be quiet since the meeting's already started.

"Glad you could make it, Marisol," she says, picking up a folder. She holds it out toward me, magenta nails pointing like tiny arrows. I walk around the table and take it.

"She *told* you she got off work at six so she couldn't be here right then," Gavin points out.

Valerie doesn't respond. I don't get the sense that this meeting is going very smoothly, and I sit in an empty chair next to Gavin.

"You two are taking a break," Valerie says, directly to me.

Under the table, Gavin puts one hand on my knee and rubs my kneecap with his thumb. I swallow as warmth prickles down through my body.

"I still think that's a stupid mistake," Gavin says. "The rags have just accused me of paying her to go on dates with me, it'll just look as if we've been caught and we've given up the jig."

Valerie sighs. It's very dramatic.

"I understand why you think that," she says, lacing her fingers together in front of her, acting as though she's speaking to a child. "But the media these days is very, very savvy and they know when they're being bullshitted. Frankly, I'm amazed they didn't pick up on this before."

Everyone else at the table, excepting Nigel, looks down all at once, like they're trying not to smile. Poor

Nigel, his windbreaker over the back of his chair, looks skyward.

"But this is just *admitting* that they're right and it's fake," Gavin says.

"No, this is you *requesting privacy at this difficult time*," Valerie says. "Public relations is three-dimensional chess, Gavin. You've got to out-maneuver and *outfox* your opponent."

Somehow, I manage not to laugh.

"Can't we just go on acting like a regular couple until they give up and find someone else to bother with?" he says. "Sooner or later they're going to stop wanting to have all eyes on two adults enjoying one another's company."

He leans back in his chair, his hand leaving my knee, though the warm spot stays.

"Listen, Gavin, I *get* you," Nigel says.

He leans forward, elbows on the table, hands out as he looks through his gold-rimmed glasses.

Poor Nigel, I think reflexively. I think that every time I see him.

"You just want to carry on until this all blows over, and that totally makes sense," Nigel goes on. "But the thing is, with all these revelations, you'll be under loads more scrutiny than you were before. If you think that on-camera kiss was bad—"

"It was," Valerie interjects.

"—then just wait for the garden of hellish delights you two will be in for now. You're a musician, not an actor, mate."

I make a mental note to ask Gavin about the *garden of hellish delights* later, glancing sideways at him. I'm nearly positive he hasn't told Nigel and Valerie about *us* yet, though I have no idea what that would change.

I do know I'm not interested in *loads more scrutiny,* though.

He opens his mouth, but I nudge his foot under the table.

"I don't think it's a bad idea," I offer. "We won't be seen together for a while, and then we could quietly start showing up to out-of-the-way places and act like we're not *trying* to be seen."

"She gets it," Valerie says.

Gavin looks at me steadily. I nudge his foot with mine again, hoping that I can properly communicate *we don't have to really take a break, it's just pretend* with the motion.

After a moment, he turns to the table at large.

"Is everyone against me on this?" he asks.

"Yes," Darcy says, wiggling a pen between two fingers.

"I think Valerie and Nigel have a good point," Trent says.

Eddie's not paying any attention at all.

"Fucking hell," he says mildly, like he's more surprised than anything. "All right then, I'm outvoted."

I nudge his foot again, and he nudges me back with his knee.

"But no fucking around," Valerie says, pointing a magenta-tipped finger at us. "That goes for both of you. You're just staying out of the limelight for a little while, I don't want this to be a damn disaster when we re-introduce you."

Re-introduce. I think they do that with wildlife, when a species has gone extinct in a specific area.

"Got it," Gavin says. His face is dead serious but he's got the telltale crinkles around his eyes that mean he's trying not to smile, and he's still got his knee against mine.

"Sure," I agree, trying not to turn pink because Gavin's playing footsie with me.

"Good," Valerie says. "Okay. On to the next thing. Eddie, you've got a *shitload* of interviews to do in the next few days, and you'd better be stone cold sober and you'd better bring up your cute dog every other sentence..."

Now that someone else is on the hook, Gavin looks over at me and winks. I wink back.

CHAPTER THIRTY-ONE
Gavin

"All right," Valerie says, checking the time on her phone and lacing her fingers together. "I've got to go get dinner with a client at The Melrose, so unless anyone's got anything else to discuss, I think we're all done here."

I force myself not to roll my eyes at her ridiculous name-dropping, but I've been here almost an hour and a half and I'm quite finished with this meeting. Even Marisol, who's capable of focusing on something boring for an impressive amount of time, is doodling on her folder while playing footsie with me.

Valerie looks around. No one speaks up.

"Great!" she says, and rises from her chair. "Those champagne cocktails are *calling* my *name*."

She bustles out of the conference room, through the lounge, and out the door.

"Right," Nigel says, shrugging on his jacket. "We've all been given marching orders, yeah?"

Everyone who's left nods. We all rise and walk for the door, and Nigel sighs dramatically.

"...Could use a bleeding cocktail myself..." he mutters, leaving. Eddie's right behind him, and then the door shuts.

Trent and Darcy stop, then turn toward Marisol and me.

I put my arm around her, because even though they're my bandmates, they did hate my last girlfriend. Though she was also an unpleasant junkie slag.

"*So*," Darcy says. "Are you okay? You seem okay."

"I'm fine," Marisol says. "Is... Eddie okay?"

"I'm sure he'll be fine," Trent says calmly. Darcy glances at him, but says nothing.

"Okay, question," she says. "Are we not telling Valerie and Nigel that you two are..."

Don't say 'banging.'

"...banging?" she says.

Marisol pushes her hands into her pockets and looks up at me, mischief written on her face.

"*Are* we not telling Valerie and Nigel that we're banging?" she asks.

Darcy and Trent both look *much* too pleased at this.

"We can if you'd like a press release about it," I say.

"I think I'd like a press release about it," Trent offers. "'The members of Dirtshine are excited and honored to announce that frontman Gavin Lockwood has recently begun boning a law student...'"

"'...who is thrilled and honored to be hopping on the D...'" Darcy adds.

"'...and will be staying on through repeated upcoming *releases*.'"

"Okay," I say, but both of them are already laughing at their own dumb joke.

Marisol's pink, but she's *also* laughing. I give in.

"You know how those two are," I say. "Her first question would be whether we'd be willing to release a sex tape."

"Are you?" Trent asks.

"The fuck do you think, mate?"

He just shrugs, still grinning.

"You should see the emails she's sent us," Marisol chimes in. "There were bullet-pointed 'physical affection benchmarks.'"

"Holy shit," Darcy breathes.

"Hand-holding was date one, but hand-holding *on the table during dinner* was date three," Marisol goes on. "And she repeatedly demanded that we achieve 'lip-on-lip.'"

"Tell me that's not a kiss," Darcy says.

"It is," I confirm.

There's a moment of silent horror.

"That's how an alien would describe kissing," Trent says.

Marisol laughs.

"That would explain a lot about Valerie," she says.

The two of them stick around for a few more minutes, and then finally, Trent pulls out his phone and checks the time.

"I've got to meet a very famous, important person for champagne cocktails soon, so I should get going," he says.

Darcy snorts.

"Go ahead," I say, rising from the couch. "I'm going to use the restroom and I said I'd give Marisol a ride home."

"Cool," Darcy says. "We should figure out rehearsal soon. And if we had new material..."

She raises both eyebrows.

"We will," I say.

"Be safe, kids," Trent says opening the door.

"Use protection!" Darcy shouts, and then the door shuts.

Still pink, Marisol turns toward me.

223

"They're—"

I kiss her before she can finish the sentence, and she says *mmmph* into my mouth but wraps her arms around me instantly, so I grab her ass and lift her until her legs are wrapped around me, squeezing my rock-hard cock, her face just above mine.

She pulls back slightly, laughing.

"Whatever you're laughing at it's quite serious and not at all funny," I say.

Marisol grins, her nose to mine.

"You got *busted*," she laughs. "They knew exactly what you were doing."

"*We* got busted."

"But mostly you."

She kisses me again, tightening her legs, and opens her mouth against mine, her hand on the back of my neck. I slide my hand onto her back, underneath her shirt, my cock throbbing so hard I can barely think straight.

I swear she does things to me I don't even understand.

"When you spend months in a van with someone on tour, they get to know you," I murmur. "And I don't give a fuck that they know what we're doing right now."

Marisol bites my lower lip *just* hard enough to send a surge of desire through my veins, sizzling over my nerve endings, and I *growl* at her in response.

I pull her shirt over her head. Before it lands I'm already on her neck, kissing and sucking the soft, delicate skin there, forcing myself not to leave a mark, no matter how badly I want to be just a little rough and reckless.

She moans. I press my fingers into her back as hard as I can, and she rocks her hips against me, one hand pressing my head to her neck as I move my mouth down. My teeth find her skin, and she gasps, but I keep going. I get her bra off one-handed — a skill I did practice, thanks — and before she can say anything, I toss her onto the couch and follow, her thighs still around me, her breasts still bouncing from the impact.

I take one perfect, dark nipple in my mouth and swirl the tip of my tongue around it, listening to Marisol's gasp as it puckers for me and I harden in response, so hard it's nearly painful. Her hand is on my head, gripping my hair, her hips moving under me.

My other hand finds her other nipple and that one stiffens too as a strangled moan escapes Marisol's lips. I bite down, gently at first, and then harder little by little until her back arches and her hand tightens in my hair, and then I flick my tongue over it until her breathing gets ragged, pinching and rolling the other at the same time.

I open my eyes, her nipple still in my teeth. She's got her head thrown back, and I can barely see her, but her eyes are closed, her lips parted and it's the most beautiful thing I've ever seen. I think I could stay here forever and just *watch* her, and I'm tempted, but instead I flatten my tongue and slide the length of it over her nipple.

Marisol grabs the back of my shirt and *pulls*, and then I'm taking it off and throwing it somewhere and she's biting her lip and running her hands down the tattoos on my torso. The look in her eyes is pure, deep *hunger*, and it darkens when her hands reach my pants and she slides one palm over my achingly hard cock.

I groan and press myself against her hand, my own body no longer under my control, and Marisol lifts herself on one elbow, her mouth seeking mine, her body pressing insistently against me. I can feel every breath she takes, her lungs expanding and contracting, every movement of her skin on mine stoking an unquenchable fire.

She lies back, looking at me, her eyes pools of lust as she unbuttons my pants. Before I kick them off I take the condom I brought out of my pocket and toss it onto the coffee table.

Marisol laughs, and I grin at her, grab her by the belt of her jeans and unbutton them, planting a kiss on her chest, in the valley of her heartbeat.

"I've had time to plan this ever since you left this morning," I say, my lips brushing against her skin as I pull down her zipper and she lifts her hips off the couch, helping me get her pants off.

My cock twitches and throbs. I throw her pants into a ball on the floor and she sits up, takes my cock in her fist, and kisses me deep.

I *groan* into her mouth as she strokes me, long and hard. My vision goes white for a second with the perfect, pure pleasure of Marisol naked in front of me, her legs around me again, my cock in her hand, and it's all I can do to keep myself from pulling her onto me and pushing myself inside her right there and then.

I don't. I run my fingers up her wet slit, circle her clit once and then slide three inside. Her hand closes around the back of my neck and she moans, her grip tightening on my cock as her hips move, her tight channel pulsing around me like she's trying to take me even deeper.

My fingers push deeper, stroking her inner wall. She moans softly, like she can't stop herself, her hips bucking and writhing, and I know I can't control myself much longer so I grab the condom, unwrap it, unroll it onto the tip and Marisol pushes it the rest of the way down as I take my fingers out of her.

We tumble together, a scramble of limbs, but then I'm on top of her and her hand's on my cock again, guiding me in, and as I sink myself inside her with a perfect, delicious thrust. She moans, the noise coming from somewhere low in her chest, her eyes fluttering closed.

Everything is white hot. I'm buried in her, tight and hot and completely perfect, and I bite her shoulder until she gasps, her fingernails on my back. I pull her knees against my body and thrust again, hard and *deep* and she cries out so I do it again, the same way, again and again until the noise is one continuous moan.

Marisol's got one knee over my shoulder. I don't know how it got there but it feels fucking *good*, feels like I'm deeper inside her than I've ever been in anyone, and all I want is more, for this to go forever and never end. We keep going, hard and deep, and I'm pretty sure we're both being loud as *fuck* and we might break this couch but I couldn't care less because with every thrust, her muscles grab me like she's pulling me in, more insistent with every stroke as they flutter around my cock.

She gasps, even louder. I drive myself deep, as hard as I can, and her nails rake down my back, her muscles fluttering and clenching around me. I keep going, not that I could stop if I wanted to.

This time she throws her head back and moans so loud it's a shout. Her muscles clamp down on my cock like a fist, and I thrust one more time and then I can't control myself any longer. I just fuck her as hard as I can while she shudders and moans, her whole body writhing, and I come into her again and again, as hard as I've ever come.

At last, I'm spent. Still inside her, I can feel the aftershocks running through Marisol's body, her leg still over my shoulder. I stroke her thigh gently, kiss the inside of her knee. She opens her eyes and looks at me, removes her knee from my shoulder.

We kiss. I don't move, still inside her and on top of her, because I like being close to her, my bare skin on hers. I like her arms around my back, her fingers tracing slow patterns.

I like the way she smiles when I put my forehead to hers, as if the only world that exists is the two of us, right here on this couch in this hotel.

I like *her*.

CHAPTER THIRTY-TWO
Marisol

Gavin sits up after a moment, and I untangle myself from him, swinging my knee off his shoulder and wiggling my toes since my foot started to go to sleep. Not that I particularly care.

I sit up too and lean against his arm as he takes the condom off, ties a knot, and then tosses onto the coffee table.

"Oh, ew," I say.

He laughs and puts his arm around me.

"Sex is perfectly natural," he teases.

"But people *eat* off that," I point out. "You're getting ...fluids... on it."

"Someone will clean it," he says. "That's their job."

Right. *Someone.* For a split-second I picture the *someone* who'll be coming in here to wipe my vaginal secretions off this table. Since we're in Los Angeles, there's a good chance that *someone* is going to look a lot like me.

I stand, grab the condom by the very end, and head for the bathroom.

"Marisol, I'll get it," Gavin says, the couch creaking as he gets up.

I wrap it in toilet paper and then throw it in the trash, wash my hands, and come back.

"I wasn't going to *leave* it there," he says.

I wrinkle my nose.

"I know," I say. "I'm just weird about stuff like that."

He sits on the couch again, putting his feet on the coffee table, and I sit in the crook of his arm.

"Okay," he says. "No used condoms on the furniture. Got it."

I'm silent for a moment, trying to put my sudden squeamishness into the right words.

"My mom cleaned hotel rooms when she first got to the U.S.," I say. "Or, when she and my dad first became residents, I should say. She picked strawberries outside Oxnard on a migrant worker visa before that."

I swallow, still staring at the tiny wet spot on the coffee table, because I don't share my parents' story a lot. People love to praise diversity, and God knows that in law school I've met tons of people who think it's *so great* that I'm a first-generation American, but no one wants to think about who cleans their hotel rooms or how they get strawberries.

My parents still can't eat them, by the way. The smell reminds them too much of days spent bent over in the sun.

"I wasn't thinking," Gavin said, and I shake my head.

"It's fine," I say. "I just... have a thing about leaving places clean. She's told me some gross stories and I'm sure I haven't even heard the worst."

Gavin's quiet for a long moment.

"I've trashed a few hotel rooms," he finally admits. "Not *trashed*. I've never thrown the telly out the window

230

or a chair into a pool, but I've certainly left some bad messes behind."

"How rock and roll."

"Liam's the one who would just fucking wreck a place, though," Gavin admits. "And it's not as if I ever stopped him. Though he only threw the TV into the pool once and he did wind up paying quite a hefty fee for it."

"It probably became the pool boy's problem at that point," I say.

"I've no idea who had to fish it out," Gavin says. "As well as a chair and, I think, a suitcase full of clothing, though that last point is hazy."

"Why'd he throw it into the pool?" I ask.

"Because cocaine is quite a drug," he says. "And there was someone on TV he didn't like, so he solved that problem by throwing it off the balcony and into the pool, and then *that* made a lovely splash so he followed it with a few more things until hotel security came barreling in."

"And you were helping?"

"I was sitting on the bed laughing hysterically, also high as a fucking kite," he says. "Though I think Liam started drinking a few hours before I joined his party and he can be an unpleasant drunk."

I wiggle my toes, feet resting on the coffee table, and hesitate for a moment. I've only met Liam once, the time he set my book on fire, and he didn't make a very good impression. Gavin only talks about him obliquely, when he's telling me a story about something else, and I don't know what to make of it.

They *were* friends. It sounds like they were best friends, practically brothers, judging by Liam's presence at every stage of Gavin's life, but Gavin never brings Liam up directly. It's like he's trying to avoid thinking about the other man.

I'm not sure I blame him. I haven't asked yet about the details of Liam's downfall, how he almost died and then got kicked out of Dirtshine, but I know Gavin's still hurt about it. I think he's avoiding the topic of Liam because they were *so* intertwined, and because Liam was so present for... well, everything, but especially the years Gavin spent as an addict.

"Did your parents meet in the states or in Guatemala?" he asks.

"They met on the truck from the worker quarters to the strawberry fields," I say. "My mom was nineteen, my dad was twenty, and he was aghast that her family had let her come to the United States alone to earn money for them with no one to protect her."

"If your mother's anything like you, I don't imagine that went over too well," Gavin muses.

"That depends on which of them you ask," I say, grinning. "My mom says that she politely informed him that she was the oldest of four children, her father was too crippled to work, and the family needed money so off she went."

"And your dad says?"

"My dad says she gave him a piece of her mind about a woman's place in the *modern* world, the whole truck went silent and simply stared at her, and that's when he fell in love."

"Who do you believe?"

"Him, of course," I laugh.

"Have you found them a house yet?" he asks.

I close my eyes and lean back against his arm, because I still haven't quite told Gavin the whole truth. He knows I agreed at the beginning of this so I could buy them a house. He *doesn't* know that they're being evicted in two more weeks — before I even *get* the million dollars — and despite our best efforts, my sister and I still haven't found them another place to live.

I've almost told him a dozen times, but he's already giving me a million dollars, and if I tell him I'll feel like I'm asking for charity from him and that's the last thing I want. Especially *now*, naked on a hotel room couch together.

"Not yet," I say. "I'm still doing the research part."

"It *is* your favorite."

"I find information very soothing," I say.

We're quiet for a moment. I'm leaning into him, my right side against his left, and even though I've got homework and studying tonight, a full day tomorrow, and a test on Friday that I'm only half prepared for not to *mention* my parental apartment problems, I don't want to move. I just want to stay there, warm and safe and tucked against him until everything I don't like disappears.

Somewhere, a phone buzzes. Gavin sighs.

"You or me?" I ask.

"I don't know," he says, so we both sit up and reach for our pants.

It wasn't my phone that buzzed just now, but I've got a series of texts from my sister Sandra, all apartment listings. Then, at the top, I've got three missed calls from her.

I frown. *That's* weird. Sandra hates the phone.

"Bugger me with a dirty spoon," Gavin mutters, and I look over at him as he holds his phone up to his ear and stands.

"Eleven missed calls and four voicemails from a number I don't—"

He goes quiet, listening as the voicemail starts, and as he listens his jaw tightens and something in his face hardens. He listens to another voicemail, then another, and pulls the phone away from his face and takes a deep breath.

"That was the security company," he says, his voice flatter and harder than usual. "Seems someone's broken a window into my house."

My mouth drops open, chest squeezing.

"Did they take anything?" I ask, standing as well.

Gavin swallows, not quite looking at me as he pulls his boxers and jeans on.

"Not that they can tell but I don't know yet," he says. "Whoever the wanker was that broke in has left a good amount of blood on the floor and the sofa, though."

"Did they cut themselves on the window?" I ask. "Did they know it was your house? Was it just a burglary gone wrong, or a crazed fan, or...."

"I really don't know yet," he says, pulling on his shirt. "It sounds as though the police are there now, but I've got to call them on the way back."

I nod, still naked but dumbstruck. Gavin walks over, finally looking me in the face as he pulls me to him.

"Sorry," he says.

"Gavin, your house got broken into," I say. "*Go.*"

He gives me a long, lingering kiss on the lips, then strokes his thumb over my cheek.

"I'll call you," he says.

"Good," I say. "Now go talk to the police."

I get one more peck on the lips, and then he's out the door. I shake my head, trying to clear the fuzz out of it, and search for my underwear.

CHAPTER THIRTY-THREE
Gavin

I shouldn't have lied to her, I think as I walk down the hall. *I should have just told her the truth.*

There's time. Go back and confess. She'll be disappointed but that's not so bad, right?

I keep walking, hit the button for the elevator, and wait. It comes. I get on and head down to the parking garage, guilt gnawing away at me.

I can handle this, I tell myself. *After this, I'll boot him, it'll be like this never happened, and I'll never have to tell her anything because it'll be over.*

You didn't even lie.

You just didn't tell Marisol the entire truth. That's different, isn't it?

The heavy, prickling sensation in my gut right now says *no, not really.*

• • •

"Thanks," I say aloud in my car, my phone on the passenger seat, connected somehow to the speakers. Wizardry, I think.

"Not a problem," says the professional-sounding man on the other end. "Glad we could get a hold of you, Mr. Lockwood. Have a nice day."

We both click off the line, and I expel all the air from my lungs, gripping the wheel as hard as I can.

Fucking Liam.

Of course it wasn't a random burglar or a crazed fan who broke the window. Apparently, the police found a "very inebriated man with a strong British accent" bleeding all over the sofa, and he's being attended to by paramedics.

After which he'll likely be hauled off in handcuffs, though it sounds as if that depends somewhat on what I say.

I half hope it happens. If Liam's in jail at least I won't have to deal with him for a day or two, and he's been getting worse lately. Despite my *no alcohol in the house* rule I did find a plastic jug of cheap vodka far in the back of the pantry the other day. I poured it out, but God only knows what he's hidden in the guest room where he's staying.

I don't go in there. I don't want to find it.

I spend the rest of my drive seething and coming up with what I'm going to say to him.

There's an ambulance parked in my driveway, so I pull up on the side of the road next to my tall wooden fence and walk in. It's nearly ten o'clock, so the rotating red lights are bright against the dark houses and trees, and I'm *quite* sure all my neighbors are perfectly aware that there's a spectacle in progress.

Liam's sitting up on a stretcher, white bandages encasing his arm from bicep to wrist. He's pale and nearly gray, the color of concrete or something, and his clothes are covered in huge splotches of blood. There's two policemen standing to one side, a paramedic on the other.

He looks up at me as I walk over, lifting his bandaged arm.

"Lookit," he says. "Now I've not got to worry about running out of toilet paper while I take a shit."

And he's *trashed*, his northern accent thick as mud, his words slurred together. The police both turn in my direction as I close the distance, but I don't pay them any mind.

"Are you fucking joking right now?" I ask, my voice rising.

"You do look like you could use a laugh—"

I grab him by the front of the shirt, sticky with his blood.

"You fucking *dickhead*," I say, my voice rising.

"Whoa!" says one of the cops.

"You move into *my* house, then you trash the place and *fucking* bleed all over half my *fucking* furniture and now you're here telling me jokes about taking a shit?"

"Calm down," says a cop. I ignore him.

"Who's gone and rammed a stick up your arse?"

"This is why you've got no one left, you stupid twat, because you don't give a shit about—"

"—Did you let your fake girlfriend stick it up there? Heard a rumor you liked that—"

"—Anyone else, so you've got no choice but to crawl back to me but I've *fucking* had it, Liam—"

"Hey now," says a cop.

"—Forgot I was talking to fucking King of Everything Gavin, maybe you could punch me now and I'd be famous again for ten minutes—"

A siren sounds for a split second, and we both jump. One of the cops is standing next to the car, his finger on a button.

"You need to unhand the suspect," he says.

I do it and step back, not looking at Liam. I'm afraid I'll punch him in his idiot face, and I don't need to do that in front of the police.

"Now," the other cop says. "If you could please come with me I'll show you the scene and then I've got a few questions."

. . .

It takes ages. I knew it would, but three hours later I'm still there, still describing my relationship with Liam to the police, confirming for the millionth time that yes, he is currently residing on the property. For his part, Liam passes out on the stretcher, and though the paramedic occasionally looks over at him with some concern, the rest of us leave him alone.

He's clearly not an escape threat.

When they're finished asking questions, the cops get in their car and then sit there, filling out a report. The paramedics wake Liam, push him off the stretcher, get into the ambulance, and leave. I sit on the front steps of the house — which is a rental, so now I've got to call the company I'm renting from and explain *this* fucking mess — and just *wait*.

Liam totters over, still drunk, barely awake, and certainly worse for the wear.

"I've got nothing to say to you," I tell him.

He sits next to me anyway.

"I'm sorry, mate," he says.

There's a raw note in his voice. I flex one hand into a fist, as if I can fight it off.

"I've fucked up again," he goes on. "Things here were going so well and I went off and ruined everything."

I don't respond.

"I fuck up everything I touch," he says, his voice barely a whisper. "It's like I want to be better but I don't want to be better at the same time. I'm dragging myself down and I can't stop."

He takes a deep, shaky breath.

"I'm so fucking sorry, Gavvy," he says. "You're right. You're right about everything, I've got no other friends because I've fucked them all over sooner or later, I haven't got any work, the band hates me and they're bloody right to hate me—"

"We don't hate you," I mutter.

"— it was the best thing that's ever happened to me and I threw it away and now I've got *nothing*."

I look over at him from the corner of my eye. His bandaged arm is hanging at his side, he's got his face in his other hand, his elbow propped on his knee, and he's crying.

"I can't stop myself," he mutters. "I fucking *killed* someone and I still can't stop myself."

I swallow hard. It's tempting to think that Liam's just faking to manipulate me into feeling sorry for him, but I've known him for more than half my life and Liam's not got a manipulative bone in his body. Everything he does is pure id, driven by whatever he's thinking or feeling at the moment.

And right now, he's drunk, probably high, his arm probably fucking hurts, and he knows he's a goddamn train wreck.

"You didn't kill Allen," I tell him.

I've told him that over and over again. Sometimes he seems like he believes me and sometimes he doesn't.

"I gave it to him," he says miserably. "I fucking handed him the needle. I told him it wasn't as much as it looked."

239

I look over at the cop car so I don't have to think about that night. One cop's got a laptop out, determinedly pecking away with two fingers.

"He'd never so much as snorted coke before I met him," Liam says, sniffing hard. "He—"

Liam grabs the bottom of his blood-covered shirt, puts it to his nose, and blows.

"Jesus *Christ*," I say, and jump up, heading through the door. I don't think I've got tissues anywhere, but there's a roll of paper towels on the counter and I grab those.

Out on the counter is a bottle of whiskey, a brand I've never heard of.

All the same it fucking *calls* to me. Just one shot, quick, no one would ever know but it would make Liam so much easier to deal with, the cops easier to take, muffle all the bullshit of this stupid night.

I pick it up. It's half-empty, the glass cool and heavy in my hand, the liquid inside sloshing slightly. Just *one* drink.

But then I think of the books on Marisol's nightstand. Of being in her bed, her head on my chest, her hair tickling my nose.

I put the whiskey down and walk back to the door.

Liam blows his nose into a towel, then stares into it like he can read the future in his snot, and he's quiet for a long time.

"I've still not worked out why you could do it and I couldn't," he finally says, his voice low and raw with misery. "I thought we were the same, we'd come up together and had our problems together and you were just a much of a wreck as me but then..."

He waves the snotty towel at his bandaged arm.

"Fucking look at this," he says.

240

I take a deep breath. I don't feel like a success, not yet, not when thirty seconds ago I looked at a bottle of cheap whiskey and had to practically drag myself away.

"Let me send you to rehab again," I say.

"It didn't fucking work."

I rub my hands together, staring down at the ground.

"Research shows that people often have to go more than once, and it rarely sticks on the first try, but it *does* often stick," I say.

Liam looks at me, eyes watery and bloodshot.

"Research shows?" he says incredulously. "Who the tits are you, some pompous university wanker?"

"No, I'm fucking sober while you're snot-crying on my front steps," I snap.

He swallows.

"Sorry."

"Marisol's been doing a lot of reading on addiction and heroin and all that," I say. "And rehab is one thing that's really excellent at breaking the cycle."

"Is that the false girlfriend?"

I sigh, because I've got the feeling that the truth is too intricate for Liam right now, but I may as well give it a go.

"We really are dating," I say.

"It's *me*, mate," he says. "Fucking lie to someone else."

"It did start out that way," I say. "But it turned out we quite liked each other, and... are now *actually* dating."

He just rolls his eyes.

"You honestly think anyone's going to believe that story?" he asks, and then pitches his voice higher. "'Oh, right, we weren't dating until we were caught in a sham but *now* it's real.'"

"That's not what I sound like," I say, because it's clear that I'm not going to convince Liam of anything right now, and besides, I don't really give a flying fuck *what* he believes.

"It is when you're trying to get one over on me."

"I'm not."

A car door slams, and we both look over. The cops are walking toward us, so we stand. They look from me to Liam and back again.

"I'm guessing you're not interested in pressing charges," the taller one says.

I glance over at Liam. For a split-second I wonder if I ought to, teach him some sort of lesson or something, but I haven't got the stones for it. I'm a fucking soft-hearted kitten.

"No," I say.

Both cops nod, officially.

"All right then," the one on the left says. "Then we'll be leaving you two alone, and I hope your Tuesday is better than your Monday was."

"Thanks," I say. "I hope so as well."

I think they're going to leave, but they simply stand on my drive for another long moment before the one on the right clears his throat.

"Listen, I hate to do this," he says. "But my daughter's seventeen and she's a *huge* Dirtshine fan, and I wonder if you'd mind signing something for her?"

I'm exhausted, it's near two in the morning, and I've still got a broken window to deal with, but I make myself smile.

"Of course, mate," I say. "If you can hold on a tic I've got some posters inside the house."

CHAPTER THIRTY-FOUR
Marisol

I wait until I get home to finally call Sandra back, because I hate it when people are on the phone on the bus, and because she *knows* me too well. I'm a little afraid that the second she answers the phone she'll know I got laid, and I've always been bad at keeping secrets from her.

It's why we haven't talked much the past month, which I think she's upset about. But I still haven't told my family that I'm seeing someone, *let alone* pretending-to-date-and-now-really-dating an actual rock star.

Sandra answers her phone on the second ring.

"Yo," she says.

"I looked at those listings," I say. "Is that an okay area? I don't really know Brea Park."

Sandra groans, and I can hear the sound of her dramatically flopping onto her bed. She lives in North Hollywood with two roommates, where she has three separate part-time jobs and also does freelance graphic design.

"I think it's not that bad of an area," she says. "To be honest, I don't really know it either, but it looks kinda nice. The one building even had a cute little courtyard?"

"I can't get out there to help until this weekend," I say.

My parents aren't exactly internet-savvy. They've got smartphones, but only because that's the only kind of phone you can even buy now. They don't own a computer, and they don't have a clue how to search Craigslist or anything.

"I'm not working Thursday morning, so I could go then," she offers.

We hash out the details. Silently, I pray that one of these is the apartment that works out, because we're running out of options quickly. They're out of their current apartment in two and a half weeks, and since they were given proper notice, that's the day the police can escort them out.

I'm fully aware that I'm dating a wealthy rock star. I'm fully aware that he's giving me a million dollars, and that if I asked for an advance, I think he'd hand it over in a heartbeat, but I *hate* the thought of that. I want to solve this on my own, without feeling as though I'm using my boyfriend like an ATM.

So I haven't told him anything about this.

"Once they're in a new place I swear we should buy them a computer," Sandra says. "I'll pick up some extra gigs, you edit a few more shitty undergrad papers, *voila*, they find their own next apartment."

"As long as you configure their internet and teach them to use it," I say, lying on my back, staring up at the ceiling.

The pillow smells a little like Gavin, and my heart thumps.

"Oh, God, I hadn't thought of that," Sandra says.

She's quiet for a moment.

"We can just keep helping them with apartments," she says, and I laugh. "I tried to show my manager Instagram today and it did *not* go well, Marisol. She kept trying to — oh! Holy shit, that reminds me, I called you earlier because *are you on TMZ?!*"

I go dead quiet.

"*Marisol*," she says.

"Probably?"

"Okay," she says.

More silence.

"That was an invitation for *you to explain*!" she half-shouts into the phone, and I can practically see my little sister, flopped on her bed, waving one hand in the air. "You're dating the guy from Dirtshine but not really and he's having a fight with the drummer who's new and not the original drummer that everyone thought was kind of cute? And they're fighting over you?!"

"Kinda," I say.

"I swear to God, Mar—"

"Okay, *okay*," I say.

I explain the whole ludicrous situation, top to bottom, starting with the secret concert at the Whiskey Lounge and ending with tonight's meeting, though I leave out our afterparty. When I finish, there's a long silence on the other end.

"I swear they used that plot on *Pasión Prohibida* last week," she says. "Are you sure no one got jilted at the altar so you could go full telenovela?"

"Shut up," I say.

"No wonder you don't want mom and dad to have the internet," she says.

"Please don't tell them," I say. "I'm going to, but it's all kind of weird and ridiculous right now."

"I could blackmail you," she says, laughing.

"Do *not* blackmail me."

"Just for dumb shit," she goes on. "One of mom's pork tamales left in the freezer? Sure, Marisol, you can have it if you want me to tell..."

"You're a monster," I say, rolling my eyes.

Sandra just laughs.

"It's pretty fucking weird, but if he treats you right and you're happy, we're good," she says.

I smile up at my ceiling.

"We're good," I say.

．　．　．

And then maybe the weirdest thing of all happens, and life is... *normal*. Sure, I'm dating someone who was shirtless on the cover of Rolling Stone, but I go to class, do my homework, and correct bad undergraduate essays until I think my eyes might bleed. Finals start in a few weeks, and even though I know I'm already pretty prepared and I'll be fine, I start worrying anyway.

Well, also, my parents need a place to live, and I still haven't told Gavin the whole truth.

And, some of my fellow students have started getting called for job interviews and I haven't. It's only one or two, but it still hurts. *I* wanted to be the first person called, at the top of every firm's list.

So it's not like my life is stress-free, but it's *good*.

We do normal couple stuff. I take him to a loud, crowded Oaxacan restaurant where we stuff our faces with mole, listen to a band play and no one even gives him a second glance. We go see a black-and-white movie at Grauman's Egyptian Theater and split a massive bucket of popcorn. I take him hiking in Griffith Park, up to the Observatory, where you can see practically all of L.A., and I point the city out to him and we stand there, looking over the Los Angeles basin, his arms around me and his chin on top of my head.

"You know I didn't like it here at first?" he says.

"And now?"

"I think I'm coming around."

I lean back against him. There are planes coming in to land at LAX, flying east to west, and I watch one as it lowers across the sky.

"Why?"

"Guess," he says, and kisses the top of my head.

A few girls in their early twenties look over at us, eyes narrowed in an is-that-a-famous-person expression, but they look away.

We spend a lot of nights at my place. I get used to studying while he lounges on my bed, headphones on, and reads. He starts with the books I borrowed about addiction, but moves onto the novels on my bookshelves. It's oddly relaxing and kind of intimate in a weird way, sitting together in silence for hours.

He stays over a lot, though I've still never been to his house. But all my school stuff is here, not there, so it really makes sense — besides, it hasn't even been two weeks.

My parents don't find a place. I'm on the phone with them every other day, with my sister, trying to figure out a plan. I can't *believe* this is happening — there are so many apartments in Los Angeles, how can we not find *one*?

But we can't. Not that they can afford. I start searching for apartments when Gavin's not around, doubling down on my determination not to tell him. I don't know why. Pride, probably.

• • •

The next Thursday I've got a test — cruel this close to finals, but not surprising — and then a paper due Friday, so I don't see much of Gavin for a few days. I feel bad, but this is temporary, and besides, he'll still be there this weekend.

Wednesday night at eight there's a loud knock on my door, and I jump in my chair, tearing my headphones off. My brain runs through all the bad scenarios that could be happening — landlord didn't get my rent check and is evicting me, police are here to tell me someone's dead, burglars, rapists — but when I look through the peephole, I see Gavin's grinning face.

He holds up a plastic bag.

I sigh and open the door, partly annoyed and partly thrilled that he's here. It's not that I didn't want to see him. Not at all. He's just a *distraction*, no matter how nice.

"You do need to eat," he says. "You like Thai, right?"

He looks over my shoulder and his eyes land on the jar of peanut butter, spoon stuck inside, sitting on my desk.

The bag he's holding smells *amazing*.

"All right, fine, you can come in," I say, smiling.

"Twenty minutes and I'm gone," he says, bending to kiss me. "I just wanted to see you and thought maybe I could barter for entry."

His eyes crawl down my body, and instantly, I heat up, thinking about exactly which kind of *entry* I'd like to give him.

We eat on the couch, because I only have one chair and no table that isn't my desk, currently strewn with notes, books, and my laptop. He explains why Led Zeppelin were geniuses and I go into the finer points of asylum law.

Before I know it, we're finished, he's throwing away empty containers and putting the leftovers in my fridge, and I'm sitting on my couch in pajama pants and an old t-shirt while a famous rock star is in my apartment.

I grab him and pull him back down to me.

"You going already?" I ask.

"It's been twenty-five minutes," he points out, even as he grabs my ass. "I did promise twenty and I don't want to overstay my welcome."

His lips taste like lemongrass, but mine probably do too. He's already hard as a rock and just his presence in my apartment has me aching and wet, so before I know it we're pulling each other's clothes off, he's grabbed a condom from my drawer, and I'm riding him hard and fast on my couch.

I come *shouting*.

When we finish, I stay half on his lap, leaning against him, and as pleasant and peaceful as the moment is, the test tomorrow starts creeping back into my brain.

"You can stay if you want, but I need to get back to work," I say, tracing a tattoo on his chest.

Gavin just laughs.

"I honestly just meant to bring you dinner," he says. "I had every intention of leaving afterward and just having a wank at home."

I laugh.

"I didn't mind that particular distraction," I say. "I just have some more studying to do."

He kisses me, then untangles himself and stands, picking his pants up off the floor.

"You study," he says. "I'll see you Friday. I've got a surprise."

"What's the surprise?" I ask, still naked on the couch.

He buttons his pants, then picks up his shirt. Even though I'm spent I can't help but enjoy the view, the long, hard muscles in his body, the easy, confident way he moves.

"It's a *surprise*," he says, pulling the shirt on. "Pick you up at five. Pack an overnight bag."

"An overnight—"

He kisses me.

"*Surprise*," he says, grinning. "Friday."

He lets himself out.

CHAPTER THIRTY-FIVE
Gavin

I spend the day Friday alone and working on the album. I've got the phone off, Liam's somewhere else and has been well-behaved for the past few days to boot.

More and more over the past few weeks, I've been fiddling around here and there, recording bits and pieces, melody and lyrics and bridges, but now I sit down in the spare room I'm using as shitty studio and work on putting things together.

It's not *easy*. I still spend hours working on chords and melodies, and there's the underlying sense that what I'm playing isn't always what's in my head and I don't quite know how to get it *there*, but all that's normal.

But I'm no longer stunted. I don't just pick up a guitar and have my mind go blank, or worse, avoid instruments altogether as I did for months. By the time I leave to go pick up Marisol, I've got the demos of two songs written and recorded on the ancient tape recorder I still prefer to anything digital, another few tapes filled with snippets of nonsense, half-sung lyrics.

I'm relieved, more than anything, because what I've feared most all along isn't true.

It wasn't *junkie* Gavin writing the songs. It was just Gavin.

• • •

When I get to Marisol's place she's out on the front steps, wearing a dress, sandals, sunglasses, and waiting with an overnight bag. It still irks me that I can't pick her up properly by knocking on her apartment door, but in nearly a month I've never once found a parking spot within a half mile of her building. If I'm coming over the spend the night I've started simply taking an Uber.

But I *do* double park, open her door for her, and give her arse a nice squeeze hello.

"How was your test?" I ask, putting the car into gear and listening to the engine growl.

"I think it went well," she says, exhaling and leaning her head against the headrest. "There were no surprises, and that's always good. I might have flubbed the essay a little, but I don't think it was too bad."

She turns toward me.

"How was your day?" she asks.

I tell her about finally working again, that I feel good about this album for the first time in a long time. I explain song structure and she tells me about how Disney more or less controls copyright law in the United States. Then we're on the freeway, heading west, sun shades flipped down.

"So we're *not* going to your house," she says.

Lately she's been ribbing me that I'm a celebrity with a beautiful house and yet we spend all our time in her tiny flat. It's not exactly true — I've only been there a handful of times, and always because that's just what made sense — but it makes me uneasy, because I know

I've not got long before my reticence to bring her home gets suspicious.

I need to get Liam out, but he's been all right the past few days and I'd hate to fuck him up again.

"You'll like this much better than my house," I say. "Besides which, you're in for a massive disappointment when I do finally let you in because it's not the Xanadu you're picturing."

"Is this your way of telling me you live in a basement apartment with four other guys or something?" she asks.

"I don't any longer," I say.

"Maybe you're one of those weird rich people who lives in a van and hoards all his money."

"Right," I say. "It's purple, has got a green dragon and a naked lady painted on it and in big letters on the back it says *don't come a-knockin if this van's a-rockin.*"

"But is the inside velvet?"

"The fuck do you take me for, Marisol? Of course the inside's velvet, I'm not a philistine."

She laughs, the sound filling my car, and my stress about Liam dissolves.

• • •

The surprise is The Dune, an oceanfront inn up in Malibu. All the rooms have balconies overlooking the ocean, and they're known for *actually* being discreet.

Plus, it's posh as fuck. Someone valet parks my car for me, takes our bags and disappears with them. The lobby is all blue and white with furniture that I'm sure cost a ridiculous amount, and in the center is a large wood-burning fireplace with seating all around. As if anyone in Southern California has ever needed a fireplace.

While I check in, Marisol wanders out to the deck and leans against the glass railing, gazing out at the ocean. The sunset frames her body, and for a moment I just *stare*.

"Mr. Lockwood?" the man behind the counter says, and I realize he's *been* saying it. "If you could please sign here..."

I finish, gather our keys, and join Marisol on the deck. She's wearing a deep blue dress that's perfectly tasteful but hugs her body in exactly the right way to make my mouth go dry every time I look at her, and she turns around as I walk out, leaning against the railing to face me.

"What now?" she asks, her eyes sparking.

I lean my elbows on the railing next to her, looking out over the beach and the ocean.

"There's a few options," I say. "We could take a long walk on the beach. We could head into town and see if anything exciting's going on. I think I saw a sign for one of those art classes where you paint a landscape while you drink wine."

She gives me an are-you-kidding-me look, and I grin at her.

"Though I don't drink wine, so I'd just be painting a landscape," I say.

"Those are the options?" she teases, inching closer to me. "Those are *all* the options?"

I slide one hand over her waist and pull her in toward me.

"I don't think Malibu's got a bowling alley or I'd say we should do that," I say, playing it as straight as I can.

"Should we go check on the room?" she asks, like she's trying to be subtle.

I grin.

"Why?"

Marisol turns faintly pink. I'm determined to make her say *because I'd like to have sex with you*, even though we both know what she's getting at.

"To see if..."

She trails off. I raise my eyebrows.

"To see if there's enough towels? I'm sure there's plenty."

Now she's glaring at me, but trying not to laugh.

"You know," she says, still pink as she picks up my hand and threads her fingers through mine. "*Alone* time?"

I lift our hands to my lips and kiss her knuckles. Even if she's not saying it, I'm getting hard as a rock from sheer anticipation

"We're alone *now*," I point out. It's close to true. There are a few other people on this deck, but they're fairly far away.

"*Damn* it," she says, and now I laugh.

"I've no idea what you're getting at so you're *just* going to have to tell me," I say.

"I'm getting at sex first and *then* bowling," she says, rushing the words a little and turning slightly pinker.

"You should have *said* that," I tease her, my voice lowering. "We don't even have to bowl."

I kiss her, sliding one hand around her hip. I know we're in public, sort of, but I can't help myself sometimes.

When we pull back she's just looking at me, eyebrows raised.

"Well?" she teases.

• • •

It's a miracle we make it down the hall and get into the room. I've got my hands up Marisol's dress before the door to our room even closes, my fingers digging into her soft skin as she presses herself against me, her mouth on mine.

I push her against the wall of our room's entryway, opposite an enormous mirror and hook my thumb underneath the band of her underwear, pulling it down.

"You should wear more skirts," I say. "I *like* it when you wear skirts."

"I like it too," she murmurs, pulling at my shirt. I get it over my head and toss it away, my hand underneath her dress again as I kiss her on the lips, my tongue in her mouth. I slide my fingers between her legs, just barely grazing the slick edges of her lips, and she digs her fingers into my back and gasps.

"You're going to shred me to ribbons one of these days," I say, her fingernails pinpricks in my back.

"It's your own fault," she murmurs, pulling me down for another kiss.

I circle her clit slowly, lazily. She moans into my mouth and flattens one palm against my aching cock, grabbing me through the rough denim of my jeans, making me groan before she finally undoes them, reaches in, and gives me a long, hard stroke.

I want her *now*, right here, up against this wall. I don't care that we're still half-clothed and in the hotel room's entry way, I'm goddamn *pulsing* with the desire to sink myself inside her as I watch the way her eyes darken with pleasure.

There's a condom in my pocket. I pull it out, but before I can open the foil package Marisol's already snatched it from me and has it in one fist.

Then she kisses my shoulder, a slow, lingering kiss. She kisses my collarbone, my chest, then she lets me go, whirls me around, pushes me back against the wall so I'm facing the mirror and she kneels.

I'm panting for breath, every muscle tight with anticipation. She strokes me again with her lips on my belly, my hip, and then she tilts her head, and runs her tongue up the underside of my cock, looking me straight in the eyes.

"*Fuck*, Marisol," I whisper, my voice rough.

Then she takes me in her mouth and I nearly shout, her lips sliding down the shaft until I hit the back of her mouth and *groan*. She looks up at me again as she pulls back, swirls her tongue around the tip, takes me in again.

I watch her from two angles, from above and in the mirror, and she's beautiful and intoxicating and *Jesus*, this feels good, so good it's nearly impossible to stop her but I do, one hand in her hair as she pulls back.

"I'm gonna come if you don't stop," I say.

"And?"

I bend down, kiss her on the mouth, hand still in her hair. She tastes like me, faintly musky, and God help me it's fucking *sexy* that she does.

"*And*, for days I've been thinking of how it feels when you come while I'm inside you," I murmur, and she wraps her hand around the back of my head, pulling me down.

Before I know it I'm on the floor as well and we're tangled, her half on top of me. My pants are still on and she's still got the condom in one hand as I try to push her dress over her head, but there's a belt or something.

"It unties," she explains breathlessly, pulling back. She pulls the bow at one side and it loosens, a widening stripe of skin down the middle before she pulls the whole thing off, following it with her bra. I pull her forward, pressing my lips to her soft, warm skin in the valley right between her breasts, her belly, moving with every breath.

And then I spin her around so she's facing the mirror, me on my knees behind her as I slide both hands over her breasts, pinching her nipples between my fingers, my cock hard as steel against her back. I kiss the side of her neck, still watching her in the mirror as her eyelids lower and she leans back against me, head against my shoulder.

"We can move," I whisper, thinking of what she told me about mirrors on our first date. "But you're sexy as fuck and God help me, I like watching you."

She turns her head toward me and pulls my lips to hers.

"I like it here," she says, and holds up the condom.

In a split second, I've got it open and I'm unrolling it onto my cock, kicking away my jeans. Marisol arches against me, watching herself in the mirror as I kiss her shoulder.

"I get the feeling you like watching as well," I say, whispering into her ear.

"I don't know yet," she says, a smile in her voice. "Convince me."

She grabs my cock. I wrap one arm around her chest, holding onto her tight, and my other hand around hers, sliding the tip between her lips, just to tease her, then circling her clit once. I wish for a moment that I could *really* feel her, bare, skin-to-skin.

But then I'm back at her entrance and I sink myself into her with a single stroke, burying myself to the hilt, and forget everything else. Marisol groans softly, the same noise she makes every time I enter her.

I fucking *live* for that noise.

I grab onto her shoulder tighter, pull her against me harder, get as deep as I possibly can. Marisol whimpers, grabbing the back of my neck with one hand as we start moving together.

I don't take my eyes from the mirror. I can't. Watching Marisol get fucked like this, back arching, toes curling, is intoxicating and seeing myself do it to her is almost unbelievable.

My hand on her shoulder slips, and she pushes it away, getting to her hands and knees, rocking back

258

against me so hard I see stars and she *shouts*, tightening around me.

"Harder," she gasps.

She's never said *that* before. I drive myself into her and she falls to her elbows on the floor but moans.

"Sorry," I gasp out.

"Don't stop."

There's not a fucking chance of *that*. I grab my jeans and shove them under her hips without stopping, and in moments we're collapsed onto the floor, her back arched and hips up as her hands claw the carpet and I fuck her as I've never fucked anyone before.

It's fast and hard and deep and *raw*. Marisol sparks some sort of pure, primal, *animal* desire in me, something bone deep that I can't even name but that I can sure as hell feel, like electricity through my veins. I grab her hip and her shoulder and simply drive myself as deep as I can and she moans explosively, so loud I'm certain they can hear her in the hall.

"Gavin," she whimpers, and a thrill races through me at the way she says it, her head to one side, her eyelids fluttering.

"Say it again."

"Gavin," she breathes, her eyes unfocused. "This feels so fucking good."

I'm on the brink, gritting my teeth together because it's nearly impossible *not* to come in a hard rush when she says my name like that, but I can tell she is too.

"Again," I tell her, because I fucking love how she says it, because I want to hear it as she comes.

"I'm gonna come," she says instead, her voice barely a whimper. "Don't stop, don't stop, *please* don't stop oh my God, Gavin—"

Her whole body tenses and Marisol shouts into the carpet, squeezing me like a fist as she comes, her whole body rocking at once.

I explode. I shout her name and come like fucking Vesuvius blowing apart, thrusting until I can't anymore, until I'm so spent I'm trembling and I can barely move.

I feel as if I've broken to pieces and been glued back together and I'm not quite sure it's done right, and for a long second, I'm not even certain where I am, except atop Marisol. The nape of her neck is in front of me so I kiss her there, then turn my head toward the mirror.

She's looking at me, eyes half-closed, and she gives me a slow, lazy smile. I find her arm with my hand and follow it to hers, lace my fingers through hers, and then give up on moving for a bit.

CHAPTER THIRTY-SIX
Marisol

"So *are* we going bowling?" I call, flopping back onto a couch. I'm finally dressed again, because we've got to eat, but I'm still feeling impossibly lazy, like even standing is more effort than I can put in right now.

"I told you, there's no bowling in Malibu," he says, walking out of the bathroom, a towel wrapped around his waist.

We got... somewhat sweaty, so we both took showers. Though I don't know why he's bothering with the towel.

"Did you actually check?"

"I did," he confirms, walking around the huge bed, clearly looking for something. "That's something normal couples do, yeah?"

"I haven't been bowling since I was ten."

"Then you've *clearly* had boring boyfriends who don't know how to show you a proper good time," he says, still looking. "Do you know where you threw my shirt?"

261

"Didn't you bring another one?"

"That's for tomorrow. I'm looking for the Pixies shirt I was wearing earlier. Nevermind, there it is."

He grabs that, jeans, and boxers, and walks back into the bathroom. I frown, and a few minutes later, he comes back out.

"Did you really just go get changed in the bathroom?" I tease.

He stops short, then looks sheepish for a moment.

"Force of habit," he says. "I've shared a lot of hotel rooms with other blokes."

"It would be pretty weird if I saw you naked," I deadpan.

"Can I do *nothing* without commentary?" he teases.

"Not that."

He holds out one hand.

"What about take you to dinner?"

I take it, and he pulls me up effortlessly, the muscles in his arm bunching. Something warm prickles up my back.

"Depends on the dinner," I tease.

• • •

We drive out of Malibu proper and up a canyon road, Gavin's fancy car growling and purring and hugging the turns as he plays me Bon Jovi and explains why it's terrible.

I argue that it's catchy. He tells me why it's bullshit. I hum *Livin' on a Prayer* over him until we're both giggling like children, headlights glowing on the road in front of us, the canyon deep and dark below us.

I think these moments are my favorite.

When we reach the top there's a tiny hamlet, just two buildings and a post office, but one of the buildings is an old-fashioned burger joint, and Gavin pulls into the parking lot.

"Come on," he says, grinning. "We're having a *date*."

Inside there's kitsch covering every wall, red-checked tablecloths and an actual jukebox in one corner playing at top volume. I'm half expecting the waitresses to be wearing poodle skirts and roller skates, but they're dressed normally.

We sit in a booth and Gavin looks around, eyebrows raised.

"It looks as if 1950s America vomited and it pooled right here," Gavin says, though he's clearly entertained. Sometimes he finds America ridiculous enough to be funny.

"Gross but accurate," I say, following his gaze.

We order burgers and fries, split a milkshake, and he makes me laugh so hard it nearly comes out my nose. The place fills up slowly, but after a while it's actually pretty crowded. The jukebox is loud and full of oldies, and even though this place is a little silly I think I really *like* it.

Or maybe I just like being here with Gavin, sharing milkshakes and listening to *Daydream Believer* on the jukebox, like he's just asked me to go steady with him.

Then he catches me rearranging the sugar packets in their holder, because I like it better when each color is grouped together, and he asks if I also arrange my french fries in size order.

I throw a sugar packet at him. He ducks.

If anyone recognizes us, they don't show it. There's a few times I think people might be snapping pictures on their phones, but I can't be bothered to care.

We drive back the way we came, though this time I'm trying to explain the *Fast and Furious* franchise, and he's remaining unconvinced of its cinematic genius.

"Let me get this straight," he says. "You think *The Simpsons* is too stupid but you like these movies?"

I open my mouth. I close it. I open it again.

"Everyone needs a guilty pleasure," I finally say. "They're... good for what they are."

We come to a stop light on the coastal highway, and Gavin looks over at me, takes my hand in his, and kisses it.

"Have I told you I quite like you?" he asks.

It's simple, sweet, and makes my heart explode into a big cloud of rainbows and butterflies. I start laughing, pull our hands to my side of the car, and kiss him on the knuckles.

"I think you may have guessed," he admits.

"I quite like you as well," I say.

• • •

The next morning we walk down to the beach and sit on the sand. I dig my toes in and lean back on my hands, the sun hitting my face, and let my eyes close. We don't have long, because soon we've got to head back into the city so I can take my shift helping my parents look at apartments, but right now, right here, this is *nice*.

"Maybe I should take up surfing," Gavin muses next to me, sitting on the towels we borrowed from the hotel.

Borrowed is a strong word. Gavin took them when I wasn't paying attention, and even though he's sworn up and down to return them, I know full well they're not intended as beach towels.

"Can you even swim?" I ask, flicking a stray piece of dried seaweed off the illicitly-gotten towel.

"Course I can swim," he laughs. "Britain's an island."

"It's not so small an island that you could walk to the coast," I point out. "I thought Mountford Wye was pretty far inland."

"Well, there's lakes and all that. Plus, this innovation known as a swimming pool."

"Don't get cheeky," I laugh. "You're the one who said you could obviously swim because Britain's an island."

"I think I'd quite enjoy surfing," he says. "And then I'd blend in seamlessly with the local culture."

"You called Americans *colonials* the other night," I point out.

"It would take a bit of practice."

I just raise my eyebrows, grinning.

"Hang ten, bro," Gavin says.

He's got the worst American accent I've ever heard. I snort-laugh.

"These gnarly waves are totally radical, *dude*," he goes on, elongating his vowels and enunciating his R's as hard as he can. He sounds like he's doing a bad impression of the *Teenage Mutant Ninja Turtles* cartoon.

I'm laughing so hard I almost can't breathe.

"Let's cruise down the strip and check out some awesome babes."

I try to inhale and snort.

"I don't know what you're laughing at," he says in his normal accent, grinning. "This is what you lot sound like."

I wipe a tear from my cheek and finally inhale.

"Please say *gnarly waves* again," I gasp.

"Let's hear your British accent then."

I shake my head.

"It's only fair," he says. "Come on, look how much fun you're having."

He has a point. I catch my breath and clear my throat.

"Wot's awl thees then?" I start.

We both dissolve into laughter.

"That's *terrible*!" Gavin gasps. "Go on."

I make myself stop giggling and take a breath.

My phone rings.

"That won't save you," Gavin says. "We're coming back to this."

I stick out my tongue at him and grab it out of my bag. Sandra.

Please, please be calling because you found an apartment, I think, and answer the phone.

"This needs to be fast because I told them I was running to the bathroom," she says.

"Okay."

"We found a place, and it's actually really nice, the landlord seems on the level, it's only a couple of miles from where they live now so they won't have to spend forever on the bus to get to work, the neighborhood is fine, there's a washer and dryer *in* the apartment..."

She pauses, and my heart sinks like a rock. Gavin's looking at me, so I stand and start pacing on the sand a couple feet away. I don't want him to overhear me.

"What's the catch?" I ask, keeping my voice low.

"They want first month's rent, last's month's rent, *and* a security deposit."

Fuck.

In Los Angeles, at least, most places only want the first month's rent and a security deposit, so that's what we'd been banking on — but landlords can ask for anything.

"And it's a little more expensive than we wanted, but it's really nice, they won't get shot, they can still get to the bus and to work and god, Marisol, it's got laundry *in* the apartment, plus—"

She pauses, her voice dropping dramatically.

"Once *that thing* you told me about happens, it won't even matter, right? And between you, me, and them, we can cover an extra one-fifty a month for two more months, until we can buy them a house."

Tears prick at the back of my eyeballs and I stare up at the cars on the coastal highway, back to Gavin, trying to breathe deep and above all *not cry*.

"It's nineteen-fifty a month?" I ask.

I can *hear* her swallow.

"Yeah," she says.

Their old place, the place their shitty landlord is dubiously evicting them from, was a thousand a month. Los Angeles has rent control, and they'd been living there for fifteen years.

"So they need, what, basically six thousand dollars?" I ask, my own voice sounding hollow.

"Mom just told me they have about four thousand in savings," Sandra whispers. "I've got maybe four hundred I can pitch in after rent this month."

I *finally* have nearly a thousand dollars in my savings account. It was supposed to be my emergency fund, but I swallow the anxious lump in my throat.

"I can give them money too," I say. "But not enough."

We're still four hundred and fifty dollars short. It's not even that much, not in the grand scheme of things, and I can't believe that it's all that's in the way.

Four-fifty. *Fuck.*

I'm crying now, furious tears welling up and sliding down my cheeks, because this wasn't supposed to happen. In a few more months I'll be out of law school, I'll have taken the bar, I'll hopefully have a job making real money.

Why couldn't this happen then? Why'd this have to happen a few stupid months before I could actually help?

There's a long, long pause on the other end, and there's no *way* Mom and Dad still think she went to the bathroom.

"What if you asked Gavin for an advance?" Sandra finally says.

I knew it was coming, but I still hate it, because as stupid as it sounds, I don't want to bring money into our relationship. Even though I *know* I was here for money, I don't want him to think I'm *still* here for that. Or, worse, I don't want him to think that I "made it real" because I thought I could get *more* money that way.

His life is full of people who want something from him. I'm not one of them. I don't want to be, and I absolutely hate asking people for things like this.

It was supposed to be me, dammit. Part of the reason I went to law school was so I'd be able to help them someday, and I feel utterly helpless that this is happening before I could get there.

But I'm pretty much out of options. My *parents* are pretty much out of options. I take a deep breath and clench my toes into the sand.

"Okay," I say. "Let me call you back."

I hang up, still facing away, and lift my left hand to my right shoulder, kneading at the tension there for a moment.

Just tell him your parents are in a tight spot and need five hundred dollars, I think. *That's less than your first date cost, probably.*

"Marisol?" his voice says behind me, and I jump. "Is everything — what's *happened*?"

He lurches forward, awkward in the sand, to put his hands on my shoulders, and I start sobbing.

"Is someone hurt?" he asks, alarm written all over his face. "Your sister? Your parents? Is it—"

I shake my head, cutting him off.

"It's kind of complicated," I say.

He waits. I take a deep, shaky breath, because I hate that I'm crying and I *really* hate what I'm about to do, but I don't see a way around it.

"My parents are getting evicted from their apartment..." I start.

I tell him everything, standing there on the sand, trying not to cry while he strokes my hair. I tell him about their shady landlord, about rent in the neighborhood where I grew up spiraling out of control, the problems with gentrification, how they can't move too far away because they don't have a car and have to be able to get to work. I keep going and going until I'm at the hard part, and then the words slow to a trickle.

"So, we, uh," I get out, my voice nearly cutting out as I look away from Gavin, down the beach. "We're four-fifty short—"

"That's it?" Gavin interrupts.

"I know," I say miserably. "It's stupid, and it's pathetic that four adults can't come up with another four-fifty..."

"I'll give it to you," he says. "Marisol, you can have the whole six grand, Jesus, I wish you'd have told me weeks ago."

I shake my head again, more tears welling. I'm ashamed at asking for money, and I'm furious that I *need* to.

"I didn't want to... crap, I don't know," I say. "I didn't want you to think I was using you, and I didn't want to bother you with my problems, and I thought I could fix it myself."

He kisses the top of my head.

"You didn't want me to think that, when you agreed to date me for money, you were interested in my money?" he asks.

"I *know* how dumb it sounds."

"I'm just winding you up," he says gently. "I know how you are."

"I'm sorry," I murmur, leaning into his chest.

"I do wish you'd told me," he says. He sounds kind of hurt. "I did tell you my problems."

"I didn't mean to keep it a secret," I say. "It just happened."

"It's all right," he says, and it sounds like he's *trying* to mean it. "Let's take these towels back, yeah?"

I nod.

"Yeah," I agree.

CHAPTER THIRTY-SEVEN
Gavin

I wind up being able to simply give Marisol the money using my mobile, and though she protests that she doesn't want the whole six grand, I tell her I'm taking it out of her million and also to shut up and take it. She does.

I drive her to Highland Park and drop her off a few blocks from where her parents and sister are — her sister knows but her parents don't, and it's not exactly the time to introduce myself.

"Thanks," she says, just before she gets out of the car, looking down. "And sorry."

Her eyes have that slightly glassy post-crying look, and yet again an overwhelming, protective urge twists in my gut. I feel as if it's my job to keep Marisol from crying, and I can't.

"Tomorrow night?" I ask, as I kiss her goodbye. She smiles.

"Monday night," she says. "I don't have class next week because it's reading period for finals, but I've got that job interview at Ramirez & Chabon I told you about on Monday morning."

Meaning *we can spend the night together*.

"Good luck," I say, and she shuts the door.

I grin, watching her walk down the sidewalk away from me. There's just something *about* watching an incredibly attractive woman walk and knowing that she's yours, and I sit there in traffic, blatantly staring at her until someone honks.

But still, as I drive home, I keep turning it over in my mind. I wish she'd told me. I knew she was dating me to buy a house for her parents, but I didn't know things were so dire. Marisol did assure me that they'd have stayed with her, not been on the street, but I've been to her apartment. It's not big enough for three.

I can't help but feel lied to, even by omission. Worse, I feel as if I've laid my own problems bare, told her the worst about myself, the horrible things I've done, and she didn't trust me enough to let me help her.

Somewhere inside I've got the nagging worry that this relationship is lopsided. That I've given more of myself over to her than she has me, that I've revealed everything and she's hesitant to tell me something like this.

And yes, I know Liam's living at my house and I've not told her, but that seems different somehow. That's because I don't want her to think less of me. I don't want her to worry that I'll relapse, don't want to seem as if I'm walking toward the edge of something bad because I'm not.

Besides, it's not as if she's ever asked whether Liam's staying with me. I just haven't mentioned it.

That's a load of shite and you know it, I think.

Fucking hypocrite.

• • •

There are photographers outside my gate again, maybe ten of them, and I mutter some choice curses under my breath. They've been gone the last several days, but I guess there's no other news right now so they're back.

I slow to a crawl and wait as my gate opens. They crowd around my car, on both sides and in front of me. I can't even drive forward without hitting them, which I admit I do fantasize about briefly.

But instead, I extend one middle finger against the window and don't look at any of the cameras, inching my car forward. They can't come onto the property, because *then* I can sue, so all I've got to do is get through the gate and I'm home free.

I swear it takes several minutes, but I get in without causing anyone grievous bodily harm, and hit the button to close the gate behind me. The shouts of the photographers get a little quieter, but the they don't fade, and when I get out of the car I can still hear them.

This is why famous people move to mountaintops, I think. *All I ever wanted to do was write songs and play music.*

"Gavin!" a particularly loud one shouts over my fence. "Do you have a comment on the contract?"

I've got no clue what he's talking about. Presumably Crumble City, the record company, has made some comment on our contract now that the rumors are out about Marisol and me. But if they've not contacted me, it can't be that big of a deal.

"Is it true it's a forgery?" someone else shouts.

Why the fuck would a record contract be a forgery?

I frown, shut my car door, and pull out my mobile. Several missed calls and texts from Valerie, some from Nigel, the top two reasons I keep the damn thing on silent.

273

"What does this mean for the band?" another voice calls out.

Valerie's texts are all-caps and make no damn sense, so I google "Gavin Lockwood Contract" as I walk for the house, stomach slowly sinking because whenever those two want to talk, it isn't ever *good* news.

Result one: TMZ.

GAVIN LOCKWOOD'S SHAM SHAG

Leaked documents PROVE girlfriend was a setup!

I stop dead on my front walk, click the link. There's a slightly blurry photo, badly lit photo on the post and I enlarge it, heart thumping.

It's the final page of the contract we both signed, that day in Larry's office. I'd nearly forgotten we ever signed a contract. I barely looked at the thing, to be honest; the entire time I was mostly listening to Marisol talk, trying not to think about the way her lips looked when she said *binding clause*.

They can't have, I think, over and over again. *Someone's faked this just to set me up, but they can't have gotten this.*

But they did. And now, standing here, listening to asshole so-called reporters shout at me over my front gate, I'm looking at the signature page of it on a gossip blog, on my mobile screen. My big, looping scrawl, Marisol's smaller, neater signature, the thick bumpy line that's Larry's.

This is it. This is definitely it, and I've not got a clue how they got a hold of it.

I walk inside, and on the other side of the door, pause for a moment, listening. No noise, so Liam's either out or asleep. It's still only two in the afternoon, so the latter's a likely possibility.

Then I sit on the remaining couch — I got rid of the blood-soaked one, obviously — and call Valerie back.

"Was this you?" she snaps.

I was already quite annoyed and irritated, but in less than a second she's managed to make me *angry* with her.

"Fucking of course not," I say. "I've been following every single suggestion you've made for me to the letter and they all seem to be getting cocked up anyway."

"You punched Eddie!" she shouts.

I think it's the first time Valerie's ever shouted at me. For all her panicked and insane emails, in person or on the phone she's usually fairly calm.

"He deserved it," I snap back. "He drugged Marisol because he's a careless wanker and he left pot-laced candy about."

And he called her my fake girlfriend, I think. *Even though she was at the time.*

"I don't care if he took a machine gun to a puppy sanctuary, you can't punch your bandmates!" she says, her voice rising in pitch. "And you can't punch your bandmates and then act like you're astonished that someone thinks you might pull other bullshit!"

"Why the fuck would I do this, Valerie?" I ask. "To finish proving that we're trying to fool everyone? So I could make *certain* to fuck myself over good and properly?"

"For the press," she says, as if it's so obvious a child could see it. "You've been out of the news cycle for a couple days, so maybe you went off-book and decided to get yourself back out there."

Now I'm standing, pacing back and forth around the living room. The blood and glass from Monday night is cleaned, but there's still a large sheet of plywood over the empty window that Liam broke, and seeing that just makes me angrier.

It's as if it doesn't matter whether I try follow the right path or not, everything around me still turns to shit.

"Valerie, what the *fuck* in our working relationship would give you the slightest idea that I've enjoyed being the object of gossip?" I ask, striding from the plywood window to the remaining couch. "All I want to do is play music, and the only reason I give a *single solitary fuck* about having good publicity is because the record label is so interested in it."

"Please," she says, her voice nearly dripping with scorn. "Everyone gets a taste, then another taste, and they're hooked and they keep going back. It's like a drug. It's addictive."

I burst out laughing, alone in the house and on the phone. I probably sound unhinged, but Valerie's fucking *mad* if she thinks that's true.

"It's *nothing* like a drug," I tell her. "Drugs are at least enjoyable while you're on them."

She clears her throat. I'm still laughing.

There's a long, awkward silence.

"I apologize for the comparison," she says stiffly. "But I don't believe I'm out of line thinking that you may have—"

"I've already told you it *fucking* wasn't me," I say, though I'm hardly even angry any more. "I don't know who it was or what they want, but it wasn't me, and that's all I've got to say on it."

I hang up the phone, toss it onto the couch, and walk into the kitchen because I need a drink. Of water, even though right now I'd fucking love just a sip of something stronger.

As I'm filling a glass from the sink, I notice a piece of notebook paper on the counter. It's ripped in half and looks like it may have been crumpled at some point. But it's a note from Liam, written in sharpie in his bloody awful handwriting.

Gav—

You were right. Back in rehab. See you on the other side, brother.

Liam

I stare at it until the glass overflows onto my hand, then turn the water off and grab the note. I turn it over. There's nothing else. That's it, just *you were right, back in rehab.*

For a moment, I wonder if someone's winding me up. Maybe he's been kidnapped and this is some attempt at a ransom note, but it's definitely his handwriting. There's nothing wrong in the house. If anything, it seems a bit neater than usual — no socks and shoes strewn about.

Actually, I think the dishes that I left out yesterday have been washed and put away.

Now *that's* strange.

I read the note again and again, drinking my water. I glance around at the cleaner-than-normal kitchen. Liam's been acting all right the past few days. He's been drinking, but not getting plastered every night; I'm fairly certain he's been smoking pot in the back yard but it's now been a while since he came home wild-eyed and told me about how the Queen, the Prime Minister and the American President are all lizard people simply *wearing* human skins.

Liam's been subdued. Calm. Almost normal.

Maybe the note's true. Maybe he really *did* go back.

Despite myself, and despite everything I *know* about Liam, I let myself believe it for a moment. Maybe this time it'll work, he'll get clean, and things can go back to the way they used to be between us, before all this.

I know better than to get my hopes up, but I can't help it. I close my eyes, cross my fingers, and offer up a quick prayer to whatever deity looks after fuckups like Liam.

Please, let it work this time, I think.

CHAPTER THIRTY-EIGHT
Marisol

"I could hide in the trunk," I offer as Gavin comes to a stop sign.

He just snorts.

"I'm hoping they've given up by now," he says, his car purring around a tight curve, tall gated houses on either side of the narrow street. "There were only two when I left to pick you up and they both looked *quite* bored."

Another car comes toward us on the street, and we slow, squeezing past each other with inches to spare. I try to peer ahead in the dark, seeing if there are paparazzi outside any of the gates ahead.

"And if they haven't, I don't give a fuck," he says. "Let them puzzle over why I'm bringing my contracted girlfriend home with me."

We snake around another curve, and a tall wooden gate comes into view, a single man standing outside, holding a camera and looking at his phone.

"Maybe we should invite him in and explain over a cup of tea," I say.

"There *are* things I'd rather do," Gavin says, and raises one eyebrow in my direction.

I press my knees together, my insides fluttering just a little as the gate slides open. The photographer looks up, pockets his phone, and starts snapping away. Gavin shades his eyes and I turn my head, though it's more because the flash is blinding in the dark than because we don't want to be found together.

We've decided we're done pretending, no matter what Valerie says, no matter what the headlines are. It's real. It's happening. Sooner or later *Rockstar Goes on Normal Date With Normal Girlfriend* will stop being headline news, contract or no contract.

He pulls into his driveway, closes the gate, and we get out of his car.

"Welcome to my humble abode," Gavin says.

It's not that humble. It's not a crazy monstrosity, but it's sure not humble.

Perched in the Hollywood Hills, Gavin's rental house is one of those boxy, cement-and-wood numbers that's very sleek and modern, basically the only thing anyone is building in Los Angeles right now. The front yard is filled with succulents and gravel, and over the roof and garage I can see the glimmer of the lights of Los Angeles, though I can't see anything yet.

"It's not what I'd have chosen to buy," he admits as we walk toward the door, mounting the concrete steps. "But I was in the market for a furnished rental with a gate, this was available, and now here I am."

Gavin holds the door open and I enter, my footsteps echoing. There are no lights on, but between the half moon and the glow of Los Angeles through the wall of windows at the back of the house, I can make out a huge room with a cathedral ceiling, a couch, a TV, a big fireplace, some chairs, and a coffee table. I guess it's a living room, except it's about three times the size of most living rooms.

Halfway to the ceiling is a railing and a balcony. I guess it's the second floor. Gavin flips the lights on, and I blink.

It's *nice*. It's obviously new, all the corners still sharp, everything still shiny and new-looking. Well, except the plywood covering part of the big wall of windows to the back yard. But somehow, even that doesn't look *bad*.

"Wow," I say, taking it all in. "Explain to me again why it was better to be at my apartment than your house?"

"Your flat's cozy," he says.

"Do you *like* that the bathroom door hits the couch if you open it too wide?"

Gavin grins, tossing his keys onto a side table next to a stack of junk mail.

"It's got your stuff in it," he says, shrugging. "It feels like home, whereas this is one of those American houses built with the idea that someone might need to run a herd of buffalo through it, so better make it large and empty enough."

"Maybe you *do* live in a gross van and you only rented this place for a night to impress me," I tease.

"Don't insult the shaggin' wagon," he says. "I paid a lot of money for that tasteful airbrushed painting of a dragon making love to a woman."

I crinkle my nose, even though I'm laughing.

"If *that's* the face you're going to make then you'll never get to ride in it," Gavin teases. "Do you want the tour or what?"

"Are there secret passageways?"

"It's not a castle."

"Is there at least a bookshelf that turns around to a secret room?"

"Well, *now* I don't want to give you a tour because you're clearly going to be disappointed."

I kiss him on the shoulder, through his shirt, because that's the part of him I can reach.

"I promise not to be disappointed," I say, and raise one eyebrow. "As long as you show me where the magic happens."

Gavin waves one arm at the room we're in.

"Well, this is the living room," he says. "The room for watching telly and, I don't know, lounging about? That window is the one that—"

He pauses for just a second, like he's remembering something.

"— that someone broke before bleeding on a couch, so it's been removed and *still* not replaced. Something about the insurance."

"Even high-end landlords are shitty," I say. "Celebrities, they're just like us."

Gavin shows me around. There's a dining room with an expensive-looking modern table, a gourmet kitchen with a breakfast nook, a deck overlooking a back yard, a room with a built-in desk he says is the study, and two bathrooms — all on the main floor. It's all very clean-looking and sterile, because he obviously barely uses most of the rooms here.

I'm a little jealous. I'd use *so many* of these rooms. I swear I'd have an entire room only for paper and plastic bags, *just because I could*.

"That's it for the main floor," Gavin says, and hits a switch, lighting up the second story.

"Is *that* where the magic happens?" I ask.

"The magic happens wherever I say it does," he says, his voice lowering, a smile tugging at his lips. "Now come the *fuck* on and let me finish this tour before the magic happens on the floor for the second time this week."

Point taken. He takes my hand and pulls me up the staircase to the second-floor balcony, looking down at where we just were.

The view's even better from up here. Gavin points at a couple of closed doors across the way.

"Bedrooms with nothing in them and that one's a linen closet," he says, walking me along a hallway.

He stops in front of a double door, turns to face me, and grins. My heart speeds up, because we both know perfectly well what's behind that door.

"*This,*" Gavin says, turning the knob behind himself. "Is where the magic happens."

It's his bedroom, obviously, but the first thing I notice isn't the huge bed, the fireplace or the strategically-low lighting, it's the view. The south-facing wall is almost entirely made of glass, and from it I can see even more of Los Angeles than from downstairs, all lit up at night.

It's gorgeous. I'm a sucker for views, and *this* one is incredible.

"We're never going to my apartment again," I say, just staring out the window.

Gavin slides his arms around my waist and pulls my body against his.

"I admit I didn't even know it was here until I moved in," he says. "And then I kept the curtains closed for another month or so afterward without realizing."

I lean my head back against his shoulder and look up at him.

"You're killing me here," I tease.

He laughs, arms tightening.

"What I mean is, when I got out of rehab and needed a place I had a feeling that sooner or later I'd fall head over heels for a girl who really enjoyed scenic overlooks, so when I saw this I *knew* I had to have it," he says.

Head over heels. I get butterflies.

"So I'm glad you like it, because I absolutely got it with you in mind and not at all by accident," he goes on, laughing.

I lean against his shoulder, look up at him, and slide a hand through his hair.

"I should ask you for lotto numbers," I tease.

Gavin leans in and kisses me. He does it slowly, so slow it's almost toe-curling, then pulls back, millimeters between our lips, so I close the gap and kiss him back.

He turns me around in his arms until I'm facing him, then snakes his fingers through my hair, his other hand still on my waist. Our tongues wind together. I bite his lower lip gently when he pulls back, and he growls so softly I barely hear it.

My body is pure electricity, snapping and crackling. All I want to do is push him to the floor and let him have me there, like we did Friday night. It's unbelievable how much I want him, *all* the time — at restaurants, in the car, when we walk around the city together.

But especially right now, desire humming through my veins, a hollow ache that I can only fill one way. Gavin's forehead is against mine and he digs his fingers into my spine, his other hand cupping my chin, one thumb stroking my cheekbone.

"I'm completely fucking mad for you," he murmurs, and kisses me again, pushing me up against the cool window.

I close my fingers around his shirt, his tongue in my mouth. He slides one hand up my outer thigh slowly, finding the hem of my dress and pushing his fingers underneath it, letting his palm rasp against my skin. The leather bracelets on that wrist tickle as he moves higher and higher, and our mouths unlock.

"And for two days now, the only thing I've thought about is you, saying my name as you come," he goes on.

He hooks one finger under the side of my thong and then snaps it. I gasp, and he smiles.

"That's actually not true," he admits, his voice still low and gravelly.

He kisses my lips, kisses my jaw, kisses the spot in front of my ear.

"I also gave some thought to you telling me *harder*," he says, his lips against my ear. "I *quite* liked that as well."

I can tell that I'm bright red, but I swallow hard and take a deep breath.

"I *quite* liked... what you were doing," I say.

I'm not great at talking dirty, but Gavin laughs softly into my ear and twists the side of my thong around his fingers, teasing me and pulling it tight.

"I'm glad, because I've got every intention of doing it again, and very soon," he says, a smile in his voice as he kisses my neck below my ear.

He moves his other hand to my neck, then the pad of his thumb to the hollow of my throat before tracing my collarbone with his fingers, sliding them down my chest and underneath the very first button on my shirtdress, then over each button, all the way down.

I'm biting my lip, and my eyes go half-closed, heat spreading outward over my skin from the path his finger's traced.

"You drive me crazy," I whisper.

"Good," he murmurs back.

I lock eyes with Gavin, his fingers still under the band of my thong, and undo the top button on my dress, dragging my fingers through the opening to undo the second button. I undo the third and now he's watching me, pure hunger lighting his eyes as I lean against the window, undressing for him slowly.

When all the buttons are undone, I hold my breath and untie the belt, shrugging the dress off. I know I'm nearly naked in front of a giant window, but it's dark, the room lit mostly by the moon and Los Angeles itself.

Gavin grabs me by the hips and pulls me in, away from the window, and holds me tight against him, his enormous erection against my belly.

"How the *fuck* am I supposed to make it to the bed?" he says.

"Do you need to?" I ask, slipping my hand between us and squeezing his hard length through his jeans.

He kisses me hard, his tongue in my mouth, his cock practically throbbing against my hand. I don't care about making it to the bed, not at *all*, and I tug his shirt off over his head, his muscles taut in the low light.

"We should at least *try* the bed," he says, and before I know it he's scooping me up and carrying me the ten feet to his enormous bed, king-sized at least. I bounce slightly when he tosses me on it, and then Gavin's already on top of me, my legs around his hips.

"See?" he says. "This could be a fun new *thing* for us. Beds."

Without waiting for an answer, he kisses my neck, my throat, the spot above my belly button. I know exactly what's about to happen and my toes curl in anticipation before he even pulls my thong off. He pushes my thighs apart, sucking on the inside of one.

I'm soaking wet. His mouth still on the inside of my thigh, Gavin puts one fingertip directly on my clit.

I gasp, tensing, curling my fingers through his hair, and he slides his finger down slowly, between my lips but not inside me.

It's pure torture, and he knows it. He's watching me, watching every reaction my body has to the things he *does* to me, and he knows I'm set to explode at the slightest touch.

"You're *dripping* wet," he murmurs, his mouth so close to me that I can feel his voice buzz.

"I know," I whisper.

Not sexy, but my mind's a blank, and I swallow.

"Please," I gasp, and I'm not even finished with the word when he flicks the very tip of his tongue across my clit.

I *grunt*.

He does it again, then again, so slowly I want to scream, stroking my lips with his fingers at the same time. I unclench my hand from his hair before I pull a handful of it out as he licks me, slowly and lazily.

I'm gasping for air, my whole body tense, as I gradually get closer and closer, bit by slow, tortuous bit.

Then, when I'm *just* on the brink, both my hands clenched in Gavin's bedspread, he stops and I'm left there, panting for breath.

Seconds later he starts licking me again, his tongue moving faster this time, and he slides his fingers inside me at last as I arch my back and groan while he strokes me and licks me at the same time.

I'm at the brink again before I know it, nearly screaming, and he stops.

"Keep going," I whimper. His fingers are still inside me but he kisses me again on the thigh, the hip, the belly. I get my bra off and he laps at one nipple, sucking it between his teeth, as he starts moving his fingers in me again, stroking my sensitive inner wall. I moan, arching my back.

And he stops. Of course. I nearly scream in frustration, and he climbs over me, his body between my legs, kissing me hard even though I can still taste myself on his lips, his erection rock-hard and insistent against me.

"Are you trying to kill me?" I whisper.

Gavin laughs, nuzzling his face against mine as his hips rock into me. I roll mine against him, the hard length of his erection firm against me.

"Marisol, I'm going to make you come so hard you forget where you are and what decade it is," he murmurs into my ear.

White heat clenches inside me. I've got both hands on his back and I can feel the muscles there tense as he rocks against me again, his hard bulge against my clit. Then he moves back, standing from the bed, both hands on his belt as he undoes it and unbuttons his jeans.

I sit up on the edge of the bed, watching him. He moves slowly, watching me watch him, snaking the belt out of its loops and tossing it away. Before he can push his jeans down, over his hips, I reach out and grab him by the waistband, pull him toward me, and press my lips to the hard muscles in his chest, my palm flat against his erection.

Gavin groans, and I give him a firm squeeze before I finally push his pants off, his cock springing out. He brings his mouth down to mine as I stroke him once, root to tip, slow and hard.

I want him *now*, so much I'm nearly trembling, the empty ache inside me threatening to take over. The temptation to guide him inside me right this second is dizzying.

He breaks the kiss. He leans over, grabs a condom out of his bedside drawer, kisses me again. His tongue doesn't leave my mouth as he pushes me back against the leather headboard of his bed, my legs still around him as he pins me on top of him.

I'm half-undone, my breath coming in ragged gasps as he grabs my hips in his hands, pulling me down, the length of his cock rubbing against my clit and lips.

"I've never wanted anyone the way I want you," he whispers. "It's fucking unholy, Marisol."

"Then quit teasing me," I murmur, rocking my hips so he rubs against me again, because *God* it feels good, my whole body overheated and too sensitive.

I want him *now*. I want to just slide him inside me bare so I can feel him skin-to-skin with nothing between us. The foil packet crinkles as Gavin goes to tear it open, but instead I put my hand over it.

"How long have you been clean?" I whisper.

His hand tightens into a fist around the still-wrapped condom.

"Twenty-four weeks on Wednesday," he murmurs, locking eyes with me. "Nearly six months."

I swallow hard and put one hand on his face, my thumb tracing his bottom lip.

"And you don't... have anything?"

There's probably nothing less sexy that I could say right now, but a slight smile lights his face and he tilts his head, kissing the inside of my wrist.

"I don't," he says. "But Marisol, it's—"

"Don't use it," I whisper.

His eyes search mine for a moment, and I feel like my heart stops beating.

"I want you inside me bare," I whisper, my voice barely audible. "Please?"

"Jesus, fuck yes," he breathes. "But Marisol, it's not—"

The sentence turns to a low groan as I guide him to my entrance, back arched, because I can't take this any longer. The head of his cock pushes between my lips, and for a moment, he pauses, like he needs to collect himself.

Then Gavin pulls me down in one hard, deep stroke and my brain just about shuts off. I think I whimper, my eyes closed, but he fills me so perfectly that I feel like I can't even move or I'll come flying apart.

He holds me down, cock hilted inside me as he rocks back and forth.

"I fucking *live* for that noise," he says, his voice low and rough, his fingers digging into my hips so hard I'll probably have bruises.

"What noise?" I gasp.

He rocks again and I bite my lip, moving my hips to match him because right now, the tiniest motion is indescribably intoxicating, like he could push me over the edge with a single thrust.

"The noise you make when I first enter you," he says. "This primal *groan* as I slide my cock in that sounds as if it's all you ever wanted."

Gavin shifts slightly, pushing me harder against the headboard as he thrusts, somehow going even deeper, and I gasp again, my fingernails digging into his shoulders.

"You're going to shred me to ribbons," he says.

"Sorry," I whisper.

I unclench my hands, but the moment I do he thrusts again, hard and deep, hitting every single spot inside me so perfectly my toes curl and I grab him again, another moan escaping my lips.

"I didn't say I minded," he says. "You can tear me apart completely if it means fucking you skin-to-skin like this."

"I can't help it," I murmur. "You feel so good I lose control."

He kisses me and we keep moving together, slow and deep, even though I want him faster and harder. I *crave* letting him push me into this headboard and take me mercilessly.

It's not what happens. Instead he drives me completely out of my mind without ever speeding up, even though I'm whimpering and moaning, my nails probably opening gashes in his back because I'm on the brink and he won't let me dive off it.

"You're fucking beautiful when you're about to come," he whispers.

He thrusts again, a little harder and faster, and I moan, my eyes half-open as I reach up with one hand and grab the top of the headboard, *something* to give me leverage.

"Just don't stop," I say, the words barely audible.

He thrusts again, burying himself *hard* this time, and I feel as if parts of me are starting to crumble, like this feels so good I might just fall into pieces.

Gavin's hand snakes up my arm and his laces his fingers through mine, holding it there.

"Not a chance," he says, and drives himself into me again and again, squeezing my hand like he's hanging on for life.

"Gavin," I whimper, and then I get hit by a tidal wave. I come so hard I feel like I'm drowning, tossed up and down as it breaks over me in slow motion and breaks me to pieces. I don't even know which way is up for a moment, but I think I might be shouting. I might be shouting Gavin's name.

I come up for air, still feeling adrift and tossed, and Gavin's got his face in my neck as he hammers himself into me, so I squeeze him between my legs as hard as I can.

"Fuck, Marisol," he shouts, and then he comes, his cock throbbing and pulsing as he spends himself inside me, saying my name over and over like he's chanting it.

We stop moving slowly, our hands and bodies still locked together as an insane, *possessive* feeling steals over me.

It's the feeling that right now, no matter what, he's mine and *this* is mine, and it can't be undone. That I'll always have this, and it's beautiful and perfect and pure, and only the two of us will ever know or understand.

It's almost overwhelming. Almost.

Gavin murmurs something into my neck that I can't hear. He lowers our hands, still locked together, to our sides.

"What?" I murmur.

He kisses my neck, then my lips, but he doesn't say it again.

CHAPTER THIRTY-NINE
Gavin

I don't tell her again. The moment I said it I knew it was too soon, that it was better to let that moment be perfect and whole and beautiful the way it was.

So I stay quiet, and I kiss her again, and I feel like time has stopped and the world has slowed and there's nothing else but the two of us.

As we drift off, Marisol nestled against my shoulder with my arm around her, she reaches across me and runs her fingers down the inside of my other forearm. She plants her fingertips and then circles them around a few spots, slower and slower until she stops, finally asleep.

Track marks. Very old ones, from before I blew out those veins and had to move on. I see her looking sometimes, and when she thinks I'm asleep she sometimes runs her fingers over the scars like she's reminding herself of them, but she's never asked. I've told her she can, but she hasn't.

I fall asleep slowly, like I'm being washed out to sea.

• • •

I come awake all at once, my eyes snapping open and my body going rigid before I even know *why* I've woken up but I lay there, tense and listening, every hair on my body standing.

Then I hear it: the door opening. The beep of someone punching a code into my alarm system, muttering curses, punching the code in again.

Please be a burglar, I think, but I fucking know better and I slide out of bed as quietly as I can.

Marisol stirs, her eyes opening just a sliver.

"It's nothing," I whisper, pulling on my jeans.

She seems to accept this. Her eyes drift closed again, and I steal for my bedroom door, closing it firmly behind me.

Liam doesn't even look up at the sound of the door shutting. He's leaning with his forearm on the wall, head planted on that, and just from the way he's sagging I know he's wasted again.

I feel like I've been punched in the gut, the air out of me. Not now. Please, God, not now, not while Marisol's here. Anything but that.

"Fucking cock-arsed fuck numbers," he mutters, the glow of the panel lighting his face as it beeps again.

I race downstairs, heart pounding, every beat saying *not now, not now*.

"I forgot the bleeding code," he says as I come downstairs. Instead of answering I push him out of the way and punch it in myself, the panel turning green and blinking the time, 5:18am.

"You can't be here," I say, keeping my voice low.

He leans against the wall again, moving like his joints are all a little loose. There's still a bandage wrapped around the arm that he used to break the window, though the bandage is dirty and looks like he's been scratching at it.

In the back of my mind, an alarm starts going off.

"Fuck I can't," he says much too loudly, as if this is a joke. "I am, aren't I?"

"You said you'd gone back to rehab."

Liam just laughs, and the sound is somewhere between a hoot and a high-pitched giggle, unhinged, and unnerving.

"I thought you'd have a laugh at that," he says, pushing himself off the wall as he scratches absent-mindedly at his arm. "You know, like we used to? Rehab's for quitters, mate."

I recognize this mood of Liam's. It's Liam's come-down mood, after he's been high for a while — cocaine, booze, maybe pills, God knows what — and it starts to wear off, when he gets ugly and vindictive, sets things on fire, goes out and crashes cars.

"Get out," I say, forcing my voice to stay low and calm because I know from long experience that anger will just fuel him.

"I'm sorry I came in past curfew," he says, a nasty edge in his voice.

"Get the fuck out, Liam."

Liam just laughs, then turns, stumbling, and starts walking for the kitchen.

"Leave the palace," he says to no one, his voice a high-pitched mockery of mine.

I lurch forward, grab his good arm and yank him back. He stumbles again, tripping into the table behind him where my junk mail's sitting.

"It's not a *fucking* joke," I say, anger flaring inside me, my grip tight on Liam's arm as he tries to turn away. "Now get—"

Behind him, the mirror balanced on top of the table wobbles, then begins rolling.

Before I can even move it rolls off and crashes to the floor, shattering into a million pieces.

We both stare at it, mouths open, for a moment. Then I take Liam and *haul* him toward the front door as he starts laughing again, stumbling along.

"That's seven years, mate," he says, giggling. "Maybe now you'll get all the shit—"

I step on a shard of glass and it slices into my toe. I unhand Liam and stop, grinding my teeth together so I don't shout.

"It's started," he says. "Bloody hell, that was *fast*."

Then he stops talking for one blessed second as I try to get the glass out of my foot in the dark, dripping blood onto the floor.

"Hello," Liam says suddenly.

My head snaps up.

Marisol's standing at the bottom of the stairs, barefoot with her dress on again, staring at Liam open-mouthed.

No.

"That's why you didn't want me coming home," he says, the nasty edge back in his voice. "You should have *said* something, mate."

"Liam, just *go*," I say, still standing on one foot, my toe bleeding.

"Liam?" Marisol says.

"Meant to sneak in past curfew but forgot the bleeding security code," he says. "I did remember my key this time, though, got in through the front door."

"He's drunk and he broke in."

"You have a key?"

"Course I've got a key, I live here," Liam says, then looks over at me. "Did Gavvy fail to *fucking* mention that?"

"He needed a place to stay," I say desperately, as if that can possibly explain.

Marisol's staring at Liam's bandaged arm. I feel as if a piano's hanging above me, ready to fall.

"*You* broke the window," Marisol says, her voice quiet and strangled, still staring at Liam.

Then she looks at me, tears in her eyes.

"When you got that call you knew it was him," she says. Her voice is shaking, and she squeezes her eyes shut. "In the hotel room. After we... *God.*"

"You're the fake girlfriend," Liam says. "Is he actually sticking it to you?"

"I'm sorry," I say, and step gingerly on the floor. There's a sea of broken glass between me and her and I start navigating it, leaving smears of blood where I've been.

"This is why you didn't want me at your house," she says, watching me, her eyes filled with tears. "Because *he* was here and you didn't want me to know."

"Yeah, I'm a dirty fucking secret," Liam says. "But someone's got to give Gavvy here a bit of fun and it's certainly not you, is it?"

"Shut the fuck up," I growl.

I step on another piece of glass and swear.

"It's a dirty fucking secret that we got shitfaced last week and you went on about and on about how much you miss your ex," Liam says, starting to laugh again.

"What?" I say.

That never happened. He's just lying, the ugly, jealous, vindictive look in his eye practically a gleam.

"Yeah, you were saying how you ought to give her a call and see what she's up to, maybe you could write another song about her," he goes on, turning toward Marisol. "He'd probably have done it if he hadn't lost his phone after snorting a mountain of coke."

"He's lying," I tell Marisol.

"What's that saying? Tigers don't change their spots?" Liam says, laughing. "He can tell you whatever fancy fucking words he wants, love, but Gavvy belongs in the gutter and we all fucking know it."

"Shut the *fuck* up," I say, pulling glass from a deep cut in my foot, gritting my teeth together.

"He's been asking me where he can score smack, you know," Liam says to Marisol, his tone almost conversational. "D'you know what that is? It's heroin, and I keep telling him I don't think it's a very good idea but—"

I lurch across broken glass for Liam, but he's wearing shoes and he manages to move out of the way, laughing his head off.

"He's only not back on it because he's not found it in Los Angeles yet," Liam goes on, backing away, glass crunching beneath his feet. "He may like you but he's only got one true love. Any junkie who says otherwise is a fucking liar."

She hasn't said anything in a long time, but she's crying silently, looking from me to Liam.

"None of it's true," I say desperately. My feet are screaming, bloody footprints across my floor.

"He's not living here?" she asks, her voice strange and detached and quiet.

I hold my breath for a moment.

"He was," I say, locking eyes with her.

"I've got a whole bedroom," Liam offers. "Upstairs, first door on the right, help yourself to anything inside though I don't think there's anything left after our little celebration Saturday night."

"What happened Saturday?" she asks me.

"I went to a movie."

"We drank a handle of whiskey and then went out in Hollywood," Liam says.

"That didn't *fucking* happen—"

"—These two girls gave us some pills and I've no idea what they were but I swear they slowed down time—"

"He's lying," I tell Marisol, my voice desperate and pleading.

"—I lost Gavin for a bit and when I found him, he was in the men's shoveling something up his nose, dunno what it was, some girl on her knees in front of him—"

She turns and runs back up the stairs. I grit my teeth and follow her, stepping on more broken glass, but I don't care. Behind me, Liam's laughing near-hysterically.

"People don't *change!*" he shouts.

"Marisol, I swear to God he's lying," I say. Every step is agony — I think there's still glass in my foot — but I ignore it, following after her.

She doesn't answer, but she goes to the guest rooms and yanks the doors open one by one until she finds Liam's.

It's a fucking mess, of course, and it reeks of unwashed sheets and the vague smell of cigarettes, every surface covered with dust and ash, the bedsheets simply in a pile in the middle of the bed. Marisol just stands in the doorway for a moment, staring at it, her shoulders shaking.

"I haven't done a single thing, I haven't had a drink, you *have* to believe me—"

She goes in, grabs something off a dresser, and comes back out, her face tear-streaked and her eyes flashing fire. As she walks past me, she shoves a piece of paper at my chest.

It's the final page of our fake-girlfriend contract.

"It was him," she shouts over her shoulder, then disappears into my bedroom again.

CHAPTER FORTY
Marisol

I shove my feet into my shoes, my whole body shaking. I have to get *out* of here, run away, leave before I completely fly apart into a sobbing, hysterical mess, and the floor's covered in glass so I can't do it barefoot.

"I'm sorry," Gavin says from the bedroom door for about the thousandth time, but I ignore him and dodge past, rushing back down the stairs. My feet crunch and squeak across the glass as Liam watches, slumped on the sofa, drinking something from a plastic bottle.

"I've saved you plenty of grief, you know," he calls out.

I grab my purse and open the door.

"And you as well," Liam says as I close it behind myself.

I take a deep breath of the cold night air as I cross Gavin's front yard, pulling out my phone to call an Uber. I know I'm crying and I think I might be sobbing, nearly hysterical, but at the same time I feel strangely detached from myself, from everything that's just happened, almost like I'm watching myself from above.

Liam lives with Gavin and Gavin lied about it, I think, over and over again. *He's living with the person who dragged him into addiction in the first place, years ago, and he lied to me about it.*

Tears drip from my chin to my neck, and I wipe them off furiously, almost to the gate. The front door opens behind me, but I don't turn around.

"Marisol, *please*," Gavin says, his footsteps crossing the yard. "Don't go, I'm sorry, I should have told you—"

"I feel like a fucking idiot," I shout. "I just believed everything you said and this whole time you've been—"

I swallow and grit my teeth together against a sob, but it wracks through my body anyway.

Gavin's behind me, and he reaches for my shoulder but I step backward.

"I don't know what you lied about," I whisper, my hands balled in fists at my sides. "Everything you said about wanting to get better, about having a new life and leaving that one behind, about moving to Los Angeles to get away from your old friends? Did you mean *any* of that? Or were you out getting high with Liam and using me the rest of the time?"

Gavin looks broken.

"I meant everything," he whispers. "Every single thing I told you I meant, Marisol, Liam's a fucking liar."

I just shake my head.

"He's got a *bedroom*," I say, swallowing hard. "How long has he been there?"

"Since you kissed me on the cheek," he admits.

"A *month*?" I ask, my voice dropping to a bare whisper. I didn't think it was that long, and now I feel like even more of a gullible idiot.

301

"I've also not done a single thing I shouldn't have in a month," Gavin says, his jaw flexing. "Everything else he's lying about, getting drunk, getting high, talking about my ex—"

"How am I supposed to believe you?"

"Does it seem like I've been doing that?" he asks, flinging one arm in the direction of the house, pointing at Liam inside. "Or does it seem like I've been sober as a nun? If Liam were going to drag me back down he'd already have done—"

"He did!" I whisper-shout, since my voice won't work quite right. "He already did once, Gavin, and it only ended because that roadie died—"

"Allen."

"—because Allen died and the record company forced you into rehab, not because you *wanted* to get better."

I turn my back and hit the button on the gate. It starts rolling open.

"But I do," Gavin says. "Marisol, I swear to God."

I slither through the gate as soon as I can and walk out into the road, hoping that Gavin doesn't follow me.

He does, limping onto the asphalt.

"Don't leave," he begs. "I've meant everything I've said and should never have lied, only I—"

Headlights shine around the corner, and I glance down at my phone. It's the Uber.

"—I wanted you to think I'm a better person than I am."

The car slows in front of me, and I look at Gavin, then at the bloody footprints leading through the still-opening gate.

"Please," he whispers.

I wipe tears off my face and shake my head.

Then I get into the car and close the door behind me, burying my face in my hands.

"Uh, is everything okay?" the driver says.

"Please just go," I whisper.

We drive off.

CHAPTER FORTY-ONE
Gavin

I can only watch as the tail lights of the car drive away and disappear around a bend in the road, a hollow space opening up in my chest, threatening to swallow me whole.

You did lie to her, a small, ugly voice whispers in my head. *You had a thousand chances to tell her the truth and you never did.*

Could be that Liam's right.

I walk back through the gate, pain shooting up both legs from the broken glass. I hit the button to close the gate, then collapse against it, sliding down until I'm sitting on the ground, eyes closed.

Marisol's gone. I took in Liam, I lied to her, and now she's gone. I didn't want to tell her because I didn't want to admit to her that sometimes I'm weak, I didn't want her to think I wasn't serious about recovery, and now she's gone and I don't know if she'll come back.

Everything around me turns to shit, I think. *I can't stop fucking up, I can't fix it, and it doesn't even matter if I try.*

Because I did try. Holy *fuck* did I try, and now she's gone after I've walked through broken glass to get her back. Not that I can even blame her. It was only the smart thing to do.

There's a flat, empty blackness inside me, threatening to spill over. I want to crawl into a deep, dark hole and never come out, never bother fucking trying to do anything right again because I clearly can't.

Liam's right. He's a fucking monster and I hate him, but he's right. People don't change, least of all me.

The front door opens again. I don't open my eyes, because I can't even fucking look at him right now, but I hear his footsteps come up to me and stop.

"Fuck off," I say.

"Heads up," Liam says.

I open my eyes just in time for a plastic bottle to come flying at me, and I catch it reflexively. It's a flat rectangular bottle of Popov vodka, half empty.

"You seem like you could use it," Liam says, pulling out his own flat bottle and taking a long drink.

"I don't want it," I say, leaning back against the gate again. "I want you to fucking leave me alone and get out of my life."

I'm not even angry, though I should be. I'm shirtless in my front yard, feet shredded, and I've just fucked up the best thing that's ever happened to me, and I want to slide into a black hole and forget all about everything.

"She was always going to leave, mate," he says, sloshing the bottle to his lips again.

"Fuck off."

"If this is all it fucking took? She was going to leave anyway. You ought to be thanking me."

I throw the bottle at his head, but it's small and plastic and it bounces off his shoulder while he laughs.

"You don't want to get rid of that just yet," he says, tossing it back at me casually. "Take the edge off. Here, I'll leave for a bit so you haven't got a witness."

Liam walks back to my front door, weaving unsteadily, and walks into my house, leaving the door wide open while I look at the bottle in my hand.

Take the edge off. Just the edge.

It can't get much fucking worse, right?

I unscrew the cap. The stuff smells like paint thinner, cleaning fluid, and sweet oblivion. I close my eyes, hold it to my mouth and take a single sip.

It *burns*, all the way down, the pain and fire blossoming through my chest, the first alcohol I've had in nearly six months. It goes straight to my head and dulls all the sharp edges. It's fucking *divine*.

I take another sip. Then a gulp. I'm sitting in my front yard and it's not even six in the morning yet but I'm drinking shit vodka from a plastic bottle, letting the alcohol fall over my brain like a soft, warm, wool blanket that dulls everything out.

I finish it off, then chuck the bottle away.

Fuck it. Fuck everything.

CHAPTER FORTY-TWO
Marisol

I cry hysterically most of the way back to my apartment in the Uber, the sun coming up in a flat gray sky over downtown Los Angeles as I get home.

I hate *still* being awake at this time of day, which is usually because I've pulled an all-nighter. My eyes feel like they've been scraped out with spoons, except right now *all* of me feels like that, deflated and hollow.

How could I believe everything was that good?

Things like that don't happen to people like me. I don't get lucky, I fight and claw my way by until I force luck's hand.

I head inside my apartment. It's about the time I'd normally be getting up anyway, but I slump onto my bed.

The whole time, I keep thinking. *He kissed me and Liam was there. He told me about his past, about everything, and Liam was in his house then.*

All the dates, all the sex, everything, he was hiding Liam.

307

Why wouldn't he just tell me?

I glance over at my dresser, where I've got the addiction books stacked up. One's got a bookmark in it where Gavin was reading it last week while I studied.

I'm an idiot, I think one more time. *A total fucking idiot.*

• • •

The sun comes up. I have some coffee, some breakfast, I take a walk around my neighborhood and become capable of rational thought once more.

And I think Liam was lying. At least he was lying some, because there's no way Gavin could be getting shitfaced or doing *mountains* of cocaine and I wouldn't know.

Right?

But on the other hand, I was clueless enough to eat pot gummi bears like a moron. I'm naive as hell about drugs, and I know it, and even though he lied to me, I *still* trust Gavin. I shouldn't. The evidence is against it, but I do. But I shouldn't.

I'm making myself completely crazy.

I spend the day studying for finals, forcing my eyeballs to the page with an intensity I didn't even know I had. Drowning myself in work is the only thing that gets his face out of my head, that makes me stop thinking of him saying *I quite like you* or *I've never wanted anyone the way I want you* or even the way he teases me about needing to only touch me with rubber gloves.

Gavin doesn't call. He doesn't even text. That makes it ten times worse, the feeling that not only did he lie, he's not trying to fix it.

Maybe he doesn't care like you thought he did. Maybe he decided that being with you was a little too

308

much work, or that he needs someone cooler or more fun or more interesting.

I'm spiraling again, and I throw my phone onto my bed, out of reach, to keep myself from texting him myself.

Tomorrow, I tell myself. *Tomorrow we'll have a conversation like rational adults and we'll discuss this and I don't know, maybe it will be fine. Maybe he'll have somehow magically not betrayed me eight hours after I let him come inside me.*

Which happened because I trusted him.

God. How dumb can I be?

I take a deep breath, get out of my chair, and do twenty jumping jacks to distract myself.

Then I force myself through more class notes.

Gavin doesn't call.

CHAPTER FORTY-THREE
Gavin

I wake up when the sun hits my face, and I squeeze my eyes shut harder, trying to block it out but it doesn't quit.

I turn my head to the other side, still trying to escape, and I realize I'm on the ground, face down in the grass.

Fuck. *Fuck*. A breeze stirs the blades and they tickle my nose while I lie there, saying a quick, silent prayer that this isn't what it feels like.

Because it feels like my head's been filled with rocks, pounding and clashing every time I move it. It feels like my bones have been removed and replaced with an aching nausea. It feels like time has slowed just so that every moment can be more exquisitely painful: my head, my feet, every joint in my body.

And Marisol left. I lied, she's angry, and she's left. Fucking simple as that, though it feels like a hole's been bored through me.

I push myself to my knees, hands still in the grass, and assess. My eyes and mouth and throat are dry as the Sahara. I'm not wearing a shirt. My feet have scotch tape wrapped around paper towels around them, and there's blood soaking through.

I'm clammy and sweaty and tired and yet underneath my skin feels a little itchy and I roll my shoulders, flex my hands because it feels like I *need* to, like if I stop moving something bad will happen.

That's all to say: even though I feel like I've been punched in the gut and left on the side of the road, this is dreadfully, horrifically familiar. In a strange way, it feels like I've returned home after a long time away, and even though home is a rat-shit-filled hovel, I do know where I am.

I stand. My feet scream in pain, but I stumble toward the back door of my house, fight with the latch for a bit, then get inside. Liam's face down in the center of the living room, but he's breathing, and I lean against a wall for a moment, just glad to be out of the bright light.

Then I continue on to the kitchen. Water, coffee, see if there's any whiskey left, though the glass of water I drink makes me feel nauseous, so I grip the counter with both hands, head down, teeth gritted together, as I wait for the single-cup coffee maker to finish.

Over in the corner of the kitchen, I spot a phone. My phone, Liam's, I don't fucking know, but I make my way over and bend to pick it up like an eighty-year old man, every inch of my body protesting.

The thing's fucking shattered like someone threw it across the room, but it does turn on, and it's mine. I've got an absolute sea of notifications, and I slump against the counter, flipping through them.

All I'm looking for is her name, though I know it won't be there. I'm just hoping for a sign, a hint, *something.*

It's a long time before I notice that the date says it's Wednesday, and I stop scrolling. The gears in my head grind together, rusted together and stuck.

Wednesday?

No, it's Tuesday.

I open my phone, and even though I can barely see anything, I open the calendar. Wednesday.

It's not fucking Wednesday.

Open the news. Wednesday, everywhere. There's a bottle of something lying on its side behind the dishrack, half-hidden, and I grab it, then slide to the floor with my back against the cabinets.

I'm hungover as fuck, I'm itching inside my skin, and I'm clearly coming down from something. Cocaine at least, as that's Liam's favorite and I doubt it's hard to get in Los Angeles, but the itching tells me there may have been something narcotic.

With one hand, I unscrew the bottle, my eyes shut. I bring it to my lips and swallow, then swallow again and again. Jim Beam, I think, though I don't even bother checking.

And *there* it is, that nice soft warm blanket, everything going just a bit fuzzy and manageable. Thank *fuck*. I take a deep breath in, hand still around the bottle, exhale, taking things a moment at a time because that seems to be all I can manage, a moment at a time.

Then: Marisol in my front yard, tears running down her face, saying *I don't know what you lied about*. The way she looked at me and I felt like a monster and a worthless fucking puddle all at once.

I take another drink.

Then it's her, naked in my bed last night, whispering *I want you inside me with nothing between us* and I take two long swallows because I've fucked up the best thing that's ever happened to me and it only took eight hours.

I sit on the kitchen floor. I drink from the bottle and slowly, surely, the pieces start coming back and I begin fitting them together.

Marisol, leaving, my heart a rock in my chest. Liam tossing me the bottle, me drinking. Later, my arm around his shoulders as he took me into the house, wrapping my feet in paper towels and scotch tape, going on and on about some idea he had for a space mission.

More drinking. The sun up, bright, shining through the windows; a blanket over a window in an unused bedroom.

Liam doing a line off a sheet of notebook paper, handing me the straw, only letting me do a bump since I wasn't up to it yet.

Fuck.

Then blurred memories, gray mush. Then a girl showing up, smiling at first but uncertain the minute she saw the broken mirror in the entryway.

I hold my breath and take another drink.

No. *Please* no. Please anything but that. Heroin again but not *that.*

The girl disappears but Liam's there, pills in my hand, washing it down with more whiskey and then sitting on the couch staring at the ceiling, feeling *so fucking good.*

Then nothing. The film seems to stop there, just ending. I'm still nauseous but now I'm drunk as well, and I look at my phone again as if she could have called in the past five minutes and I'd have missed it.

I want to text her, call her, hear her voice and plead with her, but I can't call her now, like this. I've compounded fucking up with more fucking up and now I'm on the kitchen floor with a bottle of whiskey and no fucking shirt and I don't even know what pills I took last night.

I've got to fucking *do* something, get myself out of it, so I roll over onto my knees and drag myself up until I'm standing, most of my weight on the kitchen counter. Slowly, unsteadily, I walk around Liam and up the stairs, to my bedroom, so I can shower and see how fucked up my feet are, and as long as I don't look at the bed and as long as Marisol's not left anything there, it's okay.

But I'm almost to my bedroom, head spinning, when I make the mistake of looking over at the bedrooms across the hall, the one where we tacked a blanket over the window and then spent hours on the floor, reminiscing about Dirtshine's first days in London, the wretched flats we used to live in, the wretched girls, the wretched people.

And then a few last snapshots: the girl coming out of Liam's room, high as a kite, not even looking at me as she left.

A knot unwinds in my chest.

Me, standing in the doorway of the room with the blanket over the window, looking down at Liam on the floor. Syringe in the back of one hand as he pushes down the plunger and the rush of sheer *jealousy* that tore through me.

Liam leaning against the wall, eyes half-closed, his words slow and dreamy.

Sorry mate, that's all.

Me nodding and turning, even though my haze knowing that it's for the best. Then Liam's voice: *wait.*

Here.

He tosses a tiny bag full of white powder at me, and then his eyes slide shut, his face ecstasy as I catch it. Then my memory's blank again.

I barely make it to the sink in my bathroom before I vomit Jim Beam, because now I know why I feel like I'm itching inside my own skin, why my feet don't hurt as much as they should.

I sit on the toilet, shaking, and try to think, but then I hear Liam stir downstairs, get up, trip over something, curse. I think of Marisol's books on her dresser and then of Marisol, the Korean restaurant where we had our first *real* date. The night I told her everything, or almost everything, and she took me home with her anyway.

My hands are shaking, but I manage to get my phone out. The battery's nearly dead, the screen completely shattered, but after a few tries I get Nigel's number up.

I hit the green button and hold the phone to my ear.

CHAPTER FORTY-FOUR
Marisol

Wednesday afternoon I finally give in and call. I still don't know how I feel, but I know that *this* is killing me. Whatever's happened I just want to hear his voice, talk to him, because even a day without Gavin has left a strangely-shaped hole in my heart.

But it rings until it goes to voicemail. I try again an hour later and the same thing happens. Both times I hang up without leaving a message, because you don't leave a message for this kind of thing.

Hours pass. I text.

Marisol: Can we talk?

Later:

Marisol: *Please?*

Later still:

Marisol: Are you okay?

• • •

I'm eating a burrito and skimming back through lecture notes when my phone rings. I nearly knock my chair over getting to it, then nearly choke on my burrito trying to swallow.

Nigel.

I consider not answering. I'm not sure that I can have a calm, rational conversation with him about the *next steps* in Gavin and I's relationship right now. If I hear what event or restaurant or show Gavin and I are supposed to go to next, I might throw up or cry or do both at the same time.

But then I'd just have to call him back later, so I answer.

"Hi, Nigel."

"Hello, Marisol. This is Nigel."

That's why I said Hi, Nigel.

"How are you?" I ask, hoping to get to the point soon.

There's an awkward pause, more awkward than most of Nigel's pauses.

"It's about Gavin, actually," he says.

My heart feels like it's been filled with lead and it's dropping.

"What happened?" I blurt out.

"It's a bit complicated," Nigel says. "He's, well, technically he's fine, but he *has* gone back to rehab. Would it be possible for us to meet in person?"

I don't answer for a long moment, but I sit heavily on my bed, eyes filling with tears, the books I got on addiction directly in my line of sight. All I can think about is Gavin, on my bed as I studied, lying on his side, engrossed in one of them.

I remember looking over, seeing that, and thinking, *he's really trying*. I took it as evidence that I wasn't doing something stupid by being with him, but I guess I was wrong.

"Yeah," I whisper, because I don't trust my voice. "Where?"

• • •

After arguing logistics for at least twenty minutes, Nigel and I wind up at a burger joint in my neighborhood, though that means I have to listen to him complain about parking for a good five minutes, my nerves slowly being frayed and rubbed until they're down to just the electrified wire.

"I don't care!" I finally whisper-shout.

Nigel's halfway through removing his windbreaker, and he looks startled.

"I don't care where you parked or how you had to walk *four whole blocks* to get here, just tell me what happened!"

He clears his throat. He adjusts his glasses, and though he looks ruffled, he at least doesn't look *upset*.

"I'm not exactly sure as Gavin didn't enlighten me on the particulars," he says. "He simply called, said he wanted to go back to rehab, and gave me a few instructions. I haven't seen him or spoken further."

Before I grab him and shout *what were the instructions*, he puts a cardboard box about the length and width of my forearm on the table between us. I pull my hands away from it like it's filled with spiders or something, because a heavy sense of dread presses against me, threatening to suffocate me before we even order.

It feels like a goodbye. If you want to work things out with someone, you answer their calls. You don't send a delegation with a gift.

"He asked me to give you these," Nigel says.

"What is it?"

"They look like tapes."

I feel like I might puke on the box, my heart slamming in my chest, but I take a deep breath and open one flap. Nigel's right. It's half-filled with cassette tapes in plastic jewel cases, the labels on them scribbled and written over and crossed out in Gavin's terrible handwriting.

It feels even *more* like a goodbye, and I hold my breath so I don't cry, my throat slowly closing off.

"He also asked that I initiate the agreed upon transfer of funds," Nigel says, his voice a low whisper. "As we discussed, Larry's firm will be in charge of making sure that it goes through all the proper legal channels and you're credited as a consultant—"

"Am I supposed to play these?" I ask, still staring.

"I assume so?" Nigel says. "The labels are rubbish, so I've got no clue."

I pick one up and turn it over in my hand. On the label, I can just barely make out the words *shrimp heads*, and on the back, *rubber gloves*. The night we went on a secret, unplanned second date for fish and chips. We walked up and down the beach in the dark, holding hands, and even though I didn't admit it I knew there was *something*, even then.

They go on. *Bathtub. Chopsticks. Queen Bess,* all stupid nonsense phrases that couldn't possibly mean anything to anyone else, but I feel like I've been knifed through the heart.

And *now* I'm crying, tears rolling down my face helplessly as I clench my teeth together, fist in front of my mouth, trying desperately not to make a scene in the middle of a restaurant.

He's getting rid of them.

Nigel looks politely baffled at my reaction, and folds his hands on the table in front of himself.

"We can discuss the matter of your continued involvement in a few weeks when he's out again," he offers. It sounds like he's trying to be gentle, and I just nod because I don't trust myself to actually say anything out loud.

This is my fault, I think. *I shouldn't have left like that, I should have stayed and talked about it. I just...*

I swallow hard. My hands are shaking, but another label catches my eye, this one crossed out twice before it reads, simply, *say yes.* I stand, nearly knocking over my chair.

"Thanks," I manage to whisper to Nigel, my voice coming out weird and strained. "I gotta go."

"We've not even—"

I don't hear the rest of whatever he has to say, because I'm already out the door at nearly a run, desperate to get out of there before I have a full and total meltdown.

• • •

The box of tapes is sitting on my floor, and I'm on the bed, elbows on my knees, face in my hands, staring at it. I'm crying so hard that tears are running down my arms. I've got the hiccups, so every breath I take goes breath-hiccup-sob, and I'm a snotty mess to boot.

It's wretched. I hate Liam, and I hate Nigel, and I hate Gavin, but mostly I hate myself for thinking that this could work. I hate myself for believing that I could help him, that my presence was going to make any difference at all in his life.

320

Because he was always going to go back. He was always going to relapse. Junkies only love one thing, and it takes a long time to get over her.

I don't want to open the box again. I don't want to look at the labels on all the tapes, and I don't want to find a tape player in the box as well, but I do. I shouldn't pop in *shrimp heads / rubber gloves*, but I do.

It takes me a long, long time to hit play. At first it's just static. The sound of something being bumped, then resonating, a guitar maybe.

Gavin clears his throat. He strums a chord. Stops. Fiddles with the guitar for a bit. I'm on the floor next to the tape player, curled against my dresser, huddled in the dark, praying that there's nothing on this tape even though I know there is.

Finally, he starts up again and now it sounds like an actual song. Four bars in, he starts singing.

Whisper me to sleep, your fingers on my heart. Starshine on the ocean and you —

I hit the stop button, sobbing so hard I'm shaking again.

I can't do this now. I can't. Maybe in a week. Maybe in a month.

But I know that if I listen to any more of these tapes, all labeled with the things we did together, the things we said to each other, it'll destroy me.

I shove the box under my bed and cry myself to sleep.

CHAPTER FORTY-FIVE
Marisol

Two days later, on Friday, I get the letter. It's in Gavin's handwriting and it's got his name on the return address, which is for a rehab center in Malibu, and I stand in front of the row of apartment mailboxes staring at it in my hand like it might bite me.

He couldn't even talk to me, I think, the words echoing around my brain. *He had to write because he couldn't even stand to have a conversation.*

Not even over the phone.

I'm an idiot.

I'm tempted to tear it into pieces and throw it into the apartment's garbage bin, because I want to forget that I was ever naive and starstruck and *dumb* enough to fall for a man who can't even dump me properly, but I don't. I march up three flights of stairs to my apartment, open the door, shut it firmly, lock it, throw my bag on the bed, and take a deep breath.

Then I sit on the bed and open the letter as my heart tries to claw its way out of my throat.

Marisol,

I'm sorry. I keep starting this letter only to crumple it up and toss it in the bin because I don't know how to do it properly, but I've decided that this time whatever comes out of my pen will have to do, so here it is.

I fucked up. I fucked up once and then I kept at it. I fucked up until you left. When you were gone I kept fucking up and now I'm here and I'm not even allowed to make phone calls for the first week, that's how much I've fucked up.

I should have just told you about Liam. The reasons why I didn't sound stupid when I say them out loud in the bright light of day.

Forgive me if you can. Somewhere along the way I fell in love with you so hard it terrifies me. I didn't think I could do that.

I've run out of things to say except I miss you and I've fucked up and if you asked for my heart I'd rip it out of my chest with my own hands. Letter-writing has never been my strong suit. You'd be appalled at how long this single page has taken me.

I'm sorry. I love you. I'm sorry.

Gavin

P.S. Liam's a fucking liar but I've a feeling you sorted that out already.

I read it at least five times, and by the end I'm sobbing again. I miss him. I was afraid I'd never see him again, that he had gone back to England or something to deal with his problems and he'd left me here with a box of tapes and a broken heart.

But he's in rehab, he's relapsed, and that's an ocean of uncertainty. I don't know that he'll ever be *better*. I don't know if addicts get *better* or if they're always just addicts who haven't had a fix in a long time.

Gavin, I'm terrified too, I think.

• • •

There's another letter Saturday. I haven't written back yet. There are about fifty pieces of notebook paper balled up, most in my trash can, but I haven't actually gotten through a letter yet. I don't know how to say *yes but no but yes but please don't break my heart, you could, you really could.*

Or maybe I should just say that.

Marisol,

I've made several small ceramic bowls. That's what we do in rehab, at least in California: we alternate between talking about our feelings and making pottery. Sometimes baskets. There's a painting class I could take but I'm absolute rubbish at it.

I'm not permitted phone calls until next Thursday, by the way. They've taken my mobile, and I'm pretty sure sneaking a call isn't too difficult to arrange but I'm trying, for once, to follow the rules properly. It isn't my forte but I'm really giving it a go, I swear.

This letter's longer, and he just goes on about the things he's doing at rehab — half sharing what's going on, half making fun of Californians — but I read it in his voice and then I close my eyes for a moment, just wishing he were here.

It's been five days. I know it's stupid to miss him, but I do.

324

In any case, I don't recommend going to rehab if you don't need to.

Love you.

Gavin

After another fifty tries, I finally write back on Sunday.

CHAPTER FORTY-SIX
Gavin

I'm the first to admit that I don't like rehab. It's boring and full of addicts, a whole bunch of people trying to find the motivation and inspiration to sober up for *good* this time, and that means that it's like walking around inside the pages of a self-help book.

That said, I do keep a list simply titled *reasons not to do heroin*. Marisol features heavily, but one line simply says *rehab is stupid and I hate it*.

My days are structured. I'm never alone. I've even got a roommate, because being in rehab, besides being boring, is also like being a citizen of a very mild police state: there's always someone around to watch you. Luckily Greg's not so bad, but privacy *is* a bit difficult to come by and mostly occurs in the shower.

Marisol's not written me back yet. I don't know if she will. I try not to think about it too much, at least for right now, because we are to *accept the things we cannot change* et cetera. And I know that if I finish my stint in here and haven't heard from her, I'm not giving up.

She's too important. That bit about the tearing my heart from my chest was probably a bit graphic, but it was true.

• • •

I get a letter Monday, so no need for dramatics. When I find it in the mail basket on my door — already opened to make sure it's not hiding illicit substances, of course — my heart practically leaps out of my chest. I take it to the bathroom and sit on the toilet with the lid down, the only place I can *actually* be alone to read what she's written me.

Gavin,

I'm not very good at writing letters either. I've started this one about a million times too, but I keep talking about the weather or something and then crumpling them up. The weather doesn't even make sense to talk about. We live in Los Angeles. What weather?

See, I did it again.

Here goes.

I don't know what I'm doing. I'm still hurt that you lied about Liam (I figured out he's a liar, no worries), but when Nigel gave me the tapes I thought for sure that it was your way of saying goodbye to me, and I was devastated. Because somewhere between rubber gloves and the alley, I started liking you and then quite liking you, and it's really strange that you, of all people, turned out to be the one for me but there it is.

Crap, your letter was a lot better. This sounds like I'm drawing up a contract or something.

I think I need you, and I think I love you, but I'm afraid that I shouldn't feel either way, that you'll wind up relapsing again and breaking my heart. I'm not sure I can do that.

Please advise. There's the lawyer-speak again.

Love,
Marisol

Shit. It didn't even occur to me that she could think the tapes meant goodbye. I was still wasted when I told Nigel to give them to her, but it was the only way I could think of just then to tell her how I felt. To beg her not to give up on me, to wear my heart on my sleeve and lay it all out there completely, no secrets, only rough takes and me fucking around on a guitar for a long time with lyrics that will definitely need some work.

They're all about her, after all. Or mostly about her, but she's the one who unlocked me again, made those songs possible at all. I guess I forgot to tell her that part.

I read Marisol's letter one more time, trying not to laugh at her for *please advise*. I know the letter doesn't say *I'll take you back* but it does say *I think I love you*. That's not something you think, it's something you feel, but it's Marisol. Of course she's going to analyze and overthink this. Strangely, I love that about her.

I keep writing her every day, and I start getting letters back. I don't know what to say, so I tell her about the terrible crafts I've made, I make fun of the woman who runs our group therapy sessions, I tell her the sunsets are sub-par because she's not there.

She writes about helping her parents move into their new apartment. The letter starts out casually, but it's nearly four pages long. She apologizes for not telling me about their problem sooner, that it's not nearly the same level of offense as my lie about Liam, but she understands how something like that grows until it takes over.

She writes about growing up in a dangerous part of Los Angeles, about knowing early that luck happened to other people and she was always going to have to fight for everything she got. About Brianna getting married to a rich guy while Marisol was in her second year of law school, a hundred grand in debt, and crying in the bathroom at their wedding wondering if she'd picked the wrong path.

I laugh, despite myself. I'm in rehab for the second time and Marisol's wondering if *she's* gone wrong in life.

I tell her I'm glad she picked the path that led her to me, at least.

• • •

Thursday I get telephone privileges. They don't give me my mobile back, but there's a small office with a phone, a signup sheet, no door, and a nurse in the next room. I've got forty-five minutes.

I spend the first ten with Nigel, because I need to get him out of the way. He confirms that he's done everything I've asked, and then, after a long awkward classic-Nigel pause, tells me Liam's gone home.

"He hasn't got a home," I point out.

"His mum's," Nigel says, slowly. "Back in Mountford Wye."

Liam's mum is a raging alcoholic with a mean streak, and his dad's not been heard from in years. As much as everything he's done is his own choice, et cetera, he didn't start off with a strong chance.

"Nigel," I say, exhaling. "He can't—"

"He's not your problem," Nigel says, and it's the most backbone I've ever heard him have. "You've made him your problem and look where it's gotten you."

He has a point. I hate thinking of Liam there, but Nigel's got a point. After a few minutes we hang up.

I wipe my sweaty palms on my trousers, suddenly nervous, but I pick up the receiver and dial her number.

"Hello?" she answers after the second ring.

I grin at just the sound of her voice, staring at the white wall in front of me like an idiot.

"Hey, it's me," I say.

"Hey," she says.

There's a one-second pause, and then she starts laughing. I start laughing. I have no idea why I'm laughing, except that it feels so good to hear her voice again that I'm giddy, and the two of us laugh into the phone like a couple of morons.

Finally, I stop, and take a deep breath.

"I made you a ceramic bowl to your specifications," I say. "Or I tried, at least."

CHAPTER FORTY-SEVEN
Marisol

The rehab center, which is simply called Tranquility Malibu, reminds me a *lot* of Noru. I guess it caters to basically the same clientele — rich people who can afford good sushi *and* drugs. There's probably more or less a revolving door between the two.

Nigel gave me a key to Gavin's car yesterday, and when I pull the purring black machine up to the guard station, he tries not to look surprised to see a short Latina girl in the driver's seat.

"You must be Miss Gomez," he says, smiling down at me through the window.

I'm caught off guard, because I wasn't exactly expecting him to know my name.

"Yes," I manage to say. "I'm, uh, here to see—"

"Mr. Lockwood," he says smoothly. "Of course. Take the second left and park anywhere."

I thank him and drive on. This is all a bit unnerving, and it reminds me too *much* of our first date, and of feeling like there was a bright spotlight on me, pointing out the imposter. Except now I am, technically, *almost* a millionaire, though honestly I've been too busy with finals to spend any of the money yet.

And I've spent quite a lot of time doing fancy things with Gavin, so even if I'll never actually feel at home with these people, I can fake it.

There's a front desk with a pretty, smiling blond woman. She *also* knows my name, gives me a badge that says VISITOR in big letters, offers me a sparkling water, and tells me that the visitor's lounge is through the door and second on the right.

I'm heart-stoppingly nervous. I don't know what I'm going to do. I don't know what I'm going to say, because even though we've been writing and calling, this feels like the first real step down a road with no street lamps.

Besides, despite hours googling and a pile of research, I don't feel like I know what to say to him about this. *Sucks that you relapsed, I wish you hadn't? I would really prefer you not do it again?*

I want you back but I'm afraid you're broken and I'll get hurt trying to fix you?

Outside the visitor's lounge doorway, I take a deep breath. I clench and unclench my hands, trying to release some of the tension.

And I go inside. There are a few people in there but Gavin has one whole side of the lounge to himself, because he's pacing back and forth with his hands in his pockets like a caged animal.

Then he turns, sees me, and grins. All my nerves suddenly melt away, and I grin back.

In seconds I'm in his arms, and he's squeezing me so tight I can barely breathe, picking me up, and whirling me around as I yelp. He puts me down but doesn't let me go, one hand on the back of my head, and I close my eyes and inhale his scent, my nose buried in his neck.

"I missed you," he whispers. "I'm sorry."

"I missed you too," I whisper back.

He pulls back slightly, his hand cupping my face. He strokes a thumb across my cheek, his deep brown eyes gazing into mine, like there's something he's about to say, right there below the surface.

He doesn't say it. Instead he kisses me, our lips just barely touching, soft and gentle like the kiss is an apology too. I kiss him back the same way, standing on my tiptoes, slow and gentle even though my heart's hammering nearly out of my chest.

Inside I come *alive*. The second he touches me I'm a writhing sea of lava, a volcano set to explode, heat and pressure barely contained.

It's a long kiss. By the end of it my fingers are wound through his hair, my body is pressed against his, Gavin's tongue is in my mouth and we're exploring each other like it's our first kiss again. I finally pull away, eyes closed, stroking my hand through his hair while he draws circles on my back with one hand.

There's a crumpling sound to my right. We both startle and look over.

We're being watched. There are still three other people in the visitor's lounge, and all three are simply *watching* us with detached, mild interest as if we're baseball on television or something.

I swallow, and my face flushes hot. I'd totally forgotten they were there. Gavin's hand keeps making small circles on my back.

"Would you like to go for a walk?" he asks.

• • •

Tranquility Malibu has a huge, beautiful garden. It's surrounded by a ten-foot wall, but it's a classy wall, covered in climbing bougainvillea. The whole place is a faux Italian villa, complete with shaded patios and grape arbors, a manmade stream of clear water running through the careful landscaping.

I feel like I'm on vacation at a spa, not visiting someone in rehab.

"See? It hardly feels like you're in prison at all," Gavin says as we stroll under the arbor, the warm sun behind us.

"I was just thinking maybe I should develop a heroin addiction so I could—"

I stop short, holding my breath, because he is *in rehab* and the last thing I need to do is make light of the situation.

But he looks at me and starts laughing.

"Have a week at a posh spa in Malibu?" he says.

"I'm sorry," I say. "The FAQ page said that when I visited, I shouldn't make fun of rehab or talk about the negatives, just focus on keeping the patient in the moment to help your recovery."

"Well, there are better ways to take a holiday at a posh spa," he says. "Such as taking a holiday at a posh spa. You can skip the heroin all together, in fact."

He still hasn't told me what, exactly, happened after I left on Tuesday. He's alluded to it, but he hasn't told me the details, and I'm dreading having to hear them.

I don't *want* to. I want to pretend that he *is* on holiday, I'm visiting, and when he's out everything will go back to what it was before, but I know I can't. Not if this is going to work.

I change the subject and ask about Greg, his roommate, who Gavin thinks isn't taking recovery very seriously. We talk about nothing for a while, walking up and down the paths in the garden, the little fake brook burbling alongside us.

After a while, we've seen everything. We've discussed all the plants, and though it *feels* normal and nice, there's still that weird tension of things unsaid.

At the far end of the garden, there's a patch of grass under a stand of eucalyptus trees on a slight hill. Next to it is a table stacked high with white sheets. Gavin grabs one, flips it open, and spreads it out on the grass.

I watch this with my mouth open. I can't believe this place has picnic blankets stacked next to the picnic spot. That's next-level.

Gavin, on the other hand, looks faintly embarrassed.

"What?" he says, smiling, his arms crossed over his chest. "We can't just sit on the grass like the *peasantry*."

"You know I *am* the peasantry, right?"

He sits on the blanket and holds out one hand.

"Come on. It's very therapeutic."

I fold my legs under myself, careful of my skirt, and sit next to Gavin. There are a few other people wandering the gardens, though there's no one else up here on the grassy hill.

It's quiet. It's peaceful. It's lovely. It's all a bit weird. Gavin looks over at me and I don't make eye contact, but I can feel his gaze for a long time before he finally speaks.

"You've not asked me anything."

Here we go, I guess. I keep watching the people down in the garden.

"I know."

"It's not like you."

I take a deep breath and pull my knees in, careful with my skirt, tucking it between my thighs so I don't flash anyone.

"Do you remember our first date, when we got fish and chips and then walked down on the beach?"

"Of course. You were embarrassed to admit that you didn't want to have sex in front of a mirror."

I laugh, despite myself.

"I'd forgotten that."

"I hadn't. I've got a hell of a memory for everything even slightly racy you've ever said."

"So you remember me telling you I don't have a sex tape?" I ask.

"Yes, and it was a bloody relief," he says. "Not that I thought you did. Just..."

He trails off, shrugging.

"I never asked if you had one because I didn't want to know," I say, quickly, still staring down at the garden. "If you did, or you do, I knew I'd just look it up on the internet and then I'd end up watching you have sex with someone else, and I really didn't want to do that, so I never asked."

We lock eyes again.

"To the best of my knowledge I haven't got a sex tape," he says. "I wasn't always *exactly* sober during the act, but if it's not surfaced by now, it probably doesn't exist."

"That's not what I was getting at," I say, even as my eyes fill with tears.

Gavin's past with other women is something I've stayed far, far away from, but I'm more relieved than I thought I would be.

"Were you trying to explain how not knowing is better than getting hurt by the answer?" he asks.

I sniffle.

"Yeah, but you put it a lot better than I was going to," I admit.

"That's because I've been to *loads* of group therapy in the past ten days and I'm a fucking expert at discussing my feelings," he says.

A tear rolls down my face, even though I'm trying not to cry, and he reaches out and brushes my hair back from my face.

"Not all the answers are going to hurt," he says softly. "And I can't beg you to give me another chance if you don't know everything. It wouldn't be fair."

I exhale, still trying not to cry.

"Don't beg," I say, trying to make a joke of it. "It's a bad look for you."

"My point does stand."

I take a deep breath. I drag one thumb under my eye, wiping off some tears.

"Okay," I say. "Tell me everything. Start with the coma."

CHAPTER FORTY-EIGHT
Gavin

Marisol holds my gaze steadily. For a moment, I wish I'd not done this, that I'd let her continue in ignorance. But that's how I got into this in the first place, by hiding the truth because I didn't want her to see my ugliest side.

And here it goes, out into the light.

"I don't remember a lot of it," I admit, taking a deep breath. "Being in a coma and everything."

Marisol nods.

"I'll give you the short version first," I start, since I've got no idea where to begin.

The actual beginning is probably in a club in Yorkshire when I was seventeen, or when I picked up a guitar at fourteen, or when I befriended Liam in primary school because we both had black eyes and no lunch money.

"We were in Seattle, about to play a show," I say. "It was our first show back in the U.S., close to the end of the tour for *Lucid Dream*, and things had gotten a bit ugly with the band, so I'd taken to getting high before we went on stage to take the edge off, as it made dealing with Darcy and Trent a little easier. Of course, part of the reason things had gotten a bit ugly was that I had a vicious heroin problem, so I wasn't helping matters."

Marisol just watches me, her arms wrapped around her knees.

"On the tour, Liam and I had befriended one of the roadies, Allen, and when I say befriended I mean we got high together and I didn't even know his last name until I read his obituary. I think he liked hanging out with rock stars, and the two of us liked having a regular person there, as if it made us less degenerate. Anyway, Liam knew a bloke in Seattle so he went out to score, got the stuff, came back to the hotel room."

I go quiet for a moment, coming up to the edge of my memory of that night.

"I remember Allen thought Liam had gotten quite a lot," I say softly, staring off into the distance. "And Liam said he was celebrating being able to speak the language again, and besides, it wasn't much more than we'd been doing. But I took a bit less anyway, since I knew I had to stay upright for the show and couldn't hide behind a drum kit."

I swallow and rub my face with my hands. For a long time, I thought about that night constantly, but in the past month or so it's started to fade, just a little, at least until right now.

"We, you know, did the thing, shot up, and as it's going in the last thing I remember is thinking *holy shite this is fucking strong.*"

I look over at Marisol. She's just listening, cheek against her knees.

"And then I woke up in the hospital several hours later, strapped to a load of machines. Liam woke up in another twenty-four hours. They told me Allen was dead of an overdose when they found him. And then... the record label along with Darcy and Trent made it quite clear that my options were to enter rehab or have no more Dirtshine, and you know the rest."

Marisol considers this all for a moment. I think she knew the basics already, because it's not exactly a secret. It was in the news.

"Who found you?"

"Trent. He came to find us for the show, because he knew we were probably getting high and couldn't get ourselves there, and when we didn't answer the door he kicked it down."

Her eyebrows go up.

"Trent kicked down a door?"

"He did."

"He seems so... chill."

I laugh. I've seen Trent do some *spectacularly* un-chill things.

"He has hidden depths," I say.

"It must have been hard for him," she says.

"It was," I agree. "He came to visit me during my first stint and we talked it through for a good long while."

I pause for a moment.

"We both cried," I admit. "I think I cried more. Darcy cried when she visited too, though she shouted at me first. I did deserve it."

"And Liam?"

I crack the knuckles on my left hand, because this particular relationship is nothing if not *complicated*.

"Liam was my other half for nearly twenty years," I say, looking off into the distance. "He may as well be my brother. Dirtshine is his as much as it's mine. Just about everything I've ever done he's been a part of and vice versa."

"But?" she says softly.

"But when he left rehab his first stop was at a liquor store," I say. "We needed different things. I needed the band and he needed an escape, so I guess we both got what we wanted."

I swallow.

"And all the same, I couldn't turn him away when he showed up at my doorstep, even though I knew it was a bad idea. Because I always thought that, somehow, we'd get through this together. Even after I knew we wouldn't, I wanted us to. Going on without Liam just feels a bit... *wrong*."

Marisol reaches over and takes my hand. She doesn't say anything, just holds it. After a bit I lie back on the blanket and she joins me, staring up into the branches. I force myself not to think about how close she is right now, how I haven't seen her in over week, or how if I simply rolled over her body would be beneath mine, soft and warm and fucking irresistible.

"I don't really know Liam, but I think he feels the same way," she says softly. "And I think instead of getting better himself, he's trying to hold you back with him so he's not alone."

"Have you been talking to my therapist?" I ask.

"It's not exactly rocket science," she laughs.

We look up at the tree and the sky beyond together. She shifts her hand in mine, settling her fingers between my knuckles, and then, finally, she looks over at me.

"Tell me what happened after I left before I lose my nerve," she says, her deep brown eyes close to mine.

I kiss her. I can't help myself.

"You can't evade the question," she says when I pull back.

I turn my face skyward again and steel myself, because while everything that happened before was Past Gavin, this was *me*. This wasn't some drug-addicted arsehole who hurt people. This was me, hurting Marisol.

"The very first thing I did was chug half a bottle of vodka," I start.

I list everything I remember mechanically, staring up at the sky. I can't look at her, even though I feel her eyes on my face.

Tequila. Coke. The girl in Liam's room, pills, something else, whiskey, more whiskey, putting up the blanket in the spare bedroom. Sitting around drunk as fuck and high off our asses, reminiscing about wretched flats in London when we were just starting out. Huge chunks of time completely lost to my memory.

And then: walking in on Liam with the needle in his arm. Him tossing me the baggie before he nodded out.

Me being completely trashed, recklessly high, but still with that ceaseless, gnawing emptiness inside that I couldn't fucking get rid of, so I took it, only to find that snorting heroin off my bathroom sink didn't fill it either.

I stop talking. I don't tell Marisol that the gnawing emptiness faded when I got her first letter, that it shrunk when she wrote *I think I love you*. It's not fair to let her think she's in charge of keeping the darkness at bay.

She detaches her hand from mine and rolls over without talking, and for a moment I'm certain that she's leaving, but instead she straightens her dress and lays on her stomach, her right side touching my left. I reach up and stroke her cheek with one knuckle, still waiting for her to say something, my heart feeling as if it might burst from my chest.

After a bit, she takes my hand and pulls my arm in front of her, tracing my veins and tattoos and scars with a fingertip absentmindedly, like she's trying to put something into words and it's not going well.

"Is that it?" she finally asks.

"More or less," I say. "I woke up face down on the grass Wednesday morning and got halfway through a bottle of Jim Beam before I finally had the nerve to check myself in here again."

She presses her fingertips against pockmarks on my arm, one by one, until her hand is splayed out.

"Is it going to happen again?" she asks softly, not looking at me.

We both know the truth, which is that I don't know. I didn't think it would happen this time. All I *do* know is that, right now, I'd sooner walk through a burning building than relapse again. But I also know that for once, I need to lie to her.

"No," I say.

Marisol nods, still thinking. Finally, she looks at me.

"Gavin," she says, her voice shaking. "If you're going to destroy yourself, tell me now, because I can't watch."

I take her hand in mine and roll onto my side.

"I promise," I say, and kiss her.

She feels soft and small, her mouth trembling just a little as she kisses me back. It's the most vulnerable I've ever seen her, even worse than when she thought she was dissolving, and it turns something inside me to steel.

It can be easy for me to forget that this is her, too, fragile and wounded. I'm furious at myself for being the one to do this, because I should be doing the opposite. I should be *protecting* Marisol.

"I love you," I say, and take a deep breath. I don't know what I'm going to say next, because beyond that I don't even know what I *can* say.

Marisol swallows hard.

"I'm not asking you to take me back," I say slowly. She looks up at me, her eyes wide, bloodshot, and shining. "I don't deserve that. You could walk out of here right now and never speak to me again and that would be what I deserve. And I know it."

"Gavin, I…"

She trails off, because I don't think she knows what to say either.

"All I'm asking is the chance to prove myself," I go on, an enormous lump in my throat. "Let me wake up every morning and fix myself slowly, and text you and call you and take you out on dates sometimes. It's all I want. I don't give a fuck if we put a tag on it, Marisol, just let me earn a place in your life again. *Please*."

Marisol slides a finger under the leather band around my wrist. There's just one where there used to be a pile.

"You've got a start," she says.

"I kept the rest, being an optimist," I admit.

"I don't know," she finally whispers. "I mean, I know I came here, and I've been writing you letters and requesting ceramic bowls and everything, but…"

She trails off again, looking away. My breath catches in my throat and I hold it for a moment, then let it out slowly.

"You don't have to know now," I say, ignoring the weight in my chest. More than anything, I want her to say *yes, I'll give you a chance*, but it's not up to me.

"I'm sorry," she says. "It's just, that – I don't know, Gavin, this all seems really fucked."

I kiss her gently on the temple, and she inhales raggedly.

"You don't have to explain. You don't have to do anything. You came, you're here, and since rehab's all about living in the moment, it's all I could have wanted," I murmur into her hair.

"What's next?" she asks.

"I could have *sworn* I just said I was focusing on the moment," I tease gently.

Marisol just frowns at me slightly. The joke doesn't land.

"I've got an extensive recovery plan," I say. "It's got benchmarks and dates and check-ins and bullet points and *everything*."

I tell her about it. I go into details, I talk about the research and science of recovery, I point out that the books she got from the library are where I got a lot of these ideas in the first place. I tell her Liam's back in England and I haven't spoken to him.

Gradually, we fade to simply talking, about finals and her parents and the crazy noises her upstairs neighbors make. I admit that at the last group therapy session, someone broke the talking stick, so I'm excited for tonight's because it might be pandemonium.

We lie there, on the grass, until visiting hours are nearly over. She still hasn't said yes or no to giving me a chance, but she's stopped crying and started laughing. Her dress has fallen against her and I can see every curve of her body in perfect detail, the skirt hiked up her legs slightly.

It's ten days I've been wanking in the shower, and despite myself, I'm disastrously hard.

"I should go," she's saying. "I assume that at the stroke of six, they release the tigers or something."

"One way to find out," I say.

Marisol takes a deep breath. She's on her back, looking at the sky, our hands intertwined.

"I'll come back tomorrow," she says.

"Don't," I say. "You should be studying for finals, not driving to Malibu to see some pathetic wretch."

"Are you trying to tell me what to do?" she asks, looking at me, a smile in her eyes. She rolls over onto her side.

I grin.

"I would never," I say. "Only suggest."

"Do you not want to…"

She catches sight of the huge bulge in my pants, and cocks one eyebrow.

"...see me?" she finishes. "You know I was *crying* earlier, right?"

"I can't help it," I say. "He's got a mind of his own, I swear."

I glance down.

"Rude," I tell my cock. "And fucking inappropriate."

Marisol laughs, even though her face is still red and splotchy.

"Obviously I want to see you," I say.

"Obviously," she says, and gives me a kiss on the lips.

She leaves without giving me an answer. It stings that I still don't know, and I carry a knot of tension in my chest all night, but she's coming back tomorrow. She requested another ceramic bowl. Those things aren't *yes, I'll let you try again*, but they're signs pointing in the right direction.

And for now, it's enough.

CHAPTER FORTY-NINE
Marisol

The next Saturday, I'm sitting in the same lounge where I first saw Gavin a week ago, waiting for him to finish up some exit paperwork.

My mind is racing. The past week was *insane*, and now that it's over I still can't get myself to relax. But I finished my finals, wrote all my papers, completed the research project I was helping a professor with, and did all my graduation paperwork.

And I got the job at Ramirez & Chabon, the immigration firm where I interviewed the day before everything went to hell. A huge relief, but bittersweet, because when I got the call, more than anything, I wanted to tell Gavin but had to wait until he called me with his allotted time.

I said yes. Despite the voice in my head telling me that it was stupid to give him another chance, I did. He's not my boyfriend, at least not yet. He won't be meeting my parents any time soon, and I won't be attending any functions with him. We're not *official*.

And he knows that this is it, the only do-over he gets. I can't let him break my heart like this again, so this is the last chance.

But I'm here, picking him up from rehab and taking him home. Because maybe it's a mistake, and maybe my heart is stupid, but I do love him.

Plus I *missed* him. I've gone through an astonishing number of batteries in the past two weeks.

"I'm free," Gavin says, walking into the lounge, a duffel bag slung over his shoulder.

I haven't seen him since Sunday, so I practically leap into his arms and give him a long, *long* kiss. The duffel bag drops to the floor and he wraps both arms around me, one hand traveling down my back and then even lower, cupping my ass and pulling me against him.

This time, there's no one else in the lounge, but it's completely open, anything but private.

"Ready to go home?" I ask, hoping I sound sultry, that my undertone of *home is where the bed is* comes through.

Gavin kisses me again. He's already rock hard, and despite the setting it stokes a fire inside me, too, and then I'm on my tiptoes, crushing myself against him, my tongue in his mouth.

Someone walks by and I pull back, surprised. Gavin doesn't even laugh, just looks at me with an expression so intense it's almost unreadable.

"I think I left something in the room," he says, his voice rough and low.

That's not what I was expecting.

"Okay?"

"Come help me look for it?"

Gavin winks, then takes my hand and pulls me along. We walk past a nurses' station, down a hall, and then into a room with two perfectly-made twin beds.

"What was it?" I ask, looking around.

He pulls me through the room and into the bathroom on the far end, closes the door and locks it.

Then he pushes me against the counter, his hands on my hips.

"Only door that locks," he says into my mouth. "I don't know if I'll make it all the way home."

A charge of electricity goes down my spine as Gavin presses his mouth against mine hungrily and I press back, feeling as if I've gone up in a *whoosh* of flame. I buck my hips against his hard length and he groans softly, curling his tongue around mine, my hands in his hair.

Then he pulls back, and I catch his bottom lip between my teeth.

I swear he growls at me, the sound low and raspy and pure, delicious, primal *sex*, and suddenly this can't happen fast enough.

Gavin shoves my skirt up over my hips and I grab him by the belt, unbuckling it as he tugs my underwear off, shoving one hand between my legs and sliding his fingers through my wetness. I hook a leg around him and unbutton his jeans, our mouths together.

I unzip him and he pushes his fingers inside me, the flat of his hand against my clit, and I gasp, taking his length in my hand and stroking him from root to tip.

He leans in and bites my earlobe, his fingers curling inside me as I bite back a moan.

"More," I whisper.

He chuckles into my ear and it makes a shiver run through my whole body.

"Marisol," he says, his voice low and rough and *demanding*. "I love you and I'm going to fuck you over this counter."

"Good," I whisper back.

He pulls his fingers out and turns me around, my hips braced against cool marble. We're facing a huge vanity mirror, Gavin behind me, and I lock eyes with him as I brace myself against the counter.

I wink.

Gavin grins at me, then lowers his mouth to my ear, still looking me dead in the eyes.

"You saucy minx," he says.

The head of his cock is against my slit, and I bite my lip and hold my breath, just *anticipating* the moment when he's finally inside me again, when he sends a shockwave all the way to my toes. But he slides it down, between my lips, spreading my wetness to my clit and sending a tremor through my body.

I swallow a moan, my hands curling around the edge of the countertop.

"Come on," I whisper.

He circles my clit once, slides back, and then he drives himself inside me so hard and deep that I *grunt* and put one hand on the mirror to steady myself.

"I fucking love that noise," he growls.

"I fucking love your cock," I gasp.

"Jesus," he whispers, and drives himself in again, crushing my hips against the countertop.

This isn't sweet, it isn't gentle, it's fast and hard and *needy*. It's what I craved, the pure expression of sweaty, moaning, desperate *togetherness*.

I'm going to have bruises tomorrow, but right now it feels so damn good that I'm already losing control, every thought in my head dwindling down to the single point of white-hot heat that's building inside me.

He grabs my shoulder, hooking his hand around me and pulling me closer and I arch my back, my hand in his hair. I think I'm moaning, or at least making noise, and my eyes slide shut again.

"Make me come," I whisper. "God, please."

He groans and *hammers* himself into me, and that's all it takes. The white heat building inside me goes off like a nuclear bomb and the explosion rushes through me. I think I shout Gavin's name and then a second later he erupts inside me and we come together, his face buried in my neck.

When I finish, I'm trembling a little. I feel wrung out, emptied, and I finally let Gavin's hair go as he leans his face against the back of my head, breathing deeply like he's trying to recover. I think I'm doing the same thing.

Finally, he looks at me again. He kisses me on the temple and then smiles, his face against mine. I slowly take my hand from the mirror, leaving a print behind, swallowing hard.

"I think we just had really loud sex in the rehab bathroom," I whisper.

Gavin starts laughing, and after a second, I do too.

"No, we *definitely* had very loud sex in the rehab bathroom," he says. "Good thing I'm no longer a patient."

I take his hand in mine, looking at him in the mirror, and kiss it.

"I missed you," I say.

"I love you," he says, pulling my body against his. "And I did miss you but I think I just made that quite clear."

Gavin holds me for another long moment. I turn my head and pull him down to me for a slightly off-kilter kiss, and then we finally detach. I pull my skirt down and find my underwear while his zips his pants again.

Then we kiss one more time, unlock the door, and go home.

CHAPTER FIFTY
Gavin

Two Weeks Later

The woman sitting in the chair to my right gives me another strange, you-seem-familiar look, and I try to ignore it. She's been glancing over every thirty seconds the whole time I've been seated here, even though I've not said a single word to her.

On the outdoor stage, across the quad, a woman with gray hair reads out another name.

"Caleb Fulton," she announces, and a young man in a graduation gown climbs the stairs, shakes her hand, takes a roll of paper from her, and descends down the other side.

Fulton. They're getting close, and I sit up straighter, trying to get the best view of the stage I can.

I'm not supposed to be here. We've discussed the matter quite a bit for the past two weeks, and we specifically decided that it wasn't the right time for

Marisol's parents to meet me, so I shouldn't come to her graduation.

I understand the logic. Marisol didn't think that two weeks after being released from rehab was the best time for her somewhat conservative parents to meet the tattooed ex-junkie still trying to win her back, and I couldn't really argue with that.

So I'm only disobeying the letter of the law, not the spirit, though if she wanted to debate it with me I'm certain I'd lose.

"Laura Gateway," the woman on stage calls.

I've scanned the crowd a few times, trying to figure out which are Marisol's parents, but the place is packed full of people. I had to pay for a scalped ticket, something I definitely never thought I'd be doing. I didn't even *know* that you could scalp tickets to a law school graduation until yesterday.

"Alice Gocert," the woman says, and a faint wave of nervousness flutters through my stomach, though it's not as if I've got to do anything. Everyone applauds Alice, who shakes hands, takes her diploma, and steps off the stage. I can see Marisol standing by the stairs, next in line, as she grins and waves to someone in the audience.

"Marisol Gomez," the woman says.

Marisol steps onto the stage. She's beaming, utterly fucking radiant as she shakes hands and accepts her diploma, giving another little wave to someone in the audience — her parents, I'm sure — before stepping down.

I want to stand up and shout *Hey everybody, she's amazing and she's going to be a lawyer*, but I don't. I sit still and don't make a fuss, watching Marisol walk back to her seat, and when the next person is called, I applaud politely once more.

• • •

I look up at the brick archway, trying to decipher the letters. The quad is a madhouse again, and rather than find Marisol and risk accidentally meeting her parents before I should, I'm just going to tell her where I am.

And also beg forgiveness for showing up, but I had to see her.

> Gavin: I know we agreed, but I came to your graduation anyway because I couldn't stand to miss it. I promise not to meet your parents, but I'm under the archway at Foyce Hall.

I send it and wait. A minute or two goes by, and I put my phone back in my pocket, leaning against the wall. The moment I do, of course it buzzes.

> Marisol: Stay there.

I do as ordered. A few people give me second looks, but I'm wearing sunglasses, a hat, a long-sleeved shirt and slacks, so I'm pretty well incognito. Yes, I had to buy slacks for the occasion.

After a few more minutes I see her, walking down the breezeway, and I wave, hoping she's not too angry.

She grins and waves back, so when we meet in the middle I sweep her up in a hug, spin her around, and give her a good, long kiss.

"What are you doing here?" she finally says, the words nearly bubbling over with giddiness.

"What you do *mean* what am I doing here?" I ask, grinning. "You think I was just passing through and happened upon your law school graduation?"

"We did agree," she points out, but she's obviously not angry.

"It's better to beg forgiveness than ask permission. And I couldn't stand the thought of missing this."

"How did you even get a ticket?"

"Marisol," I say. "Do you seriously think I couldn't get a ticket to a law school graduation?"

She rolls her eyes at me, but she's still smiling.

"Sorry, I forgot you were a big shot who's very important and *super* famous."

I bought the ticket from Craigslist for $200, but I'm not tipping my hand about that *now*.

"Terribly famous and probably one of the only people to secretly turn up at a law school graduation in disguise," I say, and kiss her again. "You should get back to your family."

"Thanks for coming," she says, looking up at me, her big brown eyes so sincere that it twists my heart.

"Even though we agreed I wouldn't?"

She laughs softly.

"Yeah," she says.

"I wasn't about to miss it. I'm proud of you. I love you. Go before we get caught and I have to explain all this."

One more kiss.

"I love you, too," she says, and then she's gone.

• • •

I start the fire when Marisol texts me that her parents are back home, and what am I up to?

I tell her to come over.

In front of the fireplace there's a vase of two dozen roses on the coffee table and a bottle of sparkling apple cider in an ice bucket next to two champagne glasses. Part of me thinks I'm overdoing it, that she probably just wants to brush her teeth and fall into my bed, but it's already there.

Since I got out of rehab, things have been... strangely *normal*. The first few days there were paparazzi outside my door all the time, but it seems as if they've finally given up. None of them had any idea what to make of the signed contract combined with the fact that Marisol and I *clearly* spent quite a bit of time together, so they mostly decided that the "fake girlfriend" story was itself a fake and gave up.

Things are largely as they were. She hasn't technically taken me back, and I'm still on probation with her, but functionally it's close to the same as it was.

And, of course, I wake up every morning thankful that I got a second chance I don't deserve.

I've shown the band some of the songs I wrote, the ones I about Marisol, and we've started rehearsing them. I'm still doing all my *replacement* activities, running and working out, and I've started attending several Narcotics Anonymous meetings per week.

I've even gotten a sponsor: Evan, a very calm, patient surfer about twenty years my senior who's been clean for ten years after twenty of heavy use. I like him because he's never once tried to blow sunshine up my ass about the whole mess of addiction. The first time we spoke he told me that he still thinks about using every single day, and that the trick is to simply keep saying no.

Marisol's met him. They get along. She even volunteered to come to a counseling session with me to meet my therapist and write down absolutely everything he said, including *no big life changes for a year* and *take a multivitamin*.

I now own multivitamins, though I mostly forget to take them.

There's a knock on the door. I tried to give Marisol a key but she wouldn't take it, saying that she didn't want to rush anything. That she wanted to give me time to adjust, so now I've got a goal: prove myself until Marisol will take a house key.

"*There's* Marisol Gomez, J.D.," I say when I open the door. "How's it feel to be an attorney?"

She comes in laughing and gives me a kiss.

"I haven't passed the bar exam yet," she says. "Don't count your chickens before they're hatched."

I know the bar exam's quite difficult, but there's a zero percent chance she doesn't pass.

"Think you can celebrate for one day before you begin worrying about that?" I ask, taking her hand.

"Maybe *one*," she says.

I lead her over to the couch and table in front of the fire, pour her cider, and sit with my arm around her as she snuggles into me.

"Thanks," she says, her head against my shoulder. "Today was good, but it was exhausting."

"Sounds like a proper finish to law school."

"Yeah, they make you run one final gauntlet before you get that piece of paper," she says, snuggling into me a little more. "Thank you."

She pauses, and we both look into the fire for a moment.

"And thanks for coming today," she goes on. "I'm glad you did."

I kiss the top of her head.

"I have got one more surprise," I admit.

Marisol raises one eyebrow.

"It's actually G-rated," I say, and she laughs.

I pull a long, thin jewelry box out and give it to her.

Her eyes flick to me a little nervously, and she flips the top open.

Inside is the piece of paper I've folded so that only MARBRI BAR REVIEW COURSE is showing. The moment she sees it, Marisol starts laughing.

I bought her an eight-week, intensive study course for the bar exam.

"Okay, you got me," she says. "It's perfect. Thank you."

"I've never seen you wear a necklace but I know *exactly* how you feel about the bar," I say, leaning in. "And you'll smash it."

She kisses me, still laughing.

"Do you mean crush it?"

"Apparently."

We kiss again. She stops laughing, and soon I've got her legs on my lap and my hand up her skirt. When we finish we stay on the couch, naked, tangled together, debating whether apples or pears are the superior fruit.

She wins the debate, obviously, and everything is perfect.

EPILOGUE
Marisol

Six Months Later

"Here's one of me stumbling drunkenly out of a nightclub at two o'clock in the morning," Gavin says.

I scoot over in the bed and hook my chin over his shoulder, looking at his phone.

"Looks a whole lot like the door of your recording studio," I say. "The similarity's remarkable, really. You'd think that a nightclub would have one or two other people around, at least."

"Sources close to me are claiming that I'm 'out of control' and careening toward certain ruin with the stress of a recording another album," he goes on, flicking his thumb to scroll along. "Someone saw me drink nearly a whole bottle of tequila last night and then disappear into the men's with a 'mystery blond.'"

"You've gotta teach me how you do that."

"Do what?"

"Be in two places at once. Or is this a Mrs. Doubtfire kind of thing?"

Gavin laughs.

"You mean, every time I left the room, was I secretly running to some nightclub, raising hell, and then coming back before the three of you noticed I was gone?"

"You *were* gone for a while that one time."

"I was playing with another woman's pussy."

"*That* would be a good headline. 'Frontman's girlfriend catches him teasing bandmate's pussy,'" I say, laughing.

"I got that pussy quite excited," Gavin says. "*And* I offered it drugs."

We were at Darcy's apartment last night, where we had dinner with her and Trent and then hung out until about one in the morning, at which point I nearly fell asleep on her floor cushions.

A month or two ago, she took in a stray cat with two differently colored eyes. His name is Bowie, and his interests include laser pointers, catnip, and scratching people who try to pet his belly.

"I'm still confused that they're not together," I say.

"People can be friends," Gavin points out.

"He knows where everything is in her kitchen better than she does," I point out.

"They're close friends, and she'd be perfectly happy to eat peanut butter sandwiches for every meal, so someone's got to know where things are."

"She reminded him about his sister's birthday."

"I think Trent's seeing someone," Gavin says, still scrolling through his phone. "He mentioned he had a date, a week or two ago."

I don't say anything, but I'm one hundred percent confident that it's not serious between him and anyone else. It's just *not*.

Gavin stops on a photo of the two of us walking out of a grocery store. It's not a flattering picture, and I make a face.

"We're on the rocks after our row at the market," he says, scanning the article. "Did you know?"

"Chunky peanut butter is an abomination and I'll never apologize for speaking my mind."

"But how do you *really* feel?"

I sigh and reach around him, scrolling the text up on his phone. It's the usual nonsense — someone took a picture of the two of us where we look annoyed, so they concocted a story about how Gavin's alleged partying is going to break us up.

Every word of it's completely untrue, but it still makes me angry. For the past six months Gavin's been working his *ass* off at staying clean. He's stuck to his recovery plan religiously.

About two months after he got back from rehab, he turned down sex with me because he didn't want to be late to meet his sponsor. It's *that* serious.

When he got back, I told him I wanted to be official again.

For a while he wasn't in the press at all, but with the new album well underway Valerie's been sending press releases again, and it's reminded the gossip news that he exists.

"Oh, and I'm leaving you for an older man I was seen embracing, as I'm apparently bisexual now," he goes on, looking at a picture of him giving his sponsor a hug at a restaurant.

"Evan's a catch," I say. "Was that last week?"

"We'd just had a long talk about Liam," Gavin says.

I run my fingers up his arm and take his hand in mine, my cheek still against his shoulder.

"And?"

"And Evan had a brother," Gavin says, his voice getting a little far away. "Similar situation, actually. He got better and his brother didn't. His brother died a few years ago."

I kiss his shoulder, intensely glad for Evan. There are some things about Gavin I know I'll never be able to understand or *really* help with, and this is one of them.

"Did he have any advice?"

He shifts his fingers in mine and puts his phone on the bedside table, thinking.

"He said there wasn't much advice to give, other than to know that the guilt never goes away but as time goes on I'll get used to it," he says. "And don't do drugs. He did say that as well."

"I agree with both of those things."

Gavin takes his hand out of mine and rolls me over in bed until I'm lying on my back and he's on his side, one hand stroking my hip. We're both naked because we haven't gotten out of bed yet on this lazy Sunday.

"Speaking of drugs, I completely missed Thursday," he says.

I wrack my brain for a moment, trying to remember what Thursday was. Gavin just smiles, waiting for me to figure it out.

"Was it six months?" I finally say.

"It was."

I reach up and stroke his hair, feeling awful that I forgot. Six months clean is a big deal. It's further than he got before, and here I didn't even notice.

"I'm sorry," I whisper, but Gavin just smiles.

"I don't actually mind," he says. "It feels rather good that sobriety is normal instead of cause for celebration."

"Yeah, but *I* wanted to celebrate," I say. "This stuff matters to me. I like having concrete, countable proof that..."

I trail off, because I'm never exactly sure what to say here.

"Proof that I mean it this time?" he asks, softly.

"Proof that you won't break my heart," I answer.

"I do, and I won't," he says. "Marisol, I promise. And I'm going to prove it."

I believe him. Deep down, in my bones, I believe him.

"I know," I whisper.

He leans in and kisses me softly.

"Does this mean you'll say yes this time?" he asks.

My stomach flips, and I swallow.

"Gavin, you know it's not—"

"I know," he says, laughing. "No big life changes for a year, and you *do* love following guidelines."

"They're there for a reason, you know," I tease. "I'm *helping*."

"By turning down my repeated marriage proposals?"

"You're making me sound like a monster," I laugh. "I didn't say *no*, I said *not yet*."

"So eventually I'll get you to *yes*," he says, his eyes dancing. "Through a campaign of maintained sobriety and repeated proposals."

For some reason, my heart does another flip. This isn't the first time he's proposed, even though he knew I'd say *not yet*, but it's the first time he's asked if I'd say yes someday.

"Of course you will," I say, suddenly serious.

He takes my hand in his and kisses it slowly, his eyes searching mine.

"I've been asking the wrong question," he says, a smile coming into his eyes. "I should have known."

"So, ask the right one."

"Marisol," he says, his voice quiet and serious. "If I ask you to marry me six months from now, *then* will you say yes?"

I swallow the sudden lump in my throat.

"Yes," I whisper.

We kiss again, and I roll onto my side so now we're embracing, face to face.

"And you *know* I turned you down because I love you, weird as that sounds, right?"

It's true. If all the experts and literature recommend no big changes for a year, I'm going to follow that, no matter how much I want to tell him *yes* every time he asks. Anything I can do to help, I will.

I'm still here. I still love him. Fiancée versus girlfriend is really just semantics, anyway.

He smiles, rubbing the tip of his nose against mine.

"I know," he says. "Though it's not going to stop me asking, most likely. You'll have to stand firm."

"It's harder than you think, you know," I admit.

"Good," he says, smiling, and kisses me again, his hand traveling down my back until his fingers are at the base of my spine, drawing me in. I open my mouth against his and we wind our tongues together, the familiar heat building inside me.

"I love you," he says when he pulls back. "And I promise that in six months I'll propose properly, with a ring and everything, not naked in bed moments before I ravish you."

I grin and bend my leg, sliding my knee up the outside of his thigh.

"What's wrong with this way?" I ask, laughing.

Gavin takes my thigh in his hand and pulls me against him, kissing me hard.

"Nothing," he says. "Absolutely *nothing.*"

THE END

About Roxie

I love writing sexy, alpha men and the headstrong women they fall for.

My weaknesses include: beards, whiskey, nice abs with treasure trails, sarcasm, cats, prowess in the kitchen, prowess in the bedroom, forearm tattoos, and gummi bears.

I live in California with my very own sexy, bearded, whiskey-loving husband and two hell-raising cats.

Made in the USA
San Bernardino, CA
10 February 2019